'A refreshingly new take on post-dystopia civilizations, with the smartest evolutionary worldbuilding you'll ever read'
Peter F. Hamilton

'This is superior stuff, tackling big themes – gods, messiahs, artificial intelligence, alienness – with brio' *Financial Times*

'*Children of Time* has that essence of the classic science fiction novels, that sense of wonder and unfettered imagination, but combined with this is the charm of a writer who really knows how to entertain . . . Essential science fiction, a book not to be missed'
SFBook

'The prose has Tchaikovsky's hallmark accessible but compulsive quality. The characters are believable, and in some instances, genuinely, astoundingly alien. The perspective, literally across space and time, is unique . . . A highly intriguing piece of science fiction – wonderfully done' *SFandFReviews*

'*Children of Time* is a book that is old-school SF in tone and epic in timescale, with some genuinely likeable aliens that will remain memorable after you have finished the book'
SFFWorld

'*Children of Time* is, without doubt, a standout novel of the year . . . It is beautifully written, its imaginative scope is vast and its voice is powerful' *ForWinterNights*

CHILDREN OF TIME

Adrian Tchaikovsky was born in Woodhall Spa, Lincolnshire, before heading off to Reading to study psychology and zoology. For reasons unclear even to himself he subsequently ended up in law and has worked as a legal executive in both Reading and Leeds, where he now lives. Married, he is a keen live role-player and occasional amateur actor, has trained in stage-fighting, and keeps no exotic or dangerous pets of any kind, possibly excepting his son. He is the author of the ten-book fantasy series Shadows of the Apt and *Guns of the Dawn*, a stand-alone historical fantasy novel. *Children of Time* is his first science fiction novel.

Catch up with Adrian at www.shadowsoftheapt.com for further information plus bonus material, including short stories and artwork.

BY ADRIAN TCHAIKOVSKY

Shadows of the Apt

Empire in Black and Gold
Dragonfly Falling
Blood of the Mantis
Salute the Dark
The Scarab Path
The Sea Watch
Heirs of the Blade
The Air War
War Master's Gate
Seal of the Worm

Guns of the Dawn

Children of Time

The Tiger and the Wolf

ADRIAN TCHAIKOVSKY

CHILDREN OF TIME

Ed.a

PAN BOOKS

First published 2015 by Tor

This paperback edition published 2016 by Pan Books
an imprint of Pan Macmillan
20 New Wharf Road, London N1 9RR
Associated companies throughout the world
www.panmacmillan.com

ISBN 978-1-4472-7330-1

7 9 8

A CIP catalogue record for this book is available from the British Library.

Typeset by Ellipsis Digital Limited, Glasgow
Printed and bound by CPI Group (UK) Ltd, Croydon, CR0 4YY

Visit **www.panmacmillan.com** to read more about all our books
and to buy them. You will also find features, author interviews and
news of any author events, and you can sign up for e-newsletters
so that you're always first to hear about our new releases.

To Portia

ACKNOWLEDGEMENTS

A big thank-you to my scientific advisors, including Stewart Hotston, Justina Robson, Michael Czajkowski, Max Barclay and the Entomology department of the Natural History Museum.

Also the usual thanks to my wife, Annie, my agent, Simon Kavanagh, to Peter Lavery, and to Bella Pagan and everyone else at Tor. I'm very glad of all the support for what has been a deeply, weirdly personal project.

1
GENESIS

1.1 JUST A BARREL OF MONKEYS

There were no windows in the Brin 2 facility – rotation meant that 'outside' was always 'down', underfoot, out of mind. The wall screens told a pleasant fiction, a composite view of the world below that ignored their constant spin, showing the planet as hanging stationary-still off in space: the green marble to match the blue marble of home, twenty light years away. Earth had been green, in her day, though her colours had faded since. Perhaps never as green as this beautifully crafted world though, where even the oceans glittered emerald with the phytoplankton maintaining the oxygen balance within its atmosphere. How delicate and many-sided was the task of building a living monument that would remain stable for geological ages to come.

It had no officially confirmed name beyond its astronomical designation, although there was a strong vote for 'Simiana' amongst some of the less imaginative crewmembers. Doctor Avrana Kern now looked out upon it and thought only of *Kern's World*. Her project, her dream, *her* planet. The first of many, she decided.

This is the future. This is where mankind takes its next great step. This is where we become gods.

'This is the future,' she said aloud. Her voice would sound in every crewmember's auditory centre, all nineteen of them, though fifteen were right here in the control hub with her. Not the true hub, of course – the gravity-denuded axle about which they revolved: that was for power and processing, and their payload.

'This is where mankind takes its next great step.' Her speech had taken more of her time than any technical details over the last two days. She almost went on with the line about them becoming gods, but that was for her only. *Far too controversial, given the* Non Ultra Natura *clowns back home*. Enough of a stink had been raised over projects like hers already. Oh, the differences between the current Earth factions went far deeper: social, economic, or simply *us* and *them*, but Kern had got the Brin launched – all those years ago – against mounting opposition. By now the whole idea had become a kind of scapegoat for the divisions of the human race. *Bickering primates, the lot of them. Progress is what matters. Fulfilling the potential of humanity, and of all other life.* She had always been one of the fiercest opponents of the growing conservative backlash most keenly exemplified by the *Non Ultra Natura* terrorists. *If they had their way, we'd all end up back in the caves. Back in the trees. The whole point of civilization is that we exceed the limits of nature, you tedious little primitives.*

'We stand on others' shoulders, of course.' The proper line, that of accepted scientific humility, was, 'on the shoulders of giants', but she had not got where she was by bowing the knee to past generations. *Midgets, lots and lots of midgets*, she thought, and then – she could barely keep back the appalling giggle – *on the shoulders of monkeys.*

At a thought from her, one wallscreen and their Mind's Eye HUDs displayed the schematics of Brin 2 for them all.

She wanted to direct their attention and lead them along with her towards the proper appreciation of her – sorry, *their* – triumph. There: the needle of the central core encircled by the ring of life and science that was their torus-shaped world. At one end of the core was the unlovely bulge of the Sentry Pod, soon to be cast adrift to become the universe's loneliest and longest research post. The opposite end of the needle sported the Barrel and the Flask. Contents: monkeys and the future, respectively.

'Particularly I have to thank the engineering teams under Doctors Fallarn and Medi for their tireless work in reformatting –' and she almost now said 'Kern's World' without meaning to – 'our subject planet to provide a safe and nurturing environment for our great project.' Fallarn and Medi were well on their way back to Earth, of course, their fifteen-year work completed, their thirty-year return journey begun. It was all stage-setting, though, to make way for Kern and her dream. *We are – I am – what all this work is for.*

A journey of twenty light years home. Whilst thirty years drag by on Earth, only twenty will pass for Fallarn and Medi in their cold coffins. For them, their voyage is nearly as fast as light. What wonders we can accomplish!

From her viewpoint, engines to accelerate her to most of the speed of light were no more than pedestrian tools to move her about a universe that Earth's biosphere was about to inherit. *Because humanity may be fragile in ways we cannot dream, so we cast our net wide and then wider . . .*

Human history was balanced on a knife edge. Millennia of ignorance, prejudice, superstition and desperate striving had brought them at last to this: that humankind would beget new sentient life in its own image. Humanity would no longer be alone. Even in the unthinkably far future, when Earth itself had fallen in fire and dust, there would be a legacy spreading across the stars – an infinite and expanding variety of Earth-born life diverse enough to survive any reversal of fortune until the death of the whole universe, and perhaps even beyond that. *Even if we die, we will live on in our children.*

Let the NUNs preach their dismal all-eggs-in-one-basket creed of human purity and supremacy, she thought. *We will out-evolve them. We will leave them behind. This will be the first of a thousand worlds that we will give life to.*

For we are gods, and we are lonely, so we shall create . . .

Back home, things were tough, or so the twenty-year-old images indicated. Avrana had skimmed dispassionately over the riots, the furious debates, the demonstrations and violence, thinking only, *How did we ever get so far with so many fools in the gene pool?* The *Non Ultra Natura* lobby were only the most extreme of a whole coalition of human political factions – the conservative, the philosophical, even the die-hard religious – who looked at progress and said that enough was enough. Who fought tooth and nail against further engineering of the human genome, against the removal of limits on AI, and against programs like Avrana's own.

And yet they're losing.

The terraforming would still be going on elsewhere. Kern's World was just one of many planets receiving the attentions of people like Fallarn and Medi, transformed from inhospitable chemical rocks – Earth-like only in approximate size and distance from the sun – into balanced ecosystems that Kern could have walked on without a suit in only minor discomfort. After the monkeys had been delivered and the Sentry Pod detached to monitor them, those other gems were where her attention would next be drawn. *We will seed the universe with all the wonders of Earth.*

In her speech, which she was barely paying attention to, she meandered down a list of other names, from here or at home. The person she really wanted to thank was herself. She had fought for this, her engineered longevity allowing her to carry the debate across several natural human lifetimes. She had clashed in the financiers' rooms and in the laboratories, at academic symposiums and on mass entertainment feeds just to make this happen.

I, I have done this. With your hands have I built, with your eyes have I measured, but the mind is mine alone.

Her mouth continued along its prepared course, the words boring her even more than they presumably bored her listeners. The real audience for this speech would receive it in twenty years' time: the final confirmation back home of the way things were due to be. Her mind touched base with the Brin 2's hub. *Confirm Barrel systems*, she pinged into her relay link with the facility's control computer; it was a check that had become a nervous habit of late.

Within tolerance, it replied. And if she probed behind that bland summary, she would see precise readouts of the lander craft, its state of readiness, even down to the vital signs of its ten-thousand-strong primate cargo, the chosen few who would inherit, if not the Earth, then at least this planet, whatever it would be called.

Whatever *they* would eventually call it, once the uplift nanovirus had taken them that far along the developmental road. The biotechs estimated that a mere thirty or forty monkey generations would bring them to the stage where they might make contact with the Sentry Pod and its lone human occupant.

Alongside the Barrel was the Flask: the delivery system for the virus that would accelerate the monkeys along their way – they would stride, in a mere century or two, across physical and mental distances that had taken humanity millions of long and hostile years.

Another group of people to thank, for she herself was no bio-tech specialist. She had seen the specs and the simulations, though, and expert systems had examined the theory and summarized it in terms that she, a mere polymath genius, could understand. The virus was clearly an impressive piece of work, as far as she could grasp it. Infected individuals would produce offspring mutated in a number of useful ways: greater brain size and complexity, greater body size to accommodate it, more flexible behavioural paths, swifter learning . . . The virus would even recognize the presence of infection in other individuals of the same species, so as to promote selective breeding, the best of the best giving birth to even better. It was a whole future in a microscopic shell, almost as smart, in its single-minded little way, as the creatures that it would be improving. It would interact with the host genome at a deep level, replicate within its cells like a new organelle, passing itself on to the host's offspring until the entire species was subject to its benevolent contagion. No matter how much change the monkeys underwent, that virus would adapt and adjust to whatever genome it was partnered with, analysing and modelling and improvising with whatever it inherited – until something had been engineered that could look its creators in the eye and understand.

She had sold it to the people back home by describing how colonists would reach the planet then, descending from the skies like deities to meet their new people. Instead of a harsh, untamed world, a race of uplifted sentient aides and servants would welcome their makers. That was what she had told the boardrooms and the committees back on Earth, but it had never been the point of the exercise for her. The monkeys were the point, and what they would become.

This was one of the things the NUNs were most incensed about. They shouted about making superbeings out of mere beasts. In truth, like spoiled children, it was *sharing* that they objected to. Only-child humanity craved the sole attention of the universe. Like so many other projects hoisted as political issues, the virus's development had been fraught with protests, sabotage, terrorism and murder.

And yet we triumph over our own base nature at last, Kern reflected with satisfaction. And of course, there was a tiny grain of truth to the insults the NUNs threw her way, because she *didn't* care about colonists or the neo-imperialistic dreams of her fellows. She wanted to make new life, in her image as much as in humanity's. She wanted to know what might evolve, what society, what understandings, when her monkeys were left to their own simian devices . . . To Avrana Kern, *this* was her price, her reward for exercising her genius for the good of the human race: this experiment; this planetary what-if. Her efforts had opened up a string of terraformed worlds, but her price was that the firstborn would be *hers*, and home to her new-made people.

She was aware of an expectant silence and realized that she had got to the end of her speech, and now everyone thought she was just adding gratuitous suspense to a moment that needed no gilding.

'Mr Sering, are you in position?' she asked on open channel, for everyone's benefit. Sering was the volunteer, the man they were going to leave behind. He would orbit their planet-sized laboratory as the long years turned, locked in cold sleep until the time came for him to become mentor to a new race of sentient primates. She almost envied him, for he would see and hear and experience things that no other human ever had. He would be the new Hanuman: the monkey god.

Almost envied, but in the end Kern rather preferred to be departing to undertake other projects. Let others become gods of mere single worlds. She herself would stride the stars and head up the pantheon.

'I am not in position, no.' And apparently he felt that was also deserving of a wider audience, because he had broadcast it on the general channel.

Kern felt a stab of annoyance. *I cannot physically do everything myself. Why is it that other people so often fail to meet my standards, when I rely on them?* To Sering alone she sent, 'Perhaps you would explain why?'

'I was hoping to be able to say a few words, Doctor Kern.'

It would be his last contact with his species for a long time, she knew, and it seemed appropriate. If he could make a good showing then it would only add to her legend. She held ready on the master comms, though, setting him on a few seconds' delay, just in case he became maudlin or started saying something inappropriate.

'This is a turning point in human history,' Sering's voice – always slightly mournful – came to her, and then through her to everyone else. His image was in their Mind's Eye HUDs, with the collar of his bright orange environment suit done up high to the chin. 'I had to think long and hard before committing myself to this course, as you can imagine. But some things are too important. Sometimes you have to just do the right thing, whatever the cost.'

Kern nodded, pleased with that. *Be a good monkey and finish up soon, Sering. Some of us have legacies to build.*

'We have come so far, and still we fall into the oldest errors,' Sering continued doggedly. 'We're standing here with the universe in our grasp and, instead of furthering our own destinies, we connive at our own obsolescence.'

Her attention had drifted a little and, by the time she realized what he had said, the words had passed on to the crew. She registered suddenly a murmur of concerned messages between them, and even simple spoken words whispered between those closest to her. Doctor Mercian meanwhile sent her an alert on another channel: 'Why is Sering in the engine core?'

Sering should not be in the engine core of the needle. Sering should be in the Sentry Pod, ready to take his place in orbit – and in history.

She cut Sering off from the crew and sent him an angry demand to know what he thought he was doing. For a moment his avatar stared at her in her visual field, then it lip-synced to his voice.

'You have to be stopped, Doctor Kern. You and all your kind – your new humans, new machines, new species. If you succeed here, then there will be other worlds – you've said so yourself, and I know they're terraforming them even now. It ends here. *Non Ultra Natura!* No greater than nature.'

She wasted vital moments of potential dissuasion by resorting to personal abuse, until he spoke again.

'I've cut you off, Doctor. Do the same to me if you wish, but for now I'm going to speak and you don't get to interrupt me.'

She was trying to override him, hunting through the control computer's systems to find what he had done, but he had locked her out elegantly and selectively. There were whole areas of the facility's systems that just did not appear on her mental schematic, and when she quizzed the computer about them, it refused to acknowledge their existence. None of them was mission critical – not the Barrel, not the Flask, not even the Sentry Pod – therefore none were the systems she had been obsessively checking every day.

Not mission critical, perhaps, but *facility* critical.

'He's disabled the reactor safeties,' Mercian reported. 'What's going on? Why's he in the engine core at all?' Alarm but not outright panic, which was a good finger in the air for the mood of the crew all around.

He is in the engine core because his death will be instant and total and therefore probably painless, Kern surmised. She was already moving, to the surprise of the others. She was heading up, climbing into the access shaft that led to the slender central pylon of the station, heading away from the outer floor that remained 'down' only so long as she was close to it; climbing up out of that spurious gravity well towards the long needle they all revolved around. There was a flurry of increasingly concerned messages. Voices called out at her heels. Some of them would follow her, she knew.

Sering was continuing blithely: 'This is not even the beginning, Doctor Kern.' His tone was relentlessly deferential even in rebellion. 'Back home it will have already started. Back home it is probably already over. In another few years, maybe, you'll hear that Earth and our future have been taken back for the humans. No uplifted monkeys, Doctor Kern. No godlike computers. No freakshows of the human form. We'll have the universe to ourselves, as we were intended to – as was always our destiny. On all the colonies, in the solar system and out, our agents will have made their move. We will have taken power – with the consent of the majority, you understand, Doctor Kern.'

And she was lighter and lighter, hauling herself towards an 'up' that was becoming an 'in'. She knew she should be cursing Sering, but what was the point if he would never hear her?

It was not such a long way to the weightlessness of the needle's hollow interior. She had her choice then: either towards the engine core, where Sering had no doubt taken steps to ensure that he would not be disturbed; or away. Away, in a very final sense.

She could override anything Sering had done. She had full confidence in the superiority of her abilities. It would take time, though. If she cast herself that way down the needle, towards Sering and his traps and locked barriers, then time would be something she would not have the benefit of.

'And if the powers-that-be refuse us, Doctor Kern,' that hateful voice continued in her ear, 'then we will fight. If we must wrest mankind's destiny back by force, then we shall.'

She barely took in what he was saying, but a cold sense of fear was creeping into her mind – not from the danger to her and the Brin 2, but what he was saying about Earth and the colonies. *A war? Impossible. Not even the NUNs . . .* But it was true there had been some incidents – assassinations, riots, bombs. The whole of Europa Base had been compromised. The NUNs were spitting into the inevitable storm of manifest destiny, though. She had always believed that. Such outbursts represented the last throes of humanity's underevolvers.

She was now heading the other way, distancing herself from the engine core as though the Brin had enough space within it for her to escape the coming blast. She was utterly rational, however. She knew exactly where she was going.

Ahead of her was the circular portal to the Sentry Pod. Only on seeing it did she realize that some part of her mind – the part she always relied on to finesse the more complex calculations – had already fully understood the current situation and discerned the one slim-but-possible way out.

This was where Sering was supposed to be. This was the slow boat to the future that he – in a sane timeline – would have been piloting. Now she ordered the door to open, relieved to discover that this – the one piece of equipment that was actually his particular business – seemed to have remained free of Sering's meddling.

The first explosion came, and she thought it was the last one. The Brin creaked and lurched around her, but the engine core remained stable – as evidenced by the fact that she herself had not been disintegrated. She tuned back into the wild whirl of frantic messaging between the crew. Sering had rigged the escape pods. He didn't want anyone avoiding the fate he had decreed for himself. Had he somehow forgotten the Sentry Pod?

The detonating pods would push the Brin 2 out of position,

drifting either towards the planet or off into space. She had to get clear.

The door opened at her command, and she had the Sentry hub run a diagnostic on the release mechanism. There was so little space inside, just the cold-sleep coffin – *don't think of it as a coffin!* – and the termini of its associated systems.

The hub was querying her – she was not the right person, nor was she wearing the proper gear for prolonged cold sleep. *But I don't intend to be here for centuries, just long enough to ride it out.* She swiftly overrode its quibbles, and by that time the diagnostics had pinpointed Sering's tampering, or rather identified, by process of elimination, those parts of the release process that he had erased from its direct notice.

Sounds from outside suggested that the best course of action was to order the door closed, and then lock the systems so that nobody from outside could intrude on her.

She climbed into the cold-sleep tank, and around that time the banging started; those others of the crew who had come to the same realization as her, but slightly later. She blocked out their messaging. She blocked out Sering too, who was obviously not going to tell her anything useful now. It was better if she didn't have to share her head with anyone except the hub control systems.

She had no idea how much time she had, but she worked with the trademark balance of speed and care that had got her where she was now. *Got me leading the Brin 2 facility and got me here in the Sentry Pod. What a clever, doomed monkey I am.* The muffled banging was more insistent, but the pod only had room for one. Her heart had always been hard, but she found that she had to harden it still further, and not think of all those names and faces, her loyal colleagues, that she and Sering between them were condemning to an explosive end.

Which I myself have not yet escaped, she reminded herself. And then she had it: a work-around jury-rigged release path that avoided Sering's ghost systems. Would it work? She had no opportunity for a dry run, nor had she any other options. Nor, she suspected, any time.

Release, she ordered the hub, and then shouted down all of the different ways it was programmed to ask 'Are you sure?', until she felt the movement of mechanisms around her.

Then it wanted her to go into cold sleep immediately, as had been the plan, but she made it wait. If the captain was not going down with her ship, she would at least watch its demise from a distance. *And how much distance would that need?*

There were, by then, several thousand messages clamouring for her attention. Every member of the crew wanted to talk to her, but she had nothing to say to any of them.

The Sentry Pod had no windows either. Had she wanted, it could have shown her a HUD display of the rapidly receding Brin 2, as her little capsule of life fell into its prearranged orbit.

Now she returned to the Brin's systems, her internal comms boosted by the Sentry hub, and instructed it, *Launch the Barrel*.

She wondered if it was just poor timing, but in retrospect that had probably been Sering's first and more carefully performed task – subtle enough to slip by in all her checks, because of course the actual mechanical release for Flask and Barrel was virtually beneath her notice. *On the shoulders of others*, she had said, but she had not stopped to think about those beneath her in that pyramid of achievement. Even the lowliest of them had to agree to bear her weight, or all of it would come falling down.

She saw the flare not even in her mind's eye, but through the brief flower of damage reports from the Brin 2's computers, as all of her colleagues and her facility, and Sering the traitor, and all of her work became abruptly no more than a rapidly disassociating cloud of fragments, a ghost-breath of dissipating atmosphere, with some unrecognizable organic remains.

Correct course and stabilize. She had been expecting a shockwave, but the Sentry Pod was already far enough away, and the Brin 2's energy and matter were so miniscule, compared to the distances involved, that barely any adjustment was required to ensure the Sentry Pod remained within its programmed orbit.

Show me. She braced herself for the image, but, really, at this remove it seemed almost nothing. A flash; a tiny burned boat of all her ideas and friends.

In the final analysis it had all been nothing more than a barrel of over-evolved monkeys, after all. From this distance, against the vast and heedless backdrop of Everything Else, it was hard to say why any of it had ever mattered at all.

Distress beacon, she ordered. Because they would need to know, on Earth, what had happened. They had to know that they must come and collect her, wake her like Sleeping Beauty. After all, she was Doctor Kern. She was the future of the human race, right here. They *needed* her.

Twenty long years for her signal to reach Earth. Far more than that for the rescue to come back, even with the best fusion engines employed to accelerate to three-quarter light speed. But her frail body would survive that long in cold sleep – and more than that.

Some hours later, she saw the end of it: she saw the Barrel hit atmosphere.

It was not on the planned trajectory, the conflagration of the Brin 2 having sent it off on a tangent so that it narrowly avoided being hurled forever into empty space. Its cargo would not care, in the long run. The Barrel burned, streaking like a meteor through the atmosphere of the green world. Somehow the thought of the insensate terror that its primate occupants must be going through, as they died in ignorance by fear and burning, touched her more than the death of her fellow humans. *And wouldn't Sering claim that as evidence that he was right?*

From force of habit, a redundant professional thoroughness, she located the Flask, watching as the smaller canister fell through the atmosphere at a gentler angle, delivering its viral cargo to a world devoid of the simians it was intended for.

We can always get more monkeys. That was a curious mantra, but it made her feel better. The uplift virus would last for millennia. The project would survive the treachery and death of its creators. She herself would ensure it.

Listen for a change in radio signals. Wake me when you hear it, she instructed.

The pod computer was not happy about that. It required more exacting parameters. Kern thought over all the developments back home she might want to be appraised of. Listing them all was tantamount to trying to predict the future.

Then give me options.

Her HUD streamed with possibilities. The pod computer

was a sophisticated piece of engineering, complex enough that it could feign sentience, if not quite own to it.

Upload facility, she noted. It was not the most pleasant thought in the world, but was she not always saying how much easier life would be if she could arrange everything herself? The pod could upload an image of her consciousness into itself. Albeit an imperfect copy, it would form a Kern-computer composite that would be able to react to external events in a simulation of her own best judgement. She scanned through the caveats and notes – more cutting-edge technology that they were due to have pioneered. Over time it was predicted that the AI network would further incorporate the uploaded Kern so that the composite would be able to make finer and finer distinctions. Potentially the end result would be something smarter and more capable than the simple sum total of human and machine combined.

Do it, she instructed, lying back and waiting for the pod to begin scanning her brain. *Just let them be quick with the rescue party.*

1.2 BRAVE LITTLE HUNTRESS

She is Portia, and she is hunting.

She is eight millimetres long but she is a tiger within her tiny world, fierce and cunning. Like all spiders, she has a body of two parts. Her small abdomen holds her book-lungs and the bulk of her gut. Her head-body is dominated by two huge eyes facing forwards for perfect binocular vision, beneath a pair of tiny tufts that crown her like horns. She is fuzzy with hair in broken patterns of brown and black. To predators, she looks more dead leaf than live prey.

She waits. Below her formidable eyes her fangs are flanked by limb-like mouthparts: her palps, coloured a startling white like a quivering moustache. Science has named her *Portia labiata*, just another unassuming species of jumping spider.

Her attention is fixed on another spider at home in its web. This is *Scytodes pallida*, longer-limbed and hunchbacked and able to spit toxic webbing. Scytodes specializes in catching and eating jumping spiders like Portia.

Portia specializes in eating spider-eating spiders, most of whom are larger and stronger than she.

Her eyes are remarkable. The visual acuity of a primate peers out from those pinhead-sized discs and the flexible chambers behind them, piecing together the world around her.

Portia has no thoughts. Her sixty thousand neurons barely form a brain, contrasted with a human's one hundred billion. But something goes on in that tiny knot of tissue. She has already recognized her enemy, and knows its spit will make any frontal assault fatal. She has been playing with the edge of the Scytodes's web, sending tactile lies to it of varying shades to see if it can be lured out. The target has twitched once or twice, but it will not be deceived.

This is what a few tens of thousands of neurons can do: Portia has tried and failed, variation after variation, homing in on those that evinced the most response, and now she will go about things differently.

Her keen eyes have been examining the surroundings of the web, the branches and twigs that hang over and below it. Somewhere in her little knot of neurons a three-dimensional map has been built up from her meticulous scrutiny, and she has plotted a painstaking course to where she may come at the Scytodes from above, like a minute assassin. The approach is not perfect, but it is the best the environment will allow, and her scrap of brain has worked all this out as a theoretical exercise ahead of time. The planned approach will take her out of sight of her prey for much of the journey, but even when her prey is beyond view, it will remain in her tiny mind.

If her prey was something other than Scytodes, then she would have different tactics – or would experiment until something worked. It usually does.

Portia's ancestors have been making these calculations and decisions for millennia, each generation fractionally more accomplished because the best hunters are the ones that eat well and lay more eggs.

So far, so natural, and Portia is just about to set off on her quest when movement attracts her gaze.

Another of her species has arrived, a male. He has also been studying the Scytodes, but now his acute eyes are locked on her.

Past individuals of her species might have decided that the little male was a safer lunch than the Scytodes, and made plans accordingly, but now something changes. The presence of the male speaks to her. It is a complex new experience. The crouching figure there at the far side of the Scytodes's web is not just prey/mate/irrelevant. There is an invisible connection strung between them. She does not quite grasp that he is *something like her*, but her formidable ability to calculate strategies has gained a new dimension. A new category appears that expands her options a hundredfold: *ally*.

For long minutes the two hunting spiders examine their mental maps while the Scytodes hangs patiently oblivious between them. Then Portia watches the male creep around the web's edge a little. He waits for her to move. She does not. He moves again. At last he has got to where his presence changes her instinctive calculation of the odds.

She moves off along the course that she had been plotting out, creeping, jumping, descending by a thread, and all the while her mind retains its image of that three-dimensional world, and the two other spiders inside it.

At last she is in position above the Scytodes's web, back in sight of the motionless male. She waits until he makes his move. He skitters on to the silken strands, cautiously testing his footing. His movements are mechanical, repetitive, as though he is just some fragment of dead leaf that has drifted into the web. The Scytodes shifts once, then remains still. A breeze shivers the web and the male moves more swiftly under cover of the white noise of the shaking strands.

He bounces and dances abruptly, speaking the language of the web in loud and certain terms: *Prey! Prey here, trying to escape!*

The Scytodes is instantly on the move and Portia strikes, dropping down behind her displaced enemy and sinking her fangs into it. Her poison immobilizes the other spider swiftly. The hunt is concluded.

Soon after, the little male returns and they regard one another, trying to build a new picture of their world. They feed. She is constantly on the verge of driving him away and yet that new dimension, that commonality, stays her fangs. He is prey. He is *not* prey.

Later, they hunt together again. They make a good team. Together they are able to take on targets and situations that, alone, either would have retreated from.

Eventually he is promoted from prey/not-prey to mate, because her behaviours are limited as regards males. After the act of mating, other instincts surface and their partnership comes to an end.

She lays her clutch, the many eggs of a very successful huntress.

Their children will be beautiful and brilliant and grow to twice her size, infected with the nanovirus that Portia and the male both carry. Further generations will be larger and brighter and more successful still, one after the other selectively evolving at a virally accelerated rate so that those best able to exploit this new advantage will dominate the gene pool of the future.

Portia's children will inherit the world.

1.3 THE LIGHTS GO OUT

Doctor Avrana Kern awoke to a dozen complex feeds of information, none of which helped her restore her memories of what had just happened or why she was groggily returning to consciousness in a cold-sleep unit. She could not open her eyes; her entire body was cramping and there was nothing in her mental space except the overkill of information assailing her, every system of the Sentry Pod clamouring to report.

Eliza mode! she managed to instruct, feeling queasy, bloated, constipated and overstimulated all at once as the machinery of the coffin laboured to bring her back to something resembling active life.

'Good morning, Doctor Kern,' said the Sentry hub in her auditory centres. It had assumed a woman's voice, strong and reassuring. Kern was not reassured. She wanted to ask why she was here in the Sentry Pod, but she could feel the answer continually just about to hit her and never quite landing.

Just give me something to get my memories back together! she ordered.

'That is not recommended,' the hub cautioned her.

If you want me to make any kind of decision— and then everything fell back into her head in pieces, dams breaking to unleash a flood of horrifying revelation. The Brin 2 was gone. Her colleagues were gone. The monkeys were gone. Everything was lost, except her.

And she had told the hub to wake her when the radio signals came.

She took what was intended to be a deep breath, but her chest would not work properly and she just wheezed. *About time*, she told the hub, for all that statement would be meaningless to the computer. Now it was talking to her, she instinctively felt she should converse with it as though it was human. This had always been a vexing side-effect of the Eliza mode. *How much time has elapsed, Earth standard?*

'Fourteen years and seventy-two days, Doctor.'

That's . . . She felt her throat open a little. 'That can't be . . .' No point telling a computer it couldn't be right, but it *wasn't* right. It wasn't long enough. Word couldn't have got back to Earth and a rescue ship arrived back in that time. But then the hope set in. Of course, a ship had *already* been heading for her before Sering destroyed the Brin 2. No doubt the man's status as a NUN agent had been uncovered long before, when their ridiculous uprising had failed. She was saved. Surely she was saved.

Initiate contact, she told the hub.

'I'm afraid that is not possible, Doctor.'

She tutted and called up the systems feeds again, feeling better able to cope with them. Each part of the pod opened for her, confirming its working order. She checked the comms. Receivers were within tolerance. Transmitters were working – sending out her distress signal and also performing their primary function, broadcasting a complex set of messages to the planet below. Of course, it had been intended that some day that same planet would become the cradle to a new species that might receive and decode those messages. No chance of that now.

'It's all . . .' Her croaky voice infuriated her. *Clarify. What's the problem?*

'I'm afraid that there is nothing to initiate contact with, Doctor,' the hub's Eliza mode told her politely. Her attention was then directed to a simulation of space surrounding them: planet, Sentry Hub. No ship from Earth.

Explain.

'There has been a change in radio signals, Doctor. I require a Command decision as to its significance, I'm afraid.'

'Will you stop saying, "I'm afraid"!' she rasped angrily.

'Of course, Doctor.' And it would, she knew. That particular mannerism would be barred from its speech from that moment on. 'Since you entered cold sleep, I have been monitoring signals from Earth.'

'And?' But Kern's voice shook a little. *Sering mentioned a war. Has there been news of a war?* And, on the heels of that: *Would the hub even know to wake me? It wouldn't be able to filter for content like that. So what . . . ?*

It had been there, lost amidst the profusion of data, but the hub highlighted it now. Not a presence but an absence.

She wanted to ask it, *What am I looking at?* She wanted to tell it that it was wrong again. She wanted it to double check, as though it was not checking every single moment.

There were no more radio signals from Earth. The last trailing edge of them had passed the Sentry Pod by and, radiating out from Earth at the speed of light, were already out of date by twenty years as they fled past her into the void.

I want to hear the final twelve hours of signals.

She had thought that there would be too many of them but they were few, scattered, encoded. Those she could interpret were pleas for help. She tracked them back another forty-eight hours, trying to piece it all together. The hub's rolling recorder had retained no more than that. The precise details were already lost, speeding away from her faster than she could possibly pursue. Sering's war had broken out, though; that was all she could think. It had come and begun snuffing out colonies across human space. The lights had gone out across the solar system, as the NUNs and their allies rose up and wrestled with their enemies for the fate of mankind.

That there had been an escalation seemed incontrovertible. Kern was well aware that the governments of Earth and the colonies possessed weapons of terrifying potential, and the theoretical science existed for far worse.

The war on Earth had gone hot, that much she could tell. Neither side had backed down. Both sides had pushed and pushed, pulling new toys from the box. The beginnings of the war were lost from her two-and-half-day radio window, but she had the dreadful suspicion that the entire global conflict had lasted less than a week.

And now, twenty light years away, Earth lay silent – had lain silent for two decades. Were there people there at all? Had the entire human race been exterminated save for her, or had it simply been thrown back into a new dark age, where the dumb brute people looked up at those moving lights in the sky and forgot that their ancestors had built them.

'The stations, the in-solar colonies . . . the others . . .' she got out.

'One of the last transmissions from Earth was an all-frequencies, all-directions electronic virus, Doctor,' Eliza reported dolorously. 'Its purpose was to infest and disable any system that received it. It appears that it was able to penetrate known security. I surmise that the various colony systems have all been shut down.'

'But that means . . .' Avrana already felt as cold as any human could have. She waited for the chill of realization, but there was none. The in-solar colonies and the handful of extra-solar bases were still being terraformed; they had been built early on in mankind's spacegoing history, and after the technology had been developed, the extensive presence of human settlements there had slowed the process down: so many individual toes to tread on. Tabula rasa planets were so much swifter, and Kern's World was the very first of these to be completed. Beyond Earth, mankind was terribly, terribly reliant on its technology, on its computers.

If such a virus had taken over the systems on Mars or Europa, and disabled those systems, that meant death. Swift death, cold death, airless death.

'How did *you* survive then? How did *we* survive?'

'Doctor, the virus was not designed to attack experimental uploaded human personality constructs. Your presence within my systems has prevented me being a suitable host for the virus.'

Avrana Kern stared past the lights of her HUD at the darkness inside the Sentry Pod, thinking about all the places in the greater dark beyond where humanity had once made a fragile, eggshell home for itself. In the end all she could think of to ask was, 'Why did you wake me?'

'I require you to make a Command decision, Doctor.'

'What Command decision could you possibly need now?' she asked the computer acidly.

'It will be necessary for you to return to cold sleep,' the hub told her, and now she bitterly missed the '. . . I'm afraid', which had added a much-needed sense of human hesitancy. 'However, a lack of information concerning current external circumstances means that I am likely to be unable to determine an appropriate trigger to reawaken you. I also believe that you yourself may not be able to instruct me concerning such a trigger, although you may give me any instructions you wish, or alternatively simply specify a particular period of time. In the alternative, you may simply rely on your personality upload to wake you at the appropriate time.'

The unspoken echo of that sounded in her mind: *Or never. There may never be a time.*

Show me the planet.

The great green orb that she spun about was produced for her, and all its measurements and attributes, each linking to a nested tree of additional details. Somewhere in there were the credits, the names of the dead who had designed and built each part and piece of it, who had guided its plate tectonics and sparked its weather systems into life, fast-tracked its erosion and seeded its soil with life.

But the monkeys burned. All for nothing.

It seemed impossible that she had been so close to that grand dream, the spread of life throughout the universe, the diversification of intelligence, the guaranteed survival of Earth's legacy. *And then the war came, and Sering's idiocy, just too soon.*

How long can we last? was her question.

'Doctor, our solar arrays should enable our survival for an

indefinite period of time. Although it is possible that external impact or accumulated mechanical defect may eventually result in the cessation of function, there is no known upper limit on our working lifespan.'

That had probably been intended as a pronouncement of hope. To Kern it sounded more like a prison sentence.

Let me sleep, she told the pod.

'I require guidance on when to wake you.'

She laughed at it, the sound of her own voice hideous in the close confines. 'When the rescue ship arrives. When the monkeys answer. When my undead uploaded self decides. Is that sufficient?'

'I believe I can work within those tolerances, Doctor. I will now prepare you for a return to cold sleep.'

Sleep for a long, lonely time. She would return to the tomb, and a simulacrum of herself would stand watch over a silent planet, in a silent universe, as the last outpost of the great spacefaring human civilization.

2
PILGRIMAGE

2.1 TWO THOUSAND YEARS FROM HOME

Holsten Mason started awake into a nightmare of claustrophobia, fighting it down almost as quickly as it hit him. Experience allowed him to recognize where he was and why that was no cause for alarm, but the old monkey instincts still had their moment of glory, shrieking *Trapped! Trapped!* in the halls of his mind.

Fucking monkeys. He was freezing cold and enclosed in a space that his body barely fit into, with what felt like a thousand needles withdrawing themselves from his grey and nerveless skin – and tubes being yanked from more intimate regions – none of it done with much sense of tender care.

Business as usual for the suspension chamber. He would like to think that he really hated suspension chambers, but that wasn't exactly an option for any member of the human race right now.

For a moment he thought that this was it; he was being woken up but not released, to be trapped instead behind the frigid glass, unheard and unnoticed on a vast and empty ship of iced corpses heading forever into the nowhere of deep space.

The primal claustrophobia jumped him for a second time. He was already fighting to lift his hands, to beat at the transparent cover above him, when the seal hissed and the dim, undirected light was replaced by the steady glare of the ship's lamps.

His eyes barely flinched. The suspension chamber would have been preparing his body for this awakening long before it deigned to spark his mind back to life. Belatedly he wondered if something had gone wrong. There were a limited number of circumstances in which he would have been revived, after all. He could hear no alarms, though, and the very limited status readout within the chamber had all been safe blue bars. *Unless that's what's broken of course.*

The ark ship *Gilgamesh* had been built to last a very long time indeed, using every piece of craft and science that Holsten's civilization had been able to wrest from the cold, vacuum-withered hands of their forebears. Even so, had there been an option, nobody would have trusted it, for how could anyone have faith that a machine – any machine, any work of the hands of humanity – could last throughout the appalling periods of time that would be required for this journey?

'Happy birthday! You're now the oldest man in history!' said a sharp voice. 'Now get your feet under you, you lazy tosser. We need you.'

Holsten's eyes focused on a face, nominally a woman's. It was hard, lined, with a bony chin and cheekbones, and her hair the same close crop of stubble as his own. Suspension chambers were not kind to human hair.

Isa Lain: chief Key Crew engineer of the *Gilgamesh*.

He started trying to make some joke about never thinking she'd say she needed him, but he slurred the words and lost it. She understood enough to look at him contemptuously.

'*Need* isn't the same as *want*, old man. Get up. And button your suit; your arse is hanging out.'

Feeling like a hundred-year-old cripple, he hunched and clambered and swung his way out of the coffin-shaped tank that had been his resting place for . . .

Oldest man in what, now? Lain's words came back to him with a jolt of realization. 'Hey,' he said thickly. 'How long? How far out?' *Are we even clear of the solar system? We must be for her to say that* . . . And, as if he could see through the close, confining walls, he had a sudden sense of the vast emptiness that must be out there beyond the hull, a void that no human had plumbed since before the ice age, since the millennia-ago days of the Old Empire.

The Key Crew suspension room was cramped, barely space for the two of them and the ranks of coffins: his own and two others open and empty, the rest still holding the not-quite-corpses of other vital crew, against the need for them to resume an active role aboard ship. Lain threaded her way over to the hatch and swung it open before answering, glancing back over her shoulder with all her mockery gone.

'One thousand, eight hundred and thirty-seven years, Mason. Or that's what the *Gilgamesh* says.'

Holsten sat back down on the lip of the suspension chamber, his legs abruptly insufficient to keep him standing up.

'How's the . . . how's he holding up? Have you . . . ?' The sentences kept fragmenting in his head. 'How long have you been up? Have you checked over . . . the cargo, the others . . . ?'

'I've been up for nine days now while you were being lovingly licked awake, Mason. I've gone over everything. It's all satisfactory. They did a good, solid job when they built this boy.'

'Satisfactory?' He sensed the uncertainty in that word. 'Then everyone's . . . ?'

'Satisfactory in that we have a four per cent chamber failure rate amongst the cargo,' she told him flatly. 'For just short of two millennia, I think that counts as satisfactory. It could have been worse.'

'Right. Yes, of course.' He got to his feet again and made his way over to her, the floor chilly against his bare skin, trying now to work out if they were accelerating or decelerating or if the crew section was just spinning about its axis for gravity. Certainly *something* was keeping him on the floor. If there was some sense that could split hairs between different flavours of ersatz gravity, though, it was one his forebears had somehow failed to evolve.

He was trying not to think about what *four per cent* meant, or that the handily impersonal word 'cargo' referred to a very large fraction of the surviving human race.

'And you need me for what, anyway?' Because most of the others were still asleep, and what bizarre set of circumstances could possibly require his presence when most of Command, Science, Security and Engineering were still locked in a freezing, dreamless stasis?

'There's a signal,' Lain told him, watching for his reaction carefully. 'Yes, I thought that would get you moving.'

He was nothing but questions as they negotiated the passage that led through to comms, but Lain just set a punishing pace and ignored him, letting him weave and stumble as his legs tried to betray him with every few steps.

Vrie Guyen was the third early riser, as Holsten had anticipated. Whatever the emergency, it required the *Gilgamesh*'s commander, its chief engineer and its classicist. But what

Lain had said accounted for that neatly. A *signal*. And, out here, what could that mean? Either something wholly alien, or a remnant of the Old Empire, Holsten's area of expertise.

'It's faint and badly distorted. The *Gilgamesh* took too long, really, to even recognize it for what it was. I need you to see what you can make of it.' Guyen was a thin, small-framed man, with a nose and mouth that both seemed to have been salvaged from a far broader face. Holsten recalled his command style as being a mixture of aggressive motivation and good delegating skills. It seemed like only a few days ago that Holsten had been under that stern gaze as he climbed into his suspension chamber, but when he probed his memories to determine just how many days, he uncovered an uncrossable grey area, a dim sensation that his sense of time was out of joint.

Two thousand years will do that to you, apparently. Every minute or so he was struck afresh by the revelation of how ludicrously lucky they all were just to be here. *Satisfactory*, as Lain had said.

'Where's it coming from, though?' Holsten asked. 'Is it where we thought it would be?'

Guyen just nodded, his face composed, but Holsten felt a thrill of excitement go through him. *It's there! It was real, all this time.*

The *Gilgamesh* had not just cast itself randomly into the void to escape the end of all that they had left behind. They were one step short of being quite as suicidal as that. They had been following the maps and charts of the Old Empire, looted from failed satellites, from fragments of ship, from the broken shells of orbital stations containing the void-mummified corpses of Earth's former masters. Vacuum and stable orbits had saved them while the ice was scouring the planet below.

And amongst the relics were the star maps, detailing where in the galaxy the ancients had walked.

They showed him the signal, as it was distantly received by the *Gilgamesh*'s instruments. It was a relatively short message, repeating interminably. No busy radio chatter of a bustling extra-solar colony: that would surely have been too much to hope for, given the time that had elapsed.

'Maybe it's a warning,' Guyen suggested. 'If so, and if there's some danger, we need to know.'

'And if there's some danger, what precisely do we do about it?' Holsten asked quietly. 'Can we even change our heading enough now, without hitting the system?'

'We can prepare,' Lain said pragmatically. 'If it's some cosmic event that we somehow haven't picked up, and that somehow hasn't destroyed the transmitter, then we might have to try and alter course. If it's . . . a plague, or hostile aliens or something, then . . . well, it's been a long time, I'll bet. Probably it's not relevant any more.'

'But we have the maps. Worst comes to worst, we can plot a course for the next world,' Guyen pointed out. 'We'll just slingshot past their sun and be on our way.'

By then Holsten had stopped paying attention to him and just sat hunched, listening by earpiece to the *Gilgamesh*'s rendition of the signal, looking over visual depictions of its frequency and pattern, calling up reference works from their library.

He adjusted the *Gilgamesh*'s interpretation of the signal, parsing it through all the known decoding algorithms that long-dead civilization had used. He had done this before plenty of times. All too often the signal would be encoded beyond the ability of modern cryptography to unpick. At other times there would be plain speech, but in one of those problem languages that nobody had been able to decipher.

He listened and ran his encryptions, and words began to leap out at him, in that formal, antique tongue of a vanished age of wonder and plenty, and an appalling capacity for destruction.

'Imperial C,' he declared confidently. It was one of the more common of the known languages and, if he could just get his brain working properly, it should be child's play to translate it now he'd cleaned it up. There was a message there, finally opening like a flower to him, spilling out its brief, succinct contents in a language that had died before the ice came.

'What—?' Guyen started angrily, but Holsten held up a hand for silence, letting the whole message play again and enjoying his moment of prominence.

'It's a distress beacon,' he announced.

'Distress as in "Go away"?' Lain pressed.

'Distress as in "Come and get me",' Holsten told them, meeting their eyes, seeing there the first spark of hope and wonder that he himself felt. 'Even if there's no one – and almost certainly there's no one – there will be tech, function-ing tech. Something waiting there for us for thousands of years. Just for us.'

For a moment this revelation was strong enough that their generalized low-level dislike of him almost vanished. They were three shepherds leading their human flock to a new, promised land. They were the founding parents of the future.

Then Guyen clapped his hands. 'Fine. Good work. I'll

have the *Gilgamesh* wake key personnel in time to start de-celeration. We've won our gamble.' No words said for all those left behind, who had not even been given the chance to play, or to wonder about the handful of other ark ships that had taken different courses, the Earth spitting out the last gobbets of its inhabitants before the rising tide of poison overcame it. 'Back to your slabs, both of you.' There was still at least a century of silent, death-cold travel between them and the signal's source.

'Give me just half a watch awake,' Holsten said automatic-ally.

Guyen glared at him, remembering suddenly that he had not wanted Holsten among Key Crew – too old, too fond of himself, too proud of his precious education. 'Why?'

Because it's cold. Because it's like being dead. Because I'm afraid I won't wake up – or that you won't wake me. Because I'm afraid. But Holsten shrugged easily. 'Time enough to sleep later, isn't there? Let me look at the stars, at least. Just half a watch and then I'll turn in. Where's the harm?'

Guyen grumbled his contempt at him but nodded reluc-tantly. 'Let me know when you go back. Or if you're last man up, then—'

'Turn out the lights, yes. I know the drill.' In truth the drill was a complex double check of ship's systems, but the *Gil-gamesh* itself did most of the hard stuff. All of Key Crew were taught how to do it. It was barely more taxing than reading down a list: monkey work.

Guyen stalked off, shaking his head, and Holsten cocked an eye towards Lain, but she was already going over the engineering readouts, a professional to the last.

Later, though, as he sat in the cupola and watched the

alien starfield, two thousand years from any constellations that his ancestors might have known, she came to join him, and sat with him for a fidgety fifteen minutes without saying anything. Neither of them could quite voice the suggestion then, but, by raised eyebrow and abortive hand movement, they ended up out of their shipsuits and clasped together on the cool floor, whilst all of creation wheeled gently overhead.

2.2 EARTH'S OTHER CHILDREN

The name she answers to has both a simple and a complex form. The simple form comprises a series of telegraphed gestures, a precise motion of the palps conveying a limited amount of information. The longer form incorporates a backing of stamping and shivering to add a subtle vibrational subtext to that crude flag-waving, varying with mood and tense and whether she speaks to a dominant or submissive female, or to a male.

The nanovirus has been busy, doing what it can with unexpected material. She is the result of generations of directed mutation, her presence mute witness for all those failures who never bred. Call her Portia.

To travel the forest is to travel the high roads, branch to branch, each tree a world in miniature – crossing where the branches touch: now upside down, now right side up, scaling vertical trunks then leaping where the branches give out, trailing a lifeline and trusting to the eye and the mind to calculate distance and angle.

Portia creeps forwards, judging ranges: her branch juts out into the void, and she spends a careful minute considering whether she can make the jump to the next, before deciding that she cannot. Above her the canopy fades out into a network of twigs that can't possibly bear her weight.

Portia is far larger than her tiny ancestress, half a metre from fangs to spinnerets, an arachnophobe's nightmare. The support of her exoskeleton is aided by internal cartilage once used for little more than muscle attachment. Her muscles are more efficient too, and some of them expand and contract her abdomen, drawing air actively over her book-lungs rather than just passively taking in oxygen. This permits a boosted metabolism, regulated body temperature and a life of swift and sustained action.

Below is the forest floor, no place to be crossed lightly. There are larger predators than Portia abroad and, although she is confident in her ability to out-think them, that would involve lost time and dusk is close.

She scans her surroundings and considers her options. She has the excellent eyesight of the tiny huntress she evolved from. The great dark orbs of her principal eyes are considerably larger than those of any human.

She turns her body to bring her companions into view, trusting to her peripheral eyes to warn her of danger. Bianca, the other female, is still behind at the trunk, watching Portia and willing to trust her judgement. Bianca is larger but Portia leads, because size and strength have not been their species' most prized assets for a very long time.

The third of her party, the male, is lower than Bianca, his legs spread out for balance as he hangs on the tree, looking downwards. Possibly he thinks he is keeping watch, but Portia feels he is probably just letting his mind wander. Too bad: she needs him. He is smaller than she; he can jump further and trust to more slender branches.

The three of them are out of their territory by fifty days. Theirs is a species given to curiosity. That same ability that allowed their tiny ancestors to create a mental map of their environs has become the ability to imagine, to ask what is beyond the forest. Portia's people are born explorers.

She raises her palps, white side out, and signals: *Come here!* No need to give him his name. Females do not refer to males by name. He catches the motion in his lateral eyes and twitches. He is always twitching, afraid of his own shadow – wretched creature. She has distinct opinions on him, and more complimentary ones concerning Bianca. Her world consists of over a hundred individuals – mostly females – with whom she enjoys carefully maintained relationships. The nanovirus has been driving her species hard towards a communal existence. Although her brain is decidedly smaller than a human's, just as the original Portia could use her miniscule knot of neurons to accomplish remarkable things, this distant daughter has an impressive ability to solve problems: physical, spatial, theoretical, social. Her species has proved fertile ground for the virus's attentions.

Cautiously the male crosses beneath Bianca and springs up to her branch, safety line trailing in a white thread behind him.

Bridge across, she tells him when he is close enough to communicate with properly. *Quick now*. The basic content of her speech is visual, in a rapid semaphore of the palps. A wealth of context – mostly her general dissatisfaction with him – is provided in the vibrations of her flurrying feet.

He flashes his humble acquiescence briefly and heads out as far along the branch as he dares, settling and resettling his feet over and over as he considers the jump ahead. Portia flashes her exasperation back to Bianca, but her companion is watching something below. An apparition like a walking carpet is creeping along the forest floor, another spider but a species that the nanovirus has managed to gift with a greater size and little else. As bulky as half a dozen Portias, it would kill her in a moment if only it could catch her.

Bianca is hungry. She indicates the ground-crawler and idly suggests they break their journey now.

Portia considers and finds the suggestion has merit. She waits until the male has made his jump across – easily, despite all his trepidation – and leaves him hauling himself back along his own line to begin the bridgework. Then she flashes a message to Bianca and the two of them begin to descend.

The hairy hunter below is intent on its own hunger – the forest is not short of prey species of varying sizes, many of them abortive results of the nanovirus's work. There are some surviving vertebrate species – mice, birds, dwarf deer, snakes – but the virus has tried and failed with them. Kern's experiment called for monkeys, and she ensured that the green planet's chosen would suffer no competition from close cousins. The vertebrates that the monkeys were intended to interact with were designed to reject the virus. They have changed hardly at all.

Nobody considered the invertebrates, the complex eco-system of tiny creeping things intended to be nothing more than a scaffolding by which the absent monkeys would ascend.

In so many cases – as with the great tarantula-descendant below that Portia is considering – whilst the virus was able to provoke growth, the sought-for neural complexity never arose. Often the environmental pressure to select for such a facility was simply lacking. A sense of self and the ability to contemplate the universe are not necessarily survival traits in and of themselves. Portia is a rare exception – though not the only exception – where increased cognitive capacity granted an immediate and compelling advantage.

The carpet-like hunter stops, the faintest of vibrations reaching it. The forest floor is strewn with its thread, forming a messy but effective sense organ that alerts it to the movements of its prey. Against a creature as simple as this, Portia and her kin prefer hunting methods that have not changed in thousands of years.

Portia has discerned the pattern of threads below, running through the leaf litter, almost hidden save to eyes as keen as hers. She reaches down with a foreleg and plays them carefully, speaking eloquently the language of touch and motion, creating a phantom prey, and giving it the illusion of size, distance and weight entirely conjured by her skill. She places herself in the primitive mind of the ground-hunter, as surely as if she could actually implant her thoughts there.

It advances a handful of steps, testing out this sensation, not wholly convinced. She wonders if it has had some near-escapes with her kind before. The great shaggy abdomen is up, ready to shake out a cloud of barbed hairs that will choke Portia's book-lungs and irritate her joints.

She reaches down gingerly again, prying and tugging, suggesting that the illusory prey is getting further away, soon to escape entirely. Her body is mottled and irregular as her ancestors' were, and the ground-hunter's simple eyes have not made her out.

It takes the bait suddenly, in a hairy rush across the forest floor towards nothing, and Bianca drops on its back, fangs first, driving them in where its legs meet its body, and then springing away a few body-lengths to be out of the way of any riposte. The hunter lunges after her, but stumbles even as it does so, abruptly unsteady. Moments later it is twitching and quivering as the venom takes effect, and the two females wait for it to grow motionless – though still alive – before closing in to feed. Bianca in particular remains taut for another leap to escape if need be, her abdomen heaving slightly in and out as she forces air past her book-lungs.

Up above, the male is looking down plaintively and, when Portia checks on him, he signals for permission to feed. She tells him to finish his work first.

A moment later he has dropped down practically on top of her, sending her leaping instinctively backwards, landing clumsily and flipping onto her back before righting herself angrily. Bianca has come within a whisker of killing the male, but he is stamping and signalling frantically: *Danger coming! Danger! Spitters!*

And he is right: here come her kind's ancestral foes.

The spitting spiders, the Scytodes, have marched in step with Portia's kin all the way from their miniscule beginnings. They are somewhere between her and the ground-hunter in size; but size was not the key to dominance even in the ancient days before the virus. Now she sees them creep warily forwards, a whole troop of them: six – no, eight – individuals, spread out but watching, come down off their web to hunt. They hunt in packs, these uplifted Spitters, and Portia has an understanding that they are not beasts, whilst not having achieved whatever *she* has become. They are the big, shambling killers constantly on the edge of Portia's world; brutal lurking primitives whose unseen, implicit presence keeps hatchlings from straying too far from the nest.

If the numbers had been equal, then Portia and Bianca would have contested the kill – for they see that the Spitters have been following the path of the same prey. Eight is too many, though, even with the additional tricks the three travellers can utilize. The Scytodes will throw out their sprays of sticky, venomous webbing. Although their eyesight is weak, and Portia and her kind are smart enough to anticipate and agile enough to dodge, the sheer number of nets will make the odds of their escaping poor.

Conversely, the Spitters are well aware of the danger that Portia's kind poses. The two species have clashed over untold generations, each time with more understanding of the enemy. Now both recognize that the other is something less than kin but something more than prey.

Portia and Bianca make automatic threats, lifting their forelimbs and displaying their fangs. Portia is considering whether her secret new weapon would even the odds. Her mind plays out likely scenarios, with and without the male's assistance. The enemy numbers seem too great for her to be sure of victory, and her task comes first. In her mind is a meta-plan, just the sort of A-to-B route-finding that her distant antecedents performed, save that her goal is not just a spatial location but an intangible victory condition. A fight now with the Spitters would likely leave her in no position to achieve what she has set out to do.

She signals to the other two to fall back, making her gestures large and slow enough that the inferior eyes of the Spitters will read them. Can they understand her? She does not know. She could not even say whether they have some way of communicating amongst themselves that approximates to her own visual and vibrational language. Still, they hold off – no spitting and only a minimal threat display from them, as Portia and her cohorts retreat. Bianca's feet pluck out a muttering refrain of frustration and annoyance. Being larger than Portia, she is quicker to seek physical confrontation. She is here because that has its uses, but for that same reason she knows to follow Portia's lead.

They ascend once more, aware now that they must hunt again, and hope that the Scytodes clan will be satisfied with what was left here for them. Sometimes the Spitters follow, if they have the numbers, and then it would be a choice of fast flight or turn and ambush.

By dark, they have brought down an orb-web builder, and the male jumps on an unwary mouse, neither of which makes a hearty meal. Portia's active lifestyle and altered anatomy mean that she needs considerably more food than her predecessors, pound for pound. If they were to be forced to live by hunting alone, then their journey would take far longer than it should. Amongst her baggage, however, Bianca has a quartet of live aphids. She lets the little creatures out to suck sap, fending the male off in case he forgets that they are not for eating – or not yet. After dusk, when Portia has spun a make-shift tent in the canopy, complete with warning lines in all directions, the aphids produce glutinous honeydew, which the spiders can drink as though it was the nourishing liquid-ized innards of their prey. The domesticated creatures meekly return to Bianca's webbing afterwards, understanding only that they are safe with her, not realizing that, in extremis, they themselves will become the meal.

Portia is still hungry – honeydew is subsistence stuff, nourishing without the satisfaction of taking real prey. It is difficult for her to crouch there, knowing that there are aphids – and the male – within reach, but she can look ahead and see that her long-term plan will suffer if those are consumed now. Her lineage has always specialized in looking ahead.

And in looking beyond, too. Now she squats at the entrance to the makeshift tent forming their camp, Bianca and the male nestling beside her for warmth, and looks out through the gaps in the canopy at the lights populating the night sky. Her people know them and see paths and patterns in them and realize that they, too, move. Portia understands that their celestial journeys are predictable enough to use when navigating her own. One, though, is special. One light does not tread a slow and year-long course over the heavens, but hurries past, a genuine traveller just as she is. Portia looks up now and sees that tiny glint of reflected light passing overhead, a solitary motile speck in the vast dark, and she feels a kinship with it, lending to that orbiting pinpoint as much of an arachnomorphic personality as she can conceive of.

2.3 ENIGMA VARIATIONS

This time they had all of Key Crew out of the morgue – Holsten almost the last one to appear, stumbling on numb feet and shivering. He looked better than a lot of them, though. His little jaunt – mere moments of personal time and over a century ago – had loosened him up. Most of the people he was now looking at had last opened their eyes while the *Gilgamesh* shared a solar system with the failing husk of Earth.

They were crammed into the briefing room, all grey faces and shaven heads, some of them looking malnourished, others bloated. A few had pale mottling across their skins: some side-effect of the sleep process that Holsten couldn't guess at.

He saw Guyen, looking more alert than anyone else there, and guessed the mission commander had ordered himself to be woken early, so that he could assert his bright, brisk dominance over this room full of zombies.

Holsten checked off the departments: Command, Engineering, Science, and what looked like the whole of Security too. He tried to catch Lain's eye but she barely glanced at him, nothing in her manner admitting to any century-ago liaison.

'Right.' Guyen's sharp tone drew all ears as a final few stumbled in. 'We're here. We've made it with five per cent loss of cargo, and around three per cent system deterioration according to the engineers. I consider that the greatest vindication of the human spirit and strength of will that history has ever known. You should all be proud of what we've achieved.' His tone was adversarial, certainly not congratulatory, and sure enough he went on, 'But the real work is yet to come. We have arrived and, as you all know, this was supposedly a system the Old Empire spacefleet frequented. We set our course for here because these were the closest extra-solar coordinates where we could hope to find a liveable habitat, and perhaps even salvageable tech. You all know the plan: we have their star maps, and there are other such locations within a relatively short journey of here – just a short hop compared to the distances we've already travelled without mishap.'

Or with just five per cent mishap, Holsten thought, but did not say. Guyen's belief in the extent of the Imperial presence within this system was also highly speculative, from the classicist's own perspective – and even 'Old Empire' was a maddeningly inaccurate term. Most of the others looked too groggy to really think beyond the words themselves, though. Again he glanced at Lain, but she seemed to be focused only on the commander.

'What most of you do not know is that the *Gilgamesh* intercepted transmissions emanating from this system on our way in, which have been identified as an automatic distress beacon. We have functioning technology.' He hurried on before anyone could get a question in. 'The *Gilgamesh* has therefore plotted a flightpath solution that will brake us around the star, and on the way out we'll come by slow enough for a meaningful pass close to the source of that signal – the planet there.'

Now his audience started waking up, and there was a rising babble of questions that Guyen waved down. 'That's right. A planet in the sweet spot, just like we were promised. It's been thousands of years, but space doesn't care. It's there, and the Old Empire has left a present for us too. And that could be good or it could be bad. We're going to have to be careful. Just so you know: the signal isn't from the planet itself but from some sort of satellite – maybe just a beacon, maybe something more. We're going to try and open communications with it, but no guarantees.'

'And the planet?' someone asked. Guyen indicated Renas Vitas, the head of the scientific team.

'We're loathe to commit so far,' the slender woman began – another who'd obviously been up for a while, or perhaps by nature unflappable. 'The analysis made by *Gilgamesh* on our way in suggests something only slightly smaller than Earth, at close to Earth's distance from the star, and with all the right components: oxygen, carbon, water, minerals . . .'

'So why not commit? Why not say it?' Holsten identified the speaker: big Karst, who led the security detail. His chin and cheeks were raw, red and peeling horribly, and Holsten remembered suddenly how the man had refused to lose his beard for the suspension chamber, and was now apparently paying the price.

I remember him arguing with Engineering over that, he thought. It should have seemed just days before, according to his personal waking history but, as he had noticed last time, there was clearly something imperfect about suspension. Certainly, Holsten could not feel the centuries that had passed since they abandoned Earth, but something in his mind acknowledged that lost time: the sense of a yawning, terrible wasteland, a purgatory of the imagination. He found himself reluctant to consider ever going back under.

'Why, in all honesty?' Vitas replied brightly. 'It's too good to be true. I want to overhaul our instruments. That planet is too Earth-like to be believed.'

Looking around at all the suddenly sour faces, Holsten raised his hand. 'But of course it's like Earth,' he got out. The looks turned on him were not encouraging: some merely creased with dislike, but rather more with exasperation. *What's the bloody classicist want now? Desperate for some attention already?*

'It's a terraforming project,' he explained. 'If it's like Earth, that just shows it's finished – or near finished.'

'There's no evidence the ancients ever actually practised terraforming,' Vitas told him, her tone an obvious putdown.

Let me take you through the archives: it's mentioned a hundred times in their writings. But instead, Holsten just shrugged, recognizing the showmanship of it all. 'There *is*,' he told them. 'Out there. We're heading straight towards it.'

'Right!' Guyen clapped his hands, perhaps annoyed that he had not been listening to his own voice for two minutes at a stretch. 'You each have your tasks, so go and make ready. Vitas, run checks on our instrumentation, as you proposed. I want us to conduct a full inspection of the planet and satellite as we close. Lain, keep a close eye on ship's systems as we approach the star's gravity well – the *Gil*'s not done anything but go in a straight line for a long time. Karst, get your people reacquainted with their kit, just in case we need you. Mason, you're working with my people on monitoring that signal. If there's anything active there to respond to us, I want to know about it.'

*

Hours later, and Holsten was almost the last person left in the Communications suite, his dogged academic patience having outlasted most of Guyen's people. In his ear, the signal – full of static – still pulsed its single simple message, clearer now than it had been out beyond the system, and yet saying no more. He had been sending responses regularly, seeking to spur something new, an elaborate academic's game where he formulated queries in formal Imperial C in the hope of seeming like the sort of caller that the beacon was crying out for.

He started at a sudden movement beside him, as Lain slumped into the neighbouring seat.

'How's life in Engineering?' He took out the earpiece.

'Not supposed to be about people management,' she grunted. 'We're having to thaw out about five hundred coffins from cargo to run repairs on them. Then we're having to tell five hundred recently awoken colonists that they need to go right back into the freezer. Security have been called in. It's ugly. So, have you even worked out what it says yet? Who's in distress?'

Holsten shook his head. 'It's not like that. Well, yes, it is. It says it's a distress beacon. It's calling for help, but there are no specifics. It's a standard signal the Old Empire used for that purpose, intended to be clear, urgent and unmistakable – always assuming you're even a member of the culture that produced it. I only know what it is because our early spacefarers were able to reactivate some of the stuff they found in Earth orbit and extrapolate function from context.'

'So say "Hi" to it. Let it know we've heard it.'

He sucked in the breath of the annoyed academic, starting off with the same pedantic, 'It's not . . .' before her frown made him reconsider. 'It's an automated system. It's waiting for a response it recognizes. It's not like those extra-solar listening-post things we used to have – searching for any kind of signal pattern at all. And even those . . . I was never convinced by them – by the idea that we could necessarily recognize an alien transmission for what it was. That's too rooted in our assumption that aliens will be in any way like us. It's . . . you understand the concept of cultural specificity?'

'Don't lecture me, old man.'

'It's – will you stop with that? I'm, what, seven years older than you? Eight?'

'You're still the oldest man in the universe.'

Hearing that, he was very aware that he honestly did not know how the pair of them stood, one to another. *So maybe I was just the last man in the universe, right then. Or me and Guyen, at most. Apparently it doesn't matter now, anyway.*

'Yeah, well, you'd been up for how long, before they woke me?' he goaded her. 'Keep pulling those long hours and you'll catch up real soon, won't you?'

She had no ready comeback, and when he glanced at her, her face was long and pensive. *This is no way to run a civilization*, he thought. *But of course, that's not what we are, not any more. We're a civilization in transport, waiting to happen somewhere else. Maybe here. We're the last cutting of old Earth.*

The pause stretched out between them, and he found he had no way of breaking its hold, until Lain abruptly shook herself and said, 'So, cultural specificity. Let's talk about that.'

He was profoundly grateful for the lifeline. 'So I know it's a distress beacon, but that is literally only because we've had prior contact with Imperial tech, and in sufficient context that we can make assumptions – some of which may be wrong, even. And this isn't an alien species – this is *us*, our ancestors. And, in turn, they won't recognize our signals, necessarily. There's this myth that advanced cultures will be so expansively cosmopolitan that they'll be able to effortlessly talk down to the little people, right? But the Empire never intended its tech to be forward-compatible with primitives – meaning us. Why would it? Like everyone else, they only ever intended to talk to each other. So I'm telling this thing, "Hello, here we are," but I don't know what protocols and what codes their system is expecting to receive from whatever rescuer would have been planned for, however many thousand years ago. They can't even hear us. We're just background static to them.'

She shrugged. 'So what? We get there and send Karst over with a cutting torch and open her up?'

He stared at her. 'You forget how many people died, in the early space years, trying to get at Empire tech. Even with all the systems fried by their old electromagnetic pulse weapons, there were still plenty of ways for it to kill you.'

Another lift of the shoulders, indicating a tired woman at the edge of her reserves. 'Maybe you forget how much I don't like Karst.'

Did I forget? Did I ever know that? He had a vertiginous sense that maybe he had, but that any such knowledge had fallen unnoticed from his head during the long, cold age of his suspension. And it genuinely had been an *age*. There had been whole discrete periods of human history that had not lasted so long. He found himself holding on to the console as though, at any moment, the illusion of gravity gifted by the *Gilgamesh*'s deceleration would vanish, and he would simply slip away in some random direction, with all connection lost.

These are all the people there are, with the image of that roomful of near-strangers he had never had a chance to get to know before they sealed him in the coffin. *This is life and society and human contact, now and forever.*

It seemed to be Lain's turn to find the silence awkward, but she was a practical woman. She simply got up to go, drawing away sharply as he tried to put a hand on her arm.

'Wait.' It came out more as a plea than he had intended. 'You're here – and I need your help.'

'On what?'

'Help me with the signal – the beacon signal. There's always been a lot of interference, but I think . . . it's possible there's actually a second signal clashing with it on a close frequency. Look.' He passed a handful of analyses over to her screen. 'Can you clean it up – compensate it out if it's noise, or at least . . . something? I'm running out of things to try right now.'

She seemed relieved at actually getting a sensible request from him and resumed her seat. For the next hour the two of them worked wordlessly side by side, she with what was now her task, and he in sending increasingly desperate enquiries aimed at the satellite, none of which evinced any response. Eventually he felt that he might as well just be sending over gibberish, for all the difference it made.

Then: 'Mason?' from Lain, and there was something new in her tone.

'Hmm?'

'You're right. It is another signal.' A pause. 'But we're not getting it from the satellite.'

He waited, seeing her fingers move over the panels, checking and rechecking.

'It's from the planet.'

'Shit! You're serious?' And then, with a hand to his mouth. 'Sorry, I'm sorry. Not language befitting the dignity of etcetera, but . . .'

'No, no, this is definitely a shit-worthy moment.'

'It's a distress call? It's repeated?'

'It's not like *your* distress signal. Much more complex. It must be actual live talk. It's not repeating . . .'

For a moment Holsten actually felt her hope peak, pulling the air between them taut with the untold potential of the future, and then she hissed. 'Bollocks.'

'What?'

'No, it *is* repeating. It's longer and more complicated than your distress call, but this is the same sequence again.' Hands on the move once more. 'And it's . . . we're . . .' Her bony shoulders sagged. 'It's . . . I think it's bounce.'

'Come again?'

'I think this other signal is bouncing from the planet. I . . . Well, most likely hypothesis: the satellite is sending a signal to the planet, and we're catching bounce-back. Fuck, I'm sorry. I really thought . . .'

'Lain, are you sure?'

She cocked an eyebrow at him, because he was not joining in her dejection. 'What?'

'The satellite is communicating with the planet,' he prompted. 'It's not just a bounce-back of the distress call – it's something longer. A different message sent to the planet than for the rest of the universe.'

'But it's just on a loop, same as . . .' She slowed down. 'You think there's someone down there?'

'Who knows?'

'But they're not broadcasting.'

'Who knows? It's a terraform world, whatever Vitas says. It was created to be lived on. And, even if the satellite is nothing but a call for help these days, if they seeded the world with people . . . So maybe they really are savages. Maybe they don't have the tech to receive or transmit, but they could still be there . . . on a world specifically made for humans to live on.'

She stood up suddenly. 'I'm off to fetch Guyen.'

For a moment he looked at her, thinking, *Seriously, that was the first thing you thought of?* But he nodded resignedly and she was off, leaving him to listen in on the newfound contact between satellite and planet, and try to work out what it signified.

To his great surprise it took him very little time to do so.

'It's what?' Guyen demanded. The news had brought along not just the commander but most of the Key Crew as well.

'A series of mathematics problems,' Holsten explained to them all. 'The only reason it took me as long as it did was that I was expecting something more . . . sophisticated, something informative, like the beacon. But it's maths.'

'Weird maths, too,' Lain commented, looking over his transcription. 'The sequences get quite complicated, but they're set out step by step from first principles, basic sequences.' She was frowning. 'It's like . . . Mason, you mentioned extra-solar listening posts before . . . ?'

'It's a test, yes,' Holsten agreed. 'An intelligence test.'

'But you said it was pointed at the planet?' Karst stated.

'Which raises all kinds of questions, yes.' Holsten shrugged.

'I mean, this is very old technology. This is the oldest working tech that anyone anywhere ever discovered. So what we're seeing could just be the result of a break-down, an error. But, yes, makes you think.'

'Or not,' Lain put in drily. When the others just stared at her, she continued in her snide tone: 'Come on, people, am I the only one thinking it? Come on, Mason, you've been trying to get the thing to notice you for how long now? We've rounded the star on our approach to the planet, and you're still drawing blanks. So now you say it's setting some sort of maths test for the planet?'

'Yes, but—'

'So send in the answers,' she suggested.

Holsten stared at her for a long time, then glanced sideways at Guyen. 'We don't know what—'

'Do it,' Guyen ordered.

Carefully, Holsten called up the answers he had compiled, the early problems solved easily on his fingers, the later ones only with artificial help. He had been sending plaintive signals to the distant satellite for hours. It was simple enough to dispatch the string of numbers instead.

They waited, all of the Key Crew. It took seven minutes and some seconds for the message to reach its intended destination. There was some shuffling. Karst cracked his knuckles. One of the science team coughed.

A little over fourteen minutes after sending, the distress beacon ceased.

2.4 POOR RELATIONS

Portia's people are natural explorers. As active carnivores with a considerably more demanding metabolism than their forebears, too many of them in one place will quickly over-hunt any home territory. Traditionally their family units fragment often; the females who are weakest, with the fewest allies, are the ones who venture further afield to establish new nests. Such diasporas happen regularly for, although they lay far fewer eggs than their ancestors, and although their stand-ards of care are far below human so that infant mortality rates remain high, the species population is in colossal expan-sion. They are spreading across their world, one broken family at a time.

Portia's own expedition is something different, though. She is not seeking a nesting ground, and there is a home that her present plans require her to return to. In her mind and her speech, it is the Great Nest by the Western Ocean, and several hundred of her kind – most but not all relatives of one degree or another – reside there. The basic domestica-tion of the aphids and their husbandry by the spiders has allowed the Great Nest to grow to unprecedented size, with-out the shortages that would prompt migration or expulsion.

Over several generations the social structure of the Great Nest has grown exponentially more complex. Contact has been made with other nests, each of which has its own way of feeding the modest multitudes. There has been some halting trade, sometimes for food but more often for knowledge. Portia's people are ever curious about the further reaches of their world.

That is why Portia is travelling now, following the paths of stories and rumours and third-hand accounts. She has been *sent*.

The three of them are entering already claimed territory. The signs are unmistakable – not merely regularly maintained web bridges and lines amid the trees, but patterns and designs stating by sight and scent that these hunting grounds are spoken for.

This is exactly what Portia has been looking for.

Ascending as high as they can go, the travellers can see that, to the north, the character of the formerly endless forest changes dramatically. The great canopy thins, fading away in patches to reveal startling stretches of cleared ground; beyond that there are still trees, but they are of a different species and regularly spaced, in a manner that looks jarringly artificial to their eyes. This is what they have come to see. They could simply avoid this little piece of family turf that they have come across and go look. Portia's plan, however – the step-by-step route that she has plotted from the start of their trek to its successful conclusion – specifically calls for her to gather information. For her ancestors, this would mean painstaking visual reconnaissance. For her it means asking questions of the locals.

They proceed with caution, and openly. There is a real possibility that the incumbents may chase them off; however, Portia can mentally put herself in their place, consider how she herself would look upon an intruder. She can think through the permutations enough to know that an aggressive or covert entrance will increase the chance of a hostile reception.

Sure enough, the locals are sharp enough to spot the newcomers quickly, and curious enough to make their presence known at a distance, signalling for Portia and her fellows to approach. There are seven of them, five females and two males, and they have a neat nest strung between two trees, liberally surrounded with trip lines to warn them of any over-bold visitors. Also present are a brood of at least two dozen spiderlings of various ages, hatched from a communal crèche. Fresh from the egg they are able to crawl and take live prey, and understand a variety of tasks and concepts without having to be taught. Probably no more than three or four of them will reach adulthood. Portia's people lack a mammal's helpless infant stage, and the maternal bond that accompanies it. Those that do survive will be the strongest, the most intelligent and the best able to interact with others of their kind.

The palp-semaphore language allows for communication over a mile away in clear conditions, but is not suitable for complex discussions. The more subtle step-vibration speech will not travel far across the ground or down a branch. In order to hold a free and frank exchange of views, one of the local females spins a web that stretches between several trees, large enough for everyone to rest a few feet on its many anchor points and follow the conversation as it progresses. One of the locals climbs onto the web and, at her invitation, Portia joins her.

We bring you greetings from the Great Nest on the Western

Ocean, Portia begins, meaning: we are but three, but we have friends. *We have travelled far and seen many things.* For information is often a trade good in itself.

The locals remain suspicious. They are spoken for by their largest female, who shudders upon the web and shifts her feet, saying: *What is your purpose? This is no place for you.*

We do not seek to hunt, Portia states. *We do not come to settle. We shall soon return to the Great Nest. Word has come to us* – the concept is expressed very clearly, to their minds: vibrations twanging down a taut line. They are naturally equipped to think in terms of information transmitted at a distance. *The land beyond your land is of interest.*

Unrest amongst the locals. *It is not to be travelled,* their leader says.

If that is so, then that is what we have come to discover. Will you tell us what you know?

More disquiet, and Portia is aware that her mental map of what is going on must have a hole somewhere, because they are reacting in a way she cannot account for.

Their leader wishes to appear bold, however. *Why should we?*

We will tell you things in return. Or we have Understanding to exchange. For the spiders, mere telling and 'Understanding' are two distinctly different currencies.

The locals step back off the web at a signal from their leader and huddle close, keeping several eyes on the newcomers. There is a shuffling huddle of speech, softly stepped out so that it does not reach their visitors. Portia retreats as well, and her two companions join her.

Bianca has no particular ideas, save that she is anticipating having to go up against the lead female, who is noticeably bigger. The male, though, surprises Portia.

They're afraid, he suggests. *Whatever is ahead of us, they are afraid that we may stir it up and it will attack them.*

It is natural for a male to think about fear, Portia decides. That she agrees with him makes finding out the truth about their destination all the more important.

At last the locals return to the web and negotiations resume. *Show us your Understanding*, their leader challenges.

Portia signals to Bianca, who unwraps one of the docile aphids from alongside her abdomen and displays it to the skittish surprise of the locals. The little beast is milked for honeydew, and Portia wraps up a sagging parcel of the sweet stuff and deposits it in the centre of the web, where the locals approach it.

Once they have tasted it, and once they understand Portia's mastery over the animals, they are more than ready to make some manner of deal. The value of an independent food source is immediately evident to them, especially given their mysterious northern neighbours, who might soon threaten their hunting grounds.

What of these will you trade? the local leader asks, eagerness evident in her movements.

We have two of these beasts for those that give us a full account of what lies beyond your lands, Portia offers, knowing that this is not what the locals really wish to trade for. *Also, we have eggs, but the raising and care of these creatures requires skill, or they will die young and you will have nothing.*

There is now an urgent channel of talk running between the lead female and the others, and Portia catches fragments of it along the web. They are too agitated to be careful. *You said you could trade?* the big female demands.

Yes, we can trade this Understanding, but we will ask for more in return. Portia is not referring to teaching, but to something deeper – one of the secrets of her species' continuing success.

The nanovirus itself is subject to variations in its transcription. It was designed that way in order to creatively accomplish its hardwired aim: to bring the host to a detected level of sophistication set by its creators and, once its victory conditions are met, to cease further assistance. Its creators included such safeguards so as to prevent their protégés continuing to develop into superhuman monkey-gods.

The virus was intended for a primate host, however, and so the end state that it has been programmed to seek is something that *Portia labiata* can never become. Instead the nanovirus has mutated and mutated in its inbuilt quest to reach an impossible goal, the end that justifies all conceivable means.

More successful variants lead to more successful hosts, who in turn pass on the superior mutated infection. From the microscopic point of view of the nanovirus, Portia and every other affected species on the planet are merely vectors for the onward transmission of the virus's own evolving genes.

Long ago in Portia's evolutionary history, her species' social development was greatly accelerated by a series of mutations in the reigning infection. The virus began to transcribe learned behaviour into the genome of sperm and egg, transforming acquired memes into genetically inheritable behaviour. The economic, force-evolved brains of Portia's kind share more structural logic with each other than chance-derived human minds do. Mental pathways can be transcribed, reduced to genetic information, unpacked in the offspring and written as instinctive understanding – sometimes concrete skills and muscle memory, but more often whole tranches of knowledge, ragged-edged with loss of context, that the new-born will slowly come to terms with throughout its early life.

The process was piecemeal at first, imperfect, sometimes fatal but more reliable with each generation as the more efficient strains of virus prospered. Portia has learned a great deal in her life, but some things she was either born with, or came to her as she developed. Just as all new-hatched spiderlings can hunt and creep and jump and spin, so Portia's early moultings brought with them an innate understanding of language and access to fragments of her forebears' lives.

That is now ancient history, a facility that Portia's people have possessed from back before their histories began. More recently, however, they have learned to exploit the nanovirus's enhanced capabilities, just as the virus in turn is exploiting them.

He has the Understanding, Portia confirms, a flick of one palp indicating her male follower. *But we will trade like for like. You have Understanding of how to live here and the precautions you take. That is what we seek.*

The next moment, she realizes she has overplayed her hand, because the big female goes very still on the web – a particular hunting stillness that signals raw aggression.

So your Great Nest will come to our lands after all. You are not here to hunt, and yet tomorrow your kin intend to hunt here. Because such traded Understanding would not benefit Portia herself, but only generations to come, those whose genomes are as yet unwritten.

We seek Understanding of all places, Portia protests, but the language of motion and vibration is a hard one to dissemble in. Enough unintended body language leaks into it to confirm the suspicions of the big female.

Abruptly the local leader has reared up, two pairs of legs raised high and her fangs exposed. It is a brute language unchanged for millions of years: *See how strong I am*. Her rear legs are bunched ready to spring.

Reconsider. Back off, Portia warns her. She herself is tensed up, but she is not showing submission nor retreating, nor measuring her legs against the other's.

Go now, or fight, the angry female demands. Portia notes that she does not necessarily have the wholehearted support of her fellows, who are anxiously flagging up concern or sending cautioning words along the strands of the web.

Portia creeps sideways, and feels a new dancing from behind her: a charging advance from Bianca that also serves as a kind of battle hymn. The local leader is obviously thrown by the fact that her opponents' speaker is not also their fighter, and she backs off a little, warily. Moreover, Bianca has armour.

There is a functional limit to how much Understanding any individual can inherit from the virus. New information rewrites the old, though perhaps each generation's ability to store such innate knowledge is a little greater than the last. This band of backwoods locals will have a handful of tricks all their own, carefully preserved down the years. Their individuals can learn – and teach – but their inbuilt knowledge base is limited.

A larger community like Great Nest has a great many Understandings to draw upon, different lineages passing on their mysteries and trading with others. Different discoveries, tricks and knacks can be combined and experimented with. Great Nest is more than the sum of its parts. Bianca is no artisan – not by learning nor by inherent Understanding – but she wears the fruits of others' labours; curved wooden shields she has glued to her palps, dyed in aggressive, clashing colours. She rears high, measuring legs against the big female, but then hunches down, her shields raised.

They fight in the manner of their kind: they display, threaten, bare their fangs. They dance across the web, each step sounding like a goading word. The local female is larger, and she knows how this goes. Her greater size will convince the smaller intruder to back down, because otherwise the newcomer will die.

Portia's kin share something with tool-using man: they are very able to harm each other. They were spider-killers from the first, and their venom will immobilize an enemy of their own species as easily as it would a Spitter. If matters come to that, usually the victor will give in to instinct, and feed. For this reason, they have a culture that shies away from actual violence because of the risks inherent in any clash. The danger they pose to one another has been a great civilizing influence, just as much as has that sense of kinship their shared viral heritage gifted them with.

But Bianca is not backing down, however clearly her opponent outmatches her. The threat displays become more and more aggressive, the big female leaping and darting about the web, whilst Bianca sidles sideways and keeps her shields up against the eventual pouncing strike that must be coming.

Portia, for her part, spins her thread, and readies herself to use another Great Nest innovation – this one new enough that she has had to learn it, though perhaps she may be able to virally gift it to her offspring.

The big female springs just as Portia is ready. Bianca takes the fang-strike on her shields, the impact knocking her over onto her back. The female rears up for another strike, infuriated.

The stone that strikes her knocks her clean off the web, tumbling down to hang by her safety line, twitching and convulsing. Her abdomen is cracked open on one side where the missile tore through, and the loss of fluid to her body is already causing her remaining limbs to curl in upon themselves involuntarily. Portia has already reloaded, the slingshot of silk strung in a taut 'V' between her wide-placed front feet and her powerful hind legs.

The locals stare at her. A couple have crept partway towards their injured leader, but Bianca is ahead of them, dropping to drive her fangs into her victim's cracked carapace.

Portia assesses the locals. They have adopted a submissive posture, thoroughly cowed. One of the other females – not the largest but perhaps the boldest – steps deferentially on to the web. *What do you want?* she dances out.

Good. Let us trade, Portia states, as Bianca rejoins her. *Tell us about your neighbours.*

After they are done, each side weighing what it is willing to share against the relative bargaining power of the other party, Portia's male scuttles onto the web and distils his Understanding of aphid husbandry into a neatly silk-wrapped packet of sperm. One of the local males performs a similar service with his own day-to-day knowledge of his family's territory and its aggressive neighbours. This active use of the viral transcription is not behaviour prompted by the virus itself, but a cultural tradition amongst Portia's people: information as currency, by means of a transfer that incidentally assists the virus in propagating its genetic code. At the same time, the next generation of spiderlings will share kinship, a bridge between Portia's Great Nest and this little family, part of a great web of such interrelations whose connections can be traced, community to community, across much of the planet.

What the locals now say about the north is alarming, a potential threat that Portia's Great Nest seems likely to encounter quite soon. At the same time it is intriguing, and Portia decides that the plan requires a closer personal look.

2.5 ALL THESE WORLDS ARE YOURS

The reply that came back from the satellite was not intentionally encoded, but Holsten still sweated over what seemed to him an age, trying to turn the radio signal into something comprehensible. In the end, it gave up its secrets under the combined might of Lain, the *Gilgamesh* and himself, presenting him with a curt, brief message in classical Imperial C that he could at least make a stab at translating.

Finally, he leant back in his seat, aware that all eyes were fixed on him. 'It's a warning,' he told them. 'It's saying that we're transmitting from incorrect coordinates, or something like that. It says we're forbidden here.'

'It looks as though it's warming up,' observed one of the science team, who had been taking readings from the distant object. 'I see a swift increase in energy usage. Its reactor is increasing output.'

'It's awake, then,' Guyen declared, somewhat vacuously in Holsten's opinion.

'I reckon it's still just automatic signals,' Lain guessed.

'Tell it we're responding to its distress call.'

Holsten had already phrased a reply in scholar's language which read as formally as an academy exercise, then had Lain and the *Gilgamesh* transcribe the message into the same electronic format the satellite was using.

The waiting, as the signals danced across those millions of kilometres of void, was soon stretching everybody's nerves.

'It's calling itself the Second Brin Sentry Habitat,' Holsten translated eventually. 'It's basically telling us to alter our course to avoid the planet.' Before Guyen could ask, he added, 'and it's not mentioning the distress call now. I think, because we've gone in with an answer to whatever it was signalling to the planet, it's that system we're interacting with.'

'Well, tell it who we are and tell them we're coming to help them,' Guyen instructed him.

'Seriously, I'm not sure—'

'Just do it, Mason.'

'Why would it be signalling elementary maths to the planet?' Vitas complained to nobody in particular.

'I can see all sorts of systems coming online, I think,' added her underling at the sensor suite. 'This is incredible. I've never seen anything like it.'

'I'm launching some drones, both for the sat and for the planet,' Karst announced.

'Agreed,' said Guyen.

'It doesn't *recognize* us,' Holsten reported, frantically translating the latest message from the satellite, stumbling over its antique grammar. 'It says we're not authorized here. It says . . . something about biological hazard.' And, at the shudder that went through the crew, 'No, wait, it's calling *us* an unauthorized biohazard. It's . . . I think it's threatening us.'

'How big is this thing, again?' Karst demanded.

'A little under twenty metres on its longest axis,' was the reply from the science team.

'Well, then, bring it on.'

'Karst, this is Old Empire tech,' Holsten snapped.

'We'll see what that's worth when the drones get there.' As the *Gilgamesh* was still fighting to slow down, the drones outstripped it rapidly, their own thrust hurrying them towards the planet and its lone sentinel at an acceleration that a manned craft could not have managed without pulping its occupants.

'I have another warning to divert,' Holsten reported. 'Look, I think we're in the same position as with the distress call. Whatever we're sending it just isn't being recognized by the system. Probably if we were supposed to be here we'd have the right codes or something.'

'You're the classicist, so work them out,' Guyen snapped.

'It's not like that. It's not like the Old Empire had a single . . . what, *password* or something.'

'We have archives of Imperial transmissions, don't we? So just strip some protocols from those.'

Holsten sent a glance of mute appeal towards Lain, but she was avoiding his gaze. Without entertaining any hope whatsoever, he began paring ID and greetings codes from those fragments of Old Empire recordings that had survived, and throwing them at random towards the satellite.

'I've got signal from the drones on screen,' Karst reported, and a moment later they were looking at the planet itself. It was still just a glint, barely distinct from the surrounding starfield, even with the best magnification of the drones' electronic eyes, but they could see it growing. A minute later and Vitas pointed out the tiny pinprick shadow of its moon passing across the planet's surface.

'Where's the satellite?' Guyen demanded.

'Not that you'd see it at this distance, but it's coming

round from the far side, using the planet's atmosphere and the moon to bounce its signal to us.'

'Drone parties splitting off now,' Karst reported. 'Let's take a proper look at this Brin thing.'

'More warnings. Nothing's getting through to it,' Holsten slipped in, aware that by now nobody was really listening to him.

'Karst, remember, no damage to the satellite once you contact,' Guyen was saying. 'Whatever tech's there, we want it in one piece.'

'No problems. And there she is. Starting our run right now.'

'Karst—'

'Relax, Commander. They know what they're doing.'

Holsten glanced up to see the drones fixing their aim at a point on the growing green orb's circumference.

'Look at that colour,' Vitas breathed.

'Unhealthy,' Lain agreed.

'No, that's . . . that's old Earth colour. Green.'

'This is it,' one of the engineers whispered. 'We're here. We made it.'

'Visual on the satellite,' Karst announced, highlighting a tiny glint on the screen.

'"This is the Second Brin Sentry Habitat,"' Holsten read out insistently. '"This planet is claimed by the . . ." The, what? Something . . . "*Exaltation Program*, and any interference is forbidden."'

'Exaltation what?' Lain asked sharply.

'I don't know. I . . .' Holsten was racking his brains for references, hunting through the ship's archives. 'There was something about . . . the Old Empire fell because it descended into sinful ways. You know the myth cycle?'

A few grunts of confirmation.

'The exaltation of beasts – that was one of the sins of the ancients.'

Karst let out a yelp of surprise and moments later the transmissions from his satellite-bound drones exploded into static.

'Ah, shit! Everything heading for the satellite just died!' he bellowed.

'Lain—' Guyen started.

'Already on it. Last moments of . . .' A busy silence as she worked. 'Here, this is the last one to go, by about a second. There – brief power surges – and the other drones are gone. Then this one goes right after. It just blew your drones, Karst.'

'What with? Why would it need a—?'

'Look, that thing could be serious military hardware, for all we know,' Lain snapped.

'Or it would need to be ready to track and deal with deep-space object impact,' suggested Vitas. 'Anti-asteroid lasers, maybe?'

'I'm . . .' Lain was frowning at the readouts. 'I'm not sure it did shoot . . . Karst, how open are the drone systems?'

The security chief swore.

'We are still heading towards it,' Holsten pointed out. Even as he said this, some of the other drone screens were dying – the machines Karst had been sending planetside. The satellite was snuffing them out the moment it rounded the world enough to obtain line of sight.

'What the fuck's going on?' Karst demanded, fighting for

control, sending his last pair of machines zigzagging towards the planet. A moment later there was a sudden energy spike, a colossal expenditure of power from the satellite, and one of the two surviving machines was gone.

'Now *that* was a shot,' Lain confirmed grimly. 'That atomized the bastard.'

Karst swore foully as he coded instructions for the last machine, sending it spiralling towards the planet, trying to keep the curve of the horizon between the drone and the satellite.

'Are those weapons a danger to the *Gilgamesh*?' Guyen asked, and the room fell silent.

'Probably, yes.' Vitas sounded unnaturally calm. 'However, given how much energy we've just seen, its ability to use them may be limited.'

'It won't need a second shot at us,' Lain said grimly. 'We're not going to be able to deviate from this course – not significantly. We're already decelerating as much as is safe – we have too much momentum. We're plotted to come into orbit.'

'It's telling us to leave or it will destroy us,' Holsten said tonelessly. As the *Gilgamesh*'s computers adapted, they became quicker at bringing him a comprehensible record of the signal, and he found that he was now reading the reproduction of an ancient script almost fluently. Even before any demands from Guyen, he was already phrasing his reply: *Travellers in distress. Do not initiate hostile action. Civilian transport ship requires assistance.* Lain was looking over his shoulder critically as he sent it.

'It *is* adjusting its positioning,' from the science team.

'Pointing at us,' Guyen concluded.

'It's an inexact comparison, but . . .' *But yes*, in the minds of everyone there.

Holsten could feel his heart hammering madly. *Travellers in distress. Do not initiate hostile action. Civilian transport ship requires assistance.* But the message wasn't getting through.

Guyen opened his mouth to issue some desperate order, but Lain burst out, 'Send it back its own distress call, for fuck's sake!'

Holsten goggled at her for a moment, then let out a cry of some nameless emotion – triumph inextricably mixed with annoyance at not having thought of it himself. Moments later it was done.

There were some hard minutes, then, waiting to see how the satellite would react, to see if they had been in time. Even as Holsten returned the satellite's own distress signal to it, the attack could already have been sent leaping across space towards them, fast enough that they would not even know until it struck.

Finally, Holsten sagged back in his seat with relief. The others were crowding round, staring at his screen, but none of them had the classical education to translate it, until he put them out of their suspense.

'"Please hold for further communication",' he told them, 'or something like that. I think – I *hope* – it's gone to wake up something more sophisticated.'

There was a murmur of conversation behind him, but he was counting the minutes until the next transmission arrived. When the screen filled instantly with code, he was elated for a fraction of a second before letting out a hiss of exasperation. 'It's gibberish. It's just a wall of nonsense. Why is it—?'

'Wait, wait,' Lain interrupted him. 'It's a different sort of signal, that's all. *Gilgamesh* has matched the encoding with some stuff in your archives, old man. It's . . . hah, it's audio. It's speech.'

Everyone was silent once more. Holsten glanced around at a cramped room full of bald men and women, all looking in less than good health, still shivering from the aftereffects of their unthinkably long suspension, and all unable to keep up with the revelations and emotional trauma of their current situation. *I'm honestly not sure who's even still following this.* 'Probably it's still an automated . . .' he started, but tailed off, not sure if he even had the energy for the argument.

'Right. *Gilgamesh* has done his best to decode, based on the fragments in archive,' Lain reported. 'Everyone want to hear this?'

'Yes,' Guyen decided.

What came to them from the ship's speakers was hideous: a corroded, static-spiked mess in which a female voice could just be discerned, nothing but isolated words breaking in and out of the interference – words in a language that nobody but Holsten could comprehend. Holsten had been watching the commander's face, because it had been obvious to him what they would get, and he saw a spasm of rage spike there briefly before being fought down. *Oh, that's not good.*

'Mason, translate.'

'Give me time. And if you can clean it up any, Lain'. . . ?'

'Already on it,' she muttered.

Behind them, the others began speculating cautiously. What had been speaking? Was it merely an automatic message or . . . Vitas was speculating on the Old Empire's supposed intelligent machines – not just a sophisticated autonomous engine like the *Gilgamesh* but devices that could think and interact as if they were human. Or more than human.

Holsten hunched over his console, phones to his ears, listening to the incrementally clearer versions that Lain was scrubbing for him. At first he couldn't understand more than a few words, having to slow the transmission down and focus on small slices of it, while trying to wrestle with a thoroughly unexpected intonation and pattern of speech. There was a lot of interference, too: a weird, irregular rise and fall of static that kept interfering with the actual message.

'I've got the drone into the atmosphere,' Karst announced abruptly. Everyone had almost forgotten him, as he sent instructions to his one surviving remote, with no idea of whether each refinement to its course would arrive in time to prevent its destruction. When he had the attention of the majority, he added, 'Who wants to see our new home?'

The drone's images were grainy and distorted, a high-altitude scan of a world so green that one of the scientists asked if the picture had been recoloured.

'You're seeing exactly what the drone's seeing,' Karst assured them.

'It's beautiful,' someone put in. Most others simply stared. It was beyond their experience and their imagination. The Earth that they remembered had not looked like this. Any such verdant explosion had been locked away in the years before the ice, and it never returned after the toxic thaw. They came from a planet immeasurably poorer than this one.

'All right.' The conversation behind Holsten had grown

into a hubbub of speculation, then died away into ennui in the time it had taken him to adjust to the new transmission. 'Translation, here.'

He sent it to their screens: *The Second Brin Sentry Habitation acknowledges your request for assistance. You are currently on a heading that will bring you to a quarantine planet, and no interference with this planet will be countenanced. Please provide full details of your emergency situation so that habitat systems may analyse and advise. Any interference with Kern's World will be met with immediate retaliation. You are not to make contact with this planet in any way.*

'We'll see about that,' Karst declared, and, 'Doesn't know about the last drone, then. I've set it so as to try and keep to the far side of the planet from that thing.'

Mason was still playing back the message, trying to work out what that continuing interference was. Like the distress call, it sounded as though there was some other message hitching a ride along with the satellite's signal.

'Is it still sending down to the planet?' he asked Lain.

'It is, but I've compensated for that. You shouldn't be getting . . .'

'Kern's World?' Vitas noted. 'Is that a name?'

'"Kern" and "Brin" are phonetic,' Holsten admitted. 'If they're words, then they're not in my vocabulary files. What response?'

'Will it understand if we speak to it?' Guyen pressed.

'I'll send an encoded message, like before,' Holsten told him. 'I . . . whatever it is, it's not speaking Imperial C the way the textbooks think it should be spoken. Different accent, different culture maybe. I don't think I could speak to it well enough to be properly understood.'

'Send this.' Guyen shunted over a block of text for Holsten to translate and encode. *We are the ark ship* Gilgamesh, *carrying five hundred thousand humans in suspension. It is of utmost priority that we are able to establish a presence on your planet. This is a matter of the survival of the human species. We require your assistance in preserving our cargo.*

'It's not going to work.' Holsten wondered whether Guyen had somehow heard some other message from the satellite, because that wasn't an appropriate response as far as he was concerned. He sent it off, though, and returned to listening to the previous transmission, recruiting Lain to try and parse out the rider signal, to separate out something comprehensible. And then abruptly he began to hear it, listening between the words, stock-still and gripping his console as the meaning came through to him.

The Second Brin Sentry Habitation acknowledges your request for assistance. You are currently on a heading that will bring you to a quarantine planet and no interference with this planet will be countenanced. Please provide full details of your emergency situation so that habitat systems may analyse and advise. Any interference with Kern's World will be met with immediate retaliation. You are not to make contact with this planet in any way.

Cold so cold so very long waiting waiting why won't they come what has happened can they all really have gone is there nobody nothing left at all of home so very cold coffin cold coffin cold nothing is working nothing working nothing left Eliza Eliza Eliza why won't you answer me speak to me put me out of my misery tell me they're coming tell me they're going to come and take me wake me warm me from this cold so cold so cold so cold so cold so cold cold cold cold

'Uh . . .' Mason had kicked his seat back from his position, but the voice still droned and grated in his earphones – absolutely the same voice as the main message's formal efficiency, but twisted by a terrible despair. 'We may have a problem . . .'

'New transmission coming through,' from Lain, even whilst others were demanding to know what Holsten meant.

'What should I do with the drone?' Karst put in.

'Just sit on it for now. Tell it to keep itself blocked from communications with the habitat,' Guyen told him. 'Mason—'

But Holsten was already working through the new transmission. It was a far shorter, punchier message than the first, but the word stuck in his mind. *'Habitat': that was my translation. Did the ancients mean that? They couldn't really have meant something for someone to live in. Twenty metres across, for however many millennia? No, that can't possibly . . .*

'It says, do we want to speak to Eliza,' he choked out.

Inevitably, someone had to ask, 'Who's Eliza?' as though anybody there could have answered the question.

'We do,' Guyen decided, which was just as well as Holsten had already sent the response.

Minutes later – the delay shorter each time, as they neared the planet – something new spoke to them.

Holsten recognized the same voice as before, though considerably clearer, and still with that horrible stream-of-consciousness backing constantly trying to break through. His translation for the others came swiftly. By now he reckoned he must be as fluent in Imperial C as anyone had ever been in post-glacial history.

He passed it around the others' screens: *Good evening,*

travellers. I am Eliza Kerns, composite expert system of the Second Brin Sentry Habitat. I'm sorry, but I may have missed the import of some communications that you have already sent to me. Would you please summarize what was said?

There was an interesting split in the listeners then. Command and Security remained mostly unmoved whilst Science and Engineering were thrown into sudden debate: what did the voice mean by 'expert system'? Was Holsten sure that was the proper translation? Was it actually an intelligent machine, or just something pretending to be one?

Holsten himself was busy piecing together that background message, although he felt less and less happy about it. The words, the very tone of horror and desperation in his ears, were making him feel ill.

Good evening, travellers. I am Eliza Kerns, composite expert system of the Second Brin Sentry Habitat. I'm sorry. I may have missed the import of some communications that you have already sent to me. Would you please summarize what was said?	What are you doing what are you in my mind taking taking why can't I wake up what am I seeing the void only alone and nobody nothing there is no ship why is there no ship where are there is no Eliza Kerns has stolen me stolen mine stolen mind

Holsten re-sent the *Gilgamesh*'s last substantive transmission: *We are the ark ship* Gilgamesh, *carrying five hundred thousand humans in suspension. It is of utmost priority that we are able to establish a presence on your planet. This is a matter of the survival of the human species. We require your assistance in preserving our cargo.*

And the reply:

I'm sorry, it will not be possible for you to approach or contact Kern's World in any way. This is an absolute interdiction in line with Exaltation Program guidelines. Please let me know if any other assistance may be given.

Avrana I'm Avrana's monkeys are all that matters if everyone's gone what do we have to exalt in save exaltation itself there can be no contact contamination Sering will not win we will exalt but must it be so cold slow hard to think

'Same words from a different computer,' Guyen spat angrily.

Lain was looking over Holsten's shoulder, staring at his translation of the second, hidden voice. He saw her mouth the words, *The fuck . . . ?*

'Mason, I don't care how you phrase it – dress it up as fancy as you like. It needs to understand that we are human and that we need its help,' Guyen said. 'If there's some old-world way of overriding its programming, of getting through to whatever that is, we need you to find it.'

No pressure, then; but Holsten was already planning out his response. It was not a linguistics problem, no matter what Guyen might think. It was a technological problem, but one that even Lain was surely little better equipped to deal with than he was. They were speaking to a functioning, autonomous Imperial system. The EMP-blasted hulks in orbit around Earth had contained nothing like it.

Eliza, he sent back, *we are in desperate need. We have travelled far from Earth to find a new home for that part of the human race we are responsible for. If we cannot locate such a home, then hundreds of thousands of human beings will die. Does your system of priorities allow you take responsibility for such a result? The*

Gilgamesh archives did not contain them, but Holsten had an idea that he had read somewhere of some philanthropic rules imposed on the fabled old artificial intelligences.

I'm sorry, but I cannot permit you to compromise the exaltation experiment at this time. I understand that you have other concerns and I am allowed to tender such help as my priorities allow. If you attempt to influence the planet then you will leave me no choice but to take action against your vessel.

What ship let me see the ship is coming from Earth but is it Sering's Earth or my Earth or no Earth is left for any ship to come silently they stopped sending so long so cold so let me out you bitch you witch Eliza you stole my mind my name can't keep me here let me wake let me speak let me die let me be something

So much for that. 'It really is just the same line as before. We've got nowhere, except . . .'

'What?' Guyen demanded.

'I want to try something a bit lateral,' Holsten explained.

'Is it likely to get us blown up ahead of schedule?'

'I don't think so.'

'Then you try whatever you've got, Mason.'

Holsten steeled himself and transmitted a simple, surreal question: *Is there anybody else there we could talk to?*

'You're taking the piss,' Lain said in his ear.

'Better ideas?'

'I'm Engineering. We don't do ideas.'

He managed a weak smile at that one. Everyone else was on tenterhooks, awaiting the response, save for Guyen who was glowering at Holsten as though his fierce regard could somehow inspire the classicist to greater efforts of antiquarianism.

| Would you like to speak to my sister? | Please please please please please please |

Lain swore again, and Guyen stared down at his own screen. Another murmur of baffled speculation was rising around them.

'Right, look, I have a theory,' Holsten explained. 'We're talking to some sort of automated system still, obviously, even if it's programmed to respond in a human-like manner. But there's something else there. It's . . . different. It seems less rational. So we could see if it will let us do things that the main expert system won't. Worst comes to worst, we could even turn it against the main system, somehow, I don't know.'

'But what is "it"?' Vitas asked him. 'Why would they have two systems?'

'Failsafe?' Holsten suggested, because he was keeping his worst suspicions very much to himself.

'Try it,' Guyen said. 'Karst, I want some solutions if this turns ugly. Our current course will bring us into the planet's attraction at the right speed to make orbit. The only alternative is to stop decelerating now and just fly past, and then . . . and then what?' The question was plainly rhetorical, the hard-pressed commander showing the working of his sums. 'Then we set course for the next point on the star maps, and somehow hope there's something different there? We've seen this planet now. This is going to be our home. Mason, tell it.'

Why, yes, Eliza, please let us talk to your sister. Holsten tried to match the expert system's polite and formal manner of speech.

He was not sure what they would get back, and he was

ready to shut down the comms if it was just that anguished mad babbling, because there could be no dialogue with that – no possibility of negotiating with that internalized storm of insanity.

'We're being told to stand by,' he reported, when the instruction came. After that there was nothing else for a long time; the *Gilgamesh* continued to fall inexorably towards the green planet's gravity well. The satellite was still silent when Lain and her team began their anxious watch over ship's systems, as the ancient ark ship began to creak and strain at the unnatural imposition of an external source of mass, large and close enough to claw at the vessel's structure. Everyone there felt a subtle shifting: for the whole waking portion of the journey, their perception of gravity had come from the ship's gradual deceleration. Now an alien force was reaching for them, subtly tugging with insubstantial ghost fingers, the first touch of the world below.

'All signs suggest stable orbit for now,' Lain reported tensely. There followed a slow-motion comedy as deceleration ceased and then rotation began, gravity creeping across the floor to make a new home against the wall, and the *Gilgamesh*'s consoles and fittings shudderingly adjusting. For a minute there was no point of reference; a room full of weightless people trying to remember their long-ago training, hauling on each other to get to the right surface before they could be slammed into it. In the commotion, awkwardness, and a series of minor medical calls, the whole business of their imminent destruction was almost forgotten.

'New transmission,' Holsten alerted them, as the signal came in. In his ear those same female tones sounded, but the intonation, the rhythm of the speech was quite different, and stripped free of that tortured backing.

I am Doctor Avrana Kern, chief scientist and administrator of the Second Brin Exaltation Project, was his translation. Even through the filter of archaic Imperial C, the voice was stern and proud. *What are you? What is your provenance?*

'That doesn't sound like a computer,' Lain murmured.

'Of course it's a computer,' Vitas snapped. 'It's simply a more sophisticated approximation of—'

'Enough.' Guyen cut through the argument. 'Mason?'

We are an ark ship from Earth, Holsten sent, *seeking permission to establish a colony on Kern's World.* If the thing he was talking to was in any way human, he guessed that a little flattery couldn't harm.

Whose Earth, though? Sering's Earth or my Earth? came the swift reply. Now that they were in orbit, there was barely any delay: it was almost like a real conversation.

Real conversation with a faceless machine mind, Holsten reminded himself. He sent his translation round the room, looking for help, but nobody had any suggestion as to what the satellite meant. Before he could give any kind of answer, a new transmission came in.

I do not recognize you. You are not human. You are not from Earth. You have no business here. Eliza shows me all that she sees of you and there is nothing of Earth in you but why can I not see you for myself why can I not open my eyes where are my eyes where are my eyes where are my eyes. And then an abrupt cessation of the message, leaving Holsten shaken because that was it: a segue straight into the voice of madness, without a moment's warning.

'I don't think it's a computer,' he said, but soft enough

that only Lain heard him. She was reading over his shoulder still, and nodded soberly.

Our vessel is the ark ship Gilgamesh *from Earth. This ship was built after your time,* he prepared and sent, with a bitter awareness of the sheer understatement implicit in that. He was dreading what they might receive back.

Good evening, I am Eliza Kern, composite expert system of the of the of the am instructed to require you to return to your point of origin.	Send them away I don't want them if they say they came from Earth they can go back go back go back I don't won't can't no no no no no

'It's completely deranged,' Karst stated flatly, and that with the benefit of only half of what was being said. 'Can we keep the planet between us, or something?'

'Not and retain stable orbit,' one of Guyen's team reported. 'Seriously, remember how big the *Gil* is. We can't just flit him about like your drones.'

Holsten was already sending, because Guyen had stopped dictating and it now seemed to be down to him. *Return to Earth is not possible. Please may we speak to your sister again, Eliza?*, pleading for the life of humanity in a dead language – having to make the call between artificial intransigence and what he was increasingly sure was real human crazy.

That other voice again, delivering a rant that he got down as: *Why can't you just go back where you came from? Are you Sering's people? Did we win? Did we throw you out? Are you here to finish what he started?*

'What *happened* here?' demanded Vitas incredulously. 'What's Sering? A warship?'

Earth is no longer habitable, Holsten sent, even as Lain

warned, 'That's going to push her over the edge for sure, Mason.'

He had dispatched the message even as she said it, the hollow feeling in his stomach arriving a moment later. *She's right, at that.*

But there was a measure more sanity in Doctor Avrana Kern's voice when it replied. *Nonsense. Explain.*

The *Gilgamesh* archives had histories, but whoever would have thought they would need translating into a language only historians were now interested in? Instead, Holsten did his best: History 101 for the lost time traveller, based on best guesses as to what had actually happened beyond the dawn of his recorded time, back when the Old Empire had held sway. There was so little he could actually say. The gap between the last thing Kern must know and the earliest definite fact that Holsten could rely on was insuperable.

There was a civil war between factions of the Empire, he explained. *Both sides unleashed weapons the nature of which I do not understand, but which were effective in devastating higher civilization on Earth and completely destroying the colonies.* He remembered seeing the eggshell ruins on Europa. The in-system colonies had all predated any apparent later expertise in terraforming that the Empire had come to possess. They had been hothouse flowers on planets and moons haphazardly altered to better support life, reliant on biospheres that must have required constant adjustment. On Earth people had lapsed back into barbarism. Elsewhere, when the power had failed, when the electromagnetic weapons had destroyed the vital engines, or the electronic viruses murdered the artificial minds, they had died. They had died in alien cold, in reverting atmospheres, under corrosive skies. Often, they had died still fighting each other. So little had been left intact.

He typed it all out. As though writing an abstract to a history text, he noted with dry precision that a post-war industrial society may have persisted for almost a century, and may even have been regaining some of the sophistication of its predecessors, when the ice came. The choked atmosphere that had smothered the planet in gloom had shouldered out the sun, resulting in a midnight glacial cold that had left very little of that abortive rebirth. Looking back down the well of time, Holsten could make no definite statements about those who were left, nor about the frozen age that followed. Some scientists had speculated that, when the ice was at its height, the entire remnant human population of Earth had been no more than ten thousand all told, huddling in caves and holes around the equator and staring out at a horizon rigid with cold.

He went on into more certain waters, the earliest unearthed records of what he could truly think of as his people. The ice had been retreating. Humanity had sprung back swiftly, expanded, fought its small wars, re-industrialized, tripping constantly over reminders of what the species had previously achieved. Human eyes had looked to the skies again, which were crossed by so many moving points of light.

And he told Kern why they could not go back: because of the war, the Empire's war from thousands of years before. For so long, scholars had taught that the further the ice receded, the better for the world, and yet nobody had guessed what poisons and sicknesses had been caught up in that ice, like insects in amber, the encroaching cold protecting the shivering biosphere from the last excesses of Empire.

There is no returning to Earth, he sent to the pensively silent satellite. *In the end, we could not counterbalance the increasing toxicity of the environment. So we built the ark ships. In the end all we had was old star maps to guide us. We are the human race. And we've had no transmissions from any other arks to say that they've found anywhere to stay. Doctor Avrana Kern, this is all we have. Please may we settle on your planet?*

Because he was thinking in human terms, he expected a decent pause then for his opposite number to digest all that potted history. Instead, one of the science crew shouted out, 'New energy readings! It's activating something!'

'A weapon?' Guyen demanded, and all the screens briefly went blank, then flared to life again with nonsense scattering across them: fragments of code and text and simple static.

'It's got into the *Gilgamesh* control system!' Lain spat. 'It's attacking our security – no, it's through. Fuck, we're open. It's got full control. This is what it did to your drones, Karst, the ones it didn't just vaporize. We're fucked!'

'Do what you can!' Guyen urged her.

'What the fuck do you think I can do? I'm locked out! Balls to your "cultural specificity", Mason. It's all over our fucking system like a disease.'

'How's our orbit?' someone asked.

'I have no feedback, no instrumentation at all.' Vitas sounded very slightly tense. 'However, I've not felt any change in thrust, and mere loss of power or control should not affect our position relative to the planet.'

Like all those hulks orbiting Earth, Holsten thought helplessly. *Those fried, dead ships, with the vacuum-dried bodies of their crew still in place after thousands of years.*

Abruptly the lights jumped and flickered, and then a face appeared on every screen.

It was a bony, long-jawed face; that it was a woman's was not immediately obvious. Details kept filling in: dark hair drawn back, skin shaded and textured, harsh lines about the mouth and eyes; unflattering by modern criteria but who could name the ancient aesthetics that this face acknowledged? It was a face from an era and a society and an ethnicity that time had otherwise erased. The kinship between it and the crew of the *Gilgamesh* seemed tenuous, coincidental.

The voice that rang out through the speakers was unmistakably the same, but this time it was speaking the crew's own common language, although the lips did not sync.

'I am Doctor Avrana Kern. This is my world. I will brook no interference with my experiment. I have seen what you are. You are not from *my* Earth. You are not *my* humanity. You are monkeys, nothing but monkeys. You are not even *my* monkeys. My monkeys are undergoing uplift, the great experiment. They are pure. They will not be corrupted by you mere humans. You are nothing but monkeys of a lesser order. You mean nothing to me.'

'Can she hear us?' Guyen asked quietly.

'If your own systems can hear you, then I can hear you,' Kern's voice spat out.

'Are we to understand that you are condemning the last survivors of your own species to death?' It was a remarkably mannered, patient display from Guyen. 'Because it seems that is what you are saying.'

'You are not my responsibility,' Kern pronounced. 'This planet is my responsibility.'

'Please,' Lain said, ignoring Guyen when he gestured at her to shut up. 'I don't know what you are, if you're human or machine or whatever, but we need your help.'

The face froze, nothing but a still image for a handful of heartbeats.

'Lain, if you've—' Guyen started, and then abruptly Kern's image began to break up, distorting and corrupting on screen, features bloating or atrophying and then flickering into nothing.

The voice spoke again, a plaintive whisper in its native tongue, and only Holsten could know what it was saying. *I am human. I must be human. Am I the system? Am I the upload? Is there anything of me left? Why can I not feel my body? Why can I not open my eyes?*

'The other thing, the Eliza thing, it was mentioning some other help,' Lain murmured, although surely even a whisper would be overheard. 'Can we just ask it—?'

'I will help you,' Kern said, speaking their language again, sounding calmer now. 'I will help you leave. You have all the universe except this world of mine. You can go anywhere.'

'But we can't—' Guyen started.

Then Lain broke in. 'I'm back in. Checking all systems.' A tense minute to ensure that, at the very least, the ship's computer was telling her that everything was still working. 'We've got new data flagged up. It's just dumped a whole load of stuff on us. It's . . . the *Gilgamesh* recognizes star maps. Mason, I've received some stuff in that jabber of yours.'

Holsten scanned over the jumble of data. 'I, ah . . . not sure, but it's linked to the star maps. It's . . . I think it's . . .' His mouth was dry. 'Other terraforming projects? I think the

. . . I think we've been given the keys to the next system. It's giving us destinations.' *It's selling out its neighbours*, was what he did not say, given that *it* was listening, *it's bribing us to go away*. 'I think . . . something here might even be access codes.'

'How far?' Guyen demanded.

'Just under two light years,' Vitas reported briskly. 'Just a step, really.'

Through a long, stressed silence, they waited for Guyen's decision. The face of Avrana Kern was back on some of the screens, glowering at them; twitching, distorting, reforming.

2.6 METROPOLIS

Negotiations with the locals have gone sufficiently well –
now that Portia and her party have established their
superiority – and the incumbents have lent the three travellers a male to serve as a guide in the lands to the north. The
creature is slightly smaller than Portia's own male companion, but of a quite different character, bold to the point of
impudence by Portia's standards. He has a name: call him
Fabian. Portia, whilst aware that males give themselves
names, has very seldom needed to know any, even with the
concentration of that gender to be found at Great Nest. She
guesses that in a small family unit such as these locals, males
are likely to be more self-reliant, therefore both more capable and more independently minded. Still, she finds his
brashness off-putting. Bianca appears to find him less objec-
tionable and, on their trip north, Portia catches Fabian displaying for her, a tentative offer to gift her his sperm. Bianca
has not yet shown herself receptive, but Portia notes that
she has not chased him off either.

Portia herself has put several clutches of eggs behind her
– females seldom depart Great Nest without having passed
on their lineage – and she feels this current behaviour is dis-
tracting from their mission. On the other hand, Bianca has
fought for her and probably considers playing with this new

male her reward. Portia only hopes she can keep her desires in check. It would be more diplomatically advantageous if Fabian was not killed and eaten during the throes of passion.

They do not have to travel far to the north to see just what has been growing here at the edge of the Great Nest's web of awareness. Soon they begin coming across felled trees – their trunks showing a combination of blackening, chewing and surprisingly clean cuts, often painstakingly scissored into sections. Frequently the entire root system has been unearthed as well, ensuring that nothing will regrow. The forest is under wide-scale attack, its fringes being gnawed away. Fabian can remember when there were more trees, he communicates. The clearing of land continues year to year, and Fabian's inherited Understanding suggests that it is happening faster now than in his mother's time.

Beyond that ragged edge, the other trees – the foreign trees – are set out in discrete stands. They are small and squat and bulbous, with fleshy leaves and trunks that are warty with protrusions. The exaggerated space between each copse is a firebreak – something the spiders are very familiar with. Their planet's oxygen levels are higher than Earth's – lightning-sparked fires are a constant threat.

What they are seeing is no work of nature. This is a plantation on a grand scale, and the labourers tending it are plainly visible. Everywhere Portia turns her eyes there are more of them and, if she looks beyond the chequerboard of groves, she can make out a steep-sided mound that must be the upper reaches of the plantation-owners' colony, the bulk of it being hidden underground. A pall of smoke hangs over it like bad weather.

Portia's kin are well aware that they are not the sole

inheritors of their world. Whilst they cannot know how the nanovirus has been reshaping life here for millennia, there are certain species she shares the planet with, that her people recognize as something more than animals. The Spitters are a low-end example, barely removed from a state of brute nature, but to look into their small, weak eyes is nonetheless to recognize that here is a thing of intellect – and hence, danger.

The western oceans that Portia's Great Nest looks over are home to a type of stomatopod with which her people have cautious, ritualized relations. Their ancestors were fierce, inventive hunters, equipped with unparalleled eyesight and deadly natural weapons, and used to living in colonies where negotiations over living space were common. They, too, proved fertile ground for the virus, and have developed on parallel lines with Portia's own kin. Perhaps because of their aquatic environment, perhaps because they are by nature prone to wait for prey, their society is simple and primitive by Portia's standards, but the two species have nothing to compete over, and in the littoral zone they sometimes swap gifts, the fruits of the land in exchange for the fruits of the sea.

Of more pressing concern are the ants.

Portia understands the nature of ants. There are colonies near the Great Nest, and she has both personal and genetically encoded dealings with them to draw upon. It is the Great Nest's collective experience that ant colonies are complicated neighbours. They must be dealt with decisively – left to themselves they will always expand in a manner detrimental to any species that the ants themselves have no use for, which would naturally include Portia's own. They can be destroyed – her inherited Understandings include chronicles of such conflicts – but war with even a small colony is costly and wasteful. Alternatively, preferably, they can be accommodated and limited by careful manipulation of their decisions.

Portia knows that ants are not like her people, nor like the Spitters or the stomatopods of the western shallows. She knows that individual ants themselves cannot be treated with, communicated with or even threatened. Her comprehension is coarse, of a necessity, but approximates to the truth. Each ant does not think. It has a complex set of responses based on a wide range of stimuli, many of which are themselves chemical messages produced by other ants in response to still more eventualities. There is no intelligence within a colony, but there is such a hierarchy of interacting and co-dependent instinct that it seems to Portia that *some* manner of entity is behind a colony's actions and reactions.

With ants, the nanovirus has simultaneously failed and succeeded. Amongst the ants' network of reactive decision making it has inculcated a strategy of experimentation and investigation that approaches rigorous scientific method, but it has not led to intellect such as any human or spider would recognize. Ant colonies evolve and adapt, throw up new castes, investigate and make use of resources, devise new technologies, refine them and interrelate them, and all this without anything approaching a consciousness to direct it. There is no hive mind, but there is a vast and flexible biological difference engine, a self-perfecting machine dedicated to the continuance of itself. It does not understand how what it does functions, but it constantly expands its behavioural repertoire and builds upon those trial-and-error paths that prove fruitful.

Portia's understanding of all this is very limited, but she has a grasp of how ants do and do not work. She knows that individual ants cannot innovate, but that the colony can – in a strange way – make what appear to be informed decisions. Application of force and reward, a narrowing of the colony's viable options so that the most advantageous is the one the spiders intend it to choose, can lead to a colony accepting boundaries on its territory and its place in the world, and even to become a productive partner. The colonies are perfect exponents of game theory: they will cooperate where that course is less costly and more beneficial than other strategies, such as all-out genocidal war.

The colonies that she is already familiar with, near Great Nest, are surely less than a tenth the size of what she is now looking at. Fabian explains that there were once several warring colonies here, but one has become dominant. Instead of driving its lesser neighbours to extinction, the ruling colony has incorporated them into its own survival strategy, permitting their continuance in return for making them into extensions of itself, utilizing food that they gather and technologies they have developed. It is this world's first superstate.

Portia and the others have a brief, agitated conversation. This super-colony is far enough from Great Nest not to threaten it now, but they can look ahead and envisage that its very existence here endangers their people's future. A solution must be found but, to think through a plan like *that*, Portia's kin at home will need all the information she can bring back to them.

They are going to have to continue their journey into the land of the ants.

Fabian is surprisingly useful. He has travelled further than this himself; in fact his family makes a habit of it. It is dangerous, but they have developed ways of minimizing the risk of raising the alarm, and when hunting has been lean, the ants' larders are a last resort.

A new column of ants has arrived, and they are here for timber. The spiders retreat further into the trees and watch as the insects set to work breaking up the already fallen trunks into manageable sections, using acid and the strength of their jaws. Portia is swift to spot something new: a caste that she has never seen before. Smaller branches are severed and carried off by unexceptional-seeming workers, but the large trunks are dealt with by ants with long, curved mandibles equipped with jagged inner edges. These they fix to the circumference of a trunk, and move their mouthparts in incremental opposition, scoring around and around so as to cut a circular section away. Those mandibles did not emerge from the cocoon with the rest of the ant, however. They gleam in the sunlight in a way quite unlike anything Portia has seen before: rigid, toothed sleeves that make remarkably quick work of biting and sawing the wood into pieces.

With Fabian taking the lead, the spiders ambush an ant logging party, trapping and killing them quickly and efficiently, then decapitating them and dissecting them for their scent glands. The ants are smaller than Portia – between fifteen and thirty centimetres long – and the spiders are stronger, swifter and far more efficient fighters, one on one. What they must avoid is a general alarm, where large sections of the colonies are mobilized against them.

The ants communicate principally by pheromones – to Portia's keen chemical senses the air is thick with them. They use the ants' scent to disguise their own, and they carry the severed heads with them, secured to their abdomens. In extremis they can try to divert ant attention by a morbid form of puppetry, manipulating the dead antennae of their victims in a pretence of communication.

They travel swiftly. Their victims will be missed, but the initial response will target where they were, not where they are now. Their road is the high one. They travel through the upper reaches of the ants' plantations, and whenever they reach a firebreak, one of them scuttles across the intervening ground with a thread that then forms the spine of a temporary bridge. With their own scent disguised, they travel over the ants' heads and beneath their notice.

Fabian demonstrates that the protrusions on the trunks of the ant-tended trees can be lanced with a fang to release a sweet, nourishing liquid not unlike the honeydew of aphids, a taste they know the ants relish. This plantation agriculture is obviously a useful secret, and Portia adds it to the list of observations to include in her report when she returns home.

For now, they press on towards the main colony mound, avoiding the ants where they can, killing them swiftly where they cannot. Each small alarm will contribute to a generally raised awareness across the nest, until significant insect resources are devoted to locating intruders whose presence has been deduced by the colony's ineluctable internal logic.

Portia's goal is to investigate the central colony mound, which promises more secrets. During the day the air shimmers over parts of it, and there are plumes of smoke venting from stubby chimneys. At night, some of the ants' entrances glow dimly.

In the darkness of their home, the ants start fires in the oxygen-rich atmosphere, ignited by exothermic reactions from chemicals that certain of their castes can produce. Complex arrangements of internal passageways use the temperature differentials to stimulate airflow: heating, cooling and oxygenating their nests. The ants also use fire for land clearance, and as a weapon.

Portia's world – the underlying geology that existed before the terraforming – is rich in shallow deposits of metals, and the ants dig deep to build their nests. In this colony, centuries of burning has led to charcoal production, and occasional inadvertent smelting has been systematized into the forging of tools. The blind watchmaker has been busy.

Entering the mound itself is more than Portia dares, and she is tempted to leave with all the information she has gathered. Curiosity urges her on, though. Atop the mound, beneath the hanging shroud of smoke, is a spire that gleams in the sun brightly enough to draw the eye. Like all of her kind, she is driven to investigate anything new. This reflective beacon is the highest point on the mound, and Portia wants to know what it is.

Portia finds her band of infiltrators a vantage point in the nearest plantation to the mound and considers the paths taken by the chains of ant workers. Inside the brain that bulks out the underside of her body, she has fallen into a way of thinking that her diminutive ancestress would recognize: constructing an internal map of the world, and then deconstructing that to find the best course to where she needs to go next.

I will go alone, she instructs Bianca. *If I do not return, then you must go home and report.*

Bianca understands.

Portia descends by line from the tree that provided her watchtower, and begins her journey, following the itinerary that she spent so long plotting. The ants follow particular paths that their constant travel has packed down into flat, smooth roads representing the most efficient routes. Portia navigates a delicate, cautious path between these thorough-fares. She moves haltingly, pausing, quivering, then drifting on, gauging the lightly gusting wind and letting her onward progress follow its patterns, as if she herself was nothing but some overlarge piece of wind-blown debris. The vibrations of her movement are swallowed up in the entropy of the world at large. With her scent disguised, she can ghost past the near-blind ants as though she is invisible.

The going gets more complex and more dangerous as she reaches the mound itself. Her careful plan knows constant amendment, and she comes close to discovery several times. Once she uses the detached head of one of her victims, in a brief moment of feigned contact, to put off a wandering cleaner who is paying too close attention to her.

Her painstaking progress has taken hours, and the sun has set. This leads to outdoor ant activity dropping off, and makes her progress easier; only then does she reach the summit.

The ants have built a stumpy spire here, as already observed, and atop it is something new: a pale crystal that gleams translucently in the moonlight. She has no idea what this is for, and so she waits in the hope that the ants them-selves will show her.

After the moon begins to dip towards the far horizon, they do. All of a sudden there are ants issuing out on to the mound's summit in considerable numbers, so that Portia must move rapidly, and keep moving until she has found somewhere that they do not intend to occupy, which means some way further back down the shallow gradient. The insects are forming a carpet, a net of their bodies, touching antennae and limbs. Portia is baffled.

They seem to be awaiting something – or that is how she interprets their behaviour. It is un-antlike. It concerns her.

Then another of the insects emerges from a small hole at the base of the spire and climbs up it. It flicks one antennae towards the crystal, with the other directed downwards to make contact with the general host gathered below it. Portia's wide, round eyes gather as much of the moonlight as they can, and focus on this newcomer: this small, un-prepossessing ant. It has a prosthesis on its antenna, like the tree-cutters, but this is a fine cap of the same material – metal, though Portia does not know that – that tapers to invisibility, so that the ant is now touching the crystal with a tiny, delicate, hair-like wire.

And, as Portia watches, the ants begin to dance.

She has never seen anything like it. Shivers go through the entire mat of them, apparently originating in that contact between metal feeler and crystal, and spreading through the assembled host. They are sent into constant waves of motion, each transmitting to its neighbours some rhythmic message that holds the entire congregation rapt.

Portia watches in quiet bewilderment.

She is no mathematician. She does not quite grasp the

series of arithmetical progressions, series and transformations that are represented in the waves of motion passing through the ants – no more than the ants themselves do – but she can grasp that there is some pattern there, some significance to what she is seeing.

She does her best to interpret what she sees in light of her experiences, and those experiences she has inherited, but there is nothing comparable in the whole history of her own world. The ants feel the same. Their constant exploration of possibilities has resulted in this solitary contact with something vast and intangible, and the colony processes the information it receives and attempts to find a purpose for it, more and more of its biological processing power being applied to the task, more and more ants quivering under the pulsed rhythms of a distant radio signal.

Intent on trying to find pattern and plan in the scene before her, Portia's hungry eyes note one more element, and she wonders, *Is that important?*

Like humans, Portia's people are quick to see patterns, sometimes when there are none. Hence she makes the association quickly, seeing the timing as too close to be coincidental. When the gathering of ants breaks up and hurries inside, without warning and all at once, it is just as the traveller, the swift-moving star that she has often watched coursing across the sky, is passing beneath the horizon.

She makes a plan then, swiftly and without much forethought. She is intrigued, and her species is driven to investigate anything new, just as the ants are, though in very different ways.

Once most of the ants are gone she approaches the spire carefully, wary of triggering some alarm. Lifting her palps she lets the wind ruffle them, feeling its strength and direction, and matching her movements to it.

She ascends carefully, foot over foot, until she finds the crystal before her. It does not seem so large, not to her.

She sets to spinning a complex package of silk that she holds with her rear legs. She is keenly aware of being at the very centre of the great colony. A mistake at this point would go very badly.

She has left matters almost too late. Her presence – through the vibrations of her work – has been detected. From its hole at the spire's base, the small ant that led the congregation abruptly emerges and touches one of her feet with its uncovered antenna.

Immediately it lets out an alarm, a chemical sharp with outrage and fury at finding an alien, an intruder, in this place. As the scent passes outwards it is picked up by tunnel guards and other castes that have remained close to the exterior. The message is passed on and multiplied.

Portia drops on the ant beneath her and kills it with one bite, removing its head as she did with the others, although she knows she cannot bluff her way out of this one. Instead she scuttles up the spire again, seeking as much height as it will give, and seizes the crystal from the top.

She secures her two trophies to her abdomen with webbing, even as the ants begin to swarm out over the exterior of their colony. She sees plenty there with tools and modifications that she is suddenly no longer sufficiently curious to investigate.

She jumps. An unassisted leap from the spire would land her in their very midst, to be savagely held and stung and dismembered alive. At the apex of her upward spring, though, her hind legs kick out their burden of carefully folded silk, forming a fine-spun net spread between them that catches the wind Portia was so carefully measuring earlier.

It is not taking her quite back towards Bianca and the others, but she has no control over that. At this moment her chief priority is to get *away*, gliding over the heads of the enraged insects as they lift their metal-sheathed mandibles and try to work out where she could have gone.

Her descendants will tell the story of how Portia entered the temple of the ants and stole the eye of their god.

2.7 EXODUS

Guyen took his time over his decision, as the *Gilgamesh* followed its long curving path around this solitary island of life in the vast desert of space, its trajectory constantly balanced between the momentum that would fling it away and the gravity that would draw it in.

The face of Doctor Avrana Kern – whoever and whatever she truly was – flickered and ghosted on their screens, sometimes inhuman in its stoic patience, at other times twisted by waves of nameless, involuntary emotions, the mad goddess of the green planet.

Knowing that Kern was listening, and could not be shut out, Guyen had no way to receive the counsel of his crew, but Holsten felt that the man would not have listened anyway: he was in command, the responsibility his alone to bear.

And of course there was only one answer, for all the agonized pondering that Guyen might give to the question. Even if the Sentry Habitat had not possessed weapons capable of destroying the *Gilgamesh*, the ark ship's systems were at Kern's mercy. The airlocks, the reactor, all the many tools they relied on to keep this bubble of life from the claws of the void; Kern could just switch it all off.

'We'll go,' Guyen agreed at last, and Holsten reckoned he wasn't the only one who was relieved to hear it. 'Thank you for your help, Doctor Avrana Kern. We will seek out these other systems, and attempt to establish ourselves there. We will leave this planet in your care.'

Kern's face sprang into animation on the screens, though still moving almost randomly, and completely divorced from the words. 'Of course you will. Go take your barrel of monkeys elsewhere.'

Lain was murmuring, 'What is this business about *monkeys*?' in his ear, and Holsten had been wondering the same thing.

'Monkeys are a sort of animal. We have records regarding them – the Empire used them in scientific experiments. They looked something like people. Here, I've got images . . .'

'*Gilgamesh* has got a course plotted,' Vitas stated.

Guyen looked it over. 'Re-plot. I want us to swing by this planet here, the gas giant.'

'We won't be able to gain anything useful by slingshotting—'

'Just do it,' the commander growled. 'Here . . . get me an orbit.'

Vitas pursed her lips primly. 'I don't see what would be served by an orbit—'

'Make it happen,' Guyen told her, glowering at one of Kern's images as though waiting for it to challenge him.

They felt the change of forces as the *Gilgamesh*'s fusion reactor brought the engines back online, ready to coax the vast mass of the ark ship off its comfortable orbit and hurl it out into space once more.

Without warning, Kern's face was gone from the screens, and Lain quickly ran a check of all systems, finding no trace of the intruder's presence there.

'Which is no guarantee of anything,' she pointed out. 'We could be riddled with spy routines and security back doors and who knows what.' She did not add, *Kern could have set us to explode somewhere in deep space*, which Holsten reckoned was generous of her. He saw the same thought on everyone's face, but they had no leverage, no options. Just hope.

Pinning the whole future of the human race on hope, he considered. But, then, hadn't the whole ark ship project been just that?

'Mason, tell us about the monkeys,' Lain suggested.

He shrugged. 'Just speculation, but the thing was talking about an "exaltation program". Exaltation of beasts, the old stories say.'

'How do you exalt a monkey?' Lain was studying the archive images. 'Funny-looking little critters, aren't they?'

'The signal to the planet, and the mathematics,' Vitas mused. 'Are they expecting the monkeys to respond?'

Nobody had any answers.

'You've set our course?' Guyen demanded.

'Naturally,' came Vitas's immediate reply.

'Fine. So the whole universe is ours except the one planet worth living on,' the commander stated. 'So we don't stake it all on whatever's at this next project we're being sent to. We'd be fools to – it could be as hostile as here. It could be worse. There might not be anything there. I want us – I want *humanity* to have a foothold here, just in case.'

'A foothold *where*?' Holsten demanded. 'You said yourself that was the only planet—'

'Here.' Guyen brought up a representation of one of the system's other planets: a streaky, bloated-looking gas giant like some of the outer planets of Earth's system, then narrowing in on a pallid, bluish moon. 'The Empire colonized several moons back in Earth's system. We have automated base units that can carve us out a home there: power, heat, hydroponics, enough to survive.'

'Are you proposing this as the future of the human race?' Vitas asked flatly.

'*The* future, no. *A* future, yes,' Guyen told them all. 'We will head off first to see if this Kern has sold us something of worth or not – after all, whatever's there isn't going anywhere. But we're not betting all we have on that. We'll leave a functioning colony behind us – just in case. Engineering, I want a base unit ready to deploy once we arrive.'

'Hm, right.' Lain was running calculations, looking at what the *Gilgamesh*'s sensors could say about the moon. 'I see frozen oxygen, frozen water, even tidal heating from the gas giant's pull, but . . . it's still a long way short of cosy. The automated systems are going to take . . . well, a long time – decades – to get everything set up so that someone can be *left* there.'

'I know. Detail a roster of Science and Engineering to be woken at regular intervals to check progress. Wake *me* when it's near completion.' At the general groan, Guyen glared around at them. 'What? Yes, it's back to the chambers. Of course it is. What did you think? Only difference is, we've one more wake-up call before we set off out of the system. We maximise our chances as a species. We establish ourselves here.' He was looking at the screens, where the gradually receding green disc of Kern's World was still showing. The unspoken intent to return was plain in both his face and his tone.

Vitas had meanwhile been running her own simulations.

'Commander, I appreciate your aims, but there was limited testing of the automatic base systems, and the environment they will be deployed into does seem extreme . . .'

'The Old Empire had its colonies,' Guyen stated.

Which died, Holsten thought. *Which all died.* True, they had died in the war, but they had primarily died because they were not stable or self-sufficient, and when the normal business of civilization was interrupted, they had not been able to save themselves. *You won't get me living there, if I have any choice in the matter.*

'All doable,' Lain reported. 'I've a base module ready for jettison. Give it long enough and who knows what we might cook up down there? A regular palace, probably. Hot and cold running methane in every room.'

'Just shut up and do it,' Guyen told her. 'The rest of you, get ready to go back to suspension.'

'First off,' Karst interrupted, 'who wants to see a monkey?'

They all looked at him blankly and he grinned. 'I'm still getting signals from the last drone, remember? So let's look around.'

'Are you sure that's safe?' Holsten put in, but Karst was already sending the images to their screens.

The drone was moving over an unbroken canopy of green, that unthinkable wealth of foliage that had been denied to them.

Then the viewpoint dipped, and Karst was sending the drone down, corkscrewing it through a gap in the trees, zigzagging its way delicately around a lattice of branches. The world now revealed was awe-inspiring, a vaulted cathedral of forest overshadowed by the interlocking boughs above, like a green sky held up by the pillars of tree trunks.

The drone glided on through this vast and cavernous space, keeping ground and canopy equally distant.

The expressions of the *Gilgamesh* crew were hungry and bitter, staring at this forbidden birthright, an Eden not made for human touch.

'What's that ahead?' Lain asked.

'Detecting nothing. Just a visual glitch,' Karst replied, and then abruptly their viewpoint was swinging wildly, wheeling in mid-air with frustrated forward momentum.

Karst swore, fingers flying as he tried to send new instructions, but the drone seemed to be caught on something invisible – or near-invisible. Holsten could only see brief glints in the air as the drone's viewpoint spun and danced.

It happened very swiftly. One moment they were staring out into the clear space ahead that the drone was being inexplicably denied, and then a vast hand-like shadow eclipsed their view. They had a moment's glimpse of many bristling legs spread wide, two fangs like curved hooks striking savagely towards the camera with ferocious speed and savagery. On the second impact, the picture shattered into static.

For a long while nobody said anything. Some, like Holsten, just stared at the dead screens. Vitas had gone rigid, a muscle ticking frantically at the corner of her mouth. Lain was replaying the last seconds of that image, analysing.

'Extrapolating from the drone and its camera settings, that thing was the best part of a metre long,' she remarked at last, shakily.

'That was no fucking monkey,' Karst spat.

Behind the *Gilgamesh* itself, the green world and its orbiting sentinel fell away into obscurity, leaving the ark ship's crew with, at best, mixed feelings about it.

3
WAR

3.1   RUDE AWAKENING

He was hauled unwillingly into consciousness within the close confines of the suspension chamber, with the thought in his mind: *Didn't I do this before?* The question came to him substantially before he recalled his own name.

Holsten Mason. Sounds familiar.

Fragmentary understanding returned to him, as though his brain was ticking off a checklist.

. . . with Lain . . .

. . . green planet . . .

. . . Imperial C . . .

. . . Would I like to speak to Eliza? . . .

. . . Doctor Avrana Kern . . .

. . . Moon colony . . .

Moon colony!

And he jolted into full comprehension with the absolute certainty that they were going to send him to the colony, to that freezing wasteland of frozen-solid atmosphere that Vrie Guyen had decided would be humanity's first stab at a new home. Guyen had never liked him. Guyen had no more use for him. They were waking him now to transport him to the colony.

No . . .

Why would they wake him before dispatch? What could

he contribute to the founding of a lunar colony? They had *already* taken him there, insensible in his chamber. He was waking in the eggshell confines of the base structure, to tend the myoculture vats forever and forever and forever.

He could not keep the conviction at bay, that they had already done this to him, and he tried to thrash and kick in the close interior of the suspension chamber, shouting loud in his own ears, battering at the cool plastic with shoulders and knees, because he could not get his arms up.

'I don't want to go!' he was shouting, even though he knew he had already gone. 'You can't make me!' Even though they could.

The lid opened suddenly – wrenched up as soon as the seal broke – and he nearly jackknifed out entirely to hit the floor face first. Arms caught him, and for a moment he just stared around him, unable to work out where he was.

No, no, no, it's all right. It's the Key Crew room. I'm still on the Gilgamesh. *I'm not on the moon. They haven't taken me—*

The arms that had caught him were being none too gentle about setting him on his feet, and when his knees buckled, someone grabbed him and shook him, ramming his back against the chamber so that the lid slammed shut and trapped a fold of his sleep-suit.

Someone was shouting at him. They were shouting at him to shut up. Only then did he realize he was screaming at them – the same words over and over, that he didn't want to go, that they couldn't make him.

As if to give the lie to that, whoever was manhandling him slapped him across the face, and he heard his voice wind down to a puzzled whimper before he could get control over it.

Around then, Holsten realized that there were four people in the room and he didn't know any of them. Three men and a woman: all strangers, total strangers. They wore ship-suits but they weren't Key Crew. Or if they were, Guyen hadn't woken them for the pass at the green planet.

Holsten blinked at them stupidly. The man who held him was tall, lean and long-boned, looking around Holsten's own age, with little scars around his eyes that spoke of recent surgical correction – recent presumably meaning several thousand years ago, before they put him to sleep.

The classicist's eyes passed over the others: a young-looking woman, heavily built; a small, thin man with a narrow face that was withered up on one side, perhaps a suspension chamber side-effect; a squat, heavy-jawed man standing by the hatch, who was constantly glancing outside. He was holding a gun.

Holding a *gun*.

Holsten stared at the weapon, which was some sort of pistol. He was still having difficulty interpreting what he was seeing. He could think of no reason whatsoever why there would be a gun involved in this scenario. Guns were on the manifest for the *Gilgamesh*, certainly. He was aware that, of all the trappings of old Earth carried on to the ark ship, guns had certainly not been left behind. On the other hand, they were surely not something to be carried about aboard a spaceship full of delicate systems, with the killing vacuum waiting just outside.

Unless the gun was there to force him to go down to the moon colony – but it would hardly take a gun. Karst or a couple of his security detail would surely suffice, and run less risk of damaging something vital aboard the *Gilgamesh*. Something more vital than Holsten Mason.

He tried to phrase an intelligent question, but managed just a vague mumble.

'You hear that?' the tall, lean man told the others. 'He doesn't want to go. How about that, eh?'

'Scoles, let's *move*,' hissed the man at the door, the one with the gun. Holsten's eyes kept straying to the weapon.

A moment later he found himself strung between Scoles and the woman, being awkwardly push-pulled through the hatch, the gunman leading, pointing his weapon along the corridor. In Holsten's last glimpse through the hatch before withered-face closed it, he saw that the status panels for the other Key Crew chambers were all showing empty. He had been the only person left to sleep late.

'Someone tell me what is going on,' he demanded, although it came out sounding like babble.

'We need you—' the woman started.

'Shut up,' snapped Scoles, and she did.

By that time, Holsten reckoned he could have stumbled along under his own power, but they were hustling him along faster than he could get his feet under him. A moment later he heard some loud noises from back the way they had come, as if someone had dropped something heavy. It was only when the gunman turned back and began returning fire that he realized the sound had been shooting. The pistol made little tinny noises that were oddly unimpressive, like a big dog with a tiny bark. The answering sounds were thunderous booms that shook the air and rattled Holsten's eardrums, as though the wrath of God was being unleashed in the next room. Disruptors, he recognized: crowd-control weapons relying on detonating packets of air. Theoretically non-lethal and certainly less dangerous to the ship.

'Who's shooting at us?' he got out, and this time the words sounded clear enough.

'Your friends,' Scoles told him shortly, which ranked amongst the world's least comforting answers, in the circumstances, leaving Holsten with the twin assurances that his current company did not consider him a friend, and that his actual friends – whoever they were – were ambivalent at best about hurting him.

'Is the ship . . . is something wrong with the ship?' he demanded, his tone telling him second-hand how frightened he must be. His emotions seemed to be buzzing about somewhere else in his mind, kept apart from his higher brain by the slowly thawing wall of the suspension chamber.

'Shut up or I will hurt you,' Scoles told him, in a tone suggesting that he would enjoy doing so. Holsten shut up.

The one with the withered face had been lagging behind them, and then suddenly he was down on the ground. Holsten thought the man had tripped – he even made an abortive, automatic motion to try and help before he himself was dragged away. Withered-face was not getting up, though, and the gunman knelt by his corpse, dragged a second pistol from the back of the dead man's belt and then levelled both weapons at attackers Holsten had not even seen.

Shot. No disruptor burst for withered-face. Someone on the other side – Holsten's *friends* purportedly – had apparently run short of patience, prudence or mercy.

Then there were two other people passing by to give the gunman assistance – a man and a woman, both armed – and the amount of gunfire from behind increased dramatically, but it was plain from Scoles's slowing pace that he reckoned he was safer now. Whether that translated into any greater safety for Holsten himself seemed to remain a live question. His mouth instinctively thronged with all manner of protests, questions, pleas and even threats, but he bit them all back.

He was hauled on past another half-dozen armed people – all strangers, all in shipsuits – before being shoved through a hatch, and sent sprawling unceremoniously across the floor of a small systems room, which was just a narrow space between two consoles with a single screen taking up most of the back wall.

There was another gunman there, whose startled reaction to his appearance was probably the closest Holsten had yet come to actually being shot. There was also another prisoner, sitting with her back to one of the consoles, with hands secured behind her. The prisoner was Isa Lain, chief engineer.

They dumped him beside her, restraining his arms in the same way. Scoles then seemed to lose all interest in him, stepping outside to join a hushed but heated discussion with some of the others, of which Holsten could only catch the odd word. He heard no more gunfire.

The woman and the gunman who had brought him in were still in the room, meaning that there was barely space for anyone else. The air was stuffy and close, smelling strongly of sweat and faintly of urine.

For a moment Holsten caught himself wondering if he had simply dreamt all that he remembered since leaving Earth – if some defect of the suspension chamber had drawn him into some grand hallucination where he, the classicist, was suddenly considered a necessary and useful figure among the crew.

He glanced at Lain. She was regarding him miserably. It struck him that there were lines on her face that were foreign to him, and her hair had grown to something more than mere stubble. *She is – she's catching me up. Am I still the oldest human in the universe? Perhaps just.*

He eyed their guards, who seemed to be paying far more attention to what Scoles was saying outside than to their two charges. He essayed a whisper: 'What's going on? Who are these maniacs?'

Lain eyed him bleakly. 'Colonists.'

He considered that one word, which opened a door on to a hidden past where someone – Guyen probably – had royally screwed up. 'What do they want?'

'Not to be colonists.'

'Well, yes, I could have guessed that, but . . . they've got guns.'

Her expression should have curdled into contempt – stating the obvious when every word might count – but instead she just shrugged. 'They got into the armoury before it kicked off. So much for Karst's fucking *security*.'

'They want to take over the ship?'

'If they have to.'

He guessed that Karst and the security detail were trying to redeem themselves by doing their best to stop that happening, which had apparently now escalated to pitched gun battles in the fragile corridors of the ship. He had no idea of the numbers involved. The moon colony would house several hundred colonists at least, perhaps with more being kept in suspension there. Surely there weren't half a thousand mutineers currently running loose on the *Gilgamesh*? And how many did Karst have? Was the man waking up secondary crew to use as foot-soldiers and shoving guns into their cold hands?

'What happened?' he demanded, the question aimed more at the universe than anyone in particular.

'Glad you asked.' Scoles pushed into the room, virtually elbowing the gunman out to give himself space. 'What was it you said, when we hauled you out of bed? "I don't want to go," was it? Well, join the club. Nobody here signed on for this journey to end up freezing in some death-trap on a moon without an atmosphere.'

Holsten stared at him for a moment, noticing the lean man's long hands clenching, seeing the skin round his eyes and mouth twitch involuntarily – he guessed it was the mark of some drug or other that had been keeping the man awake and going since who knew how long. Scoles himself held no gun, but here was a dangerous, volatile man who had been pushed about as far as he could go.

'Ah, sir . . .' Holsten began, as calmly as he could manage. 'You probably know that I'm Holsten Mason, classicist. I'm not sure if you actually wanted me, or if you were just after whoever you could get for . . . for a hostage, or . . . I don't really know what's going on here. If there's anything . . . any way that I—'

'Can get out with your skin intact?' Scoles interjected.

'Well, yes . . .'

'Not up to me,' the man replied dismissively, seeming about to turn away, but then he refocused and looked at Holsten again as if with fresh eyes. 'Fine, last time you were about, things were different. But, believe me, you do know things – very valuable things. And I appreciate you're not to blame, old man, but there are lives at stake here, hundreds of lives. You're in this, like it or not.'

Not, decided Holsten grimly, but what could he say?

'Signal the comms room,' Scoles ordered, and the woman twisted her way over to one of the consoles, virtually sitting on Holsten's shoulder as she sent the commands.

A long moment later, Guyen's louring face appeared on the wall screen, glaring thunderously at all and sundry. He, too, looked older to Holsten's eyes, and even more lacking in human kindness.

'I take it you're not about to lay down your arms,' the *Gilgamesh*'s commander snapped.

'You take it right,' Scoles replied levelly. 'However, there's a friend of yours here. Perhaps you want to renew your acquaintance.' He prodded Holsten in the head to make his point.

Guyen remained impassive, narrow-eyed. 'What of it?' There was no real clue that he recognized Holsten at all.

'I know you need him. I know where you're intending to jaunt off to, once you've consigned us all to that wasteland,' Scoles told him. 'I know you'll need your vaunted classicist when you find all that old tech you're so sure of. And don't bother searching the *cargo* manifests,' this was said with bitter emphasis, by a man who until recently had been merely a part of that cargo, 'because Nessel here is the next best thing – not an expert like your old man, but she knows more than anyone else.' He clapped the woman beside him on the shoulder. 'So let's talk, Guyen. Or else I wouldn't give much for your classicist and your chief engineer's chances.'

Guyen regarded him – all of them – without expression.

'Engineer Lain's team is quite capable of covering for her, in her absence,' he said, as though she had simply gone down with some transient infection. 'As for the other, we have the codes now to activate the Empire installations. The science team can handle it. I will not negotiate with those who defy my authority.'

His face vanished, but Scoles stared at the empty screen for a long time afterwards, hands clenched into fists.

3.2 FIRE AND THE SWORD

Generations have passed this green world by, in hope, in discovery, in fear, in failure. A future long foreseen is coming to pass.

Another Portia from the Great Nest by the Western Ocean, but a warrior this time, in the manner of her kind.

Her surroundings right now are not Great Nest but a different metropolis of the spiders: one she thinks of as Seven Trees. Portia is here as an observer, and to lend what aid she might. All around her, the community is a hive of furious activity as the inhabitants scurry and leap and abseil about their frantic business, and she watches them, her scatter of eyes taking in the chaos on all sides, and compares the sight to a disturbed ant's nest. She is capable of the bitter reflection that circumstances have now dragged her people down to the level of their enemy.

She feels fear, a building anxiety that makes her stamp her feet and twitch her palps. Her people are more suited to offence than defence, but they have been unable to retain the initiative in this conflict. She will have to improvise. There is no plan for what comes next.

She may die, and her eyes look into that abyss and feed her with a terror of extinction, of un-being, that is perhaps the legacy of all life.

There are signals being flagged by messengers and look-outs posted high in the trees above, as high up as Seven Trees' silk scaffolding extends. They signal regularly. The signal is time counting down: how long this place now has left before the enemy comes. The message wires that are strung between the trunks and their multitude of spun dwellings thrum with speech, as though the community is raging against the inevitability of its destruction.

Neither Portia's death nor Seven Trees' destruction is inevitable. The community has its own defenders – for in this time, in this age, every spider conurbation has dedicated fighters who spend their time training for nothing other than to fight – and Portia is here along with a dozen from Great Nest, in support of their kin. They wear armour of wood and silk, and they have their slingshots. They are the diminutive knights of their world, facing an enemy that outnumbers them by hundreds to one.

Portia knows she needs to calm herself, but the agitation within her is too great to be suppressed. She needs some external reassurance.

At the high point of the nest's central tree she finds it. Here is an expansive tent of silk whose walls are woven with complex geometric patterns, the crossing threads drawn out according to an exacting plan. Another handful of her kind are already there, seeking the reassurance of the numinous, the certainty that there is something more to the world than their senses can readily grasp; that there is a greater Understanding. That, even when all is lost, all need not be lost.

Portia crouches down with them and begins to spin, forming knots of thread that make a language out of numbers, a holy text that is written anew whenever one of her people kneels in contemplation, and that is then consumed when they arise. She was born with this Understanding, but she has learned it anew as well, coming to Temple at an early age just as she has come here now. The innate, virus-hardwired Understanding of these mathematical transformations that she inherited did not inspire her in the same way as being guided through the sequences by her teachers, slowly coming to the revelation that what these apparently arbitrary strings of figures described was something beyond mere invention – was a self-evident and internally consistent universal truth.

Of course in Great Nest, her home, they have a crystal that speaks these truths in its own ineffable way – just as most of the greatest nests have now, that pilgrims from lesser communities often journey great distances to see. She has watched as the votive priestess touches the crystal with her metal probe, feeling the pulsing of the message from the heavens, dancing out that celestial arithmetic for the benefit of the congregation. At such times, Portia knows, the Messenger itself would be in the skies overhead, going about her constant journey – whether at night and visible, or hidden by the brightness of the daytime sky.

Here in Seven Trees there is no crystal, but to simply repeat that message, in all its wondrous but internally consistent complexity, to spin and consume and spin again, is a calming ritual that settles Portia's mind, and allows her to face whatever must soon come, with equanimity.

Her people have solved the mathematical riddles posed by the orbiting satellite – the Messenger, as they think of it – learning the proofs first by rote and then in true comprehension, as a civic and religious duty. The intrusion of this signal has seized the attention of much of the species in a relatively short period of time, because of their inherent curiosity. Here is something demonstrably from beyond, and it fascinates them; it tells them that there is more to the world than they can grasp; it guides their thinking in new ways. The beauty of the maths promises a universe of wonders if they can but stretch out their minds that bit further: a jump they can almost, but not quite, make.

Portia spins and unravels and spins, soothing away the trepidation consuming her, replacing it with the undeniable certainty that there is *more*. Whatever happens this day, even if she should fall beneath the iron-clad mandibles of her foes, there is a depth to life beyond the simple dimensions that she can perceive and calculate in, and so . . . who knows?

Then it is time, and she backs out of temple and goes to arm herself.

There is considerable variation in the settlements of Portia's people, but to human eyes they would look messy, possibly nightmarish. Seven Trees now encompasses more than the original seven, the thicket of trunks interlinked by hundreds of lines, each part of a plan, each assigned a specific purpose, whether structural, as a thoroughfare, or for communication. The vibratory language of the spiders transmits well down silk threads over some distance, and they have developed nodes of tensioned coils that amplify the signal so that speech can pass for kilometres between cities in calm weather. The dwelling places of her kin are silk tents pulled taut by support lines into a variety of shapes, suitable to a species that lives its life in three dimensions and can hang from a vertical surface as easily as resting on a horizontal one. Meeting places are broad webs where a speaker's words can be transmitted to a crowd of listeners along the dancing of the strands. In the high centre, shadowing much of the city, is the reservoir: a watertight net spread wide that catches rain and run-off from a grand area around Seven Trees, the water channelling to it through troughs and pipes from a multitude of smaller rain-catchers.

Around Seven Trees the forest has been cut back by the semi-domesticated local ants. Previously this has been a fire-break. Soon it will be a killing ground.

Portia crawls and leaps her way through Seven Trees, and sees that the sentries are signalling first contact with the enemy: the settlement's automated defences have been triggered. All around her the evacuation is ongoing, those who are not dedicated fighters gathering what they can – supplies and those few possessions they cannot simply recreate – and abandoning Seven Trees. Some carry clutches of eggs glued to their abdomens. Many have spiderlings clinging to them. Those young that are not sensible enough to hitch a ride are likely to die.

Portia swiftly draws herself up to one of the lofty watch towers, looking out towards the treeline. Out there is an army of hundreds of thousands advancing towards Seven Trees. It is an independent arm of the same great ant colony her ancestress once scouted out; a centuries-old composite life form that is taking over this part of the world day by day.

The nearby forest is riddled with traps. There are webs to catch incautious ants. There are springlines, pulled taut between ground and canopy, that will stick to a passing insect, then detach and whip the luckless creature upwards, to trap it in the high branches. There are deadfalls and pits, but none of them will be enough. The advancing colony will meet these dangers as it meets all dangers, by sacrificing enough of itself to nullify them, with the main thrust of its attack barely slowing. There is a particular caste of expendable scout now ranging ahead of the ants' main column, specifically to suicidally disarm these defensive measures.

Now there is movement in the trees. Portia focuses on it, seeing those scouts that survive washing forwards in a chaotic mass, obeying their programming. The ground between them and Seven Trees is only lightly trapped, but they have other difficulties to face. The local ants are on them instantly, sallying forth valiantly to bite and sting, so that within metres of the treeline the ground becomes messy with knots of fighting insects, insensately dismembering each other and being dismembered in turn. To human eyes, the ants of the two colonies would seem indistinguishable, but Portia can discern differences in colouration and pattern, extending into the ultraviolet. She is ready with her slingshot.

The arachnid defenders start their barrage with solid ammunition, simple stones gathered from the ground, chosen for their convenient size and heft. They target those scouts that break loose from the ant melee, picking them off with deadly accuracy, each shot plotted and calculated exactingly. The ants are incapable of dodging or reacting, unable to even perceive the defenders at their high vantage points. The death toll amongst the insects is ruinous, or it would be if this host was anything but the disposable vanguard of a much greater force.

Some of the scouts reach the foot of Seven Trees, despite the bombardment. But, after a metre or so of bare trunk, each tree boasts sheer web skirts that angle up and out, a surface that the ants cannot get purchase on. They climb and fall, climb and fall, initially mindless in their persistence. Then a sufficient concentration of messaging scent builds, and they change their tactics, climbing up over one another to form a living, reaching structure that extends blindly upwards.

Portia stamps out a call to arms and her sisters from Great Nest muster around her. The local defenders are less well armed, lacking both experience and innate understanding of ant-war. She and her fellows will lead the charge.

They drop swiftly from the heights on to the ant scouts, and begin their work. They are far larger than the attackers, both stronger and swifter. Their bite is venomous, but it is a venom best used against spiders, so they now concentrate on using their fangs at the intersections of the insects' bodies, between head and thorax, between thorax and abdomen. Most of all, they are more intelligent than their enemies, better able to react and manoeuvre and evade. They tear apart the scouts and their bridge-building with furious haste, always moving, never letting the ants latch on to them.

Portia leaps back to the trunk, then scuttles over to cling effortlessly to the same silk underhang that the ants could not climb. Upside down, she sees fresh movement at the treeline. The main column has arrived.

These new ants are larger – though still smaller than herself. They are of many castes, each to its own speciality. At the head of the column, and already accelerating along the scouts' scent trail towards Seven Trees, come the shocktroopers. Their formidable mandibles sport barbed, sawedged metal blades, and they have head-shields that spread back to protect their thoraxes. Their purpose is to monopolize the defenders' attention and sell their lives as dearly as possible, so as to allow more dangerous castes to close the distance.

More of the enemy are even now entering the tunnels of the local ants' nest, spreading confounding chemicals that throw the defending insects into confusion, or even enlist them to the cause of the attacker. This is one way that the mega-colony grows, by co-opting rather than destroying other ant hives. For foreign species such as Portia, though, there is no purpose and no mercy.

Back in Seven Trees, the remaining local males are hard at work. Some have fled, but most of the evacuees are female. Males are replaceable, always underfoot, always too numerous. Many have been instructed to remain in the city until the last, on pain of death. Some have fled anyway, to take their chances, but there are still plenty to cut any remaining lines between the settlement and the ground, to deny the ants easy access. Others are hurrying from the reservoir with silk parcels bulging with water. Portia notes such industry with approval.

The front ranks of the column are nearing. The armoured ants suffer less from the slingshots, but now other ammunition is brought into play. Portia's people are chemists of a sort. Living in a world where scent is so vital – a small part of their language but a very large part of the way the rest of the world perceives itself – they have developed numerous inherited Understandings with respect to the mixing and compounding of chemical substances, most especially pheromones. Now the slingers are sending over silk-wrapped globules of liquid to splash amongst the advancing ants. The scents thus released briefly cover up the attackers' own constant scent language – denying them not only speech, but thought and identity. Until the chemicals dissipate, the affected sections of the attacking army are deprogrammed, falling back on base instincts and unable to react properly to the situation around them. They blunder and break formation, and some of them fight each other, unable to recognize their own kin. Portia and the other defenders attack swiftly, killing as many as they can while this confusion persists.

The defenders are taking losses now. Those metal jaws can sever legs or tear open bodies. Portia's warriors wear coats of silk and plates of soft wood to snare the saw teeth, shedding this armour as they need to, repairing it when they can. The column is still advancing, despite everything the defenders can do.

The males are splashing water about the lower reaches of Seven Trees, proactive fire-fighting, for the ant colony is now deploying its real weapons.

Near to Portia there is a flash and gout of flame, and two of her comrades are instantly ablaze, like staggering torches kicking and shrivelling and dying. These new ants brew chemicals inside their abdomens, just like certain species of beetle. When they jut their stingers forwards and mix these substances there is a fierce exothermic reaction, a spray of heated fluid. The atmosphere of Portia's world has an oxygen content a few per cent higher than Earth's, enough for the searing mixture to spontaneously ignite.

The technology of Portia's kind is built on silk and wood, potential energy stored in tensioned lines and primitive springs. What little metal they use is stolen from the ants. They have no use for fire.

Portia gains height and reverts to her sling. The flame-thrower ants are lethal at short range but vulnerable to her missile fire. However, the ants now control all the ground around Seven Trees and they are bringing forward more far-reaching weapons.

She sees the first projectile as it is launched, her eyes tracking the motion automatically: a gleaming sphere of a hard, transparent, fragile material – for the ants have stumbled upon glass in the intervening generations – now arcs overhead and shatters behind her. Her lateral eyes catch the flare as the chemicals within it mix and then explode.

Below, behind the shielded shock-troopers, the artillery is at work: ants with heads encased in a metal mask that includes a back-facing tongue – a length of springy metal that their mouthparts can depress and then release, flicking their incendiary grenades some distance. Their aim is poor, blindly following the scent clues of their comrades, but there are many of them. Although the males of Seven Trees are rushing with water to douse the flames, the fires spread swiftly, shrivelling silk and blackening wood.

Seven Trees starts to burn.

It is the end. The defenders who can do so must leave, or roast. For those that leap blindly, though, the metal jaws of the ants await.

Portia scales higher and higher, racing against the flames. The upper reaches of the settlement are cluttered with desperately reaching bodies: warriors, civilians, females, males. Some shudder and drop as the smoke overcomes them. Others cannot outstrip the hungry fire.

She fights her way to the top, jettisoning the wooden plates of her armour while spinning frantically. Always it has been thus, and at least she has one use for the inferno that is stoking itself below her: the thermals will give her height so that she can use her self-made parachute to glide beyond the reach of the rapacious ant colony.

For now. Only for now. This army is closing on Great Nest, and after that there will only be the ocean. If Portia's kind cannot defeat the mindless march of the ants, then nobody will be around to write the histories of future generations.

3.3 ROCK AND A HARD PLACE

There was an awkward silence for some time after Scoles left. The unnamed gunman and the woman, Nessel, went about their duties without speaking to one another; she bent over the computer displays, he scowling at the prisoners. Having confirmed to his own satisfaction that furtive squirming resulted only in the restraints cutting deeper into his wrists, Holsten became more and more oppressed by the silence. Yes, there was a gun pointing his way. Yes, the *Gilgamesh* was obviously playing host to a conflict that could plainly get him killed at any moment, but he was *bored*. Just out of suspension, freshly woken from decades of involuntary hibernation, and his body wanted to *do* something. He found he had to bite his tongue to stop himself speaking his thoughts aloud, just to vary the tedium.

Then someone varied it for him. There were some distant bangs that he identified, after the fact, as gunshots, and someone passed by the hatch with some muttered instruction he missed hearing. The gunman caught it, though, and was out on the instant, running off down the corridor and taking his gun with him. The small room seemed remarkably more spacious without it.

He glanced at Lain, but she stared at her feet, avoiding his gaze. The only other person there was Nessel.

'Hey,' he tried.

'Shut up,' Lain hissed at him, but still looking away.

'Hey,' Holsten repeated. 'Nessel, is it? Listen . . .' He thought she would just ignore him, but she glanced over sullenly.

'Brenjit Nessel,' she informed him. 'And you're Doctor Holsten Mason. I remember reading your papers back when . . . Back when.'

'Back when,' Holsten agreed weakly. 'Well, that's . . . flattering, I suppose. Scoles was right, then. You're a classicist yourself.'

'Student,' she told him. 'I didn't follow it up. Who knows, if I had, maybe we'd be in each other's places right now.' Her voice sounded ragged with emotion and fatigue.

'Just a student.' He remembered his last classes – back before the end. The study of the Old Empire had once been the lifeblood of the world. Everyone had been desperate to cut a slice off the secrets of the ancients. In Holsten's time it had fallen out of favour. They had seen the end coming by then, and known that there would not be enough broken potsherds of lore from the old days to stave it off; known that it was those same ancients, with their weapons and their waste, that had brought that long-delayed end upon them. To study and laud those antique psychopaths during the Earth's last toxic days had seemed bad taste. Nobody liked a classicist.

Nessel had turned away, and so he spoke her name again, urgently. 'Look, what's going to happen to us? Can you tell us that, at least?'

The woman's eyes flicked towards Lain with obvious distaste, but they looked kinder when they returned to Holsten.

'It's like Scoles says, it's not up to us. Maybe Guyen will end up storming this place, and you'll get shot. Maybe they'll break through our firewalls and cut off the air or the heat or something. Or maybe we win. If we win, you get to go free. *You* do, anyway.'

Another sidelong glance at Lain, who now had her eyes closed, either resigned to her situation or trying to unmake it all, to just blot out her surroundings.

'Look,' Holsten tried, 'I understand you're fighting Guyen. Maybe I'm even sympathetic about that. But, she and I, we're not responsible. We're not a part of this. I mean, nobody consults me about these things, do they? I didn't even know this thing was . . . that any of this was going on until you slapped me awake back there.'

'You? Maybe,' Nessel said, abruptly angry. 'Her? She knew. Who'd the commander have overseeing the technical details, then? Who was arranging to ship us down *there*? Who had her fingers in every little piece of the work? Only the chief engineer. If we shot her right now, it'd be justice.'

Holsten swallowed. Lain continued to be no help, but maybe he could now see why. 'Look,' he said again, more gently, 'surely you must see that this is crazy?'

'Do you know what I think is crazy?' Nessel returned hotly. 'It's setting up some fucking icebox of a base on a moon we've no use for, just so Guyen can run a flag up his dick and say he's claimed this system for Earth. What I think is crazy is expecting us to go there peaceably, willingly, and just live there in that artificial hell, while the rest of you just fuck off on some wonder-trip that'll take you how many human lifetimes to get there and return? If you ever *do*.'

'We're all a lot of human lifetimes from home,' Holsten reminded her.

'But we *slept!*' Nessel shouted at him. 'And we were all together, all the human race together, and so it didn't *count*, and it didn't matter. We brought our own time with us, and we stopped the clock while we slept, and started it when we woke. Why should we care how many thousands of years went by on dead old Earth? But when the *Gil* heads off for wherever the fuck it's going, us poor bastards won't get to sleep. We're supposed to make a life down there, on the ice, inside those stupid little boxes the automatics have made. A *life*, Doctor Mason! A whole life inside those boxes. And what? And *children*? Can you imagine? Generations of ice-dwellers, forgetting and forgetting who we ever were, wasting away and never seeing the sun except as just another star. Tending the vats and eating mulch and putting out more doomed generations who could never amount to anything, while *you* – all you glorious star-travellers – get to sleep wrapped in your no-time, and wake up two hundred years later as if it's just the next day?' She was shouting now, almost shrieking, and he saw that she must have been awake for far too long; that he had cracked the dam, let it all pour out after his thoughtless words. 'And when *you* woke up, all of you *chosen* who weren't condemned to the ice, we'd be dead. We'd be generations dead, all of us. And why? Because Guyen wants a presence on a dead moon.'

'Guyen wants to preserve the human race,' Lain said sharply. 'And whatever we encounter at the next terraforming project could obliterate the *Gilgamesh*, for all we know. Guyen simply wants to spread our chances as a species. You know this.'

'Then let *him* fucking stay. And *you* can stay too. How about that? When we win control, when we take the ship, the two of you can go keep the species going in that icebox, on your own. That's what we'll do, believe me. If you live that long, that's just what we'll do with you.'

Lain did her best to shrug it off, but Holsten could see her jaw clench against the thought.

Then Scoles came ducking back in, snagging Nessel's arm and dragging her aside for a muttered conversation in the doorway.

'Lain—' Holsten started.

'I'm sorry,' the woman said flatly, wrong-footing him. He was not sure what she was apologizing for.

'How far does this go?' Holsten murmured. 'How many of them?'

'At least two dozen.' He could barely make out Lain's whispered words. 'They were supposed to be the pioneers – that was Guyen's plan. They'd go down awake, to start everything off. The rest would be shipped down as freight, to be awoken as and when.'

'I see that all worked out beautifully, then,' Holsten remarked.

Again her expected caustic response did not come. Some barbed edge seemed to have been filed off Lain since he had last seen her, all those decades before.

'How many's Karst got?' he pressed her.

She shrugged. 'The security detail's about a dozen, but there's military he could wake up. He'll do it, too. He'll have an army.'

'Not if he's got any sense.' Holsten had been pondering this. 'Why would they take orders from him, to start with?'

'Who else is there?'

'Not good enough. Have you actually *thought* about what we're doing, Lain? I don't even mean *this* business,' a jerk of the head towards Scoles, 'but the whole show. We don't have a culture. We don't have a hierarchy. We simply have a *crew*, for life's sake. Guyen, who someone once considered fit to command a large spaceship, is now titular head of the human race.'

'It's the way it's got to be,' Lain replied stubbornly.

'Scoles disagrees. I reckon the army will disagree too, if Karst is stupid enough to start waking people up and putting guns in their hands. You know what's a good lesson of history? You're screwed if you can't pay the army. And we don't even have an economy. What could we give them, as soon as they realize what's going on. Where's the chain of command? What authority does anyone have? And once they've got guns, and a clear indication of where they might wake up next, why should we ever expect them to go back to the chambers and sleep? The only currency we have is freedom, and it's plain that Guyen's not going to be handing that out.'

'Oh, fuck off, historian.' At last he got a rise out of her, though he wasn't looking for it by then.

'And although I don't want to think about what happens if Scoles wins, what happens if he loses?'

'*When* he loses.'

'Whatever – but what then?' Holsten insisted. 'We end up shipping all those people down to a – what – a penal colony for life? And what happens when we return? What do we hope to find down there, with that for a beginning?'

'There won't be any *down there*, not for us.' It was Scoles

147

again, pulling that trick of suddenly being in front of them, now squatting on his haunches, hands resting on his knees. 'If the worst comes to the worst, we still have a plan B. Thanks to you there, anyway, Doctor Mason.'

'Right.' Looking the man in the face, Holsten didn't know what to make of that. 'Maybe you'd like to explain?'

'Nothing would please me more.' Scoles smiled thinly. 'We have control of a shuttle bay. If all else fails, we're getting ourselves off the *Gil*, Doctor Mason, and you're coming with us.'

Holsten, still thinking slowly after the suspension, just goggled at him. 'I thought the point was *not* to go somewhere.'

'Not to go to the ice,' Nessel said from behind Scoles. 'But we know there's somewhere else in this very system, somewhere *made* for us.'

'Oh.' Holsten stared at them. 'You're completely mad. It's . . . there are monsters there.'

'Monsters can be fought,' Scoles declared implacably.

'But it's not just that – there's a satellite. It came within a hair's breadth of destroying the whole of the *Gilgamesh*. It sent us away. There's no way a shuttle can . . . possibly get . . .' He stammered to a halt, because Scoles was smiling at him.

'We know all this. *She* told us,' a companionable nod towards Lain. 'She told us we'd never make the green planet. That the ancient tech would get us first. But that's why we have you, Doctor Mason. Maybe Nessel's grasp of the ancient languages would be enough, but I'll not take that chance. Why should I, when you're right here and desperate to help us?' The chief mutineer stood up easily, still with that razor grin on his face.

Holsten looked at Lain, and this time she met his gaze and he read the emotion there at last: guilt. No wonder she'd been easy on him. She was cringing inside, knowing that she had brought him here.

'You told them I could get them past Kern?' he demanded.

'No!' she protested. 'I told them it couldn't be done. I said that, even *with* you, we barely made it. But I . . .'

'But you managed to get them thinking of me,' Holsten finished.

'How was I to know these fuckwits would just—' Lain started, before Scoles stamped on her ankle.

'Just a reminder,' he growled, 'of who you are and why you deserve all you get. And don't worry, if we have to take the shuttle, you'll be right there with us, Chief Engineer Lain. Perhaps then you might feel like using your expertise to prolong your own life, for once, rather than just to ruin other people's.'

3.4 BY THE WESTERN OCEAN

The Great Nest. The greatest metropolis of Portia's kind. Home.

Returning like this, at the head of a band of defeated stragglers – those lucky enough to escape the flames of Seven Trees – Portia feels something analogous to shame. She has not stopped the enemy, or even slowed it down. Each day, the ant colony will march closer to Great Nest. Looking across the expanse of her beloved birthplace, she finds herself picturing it in the throes of evacuation. In her mind's eye – a faculty already present in some form even for her tiniest ancestress – she sees her home burning. The ants do not know where Great Nest is, of course – their spread across the world is methodical but mindless – but they will reach the coast soon. The days are counting down to when they will arrive at the gates.

Great Nest is vast, home to several thousand spiders. The natural forest is still thick here, but great effort and artifice has gone into erecting artificial trees to provide more living room. Great pillars made from felled trunks, sheathed and strengthened with silk, spread out from the living copse at the city's centre – and even out into the sea itself, allowing the webwork of the city to reach out across the waters.

Space is at a premium and, over the last century, Great Nest has grown exponentially in all directions, including up.

Beyond the city proper, there lies a patchwork of farms: aphids for honeydew, mice for meat, and stands of the blister-trunked trees cultivated by the ants, another secret stolen from the enemy. The seas throng with fish ready for the netting, and offshore there is a sister-settlement on the sea-bed; relations with the marine stomatopod culture are cordial and mutually profitable, in a minimal sort of way. A generation ago there was friction as the spiders began to expand their city seawards. The sunken bases of the pillars, however, have enriched the marine environment, providing an artificial reef that sealife has quickly taken advantage of. In retrospect, the sea-dwellers concede that they have gained from this situation, however inadvertently.

Portia and her band get aloft quickly, clambering up towards the city on lines strung over the outlying farmland. She has brought back some warriors, and a reasonable number of males, though few will thank her for returning with the latter. The smaller males are better able to parachute to safety: they survived when many of their sisters did not. And they fought, Portia concedes. The idea of a male warrior is absurd, but they are still stronger and faster and more intel-ligent than ants. For a moment she has a mad idea: arm and train the males, thus vastly increasing the number of fighters available to Great Nest. But she shies away from the idea instantly – that way anarchy lies, the reversal of the natural order of things. Moreover, even that way their numbers would not be enough. Arm every male in the city and the spiders would still be only a drop against the ant colony's ocean.

She reaches a high vantage point, looking down at the great elegant sweep of her home, the myriad threads that link it all together, Down in the bay she sees a great balloon of silk half-submerged in the water, sagging and rippling as it is filled with air. An embassy to the stomatopods, she knows: a diving bell allowing inquiring minds amongst her people to visit their underwater counterparts. There can be no exchange of Understandings with the sea-dwellers, of course, but they can still teach and learn via the simple language of gestures that the two cultures have worked out between them.

Seek out your peers, she instructs her fellows, the returning warriors. *Await the call.* The males she leaves to their own devices. If they possess any initiative, they will find work and get fed. In a vast city like Great Nest there is a constant need for maintenance – lines and sheets of silk needing repairs. An industrious male can make himself useful enough to be rewarded. The alternative for him is to make a living through courtship and flattery, which involves less effort but considerably more danger.

Portia sets off through the city, creeping and jumping from line to line, seeking out her peer house.

Using communal crèches and lacking any maternal instincts, Portia's people have no strict family units. The youngest spiderlings, still confined to the crèche, are provided with food by the city, but this period of free bounty does not last long. The fast-maturing young are expected to become independent within their first year. Like the males, they must make themselves useful.

Because a spider alone is vulnerable, always at the mercy of bullying from her larger kin, these maturing spiderlings tend to band together into peer groups formed from those who hatched from the same crèche at around the same time. The bonds made between juveniles, who aid and rely upon one another, persist into adulthood. Unions of such peers form the base social unit in most spider settlements, and these peers then tend to found a crèche between them, looking after one another's eggs, and so inadvertently perpetuating a continuity of heredity down the female line. The social bonds within such peer groups are strong, even after the individuals have gone their separate ways and taken up their particular trades and specialities. All the larger peer groups maintain peer houses within the city – 'house' here meaning a complex of silk-walled chambers.

Males do not form such groups – for who would have any use for a large group of males? Instead, juvenile males do their best to attach themselves to the periphery of a female peer group, playing at flirting, running errands, paying in utility and amusement value for the scraps of food that might get thrown their way. Portia is vaguely aware that males fight each other, and that the lower – less desirable – reaches of the city play host to countless little dramas between males struggling over food or status. She has very little interest in the subject.

She is bitterly exhausted when she crawls through the entrance of her peer house, located at the lowest point of the series of bubble chambers in which her fellows dwell and meet. Another couple of rooms have been added since she was last here – re-structuring is no major chore for her kind – and for a moment she feels proud and happy that her peers are doing well, before her treacherous memory goads her with the thought of the ants' inexorable advance. Building more just means more to lose.

Those of her peers who are currently in residence greet her warmly. Several of her closer friends are holding court there at the centre of a worshipful knot of younger females and fluttering, dancing males. Their dances are courtship rituals that they constantly almost, but not quite, consummate. Other than menial labour, this is the place of a male in Portia's society: adornment, decoration, simply to add value to the lives of females. The larger, more notable or more important a female is, the more males will dance attendance on her. Hence, having a crowd of uselessly elegant males around one is a status symbol. If Portia – the great warrior – were to stay still long enough, then she would attract her own entourage of hopeful parasites; indeed, if she cast them off and refused their attentions she would be diminishing herself in the eyes of her peers and her culture.

And sometimes the courtship will proceed as far as mating, if the female feels sufficiently safe and prosperous to start work on a clutch of eggs. The act of courtship is consummated as a public ritual, where the hopeful males – in their moment of prominence – perform in front of a peer group, or even the whole city, before the female chooses her partner and accepts his package of sperm. She may then kill and eat him, which is thought to be a great honour for the victim, although even Portia suspects that the males do not quite see it that way.

It is a mark of how far her species has come, that this is the only openly acceptable time when killing a male is considered appropriate. It is, however, quite true that packs of females – especially younger ones, perhaps newly formed peer groups seeking to strengthen their bonds – will descend to the lower reaches of the city and engage in hunting males.

The practice is covertly overlooked – girls will be girls, after all – but overtly frowned upon. Killing a male, sanctioned or not, is a world apart from killing a beast. Even as the fang strikes, the killer and the slain know themselves to be part of a grander whole. The nanovirus speaks, each to each. Portia's culture is strung between base spider nature and the new empathy the nanovirus has inflicted upon them.

There are more of her peers here than Portia had expected to see. One of her seniors is entering her time and therefore must retire from society for a month or so, and her sisters are rallying round her to make the ordeal as painless as possible. Portia ascends to one of the inner chambers to witness the rite, because it will at least give the illusion that life here is proceeding according to age-old patterns, and so might continue in the same way for generations to come. She arrives just in time to see her ailing sister retreat into her cocoon. In ancient, primitive times she would have been left alone in some high, safe spot, spinning her own retreat before retiring in lonely secrecy. Now she has sisters to create her haven for her, and then keep her company while she moults.

Portia's kind must shed their skins in order to grow. When it is time for a large female to cast off her skin – when she feels it too tight at each joint and with each breath of her abdomen – she retires to her peer house, to the company of those she trusts, and they spin her a cocoon that will support her expanded frame until her expanded skin has hardened again.

As Portia watches, the retiring female begins the difficult, painful task of ridding herself of her skin, first flexing her abdomen until the shell cracks there, and then peeling herself from back to front. The process will take hours, and her sisters stroke the cocoon with messages of solidarity and support. They have all been through this.

It must be difficult for males, who presumably undergo the ordeal alone, but then males are smaller, and less sensitive, and Portia is honestly not sure how capable they are of finer levels of thought and feeling.

A handful of her sisters notice Portia there and scurry over to talk. They listen with agitation to her news of Seven Trees – news that will be all over Great Nest by now, because males can never keep their feet still when they have something to say. Her fellows touch palps and try to tell her that what happened to Seven Trees cannot happen here, but nothing they say can remove those images from Portia's memory – the flames, the whole structure of a thriving settlement just withering in the heat; the reservoir fraying and splitting, its waters cascading down amid a rising curtain of steam; those who could not jump or glide far enough being overwhelmed by the roiling tide of ants, to be dismembered while still alive.

She performs a careful calculation based on her count of days and the elevation of the sun outside, and tells them that she is going to the temple. She badly needs peace of mind, and the Messenger will be passing soon.

Go quickly. There will be many others seeking the same, one of her sisters advises her. Even without Portia's personal experience, the population of Great Nest is fast becoming aware that they face a threat seemingly without limit. All their centuries of culture and sophistication may become nothing but a fading memory in the minds of the stomatopod sea-dwellers.

The temple at Great Nest is the city's highest point, a space without walls, strung between the extremity of the canopy above with an inward-sloping floor below. At its centre, on the apex of one of the city's original trees, is the crystal that Portia's own ancestress wrested from the ants, a deed that has since become legend. If Portia reaches inside herself, she can even touch that other Portia's Understandings, a private retelling of the well-known story through the lens of first-hand experience.

She arrives ahead of the Messenger's appearance, but there is already barely room for her amongst the crouching multitude, thronged all the way up to the central trunk. Many have the look of refugees – those who escaped Seven Trees and other places. They are come here to find hope because the material world outside seems to hold little of it.

How Portia's people regard the Messenger and its message is hard to say: theirs is an alien mindset, trying to unravel the threads of a phenomenon they are equipped to analyse and yet not understand. They gaze up at the Messenger in its fleet passage across the sky, and they see an entity that speaks to them in mathematical riddles that are aesthetically appealing to a species that has inherited geometry as the cornerstone of its civilization. They do not conceive of it as some celestial spider-god that will reach down into their green world and save them from the ant tide. However, the message *is*. The Messenger *is*. These are facts, and those facts are the doorway to an invisible, intangible world of the unknown. The true meaning of the message is that there is *more* than spider eyes can see or spider feet can feel. That is where hope lies, for there may yet be salvation hidden within that *more*. It inspires them to keep looking.

The priestess has emerged to dance, her stylus hunting out the connection points on the crystal as, invisibly, the

Messenger crosses the blue vault of the sky while broadcasting its constant message. Portia spins and knots, reciting the mantras of numbers to herself, watching the votary begin her elegant visual proofs, each step, and every sweep of her palps speaking of the beauty of universal order, the reassurance that there is a logic to the world, extending beyond the mere chaos of the physical.

But, even here, there is a sense of change and threat. As Portia watches the dance, it seems to her that the priestess halts sometimes, just for a second, or even stumbles. Ripples of unease pass through the close-packed congregation, who spin all the harder, as if to cover over that slip. *An inexperienced priestess*, Portia reassures herself, but she feels dreadfully afraid deep within herself. Is the doom that threatens her people in the material world now being reflected in the heavens? Is there a variation in the eternal message?

After the service finishes, and feeling more shaken than reassured, she finds a male in her way, frantically signalling his good intentions and that he bears a message for her.

You are needed, the little creature tells her, coming close enough to brave her fangs in his insistence. *Bianca asks for you.*

Bianca – this particular Bianca – is one of Portia's peer group, but not one that she has spoken with in a long time. No warrior but instead one of the foremost scholars of Portia's people.

Lead me, Portia directs.

3.5 BEARING A FLAMING SWORD

Holsten and Lain had been left to their own limited devices for some time, constantly overseen by one or other of Scoles's people. Holsten had been hoping to have more words with Nessel, on the basis that he might just be able to trade enough on his doctorate to gain some sort of cooperation from her, but she had been redeployed by her leader, perhaps for that exact reason. Instead there had been a succession of taciturn men and women with guns, one of whom had bloodied Holsten's lip just for opening his mouth.

They had heard distant shots on occasion, but the anticipated crescendo never seemed to arrive, nor did the fighting recede entirely out of earshot. It seemed that neither Scoles nor Karst was willing to force the matter to any sort of conclusion.

'It's times like these . . .' Holsten started, speaking softly for Lain's benefit only.

She raised an eyebrow. 'Times like what, Mason? Being held hostage by lunatic mutineers who might kill us at any second? How many times like those have you had, exactly? Or is the world of academia more interesting than I thought?'

He shrugged. 'Well, on the basis that we were all under a death sentence on Earth, and then, the last time we were working together, a mad computer-person hybrid thing

159

wanted to kill us for disturbing its monkeys, I think it's been times like these all the way, to be honest.'

Her smile was faint, but it was there. 'I'm sorry I got you into this.'

'Not half as sorry as I am.'

At that point Scoles burst in with a half-dozen followers crowding the hatch behind him. He shoved something into the hands of the guard that the man quickly donned.

A mask: they were all putting on oxygen masks.

'Oh, fuck,' Lain spat. 'Karst's got control of the air vents.' From her tone it was something that she had been anticipating for some time.

'Cut him loose.' From behind the mask, Scoles's voice emerged with the tinny precision of his radio transmitter. Immediately someone was bending over Holsten, severing his restraints, hauling him to his feet.

'He's coming with us,' Scoles snapped, and now Holsten could hear gunfire again, and more of it than before.

'What about her?' A nod towards Lain.

'Shoot the bitch.'

'Wait! Hold on!' Holsten got out, flinching as the gun swung back towards him. 'You need me? Then you need her. She's the chief engineer, for life's sake! If you're going anywhere on a shuttle . . . If you're serious about going up against Kern – against that killer satellite – then you need her. Come on, she's Key Crew. That means she's the best engineer on this ship.' And, despite his words, when the gun swung back towards Lain: 'No, seriously, wait. I . . . I know you can force me to do whatever you want, but if you kill her, I'll fucking fight you to my last breath. I'll sabotage the shuttle. I'll . . . I don't know what I'll do but I'll find something. Keep her alive and I'll do everything you need, and everything I can think of, to keep you alive. To keep us *all* alive. Come on, it makes sense. Surely you can see it makes sense!'

He could not see Scoles's expression, and for a moment the chief mutineer just stood there, statue-still, but then he nodded once, and exceedingly grudgingly. 'Get them both masks,' he snapped. 'Get them up. Re-secure their arms and bring them along. We're getting off this ship right now.'

Outside in the corridor waited a dozen or so of Scoles's people, most of them also wearing masks. Holsten looked from one set of visor-framed eyes to the next until he picked out Nessel – not quite a familiar face but better than nothing at all. The rest of them, men and women both, were strangers.

'Shuttle bay, *now*,' was Scoles's order, and then they set off, shoving Lain and Holsten ahead of them.

Holsten had no idea about much of the *Gilgamesh's* layout, but Scoles and his party seemed to be taking a decidedly circuitous route to wherever they were going. The chief mutineer was constantly muttering, obviously in radio contact with his subordinates. Presumably there was some serious offensive by Security going on, and certainly the pace quickened, and quickened again – *First to the shuttle bay wins?*

Then one of the mutineers stumbled and fell, leaving Holsten wondering if he'd missed the sound of a shot. Nessel dropped to one knee beside him and began fiddling with his mask, and a moment later the man was stirring drunkenly, staggering to his feet with Scoles roundly cursing him.

'Since when did we have poison gas on the ship?' the classicist demanded wildly. Again, the whole episode was assuming a dreamlike quality.

Lain's voice sounded right in his ear. 'Idiot, just fucking with the air mix would do it. I'd guess these monkeys have been fighting for control of the air-conditioning since they made their stupid stand, and now they've lost. This is a space-ship, remember. The atmosphere is whatever the machines say it should be.'

'All right, all right,' Holsten managed to reply, as someone shoved him hard in the back to get him to pick up speed.

'What?' the man beside him demanded, shooting him a suspicious look. Holsten realized that Lain's voice had not broadcast to the rest of them, only to him.

'I despair of you, old man,' came her murmur. 'These masks do have tongue controls, you realize? Of course you don't, and neither do these clowns. You have four tabs by your tongue. Second one selects comms menu. Then third for private channel. Select 9. It'll show in your display.'

It took him the best part of ten minutes to get through that, slobbering over the controls and terrified that one false drool would turn his air supply off. In the end it was only when their escorts halted abruptly for a furious discussion that he was able to work it out.

'How's this?'

'Clear enough,' came Lain's dry response. 'So how fucked are we, eh?'

'Was that seriously what you wanted to say?'

'Look, Mason, they hate my guts. What I really want to say is that you should talk them into letting you go. Tell them you're a crap hostage, or that they don't need you, or something.'

He blinked, seeking out her eyes but finding only the lamps reflecting in the plastic of her visor. 'And you?'

'I am more fucked than you by an entire order of magnitude, old man.'

'They are all f . . . they're all in big trouble,' he came back. 'Nobody's getting on to that planet.'

'Who knows? I wasn't exactly planning anything like this, but I have been thinking around the problem.'

'Get moving!' Scoles suddenly snapped, then people were shooting at them from ahead.

Holsten had a glimpse of a pair of figures in some sort of armoured suit, dark plastic plates over shiny grey fabric, presumably the full security-detail uniform. They were lumbering forwards, holding rifles awkwardly, and Scoles hauled Lain in front of him.

'Back, or she goes first!' he yelled.

'This is your one and only chance to give yourselves up!' came what might have been Karst's voice, from one of the suits. 'Guns down, you turds!'

One of the mutineers shot at him, and then they were all at it. Holsten saw both figures stagger; one was knocked flat over on to its back. It was only the frustrated momentum of the bullets, though. There was no sign of penetration, and the fallen security man was already sitting up again, levelling his gun.

'Faceplates! Aim for the face!' Scoles shouted.

'Still bulletproof, you moron,' Lain's taut voice in Holsten's ear.

'Wait!' the classicist yelled. 'Hold it, hold it!' and Lain convulsed in Scoles's grip with a howl that was abominably loud in Holsten's ear.

'You twat! I'm half-deaf!' she snapped. The man next to Holsten grabbed at his arm to try and rope him in as a second human shield and the classicist pulled away instinctively. A moment later the mutineer was on the ground, three dark patches spread across his shipsuit. It was too quick for Holsten to feel any reaction.

Another mutineer, a woman, had managed to close with Security, and Holsten saw a knife flash out. He was in the middle of thinking what a feeble threat that must be when she got the blade into one of them, and ripped a gash down the man's arm, the grey material parting stubbornly, armour plate peeling back. The injured security man flailed, and his companion – Karst? – turned and shot at her, bullets scattering and ricocheting from his companion's armour.

'Go!' Scoles was already moving on, hauling Lain behind him. 'Get a door closed between us and them. Get us time. Have that shuttle warmed up and ready!' The last words presumably directed to some other follower already sitting in the bay.

Shots followed them, and at least one other mutineer simply dropped, sprawling, as they fled. But then Nessel had a heavy door sliding down behind them, hunching over the controls presumably to try and jam them in some jury-rigged way to delay Security that little bit more. Scoles left her to it, but she caught up with the main pack soon after, showing a surprising turn of speed.

No waiting for stragglers once we're at the shuttle, then. Holsten was seeing his opportunity to make a stand diminishing. He lunged at the mask tongue controls until he was on general broadcast again.

'Listen to me Scoles, all of you,' he started. One of the mutineers cuffed him across the head but he bore it. 'I know you think there's some chance if you can get off the ship and head for the terraform project. Probably you've seen the pictures of that spider thing that lives there, and yes, you've got guns. You'll have all the tech from the shuttle. Spiders no problem, sure. Seriously, though, that satellite will *not* listen to anything we've got to say. You think we'd be anywhere *but* that damn planet otherwise? It was within a hair of carving up the whole *Gilgamesh*, and it blew up a whole load of spy-drones that tried to get near. Now, your shuttle's way smaller than the *Gil*, and it's way clumsier than drones. And, I swear, I do not have anything I can say that will work on the insane whatever that's in that satellite.'

'Then think of something,' was Scoles's cold response.

'I am *telling* you—' Holsten began, and then they spilled out into the shuttle bay. It was smaller than he had thought, just a single craft there, and he realized he knew nothing about this side of the ship's operations. Was this some special yacht for the commander to gad about in, or were all the shuttles in their own separate bays, or what? It was an utter blank to him – not his area, nothing he had needed to know.

'Please listen,' he tried.

'They made the mistake of showing us what our new home was going to be like,' came Nessel's voice. 'I swear the commander never imagined that anyone might defy his almighty wisdom. You can say what you like, Doctor Mason, but *you* didn't see it. You didn't see what it was like.'

'We'll take our chances with the spiders and the AI,' Scoles agreed.

'It's not an AI . . .' But he was already being bundled into the shuttle, with Lain right alongside him. He could hear more shooting, but certainly not close enough to change things now.

'Get the bay doors open. Override the safeties,' Scoles ordered. 'If they're after us, let's see if those suits of theirs can handle vacuum,' and, even as Lain was muttering, 'They can' for Holsten's ears only, he felt the shuttle's reactor begin to shift them forwards. He was about to leave the *Gilgamesh* for the first time in two thousand years.

The shuttle cabin was cramped. Half the mutineers had decamped to the hold, where Holsten hoped there were belts and straps to secure them. Acceleration was currently telling every loose object – or person – that *down* was the rear of the ship, and when they reached whatever speed fuel economy dictated was their safe maximum, there would be no effective 'down' at all.

Holsten and Lain occupied the rearmost two seats of the cabin, where people could keep an eye on them. Scoles himself had the seat next to the pilot, with Nessel and two others sitting behind him at the consoles.

Holsten's gut lurched under the pressure of the acceleration, as they made their getaway. For a moment he thought he was about to lose his stomach contents through the hatch into the hold behind him, but the feeling passed. His bloodstream was still swimming with suspension-chamber drugs that fought hard to stabilize his sudden feelings of instability.

The first thing Lain said to him once the shuttle got clear was, 'Keep the mask. We need a secure channel.' Her tightly controlled tones came through the receiver beside Holsten's ear. Sure enough, the mutineers were removing their breathing masks now they were in an environment they had full control of. One of them reached back for Lain's, and she bucked her head upwards sharply as he grabbed it, so that she ended up wearing the thing as a sort of high-tech bandanna covering her mouth. Holsten tried the same trick but just ended up in an awkward pulling match with the man, without achieving anything.

'Sod you, then,' he was told. 'Suffocate if you like.' Then the mutineer turned away. Lain leant over quickly, teeth digging into the rubber seal so she could yank his mask down like hers. For a moment she was cheek to cheek with him, eye to eye, and he had a weird feeling of horribly inappropriate intimacy, as though she might kiss him.

Then she regained her balance, and the two of them sat there with masks in identical, awkward positions, Holsten thinking, *How much more like conspirators could we look?*

The mutineers had other priorities, though. One of the men sat at a console apparently fighting the *Gilgamesh*'s attempts to override control of the shuttle, whilst Nessel and another woman were giving reports on the systems powering up. After listening awhile, Holsten realized that they were waiting to see if the ark ship had any weapons it could bring to bear. *They don't even know.*

Are they wondering if Lain and I will save them by being here? Because, if so, they weren't listening to Guyen closely enough before.

At last, Lain piped up for all to hear, although her voice echoed hollowly over Holsten's mask speaker as well: 'The *Gilgamesh* only has its anti-asteroid array, and that's forwards-facing. Unless you decide to moon the front cameras there's nothing able to come your way.'

They regarded her distrustfully, but Nessel's reports seemed to confirm the same.

'What would happen if an asteroid was going to hit us in the side?' Holsten asked.

Lain gave him a look that said eloquently, *And that's what's important right now?* 'The odds are vanishingly unlikely. It wasn't resource-effective.'

'To protect the entire human race?' Nessel demanded, more as a jab at Lain than anything else.

'The *Gil* was designed by engineers, not philosophers.' Isa Lain shrugged – or as much as she could with her hands still secured. 'Let me free. I need to work.'

'You stay right there,' Scoles told her. 'We're clear now. It's not like they can just turn the *Gil* around and come after us. We'd be halfway across the system before they could build up any speed.'

'And how far is this tin box going to get you exactly?' Lain challenged him. 'What supplies do you have? How much fuel?'

'Enough. And we always knew this was a one-way trip,' the chief mutineer said grimly.

'You won't even *get* one way,' Lain told him. Immediately Scoles had his seat belt undone and fell the short distance towards them, gripping hand over hand along the seat backs. The movement was fish-like, effortless enough that the man had plainly put in some training time back home.

'If the *Gil* isn't shooting, I'm feeling less and less certain why we need you,' he remarked.

'Because it's not the ship you need to worry about. That satellite out there is a killer. *It's* got a defence laser that will just carve this boat into tiny pieces. The *Gilgamesh*'s array is nothing to that.'

'That's why we have the esteemed Doctor Mason,' Scoles told her, hovering over her like a cloud.

'You need to let me loose on your systems. You need to give me full access and let me rip the fuck out of your comms panel.' Lain smiled brightly. 'Or we're all dead, anyway, even if it doesn't shoot. Mason, you tell them. Tell them about how Doctor Avrana Kern said hello.'

Their acceleration was levelling out, weightlessness replacing the heavy hand that had been pressing Holsten back into his seat. After a blank moment, then catching Lain's eye, the classicist nodded animatedly. 'It took over our systems completely. We had absolutely no control. It went through the *Gilgamesh*'s computers in seconds, locked us out. It could have opened all the airlocks, poisoned the air, purged all the suspension chambers . . .' His voice trailed off. At the time he had not quite appreciated just what might have happened.

'Who is "Doctor Avrana Kern"?' one of the mutineers asked.

Holsten exchanged looks with Lain. 'It . . . she is what's in the satellite. She's one of the things in the satellite, rather. There are the basic computers, and then there's something called Eliza which I . . . maybe it's an AI, a proper AI, or maybe it's just a very well-made computer. And then there's Doctor Avrana Kern, who might also be an AI.'

'Or might be what?' Nessel prompted him.

'Or might just be a stark raving mad psychotic human being left over from the Old Empire, who's taken it into her head that keeping us off the planet is the single most important objective in the universe,' he managed, looking from face to face.

'Fuck,' said someone, almost reverently. Evidently something in Holsten's testimony had sounded convincing.

'Or maybe she'll be having a good day and she'll just take over the shuttle's systems and fly you back to the *Gilgamesh*,' Lain suggested sweetly.

'Ah, on that subject,' the pilot broke in, 'it looks like our damage to the drone bays has paid off. There's no sign of a remote launch, but . . . wait, *Gil* is launching a shuttle after us.'

Scoles spun himself around, and coasted over to see for himself.

'Guyen is really pissed,' came Lain's voice *sotto voce* in Holsten's ear.

'He's crazy,' the classicist replied.

She regarded him impassively, and for a moment he thought she was going to defend the man, but then: 'Yeah . . . no, he's crazy all right. Perhaps it's the sort of crazy you need to have got us all the way out here, but it's starting to go off the bad end of the scale.'

'They're telling us to cut engines, surrender our weapons and give up the prisoners,' the pilot relayed.

'What makes them think we'd do that, now that we're winning?' Scoles stated.

The look that passed between Lain and Holsten was in complete accord that here, in spirit, was Vrie Guyen's very double.

Then Scoles was hovering above them again, staring down. 'You know that we'll kill you if you try anything?' he told Lain.

'I'm trying to keep track of all the ways this venture is likely to kill me but, yes, that's one of them.' She looked up at him without flinching. 'Seriously, I am more concerned about that satellite. You need to cut us free right now. You need me isolating the ship's systems so that thing can't just walk in and take over.'

'Why not just cut the comms altogether?' one of the mutineers asked.

'Good luck on getting Mason to sweet-talk the satellite if we can't transmit and receive,' she pointed out acidly. 'Feel free to have someone looking over my shoulder at all times. I'll even talk them through what I'm doing.'

'If we lose power or control for one moment, if I think you're trying to slow us so the other shuttle can catch up with us . . .' Scoles started.

'I know, I know.'

With a scowl, the chief mutineer produced a knife and severed Lain's bonds – and Holsten's too, as an afterthought.

'You sit there,' he told the classicist. 'Nothing for you to do yet. Once she's done her work, you'll get your chance with the satellite.' Apparently he didn't feel that making overt death threats was necessary to keep Holsten in line.

Lain – clumsy in the lack of gravity – flailed over to the comms console and belted herself down in the seat next to Nessel. 'Right, what we're after here . . .' she started, and then the language between them got sufficiently technical that Holsten failed to follow. It was obvious that the work would take some time, though, both reprogramming and physically cutting connections between comms and the rest of the shuttle's systems.

Holsten gradually fell asleep. Even as he was dropping off, he felt this was a ridiculous thing to do, considering the constant threat to life and limb, combined with the fact that he had been out of the world for a century or so not so long ago. Suspension and sleep were not quite the same, however, and as the adrenaline now ebbed from his system, it left him feeling hollowed out and bone-weary.

A hand on his shoulder woke him up. For a moment, stirred from dreams he could barely recall, he spoke a name from the old world, one a decade dead even before he embarked on the *Gilgamesh*, millennia dead now.

Then: 'Lain?' because he heard a woman's voice, but instead it was Nessel the mutineer.

'Doctor Mason,' she said, with that curious respect she seemed to hold for him, 'they're ready for you.'

He undid his seatbelt, and allowed them to pass him unceremoniously hand over hand across the ceiling, until Lain could reach out and snag him, and drag him into the comms chair.

'How far out are we?' he asked her.

'It's taken me longer than I'd thought to make sure I cut every single connection to comms. And because our friends here don't trust me, and kept getting me to stop in case I was doing something nefarious. We've shielded all the shuttle's systems from any outside transmission, though. Nothing is accepting any connection that isn't hardwired into the ship itself, except the comms – and the comms don't interact with the rest of what we've got in here. The most Doctor Avrana Kern can manage now is to take over the comms panel and shout at us.'

'And destroy us with her lasers,' Holsten pointed out.

'Yeah, well, and that. But you better get on with telling her not to, right now, because the sat's started signalling.'

Holsten felt a shudder go through him. 'Show me.'

It was a familiar message, identifying the satellite as the

Second Brin Sentry Habitat and instructing them to avoid the planet – just what they'd got when they interrupted the distress beacon the first time. *But that time we'd signalled it, and it hadn't noticed us inbound. This time we're in a much smaller ship and it's taking the initiative. Something's still awake over there.*

He remembered the electronic spectre of Avrana Kern appearing on the screens of the *Gilgamesh* comms room, her voice translated into their native tongue – a facility with language that neither he nor Lain had felt the need to comment on to the mutineers. Instead, though, he decided to keep matters formal just for now. He readied a message, *May I speak to Eliza?*, translated it into Imperial C and sent it, counting the shortening minutes until a response could be expected.

'Let's see who's home,' Lain murmured in his ear, peering over his shoulder.

The response came back to him, and it was disturbing and reassuring in equal measures – the latter because at least the situation on the satellite was as he remembered.

You are currently on a heading that will bring you to a quarantine planet and no interference with this planet will be countenanced. Any interference with Kern's World will be met with immediate retaliation. You are not to make contact with this planet in any way.	Monkeys the monkeys are back they want to take away my world is only for me and my monkeys are not as they say as they seem as much as they claim to be from Earth I know better vermin they are vermin leaving the sinking ship of Earth has sunk and no word no word none

The translation came easily. Nessel, poised at his other shoulder, made a baffled noise.

Eliza, we will not interfere with Kern's World. We are a scientific mission come to observe the progress of your experiment. Please confirm permission to land. Holsten thought it was worth a try.

Waiting for the reply was just as wearing on the nerves as he remembered. 'Any idea when we'll be in range of its lasers?' he asked Lain.

'Based on Karst's drones, I think we have four hours nineteen minutes. Make them count.'

Permission to approach the planet is denied. Any attempt to do so will be met with lethal force as per scientific devolved powers. Isolation of experimental habitat is paramount. You are respectfully requested to alter your course effective immediately.

Filthy crawling vermin coming to infect my monkeys will not talk to me it has been so long so long Eliza why will they not speak why will they not call to me my monkeys are silent so silent and all I have to talk to is you and all you are is my broken reflection

Eliza, I would like to speak to your sister Avrana, Holsten sent immediately, aware of time falling away, their limited stock of seconds dropping through the glass.

'Brace yourselves,' Lain warned. 'If we didn't get this right, we might be about to lose everything, possibly including life-support.'

The voice that spoke through the comms panel – without anyone giving it permission – was sticking to Imperial C at that moment, though to Holsten its haughty tones were unmistakable. The content was little more than a more aggressive demand that they alter their course.

Doctor Kern, Holsten sent, *we are here to observe your great experiment. We will not alter anything on the planet, but surely some manner of observation is permitted. Your experiment has been running for a very long period of time. Surely it should have come to fruition by now? Can we assist you? Perhaps if we gather data you may be able to put it to use?* In truth he had no certain idea what Kern's experiment was – though by now he had formed some theories – and he was simply bouncing off what he had gleaned from Kern's own stream-of-consciousness thoughts, transmitted along with Eliza's sober words.

You lie, came the reply, and his heart sank. *Do you think I cannot hear the traffic in this system? You are fugitives, criminals, vermin amongst vermin. Already the vessel pursuing you has asked me to disable your craft so that they may bring you to justice.*

Holsten stared at the words, his mind working furiously. For a moment there he had been negotiating with Kern in good faith as though he was actually a mutineer himself. He had almost forgotten his status as hostage.

His hands hovered, ready to send the next signal, *Why don't you do just that . . . ?*

Something cold pressed into his ear. His eyes flicked sideways to catch Nessel's hard expression.

'Don't even think it,' she told him. 'Because if this ship gets stopped, you and the engineer won't live to get rescued.'

'Shoot a gun in here and you're likely to punch a hole straight through the hull,' Lain said tightly.

'Then don't give us an excuse.' Nessel nodded at the console. 'You might be the expert, Doctor Mason, but don't think I'm not catching most of this.'

Typical that now *I find an able student,* Holsten thought despairingly. 'So what do you want me to say?' he demanded.

'You heard what I heard, then – that she knows what we are. She's receiving all the transmissions from the *Gilgamesh* and the other shuttle.'

'Tell her about the moon colony,' Scoles snapped. 'Tell her what they wanted us to do!'

'Whatever we're talking to now has been in a satellite smaller than this shuttle since the end of the Old Empire. You're looking for *sympathy*?' Lain demanded.

Doctor Kern, we are human beings, like you, Holsten sent, wondering how true that latter part could possibly be. *You could have destroyed the* Gilgamesh *and you did not. I understand how important your experiment is to you* – another lie – *but, please, we are human beings. I am a hostage on this vessel. I am a scholar like you. If you do as you say, they will kill me.* The words passed into cold, dead Imperial C like a treatise, as though Holsten Mason was already a figure long consigned to history, to be debated over by academics of a latter age.

The gaps between message and response were ever shorter as they closed with the planet.

You are currently on a heading that will bring you to a quarantine planet and no interference with this planet will be countenanced. Any interference with Kern's World will be met with immediate retaliation. You are not to make contact with this planet in any way.

They are not my responsibility so heavy a whole planet is mine they must not interfere with the experiment must proceed or what was it all for nothing if the monkeys do not speak to me and my monkeys are all that's left of the human now these vermin come these vermin

'No,' Holsten shouted, 'not back to Eliza!' startling the mutineers.

'What's going on?' Scoles demanded. 'Nessel—?'

'We've . . . dropped back a step or something?'

Holsten sat back numbly, his mind quite blank.

Suddenly Scoles was speaking in his ear. 'Is that it, then? You're out of ideas?' in tones crammed with dangerous subtext.

'Wait!' Holsten said, but for a perilous moment his mind remained completely empty. He had nothing.

Then he had something. 'Lain, do we have the drone footage?'

'Ah . . .' Lain scrabbled and clawed her way over to another console, fighting for space with the mutineer already seated there. 'Karst's recording? I . . . Yes, I have it.'

'Get it onto the comms panel.'

'Are you sure? Only . . .'

'Please, Lain.'

Circumventing the comms isolation without opening the ship up to contamination was a surprisingly complex process, but Lain and one of the mutineers set up a second isolated dropbox with the data, and then patched it into the comms system. Holsten imagined the invisible influence of Doctor Kern flooding down the new connection only to find just another dead end.

Doctor Avrana Kern, he readied his next message. *I think you should reconsider the need of your experimental world for an observer. When our ship passed your world last, a remote camera captured some images from down there. I think you need to see this.*

It was a gamble, a terrible game to play with whatever deranged fragments of Kern still inhabited the satellite, but there was a gun to his head. And besides, he could not deny a certain measure of academic curiosity. *How will you react?*

He sent the message and the file, guessing that Kern's recent exposure to the *Gilgamesh*'s systems would allow her to decode the data.

Bare minutes later there was an incomprehensible transmission from the satellite, very little more than white noise, and then:

Please hold for further instructions. Please hold for further instructions.

What have you done with my monkeys? What have you done with my monkeys?

And then nothing, a complete cessation of transmission from the satellite, leaving those in the shuttle to fiercely debate what Holsten had done, and what he might have achieved.

Great Nest has no strict hierarchy. By human standards, in fact, spider society would appear something like functional anarchy. Social standing is everything, and it is won by contribution. Those peer groups whose warriors win battles, whose scholars make discoveries, who have the most elegant dancers, eloquent storytellers or skilled crafters, these garner invisible status that brings them admirers, gifts, favours, greater swarms of sycophantic males to serve as their workforce, petitioners seeking to add their talents to the group's existing pool. Theirs is a fluid society where a capable female can manage a remarkable amount of social mobility. Or, in their own minds, their culture is a complex web of connections re-spun every morning.

One key reason this all works is that the middling unpleasant labour is undertaken by males – who otherwise have no particular right to claim sanctuary within the Nest at all, if they lack a purpose or a patroness. The hard labour – forestry, agriculture and the like – is mostly undertaken by the domesticated ant colonies that the Great Nest spiders have manipulated into working with them. After all, the ants work by nature. They have no inclination or capacity to consider the wider philosophy of life, and so such opportunity would be wasted on them. From the point of view of the ant colonies, they prosper as best they can, given the peculiarly artificial environment they find themselves enmeshed in. Their colonies have no real concept of what is pulling their strings, or how their industry has been hijacked to serve Great Nest. It all works seamlessly.

Portia's is a society now pulled taut to breaking point. The fact of the encroaching ant column demands sacrifices, and there is no chain of command to determine who must make them and for whose benefit. If the situation becomes much worse, then Great Nest will start fraying apart, fragmenting into smaller fugitive units and leaving only a memory of the high point of spider culture. Alternatively some great leader might arise and take control of all, for the common good – and later, if human examples can be valid guidelines, for the personal good. But, either way, the Great Nest that Portia knows would cease to be.

It would not be the first lost metropolis. In its ceaseless march across the continent, the ant colony has obliterated a hundred separate, distinct and unique cultures that the world will never know again, exterminating individuals and over-writing ways of life. It is no more than any conquering horde has ever done in pursuit of its manifest destiny.

Portia's military exploits have won some esteem for her peer group, but Bianca is currently their greatest asset: one of the Nest's most admired and maverick scholars. She has improved the lives of her species in a dozen separate ways, for she has a mind that can see answers to problems others did not even realize were holding them back. She is also a recluse, wanting little more than to get on with her experiments – a common trait for those driven to build on their inherited Understandings – which suits Portia's peers well, as otherwise Bianca might decide that she was owed rather more of the group's good fortune.

However, when she sends a messenger, her peers come running. Should Bianca suddenly feel unappreciated, she would have her pick of the peer groups of Great Nest to join.

Bianca is not within Great Nest proper. True science demands a certain seclusion, if only so that its more unexpected results can be safely contained. Portia's people are, by ancestry, born problem-solvers, and given to varying their approach until something succeeds. When dealing with volatile chemicals, this can have drawbacks.

Bianca's current laboratory, Portia discovers, is well within the territory of one of the local ants' nests. Approaching the mound along a trail marked out for the ants to avoid, she feels herself reluctant, pausing often, sometimes lifting her forelegs and displaying her fangs without intending to. The old association between ants and conflict is hard to shake.

The chamber she finds Bianca in would have been dug by the ants themselves, before being cordoned from their nest by the application of colony-specific scents. Such measures have been attempted in the past to ward a settlement from attack by the encroaching super-colony, but never successfully. The ants always find a way, and fire does not care about pheromones.

Silk coats the walls of the chamber, and a complex distillery of webbing hangs from the ceiling, providing the mixing vessels of Bianca's alchemy. A side-chamber houses a pen of some manner of livestock, perhaps part of the experiment, perhaps simply convenient sustenance. Bianca presides over the whole enterprise from up on the ceiling, her many eyes keeping track of everything, signalling to her underlings with palps and sudden stamping motions when her direction is required. Some light falls in from the entryway above, but Bianca is above the routines of night and day, and has cultured luminescent glands from beetle larvae to glitter amid the weave of her walls like ersatz constellations.

Portia lets herself down into the chamber, aware that part of the floor is also open, giving on to the ant colony below. Through the thinnest skein of silk, she can see the constant, random bustle of those insects going about their business. Yes, they work tirelessly, if unknowingly, for Great Nest's continued prosperity, but if Portia cut through that membrane and entered their domain, then she would meet the same fate the ants reserve for all intruders, unless she had some chemical countermeasure to preserve her.

She greets Bianca with a flurry of palps to renew their acquaintance; the exchange contains a precisely calculated summary of their relative social standings, referencing their mutual peers, their differing expertise and the esteem that Bianca is held in.

The alchemist's reply is perfunctory without being discourteous. Asking Portia to wait, she turns her main eyes on the busy laboratory below them, checking that matters in hand can be left without her close attention for a few minutes.

Portia gives the activity below a second glance, and is shocked. *Your assistants are male.*

Indeed, Bianca agrees, with a stance that suggests this topic is not a new one.

I would have thought they would prove insufficient for the complexity of such work, Portia assays.

A common misunderstanding. If well coached and born with the pertinent Understandings, then they are quite able to deal with the more routine tasks. I did once employ females, but that results in so much jostling for status and having to defend my pre-eminence; too much measuring of legs against each other – and me – to get the work done. So I settled on this solution.

But surely they must be constantly trying to court you, Portia replies perplexedly. After all, what else did males actually want out of life?

You have spent too long in the peer houses of the idle, Bianca reproaches her. *I choose my assistants for their dedication to the work. And if I do accept their reproductive material from time to time, it's only to preserve the new Understandings we come up with here. After all, if they know it, and I know it, the chances are good that any offspring should inherit that Understanding as well.*

Portia's discomfort with this line of reasoning is evident in her shifting stance, the rapid movement of her palps. *But males do not—*

That males can transmit to their offspring knowledge that they learn during their lives is an established fact, as far as I am concerned. Bianca stamped harder to impose her words over Portia's. *The belief that they can only pass on their mothers' Understandings is without foundation. Be glad for our peer group that I at least comprehend this – I try to choose mates who hatched from our own crèche, as they're more likely to already possess worthwhile Understandings to pass on, and the cumulative effect is to compound and enrich our stock overall. I believe this will become common practice, before either of us pass on. When I have time, I will start trading on the Understanding of it to those few in other peer groups who are likely to appreciate the logic.*

Assuming either of us is granted so much time, Portia tells her forcefully. *I will not be remaining in Great Nest long, sister. How can I help you?*

Yes, you were at Seven Trees. Tell me of it.

Portia is surprised that Bianca knows even that much of Portia's comings and goings. She gives a creditable report, focusing primarily on matters military: the tactics used by the defenders, the weapons of the enemy. Bianca listens carefully, committing the salient details to memory.

There are many at Great Nest who believe that we cannot survive, Bianca tells her when she is done. *No peer group wishes to attract general scorn by being the first to abandon us, but it will happen. When one has gone, once that gap has been bridged, there will be a general rush to leave. We will destroy ourselves, and lose all we have built.*

It seems likely, Portia agrees. *I was at temple earlier. Even the priestess seemed distracted.*

Bianca huddles against the ceiling for a moment, in a posture of disquiet. *It is said that the message is contaminated, that there are other Messengers. I have spoken to a priestess who said that she felt a new message within the crystal at the wrong time, and without meaning – just a jumble of random vibrations. I have no explanation for that, but it is concerning.*

Perhaps that message is meant for the ants. Portia is staring down at the scuttling insects below. The sense-image of 'a jumble of random vibrations' seems apposite.

You are not the first to suggest it, Bianca tells her. *Thankfully, my own thoughts on message and Messenger are just that: my own – and they do not prevent me from working towards the salvation of our nest. Come with me. I have researched a new weapon, and I need your assistance in deploying it.*

Portia feels a sudden hope for the first time in many days. If any mind can find a way forward, it is Bianca's.

She follows the alchemist to the animal pens, seeing within them an unruly throng of ant-sized beetles – twenty centimetres at most. They are a dark red in colouration and most remarkable for their antennae, which spread out into a disc of fine fronds like circular fans.

I have seen these before? Portia says uncertainly with hesitant movements.

Great confronter of our enemies as you are, it seems likely, Bianca confirmed. *They are a species of unusual habits. My assistants have gone into the colony below, at some risk to themselves, to find them. They live amongst the ants and yet remain unmolested. They even eat the ants' larvae. My assistants' reports indicate that the ants themselves are persuaded to feed these creatures.*

Portia waits. Any communication from her at this juncture would be futile. Bianca has this entire encounter already planned out, point by point, to a successful conclusion.

I need you to gather capable and trusted warriors, perhaps twenty-four, Bianca instructs her. *You will be courageous. You will test my new weapon, and if it fails you are likely to die. I need you to confront the colony marching against us. I need you to walk right into the heart of it.*

Infiltrating an ant colony is no longer just a case of taking some heads and stolen scent glands. The super-colony has developed its defences: a blind chemical arms race run against the spiders' ingenuity. The ants now use the chemical equivalent of shifting cyphers that change over time, and in different detachments of the sprawling colony, and Portia's kin have been unable to keep up. The chemical weapons the spiders use to disrupt and confuse their enemies are short-lived, and barely an annoyance in the face of the sheer scale of the enemy.

The increased security of the colony has had a catastrophic impact on a number of other species. Ant nests are ecosystems in their own right, and many species live in uneasy communion with them. Some, like the aphids, provide services, and the ants actively cultivate them. Others are parasitic: mites, bugs, beetles, even small spiders, all of them adapted to steal from the ants' table or to consume their hosts.

The majority of such species are gone from the super-colony now. In adapting to defend against the external enemy, the increased chemical encryption used by the ants has also unmasked and eliminated dozens of unwelcome guests within the ants' domain. A very few, however, have managed to survive by ingenuity and superior adaptation. Of these, the Paussid beetles – Bianca's current area of study – are the most successful.

The Paussids have dwelt within ant nests for millions of years, utilizing various means to lull their unwitting hosts into accepting them. Now the nanovirus has been working with them and, although they are not as intelligent as Portia, they still have a certain cunning and the ability to work together, and utilize their versatile pheromonal toolkit with considerable insight.

Each individual Paussid has a suite of chemicals to manipulate the ants around it. The individual ants – sightless and living in a world entirely built on smell and touch – can be fooled thus. The Paussid chemicals artfully create an illusory world for them, guiding their hallucinations to induce sub-orned units of the ant colony to do their bidding. It is fortunate for Portia and her people that the Paussids have not yet quite reached a level of intellect that would allow them to look beyond their current existence as a self-serving fifth column amongst the ants. It is easy to envisage an alternate history where the advancing ant colony became merely the myriad-bodied puppet of hidden beetle overlords.

The changing chemical codes of the colony provide a constant challenge to the Paussids, and individual beetles exchange chemicals continuously to update one another with the most efficient keys for unlocking and rewriting the ants' programming. However, the simple feat of living undetected amongst the ants is left to the Paussid's secret weapon: a refinement of their ancestral scent that Bianca has detected and become fascinated by.

Portia has listened carefully as Bianca sets out her plan. The scheme seems somewhere in between dangerous and suicidal. It calls for her and her cohorts to seek out the ant column and ambush it, to walk straight into it past the multitude of sentries as though they were not there. Portia is already considering the possibilities: an attack from above, dropping from the branches or from a scaffolding of webbing, plunging into that advancing torrent of insect bodies. Bianca, of course, has already thought this part through. They will find the column when it is halted for the night in a vast fortress made of the bodies of its soldiers.

I have developed something new, Bianca explains. *Armour for you. But you will only be able to don it when you are about to make your attack.*

Armour strong enough to ward off the ants? Portia is justifiably doubtful. There are too many weak points on a spider's body; there are too many joints that the ants can seize upon.

Nothing so crude. Bianca always did like keeping her secrets. *These Paussids, these beetles, they can walk through the ant colonies like the wind. So will you.*

Portia's uncertainty communicates itself through the anxious twitching of her palps. *And I will kill them, then? As many as I can? Will that be enough?*

Bianca's stance says otherwise. *I had considered it, but even you, sister, could not stop them in such a way, I fear. There are just too many. Even if my protection kept you safe for that long, you could kill ants all day and all night, and still there would be more. You would not keep their army away from Great Nest.*

Then what? Portia demands.

There is a new weapon. If it works . . . Bianca stamps out her annoyance. *There is no way of testing it but to use it. It works on these little colonies here, but the invaders are different, more complex, less vulnerable. You will simply have to hope that I am correct. You understand what I am asking of you – for our sisterhood, for our home?*

Portia considers the fall of Seven Trees: the flames, the ravenous horde of insects, the shrivelling bodies of those who were too slow or too conscientious to escape. Fear is a universal emotion, and she feels it keenly, desperately wanting to flee that image, never to have to face the ants again. Stronger than fear are the bonds of community, of kinship, of loyalty to her peer group and her people. All those generations of reinforcement, through the success of those ancestors most inspired by the virus to cooperate with their own kind, now come to the fore. There comes a time when someone must do what must be done. Portia is a warrior trained and indoctrinated from an early age so that now, in this time of need, she will be willing to give up her life for the survival of the greater entity.

When? she asks Bianca.

Sooner is better. Gather your chosen; be ready to leave Great Nest in the morning. For tonight the city is yours. You have laid eggs?

Portia answers in the affirmative. She has no clutch within her ready for a male's attentions, but she has laid several in the past. Her heritage, genetic and learned, will be preserved if Great Nest itself is. In the grander scheme of things, that means that she will have won.

That night, Portia seeks out other warriors, veteran females she knows she can rely on. Many are from her own peer group, but not all. There are others she has fought alongside – whom she has sometimes fought against, in displays of dominance – whom she respects, and who respect her. Each one she approaches cautiously, feeling her way, telegraphing her intent, paying out Bianca's plan length by length until she is sure of them. Some refuse – either they are not persuaded by the plan, or they lack the requisite degree of courage, which is, after all, near-total fearlessness; a devotion to duty almost as blind as that of the ants themselves.

Soon enough Portia has her followers, though, each one then taking to the high roads of Great Nest to make the most of this night, before the morning calls upon them to muster. Some will resort to the company of their peer groups, others seek out entertainment – the dances of males, the glittering art of weavers. Those who are ready will let themselves be wooed, then deposit a clutch of eggs in their peer house, so as to preserve as much of themselves as they can. Portia herself has learned many things since her last laying, and feels some remorse that those Understandings, those discrete packets of knowledge, will be lost when she is lost.

She goes to temple again, seeking that fugitive calm that her devotions bring, but now she remembers what Bianca has said: that the voice of the Messenger is not alone, that there are faint whisperings in the crystal that worry the priestesses. Just as she has always believed that the mathematical perfection of the message must have some greater, transcendent significance beyond the mere numbers that compose it, so this new development surely has some wider meaning too vast to be grasped by a poor spider knotting and spinning that familiar tally of equations and solutions. What, then, does it mean? Nothing good, she feels. Nothing good.

Late that night, she sits in the highest reaches of Great Nest, staring at the stars and wondering which point of light up there is whispering incomprehensible secrets to the crystals now.

3.7 WAR IN HEAVEN

Kern had severed all contact, leaving the mutineers' shuttle to glide on towards the green planet, eroding the vast intervening distances a second at a time. Holsten did his best to sleep, crouching awkwardly on a chair that was ideally designed to cushion the stresses of deceleration but very little else.

He drifted in and out of slumber, because Kern's absence had not shut down radio communications. He had no idea who fired the first linguistic shot, but he was constantly being woken by a running argument between Karst – on the pursuing shuttle – and whoever was manning the mutineers' comms at the time.

Karst was his usual dogmatic self, the voice of the *Gilgamesh* with the authority of the whole human race behind him (via its unelected representative, Vrie Guyen). He demanded unconditional surrender, threatened them with a space-borne destruction even Holsten knew the shuttles were not capable of, vicariously invoked the dormant satellite's wrath and, when all else failed, descended to personal abuse. Holsten developed the idea that Guyen was holding Karst personally responsible for the mutineers' escape.

There was mention made of him and Lain, however – that was the only positive. Apparently Karst's orders did include recovery of the hostages at some level, though possibly not top priority. He demanded to speak to them, to be sure they were still alive. Lain shared a few acid words with him that both satisfied him on that issue and dissuaded him from asking any more. He continued to include their return unharmed in his list of monomaniac demands, which was almost touching.

The mutineers, for their part, bombarded Karst with their own demands and dogma, going into considerable detail about the difficulties the moon colony would face, and asserting the lack of need for it. Karst countered with the same reasons Lain had already given, albeit less coherently, sounding very much like a man parroting someone else's words.

'Why did they even give chase?' Holsten asked Lain wearily, after this slanging match over the comms had finally defeated any possible chance of further sleep. 'Why not just let us go, if they know how doomed this whole venture is? It's not just for us two, surely?'

'It's not for *you*, anyway,' she riposted. Then she relented, 'I . . . Guyen takes things personally.' She said it with an odd twist, so that he wondered just what her experience of this might be. 'But it's more than that. I accessed the Key Crew Aptitudes, once, in the *Gilgamesh*'s records.'

'Command access only,' Holsten noted.

'I'd be a pisspoor chief engineer if that could stop me. I wrote most of the access scaffolding. You ever wonder what our lord and master scored so high on, that he got this job?'

'Well *now* I'm wondering.'

'Long-term planning, if you can believe it. The ability to take a goal and work towards it through however many intervening steps. He's one of those people who's always four moves ahead. So if he's doing this now, it may look just like pique but he's got a reason.'

Holsten considered that for some while, whilst the mutineers continued ranting at Karst. 'Competition,' he said. 'If by chance we get past the satellite and on to the planet . . . and survive the monster spiders.'

'Yeah, maybe,' Lain agreed. 'We sod off to Terraform B, or whatever the place is, then come back a few centuries later to find Scoles is well established on the planet, maybe he even cuts a deal with Kern. Guyen . . .'

'Guyen wants the planet,' Holsten finished. 'Guyen is looking to beat the satellite and take over the planet. But he doesn't want to have to fight anyone else for it, as well.'

'And more – if Scoles does set up there and sends a message saying, *Come on down, the spiders are lovely*, then what if a load of people want to join him?'

'So, basically, Guyen can't ignore us.' And a thought came to Holsten on the tail end of that: 'So basically the best result for him, other than surrender, would be Kern blowing us to bits.'

Lain's eyebrows went up and her eyes flicked over to the wrangle in progress at the comms.

'Can we hear if Karst is transmitting to the satellite?' Holsten asked her.

'Don't know. I can have a go at finding out, if these clowns'll let me try.'

'I think you should.'

'Yeah, I think you're right.' Lain unclipped her webbing and pushed herself carefully from the seat, attracting the immediate attention of most of the mutineers. 'Listen, can I have the comms for a minute? Only—'

'He's launched a drone!' the pilot shouted.

'Show me.' Scoles lunged forwards, got a hand on Lain's shoulder and simply shoved her, breaking her grip on Holsten's seat back and sending her tumbling towards the back of the cabin. 'And she doesn't get *near* anything until we know what's going on.'

There was a clatter and an oath as Lain hit something and scrabbled for purchase to prevent a rebound.

'Since when do these shuttles carry drones?' Nessel was asking.

'Some of them are equipped for payload, not cargo,' came Lain's voice from behind them.

'What can the drones do?' someone demanded.

'Might be armed,' the pilot explained tensely. 'Or they could just ram us with it. A drone can accelerate faster than us, and we're starting deceleration anyway. They must have launched it now because they're close enough.'

'Why are we letting them catch us?' another mutineer yelled at him.

'Because we need to slow down if you don't want to make a big hole in the planet when we try to land, you prick!' the pilot yelled back. 'Now get strapped in!'

Amateurs, Holsten thought with creeping horror. *I am on a spacecraft intending to make a landing on an unknown planet, and not one of them knows what they're doing.*

Abruptly *down* was shifting towards the front of the shuttle as the pilot fought to cut their speed. Holsten scrabbled with his seat, sliding forwards until he got a grip.

'Drone's closing fast,' Nessel reported. Holsten remembered how swiftly the little unmanned craft had closed the distance between the *Gilgamesh* and the planet, the time before.

'Listen,' came Lain's forlorn voice as she worked her way forward again, hand over hand, 'was there any traffic between Karst and the satellite?'

'What?' Scoles demanded, and then an ear-wrenching screech erupted from the comms that had everyone clutching at their ears, Nessel slapping at the controls.

Holsten saw Scoles's lips shape the words, *Shut it down!* It was plain from Nessel's frustration that she couldn't.

Then the sound was gone, but it had paved the way for a familiar voice.

It came over the speakers with the booming volume of a wrathful god, uttering the elegant, ancient syllables of Imperial C as though it was pronouncing the doom of every hearer. Which it was.

Holsten translated the words as: *This is Doctor Avrana Kern. You have been warned not to return to my planet. I do not care about your spiders. I do not care about your images. This planet is my experiment and I will not have it tainted. If my people and their civilization are gone, then it is Kern's World that is my legacy, not you who merely ape our glories. You claim to be human. Go be human elsewhere.*

'She's going to destroy us!' he shouted. For a long moment the mutineers just stared at one another.

Lain hung on to the seat backs, pale and drawn, awaiting developments. 'So this is it, then?' she groaned.

'That's not what she was saying,' Nessel objected, although precious few people were listening to her.

Welcome to the classicist's lot, Holsten thought drily. He closed his eyes.

'The shuttle's changing course,' the pilot announced.

'Bring it back on. Get us down to the planet, no matter what—' Scoles started.

The pilot interrupted him. 'The other shuttle. The Security shuttle. We're still good, but they're . . .' He squinted at his instruments. 'Drifting? And the drone's off now . . . it's not following our course adjustments. It's going to overshoot us.'

'Unless that's what they want. Maybe it's a bomb,' Scoles suggested.

'Going to have to be an almighty big bomb to get us at the distances we're talking about,' the pilot said.

'It's Kern,' Lain declared. Seeing their baffled faces she explained, 'That warning wasn't just for us; it was for everyone. Kern's got them – she's seized their systems. But she can't seize ours.'

'Good work there,' Holsten muttered into the mask radio around his neck.

'Shut up,' she returned by the same channel.

Then Kern's voice was on the radio again: a few sputtering false starts and then words emerging in plain language, for everyone to understand.

'Do you think that you have escaped me just because you have locked me out of your computers? You have prevented me turning your vessel round and sending it back to your ship. You have prevented me dealing with you in a controlled and merciful manner. I give you this one chance now to open access to your systems, or I will have no option but to destroy you.'

'If she was going to destroy us, she'd have done it already,' one of the mutineers decided – on the basis of what evidence, Holsten did not know.

'Let me get at the comms,' Lain said. 'I've got an idea.' Once again she kicked off for the comms panel and this time Scoles hauled her to him, a gun almost up her nose. Her deceleration-weight yanked at him, and the pair of them nearly ended up crashing into the pilot's back.

'Doctor Mason, your opinion on Kern?' Scoles demanded, glaring at Lain.

'Human,' was the first word to come to Holsten's mind. At Scoles's exasperated glower, he explained, 'I believe she's human. Or she *was* human, once. Perhaps some melding of human and machine. She went through the *Gilgamesh*'s database, therefore she knows who we are, that we're the last of Earth, and I think that means *something* to her. Also, a laser like she's got must be an almighty energy sink compared to just shutting us down or telling our reactor to go critical. She won't use her actual weapons unless she absolutely has to. Even Old Empire tech has limits, energy-wise. So she'll shoot us as a last resort, but possibly she'll try to get rid of us without killing us, if she can. Which she can't at the moment because we've sealed her off in the comms.'

Scoles let Lain go with an angry hiss, and she instantly started explaining something to Nessel and one of the mutineers, something about restoring some of the links to the shipboard computer. Holsten only hoped she knew what she was doing.

'Will she try to kill us?' Scoles asked him flatly.

What can I say? Depends what mood she's in? Depends which Kern we're talking to at any given moment? Holsten unclipped his strapping and slowly crawled towards them, with the idea that perhaps he could talk Kern round. 'I think she's from a culture that wiped itself out and poisoned the Earth. I don't know what she might do. I think that she's even fighting with herself.'

'This is your final warning,' Kern's voice came to them.

'I can see satellite systems warming up,' the pilot warned. 'I reckon it's locked on.'

'Any way of getting round the planet, putting the other shuttle in the way?' from Scoles.

'Not a chance. We're wide open. I'm on our landing approach now, though. It's got a window of about twenty minutes before we'll be in the atmosphere, which might cut down on its lasers.'

'Ready!' Lain chimed in.

'Ready what?' Scoles demanded.

'We've isolated the shipboard database and linked it to the comms,' Nessel explained.

'You've given this Kern access to our database?' Scoles translated. 'You think that'll sway her?'

'No,' Lain stated. 'But I needed access to a transmission. Holsten, get over here.' There was a horribly undignified piece of ballet, with Holsten being manhandled over until he was clipped into a seat at the comms panel, leaning sideways towards the shuttle's nose as the force of their cut speed tugged at him.

'She's going to burn us up,' Lain was telling them, as she got Holsten settled. The prospect seemed almost to excite her. 'Holsten, you can sweet-talk her? Or something?'

'I – I had an idea . . .'

'You do yours and I'll do mine,' Lain told him. 'But do it *now*.'

Holsten checked the panel, opened a channel to the satellite – *assume it hasn't been eavesdropping on everything, anyway* – and began, 'Doctor Kern, Doctor Avrana Kern.'

'I am not open to negotiation,' came that hard voice.

'I want to speak to Eliza.'

There was a brief, clipped moment of Kern speaking – and then Holsten's heart leapt as it was overwritten by a transmission in Imperial C. Eliza was back at the helm.

You are currently within the prohibited zone about a quarantined planet. Any attempt to interact with Kern's World will be met with immediate retaliation.	No Eliza no give me back my voice it's my voice give me back my mind it's mine it's mine enough warnings destroy them let me destroy them

As swiftly as he could, Holsten had his reply ready and translated. *Eliza, we confirm we have no intention of interacting with Kern's World*, because he was fairly sure Eliza was a computer and who knew what the limits of its cognition and programming were?

That is not consistent with your current course and speed. This is your final warning.	They're lying to me to you let me speak let me out help me someone please help me

Eliza, please may we speak to Doctor Avrana Kern?, Holsten sent.

The expected voice thundered through the enclosed cabin, 'How dare you—?'

'And away,' Lain said, and Kern's voice cut off.

'What was that?' Scoles demanded.

'Distress signal,' Lain explained. 'A repeat transmission of her own distress signal,' even as Holsten was sending, *Doctor Kern, please may I speak to Eliza?*

The response that came back was garbled almost into white noise. He heard a dozen fragments of sentence from Kern and from the Eliza system, constantly getting chopped out as the satellite's systems tried to process the high-priority distress call.

'Almost to atmosphere,' the pilot reported.

'We've done it,' someone said.

'Never say—' Lain started, and then the comms unit went so silent that Holsten looked at its readouts to make sure it was still functioning. The satellite had ceased transmitting.

'Did we shut it down?' Nessel asked.

'Define "we",' Lain snapped.

'But, look, that means that everyone can come to this planet, everyone from the *Gil*—' the woman started, but then the comms flared with a new signal and Kern's furious voice whipped out at them.

'No, you did not shut *me* down.'

Lain's hands were immediately at her waist, fastening the crash webbing, and then scrabbling for Holsten.

'Brace!' someone shouted ludicrously.

Holsten looked back at his original seat, towards the rear of the shuttle. He actually had a brief glimpse back into the cargo bay, seeing the desperate flailing about as the mutineers there tried to fully secure themselves. Then there was a searing flash that left its image on his retinas, and the shuttle's smooth progress suddenly became a tumble . . . and from outside there was a juddering roar and he thought, *Atmosphere. We've hit atmosphere.* The pilot was swearing frantically, fighting for control, and Lain's arms were tight about Holsten, holding him to her, because she had not been able to get all his webbing secured. For his part he gripped the seat as tight as he could even as the world tried to shake him loose.

The doors to the cargo hold had closed automatically. At that point he did not realize it was because the rear half of the shuttle had been shorn away.

The front half – the cabin – fell towards the great green expanse of the planet below.

3.8 ASYMMETRICAL WARFARE

Portia's people have no fingers, but her ancestors were building structures and using tools millions of years before they attained anything like intelligence. They have two palps and eight legs, each of which can grip and manipulate as required. Their whole body is a ten-digit hand with two thumbs and instant access to adhesive and thread. Their one real limitation is that they must fashion their work principally by way of touch and scent, periodically bringing it before their eyes to review. They work best suspended in space, thinking and creating in three dimensions.

Two strands of creation have given rise to Portia's current mission. One is armour-smithing, or the equivalent in a species with access to neither fire nor metal.

The ant column has stopped for the night up ahead, forming a vast and uniquely impregnable fortress. Portia and her cohorts are twitching and stamping nervously, aware that there will be plenty of enemy scouts blindly searching the forest, attacking all they come across and releasing the keen scent of alarm at the same time. A chance encounter now could bring the whole colony down on them.

Bianca is fussing over her males as the butchers set to work killing and dismembering her pets. The males will perform their part of the plan, apparently, but they lack the nerve to form the vanguard. It is Portia and her fellows who will undertake the impossible task of infiltrating the colony while it sleeps, taking their secret weapon with them.

The collection of Paussid beetles that Bianca had accumulated have been driven here from Great Nest. They are not herding animals by nature and the going has been exasperating, meaning that they have arrived alarmingly late in the night, getting close to the dawn that will see the enemy on the move again.

Several of the inventive beetles have escaped, and the rest appear to be communicating via scent and touches of the antennae, so that Portia wonders if some mass action is being planned on their part. She has no idea if the Paussids can think, but she reckons their actions are more complex than those of simple animals. Her world is one in which there is no great divide between the thinkers and the thoughtless, only a long continuum.

The beetles have left any intended breakout too late, however. Now they are penned in and Bianca's people kill them quickly and efficiently and peel off their shells. Great Nest artisans promptly begin fashioning armour from the pieces, cladding Portia and her fellows as completely as possible in heavy, cumbrous suits of chitin mail. They use their fangs and the strength of their legs to twist and crack the individual sections of shell to make a better fit, securing each plate to its wearer with webbing.

Bianca explains the theory, as they work. The Paussid beetles seem to use numerous and very complex scents to get the ants to feed them, and otherwise provide for them. These scents change constantly as the ants' own chemical defences change. The beetles' chemical language has proved too complex for Bianca to decode.

There is a master-scent by which the beetles live, however, and that does not change. It is not a direct attack on the ants themselves, but simply functions to inform the colony *Nothing here*. The beetle does not register with the ants at all, unless it is actively trying to interact with them. It is not an enemy, not an ant, not even an inanimate piece of earth, but *nothing*. For the blind, scent-driven ants, the beetles utilize a kind of active invisibility, so that even when touched, even when the ant's antennae play over the beetle's ridged carapace, the colony registers a blank, a void to be skipped over.

The null scent persists even through death, but not for very long, hence this massacre of the beetles at the eleventh hour. Bianca cautions Portia and her fellows that they must be swift. She does not know how long the protection will last.

So we can just kill them, and they will not know, Portia concludes.

Absolutely not. That is not your mission, Bianca replies angrily. *How many of them do you think you could possibly destroy? And if you begin attacking them, their own alarm system may eventually override the scent of your armour.*

Then we will kill their egg-laying caste, Portia tells her. The ant colony on the move is still a growing organism, constantly churning out eggs to replace its losses.

You will not. You will distribute yourselves about the colony as planned, and wait for your packages to degrade.

The packages are the other part of the plan, and represent the other end of spider craftsmanship. Bianca makes them herself by brewing up a chemical from prepared compounds and the remains of the Paussids, and sealing it in globules of webbing. Again, it will not keep for long.

The alchemy of Portia's people has a long history, evolving at first from the scent markers their distant ancestors used, and then becoming swiftly more elaborate and sophisticated after contact with species like ants, who can be deftly manipulated and enticed by artificial scents. To a spider like Bianca, personally experienced and blessed with past generations of Understanding to assist her, mixing chemicals is a visual experience, her senses blending into one another, allowing her to use the formidable ocular parts of her brain to envisage the different substances that she works with and their compounds in a representational mental language of molecular chemistry. She spurs her alchemical reactions with the use of exothermic catalysts that generate heat without a dangerous open flame.

Just as the chemicals themselves have a limited lifespan, so do their webbing containers. Precisely crafted, they will release their payload within moments of each other, which is essential timing as Portia and her fellows will have no way to coordinate with each other.

Bianca hands them their weapons, and they know what they must do. The mobile fortress of the enemy is ahead of them, through the dark forest. They must accomplish their task in the short time gifted to them or they will die, and then their civilization will follow them. Still, every part of them that cares for self-preservation balks at it. Nobody enters an ant colony's travelling fortress and survives. The advance of Portia and her fellows is slow and reluctant, despite the chivvying of Bianca from behind. A fear of extinction was their birthright long before intelligence, and certainly long before any kind of social altruism. Despite the stakes, it is a hard fear to suppress.

Then the night is made day, and the spiders look up at a sky from which the stars have been briefly banished.

Something is coming.

They can feel the air shake in rage, the ground vibrate in sympathy, and they crouch inside their heavy armour, terrified and bewildered. A ball of fire comes streaking across the sky, with a trail of thunder rushing after it. None of them has any idea what it can possibly be.

When it strikes the ground, well within the ant colony's scouting range, it has lost a great deal of its speed, but the impact still resonates through their sensitive feet as though the whole world has just cried out some vast, secret word.

For a moment they remain still, petrified in animal terror. But then one of them asks what it was, and Portia reaches within herself and finds that part of her that was ever open to the incomprehensible: the fearful and the wonderful understanding that there is more in the world than her eyes can see, more than her feet can feel.

The Messenger has come down to us, she tells them. In that moment – out of her fear and her hope – she has quite convinced herself, because what has just happened is from so far beyond her experience that only that quintessential mystery can account for it.

Some are awestruck, others sceptical. *What does that mean?* one of them demands.

It means you must be about your work! Bianca hammers out from behind them. *You have little time! Go, go! And if the Messenger is here with you, then that means she favours you, but only if you succeed! If it is the Messenger, show her the strength and ingenuity of the Great Nest!*

Portia flags her palps in fierce agreement, and then they all do likewise. Staring at the trail of smoke still blotting out the night stars, Portia knows it is a sign from the sky, the Messenger's sky. All her hours spent in reverent contemplation of the mathematical mysteries of Temple, on the brink of revelation, seem to her to have led to this.

Onward! Portia signals, and she and her cohorts head off towards the enemy, knowing that Bianca and her team will be following behind. The beetle-shell armour is heavy, obscures their vision, is awkward to run in and makes jumping impossible. They are like pioneering divers about to descend into a hostile environment from which only their suits can protect them.

They hurry along the forest floor as best they can, the armour catching on their joints, hobbling and crippling them. They are determined, though, and when they come close to ant scouts scouring the area, they pass by in their black armour as though they were nothing but the wind.

The scouts themselves are agitated, already on the move, heading for that gathering smoke and fire where the Messenger has visited, no doubt ready, in their blind and atheistic way, to cut a firebreak to preserve their colony – and, unwittingly, their colony's enemies.

Then the fortress of the colony is right in front of Portia and her fellows. The fortress *is* the colony. The ants have made a vast structure around a tree trunk, covering tens of square metres horizontally and vertically, constructed only from ants. Deep within the heart of it will be hatcheries and nursery chambers, food stores, racks of pupae where the next generation of soldiers is being cast, and all of these rooms and the tunnels and ducts that connect them are built from ants, hooked on to one another with their legs and mouthparts, the entire edifice a voracious monster that will devour any intruder who dares enter. The ants are not wholly dormant, either. There is a constant current of workers coursing through the tunnels, removing waste and the bodies of the dead, and the corridors themselves shift and realign to regulate the fortress's internal temperature and airflow. It is a castle of sliding walls and sudden oubliettes.

Portia and her fellows have no choice. They are the chosen warriors of Great Nest, tough veteran females who have faced the ants on dozens of battlefields. Their victories have been few and small, though. Too often, all they have achieved is to either lose less or lose more slowly. By now they all know that mere skill at arms, speed and strength cannot defeat the numbers and singular drive of the super-colony of which this fortress is only a single limb. And for all they do not understand it, Bianca's plan is the only plan they have.

They split up as they near the fortress, each seeking a different entryway into the mass. Portia elects to climb, lugging her bulky second skin up a ladder of living ant bodies, feeling their limbs and antennae twitch as she crosses them, investigating her plated underside. So far so good: she is not immediately denounced as an intruder. She is more than able to imagine what would happen if the colony knew her for what she actually was. The very wall would become a blade-lined maw to dissect and consume her. She would have no chance at all.

Some distance away, one of her fellows meets exactly this

fate. Some gap in her armour has let out the scent of spider, and at once a pair of mandibles clenches on one of her leg joints, severing that limb at the knee. The brief rupture of fluid excites the other nearby ants, and in moments there is a full scale seething of angry, defensive insects. Whilst those parts of the spider that are still armoured are ignored, the ants follow the blood, tunnelling into the kicking intruder's innards via the wound, cutting her apart from the inside whilst letting the obscuring armour fall off piece by piece, unseen and unseeable.

Portia presses on grimly, finding one of the openings through which the fortress breathes and forcing her bulk into it, clawing at a mat of sluggish bodies for purchase. Her palps hold the slowly disintegrating package close to her to avoid snagging it on the angular shapes that make up every solid surface around her. She burrows on into the mass of the colony, following their airways and walkways, jostling the scuttling workers but attracting no attention. The armour is serving its purpose.

And yet she is aware that all is not well; she is invisible, but she causes ripples. When she blocks an airway, the colony notices. When she must pry ant bodies apart to force her way through, she adds to a slow, general sense in the ants' collective understanding that something is not quite as it should be. As she presses on into the lightless reaches of the living fortress, she is aware of incrementally greater movement and mobility around her, a disturbance that can only be a symptom of her own infiltration. The tunnels behind her are closing; the colony investigating, by its massed sense of touch, what it cannot smell.

Ahead of her she feels a quick movement that is not an

ant. For a moment she is blindly face to face with a Paussid beetle that investigates her stolen carapace and then retreats in horrified fright. Instinctively she pursues, allowing the beetle to show her the inner ways of the nest, while pushing herself to the limit. By now she is overheating, running out of strength in her muscles, her heart barely able to keep oxygenated fluids moving about the hollow inside of her body. She finds herself losing focus, moment to moment, only ancient instinct keeping her moving.

She can feel the whole colony unfolding around her, waking up.

Then it happens. A questing antenna finds a gap where her own cuticle is exposed, and at once there is a dead weight at the end of one of her legs as the ant latches on mindlessly, sounding an alarm that has the tunnel about her breaking apart into individual ants, each searching for the intruder they know must be present.

Portia wonders if she has progressed far enough. After all, her own survival is not necessary for Bianca's plan to work, even though she would personally prefer it.

She tries to bundle herself up, tucking her legs in, but the ants are all over her, and she quickly finds it hard to breathe, too hot to think. They are smothering her with their relentless enquiries.

The package she has been carefully guarding seizes this moment to come apart, its webbing fraying by carefully coordinated measures, its pressurized chemical cargo unleashing itself in an explosion of stinking, acrid gas.

Portia loses consciousness, nearly suffocated in that initial detonation. On slowly returning to herself after an unknown period of time, she finds herself on her back, legs curled in, still in most of her beetle armour and surrounded by ants. The entire fortress has collapsed and dissolved into a great drift of insect bodies, from which a handful of individual spiders are even now digging themselves free. The ants do not resist them. They are not dead: they wave their antennae hopefully and some of them make uncertain moves here and there, but something has been struck from the colony as a whole: its purpose.

She tries to back away from the quiescent colony, but they are crowding her on all sides, a vast field of fallen insect architecture. It seems to her that at any moment they must surely remember their place in the world.

Less than half her infiltration force remain alive, and they stumble and crawl over to her, some of them injured, all of them exhausted by the weight of armour they have been forced to wear. They are in no state to fight.

Then one of her fellows touches her to attract her attention. Their footing of dazed ants is too inconstant to hold a conversation upon, so she signals broadly with her palps: *She comes. They come.*

It is true: Bianca and her male assistants have arrived, and they are not alone. Trotting tamely by their side are more ants, smaller than most of the invader castes and presumably reared from the domesticated colonies that Great Nest interacts with.

Portia stumbles and drags herself over to the edge of the tumbled fortress, hauling herself from the slough of feebly-moving bodies to collapse in front of Bianca.

What is going on? she asks. *What have we done?*

I have simply saturated the area with a modified form of the Paussid beetle chemical that has protected you thus far, Bianca explains with precise motions of her feet, whilst her palps continue signalling instructions to her staff. *You and your sisters had sufficiently infiltrated the colony, and the radius of the gas was sufficiently large, that we have caught the entire column – as I had hoped. We have blanketed them in a scent of absence.*

The males are now priming the tame ants for some manner of action, by exposing them to carefully calibrated scents. Portia wonders if these little workers are to be the executioners of that great mass of their hostile brethren.

I still do not understand, she confesses.

Imagine that most of the ways the ants know about the world, all the ways that they act and react, and most importantly the way that their actions spur other ants on to action, are a web – a very complex web, Bianca explains absently. *We have unravelled and consumed that web entirely. We have left them without structure or instruction.*

Portia regards the vast host of aimless ants on every side. *They are defeated then? Or will they re-weave their web?*

Almost certainly, but I do not intend to give them the chance.

The tame herd ants are going amongst the larger invaders now, touching antennae urgently, communicating in the way of their kind. Portia watches their progress at first with perplexity, then with awe, then with something closer to fear at what Bianca has unleashed. Each ant that the tame workers speak to is immediately filled with purpose. Moments later it is about its frantic way, just like ants everywhere, but its task is simple: it is talking with other ants, reviving more of its stunned brethren, converting them to its cause. The spread of Bianca's message is exponential, like a disease. A wave of new activity courses across the face of the fallen colony, and in its wake is left a tame army.

I am weaving them a new structure, Bianca explains. *They will follow the lead of our own ants now. I have given them new minds, and henceforth they are our allies. We have an army of soldiers. We have devised a weapon to defeat the ants, no matter how many of them there are, and make them our allies.*

You are truly the greatest of us, Portia tells her. Bianca modestly accepts the compliment, and then listens as the warrior goes on: *Was it you, then, that made the ground shake? That made the light and the smoke that distracted their scouts?*

That was not my doing, Bianca admits hesitantly. *I am still awaiting news of that, but perhaps, when you have shed that ungainly second skin, you may wish to investigate. I believe that something has fallen from the sky.*

3.9 FIRST CONTACT

They were down.

The cabin section of the shuttle had still been passably aerodynamic, and the pilot had deployed braking jets and air scoops and chutes to slow them, yet still it seemed that the first human footprint on this new green world would be a colossal crater. Somehow, though, the mortally wounded craft had battled through the air, swinging with the turbulence and yet never quite spinning out of control. Holsten learned later that jettisoning the cargo hold was in fact something the vessel was *supposed* to be able to do. The pilot had dumped the last twisted stump of it just before they hit atmosphere, letting the mangled chunk of wreckage streak across the new world's sky as though signifying a new messiah.

Not to say that the landing was gentle. They had come down hard enough, and at a sufficiently unwise angle, that one of the mutineers was ripped from his straps to smash bodily – fatally – into the comms panel, while Holsten himself felt something give in his chest as physics fought to free him from the restraints Lain had finally managed to get closed over him. He lost consciousness on impact. They all did.

When he woke, he realized they were down but blind, the

interior of the cabin dark save for a cascade of warning lights telling them all just how bad it was, the viewscreens dead or smashed. Someone was sobbing and Holsten envied them, because he himself was having a hard time just drawing breath.

'Mason?' sounded in his ear – Lain speaking over the mask comms, and not for the first time from the sound of it.

'H-hh . . .' he managed.

'Fuck.' He heard her fumbling about next to him, and then she was muttering, 'Come on, come on, we must have emergency power. I can see your fucking lights, you bitch. You don't flash your fucking lights at me to tell me there's no . . .' and then a dim amber illumination seeped in from a strip that encircled the cabin near the ceiling, revealing a surprisingly tidy crash scene. Aside from the one luckless deceased, the rest of them were still strapped into their seats: Scoles, Nessel, the pilot and one other man and woman of the mutineers, plus Lain and Holsten. The fact that the landing had been survivable by mere fragile humans meant that most of the cabin interior was still intact, though almost nothing appeared to be functioning. Even the comms panel appeared to have been exorcized from Avrana Kern's malign ghost.

'Thank you, whoever that was,' Scoles said, then saw it was Lain and scowled. 'Everyone speak up. Who's hurt? Tevik?'

Tevik turned out to be the pilot, Holsten somewhat belatedly discovered. He had done something to his hand, he said; perhaps broken something. Of the others, nobody had escaped bruises and broken blood vessels – every eye was red almost to the iris – but only Holsten appeared to be seriously injured, with what Lain reckoned was a cracked rib.

Scoles hobbled from his seat, fetched medical supplies and began handing out painkillers, with a double dose for Tevik and Holsten. 'These are emergency grade,' he warned. 'Means you won't feel pain much at all – including when you should. You can end up tearing your muscles really easily by overdoing it.'

'I don't feel like overdoing it,' Holsten said weakly. Lain stripped his shipsuit down to the waist and strapped a pressure bandage about his chest. Tevik got a gel cast to keep his hand together.

'What's the plan?' Lain was asking as she worked. 'Seven of us to populate a new Earth, is that it?' When she looked up, she found Scoles was training a gun on her. Holsten saw the thought occur to her to say something sarcastic, but she wisely fought it down.

'We can do it with five,' the mutineer chief said quietly. His people were watching him uncertainly. 'And if I can't count on you, we will. If we're going to survive out there, it'll be tough. We'll all need to rely on one another. Either you're part of the team now, or you're a waste of resources that could be allotted to someone more deserving.'

Lain's eyes flicked between his face and the gun. 'I don't see that I have a choice – and I don't mean that because you're about to shoot me. We're here now. What else is there?'

'Right.' Scoles nodded grudgingly. 'You're the engineer. Help us salvage everything from this thing that's going to be useful. Anything we can use for heat or light. Any supplies here in the cabin.' A tacit acknowledgement that all the gear he had *planned* to use, to build his brave new world, had been cut from him along with the bulk of his followers, up at the atmosphere's edge.

'I've got readings from outside,' Tevik reported, having jury-rigged something on his console one-handed. 'Temperature's six over ship standard, atmosphere is five per cent oxygen over ship standard. Nothing poisonous.'

'Biohazard?' Nessel asked him.

'Who knows? What I can tell you, however, is that we have precisely one sealed suit between us, because the rest were back in the hold when it blew. And without the scrubbers working, my dial here says we've got about two hours breathable air max.'

Everyone was silent for a while after that, thinking about killer viruses, flesh-eating bacteria, fungal spores.

'The airlock'll work on manual,' Lain said, at last. While everyone else had been thinking about impending doom, she had just been *thinking*. 'The medical kit can run an analysis on the microbial content of the air. If it's alien stuff we're fucked, because it won't know what to make of it, but this is a terraformed world, so any bugs out there should be Earth-style, let's hope. Someone needs to go out and wave it around.'

'You're volunteering?' Scoles asked acidly.

'Sure I am.'

'Not you. Bales, suit up.' He prodded the other female mutineer, who nodded grimly, shooting an evil look at Lain.

'You know how to work the medical analyst?' Lain asked her.

'I was a clinician's assistant, so better than you do,' the

woman Bales replied tartly, and Holsten recalled that she had been the one to case up Tevik's hand.

They got her into the suit, with difficulty – it wasn't a hard suit like the security detail had been wearing, just a ribbed white one-piece that hung slack off her frame, given that they wouldn't need to pressurize it. The helm had a selection of visors to guard against anything ranging from abrasive dust to the searing naked glare of the sun, and enough cameras and heads-up displays to let the wearer run around blindfold, if need be. Working patiently, Nessel connected the medical scanner to the suit systems, and Lain managed to use emergency power to resurrect one of the small view-screens in the cabin to receive Bales's camera feed. Nobody said anything about the vast scope of unknown dangers that could be waiting out there for this woman, and which her suit could not possibly have been designed for.

Scoles hauled open the airlock, and then shut it behind her. With no power to the doors, she would have to do the rest herself.

They were watching through her lenses as she got the external door open, whereupon the dark of the airlock was replaced by a dull, amber glare, the camera's viewpoint swinging wildly as Bales stepped down from the hatch. When their vantage point stabilized, the scene revealed looked like some vision of hell: blackened, smoking, some of it still on fire, the external emergency lamps lighting up the choked air in an unhealthy yellowish fog.

'It's a wasteland,' someone remarked, and then Bales stopped looking back down the charred furrow the shuttle cabin had raked in the soil, and turned her lens, and her eyes, on the forest instead.

Green, was Holsten's first helpless thought. In fact it was mostly shadowed darkness, but he remembered what the planet had looked like from orbit, and this was it: this was that great verdant band that had clad most of the tropical and temperate regions. He examined his memories of Earth – distant, poisoned Earth. By his generation, there had been nothing left like this, no riot of trees towering high, stretching into a vaulted, many-pillared space, out from the splintered hole that the shuttle's fist had broken into it. It was *life*, and only now did Holsten realize that he had never really seen Earth life, as it had been intended. The home he remembered was just a dying, browning stub, but *this* . . . Gently, almost imperceptibly, Holsten felt something breaking up inside him.

'Looks better than the inside of the *Gil*,' Nessel suggested tentatively.

'But is it safe?' Lain pressed.

'Safer than suffocating in here, you mean?' Tevik asked derisively. 'Anyway, the medical scanner is working. Sampling now, it says here.'

'. . . hear me . . . ?' came a faint voice from his console, and he jumped.

'Comms is fried,' Lain said tersely. 'There's a lot of crap in here that can be repurposed as a receiver, though. Don't think we can answer yet.'

'. . . know if you're getting this . . .' Bales's voice ghosted in and out of audibility. 'I can't believe we're . . .'

'How long for the scanner?' Scoles demanded.

'It's working,' Tevik said noncommittally. 'High microbial count already. Some of it recognized, some not. Nothing definitely harmful.'

'Gather the kit and be ready to get out as soon as we get the all-clear.'

'. . . not seeing any sign of biohazard . . .' from Bales.

'Give it *time*, come on,' Tevik's answering, unheard complaint. 'All sorts of crap out there. Still no yellow lights, but . . .'

Bales screamed.

They heard it: tinny and distant as though it was some tiny person locked away within the cabin's workings. The camera view was suddenly wavering wildly, then Bales appeared to be fighting with her own suit.

'Fuck me, look at that!' Lain spat. Holsten had only a blurred view of something spiny, leggy, attached to the woman's boot. The screaming continued, and now there were audible words, 'Let me in! Please!'

'Open the airlock!' Scoles shouted.

'Wait, no!' from Tevik. 'Look, we can't flush the air out. Nothing's working. The air out there is planet-air. If there's shit in it, we get it the moment we open the inner door!'

'Open the fucking thing!'

And now Nessel was hauling on the lever, dragging the door open. Holsten had a mad moment of holding his breath against the anticipated plague before recognizing the stupidity of it.

Well, we've all got it now.

'Get the guns. Get the gear. We're here now, and it's survive outside or die inside,' Scoles snapped. 'Everybody out, and quick!'

Nessel was already dragging at the outer door, tearing open their little illusion of security. Beyond was the real world.

They could hear Bales screaming as soon as the outer door opened. The woman lay on the ground just outside, smashing both hands against her suit, kicking and flailing as though beset by an invisible attacker. Everyone except Holsten and Tevik piled out to help her, trying to get her under control. They were shouting her name now, but she was oblivious, thrashing out at them, then trying to force her helmet off as though she was suffocating. One foot was a red ruin – seeming half cut away – the leg of her suit slashed open with a weird precision.

It was Nessel that released the catch and dragged Bales's helmet off, but the screaming had already turned to a ghastly liquid sound before then, and what came out first, after the seal broke, was blood.

Bales's head flopped aside, eyes wide, mouth open and running with red. Something moved at her throat. Holsten got sight of it just as everyone else suddenly recoiled: a head rising from the ruin of the woman's throat, twin blades brandished at them under a pair of crooked antennae that flicked drops of Bales left and right as they fidgeted and danced.

Then Scoles shouted and kicked madly, flinging something away from him, and Holsten saw that the ground around them was crawling with ants, dozens of ants, each as large as his hand. Monkeys might be merely a memory of Old Empire, but spiders and ants had paced humanity to the ends of the Earth, and now here they were waiting on this distant world. In the leaping, dim light cast by the fires the insects had gone unnoticed, but now he saw them everywhere he looked. More of them were scissoring their way free of Bales's suit, each emergent head accompanied by a slick of sluggish blood from the wounds the things had carved in her.

Scoles began shooting.

He was calm, ridiculously calm, as he levelled his pistol to pick out each target carefully, but he still hit only one out of two, unable to track the insects' rapid, random movements. It was a forlorn hope. Everywhere Holsten looked on the ground there were ants, not a vast carpet of them but still dozens, and they were converging on their visitors.

'Get in!' Tevik shouted. 'Inside, now, all of you!' and he went down with a yell, rolling over, tearing at his thigh where an insect was clinging, its scissor jaws embedded in him, tail curling under itself to sting and sting. Nessel and Lain pushed past Holsten, almost knocking him out of the hatch in their hurry to get back in. Scoles was right behind them, shoving Tevik forwards and then frantically fumbling another clip into his gun. The remaining mutineer was trying to drag Bales after them.

'Leave her!' Scoles shouted at him, but the man didn't seem to hear. The ants were already crawling over him, and yet he was still hauling at the ragged weight that was Bales, as blindly single-minded as the insects themselves.

Lain had ripped the ant off Tevik, but the insect's head was left behind, still holding its grip, and the man's leg was visibly swelling where the sting had lanced through his shipsuit. He was screaming, and now the man outside was screaming too; Scoles was trying to force the airlock closed, but there were ants already inside with them, rushing about the enclosed confines of the cabin, seeking out fresh victims.

Holsten crouched by Tevik, trying to work the ant's head free of his leg and aware that his ribs should be vociferously

222

complaining right then. In the end he had to pry it out with pliers, whilst Tevik clutched at the floor, emergency pain-killers unequal to the task.

Holding up the head, Holsten stared at it. The bloodied mandibles looked weirdly heavy, metallic.

Scoles now had the airlock shut and he, Nessel and Lain had been stamping on every insect they found, whilst the cabin slowly filled up with an acrid reek from their crushed bodies. Holsten looked over just as they spotted one more ant up on the consoles.

'Don't smash the electronics,' Lain warned. 'We may need . . . was that a flame?'

There was a brief flash and flare at the ant's abdomen, which it was directing aggressively towards them.

Aiming was the word that came to Holsten's mind.

Then that end of the cabin was on fire.

The crew reeled back from the sudden jet of flame that sprayed burning chemicals across the confined space. Nessel fell back over Holsten and Tevik, beating at her arm. Suddenly there was a line of fire between them and the airlock, leaping absurdly high, seeming to burn fiercer and faster than there was any reason for. And the ant was still spewing it out; now the plastics of the consoles were melting, filling the air with throat-catching fumes.

Lain lurched to the rear, coughing, and slapped at one of the panels, hunting for an emergency release. Holsten realized that she was trying to open the shutters to the hold – or where the hold had been. A moment later the back wall of the cabin irised out into open space and Lain almost fell through.

Scoles and Nessel went straight out with Tevik between

them, and Lain hauled up Holsten under the armpits and helped him follow.

'The ants . . .' he managed.

Scoles was already looking around, but somehow the great host of insects they had seen earlier appeared to have disintegrated in just the few moments they were inside. Instead of the purposeful coalescing of an insect horde there were now just little knots of fighting insects all about – turning on one another or just wandering blankly around. They seemed to have lost all interest in the shuttle. Many were heading back into the trees.

'Did we poison them or something?' Scoles asked, stamping on the closest just to be on the safe side.

'No idea. Maybe we killed them with our germs.' Lain collapsed next to Holsten. 'What next, chief? Most of our kit's on fire.'

Scoles stared about him with the baffled, angry look of a man who has lost control of the last shreds of his own destiny. 'We . . .' he started, but no plan followed the word.

'Look,' said Nessel, in a hushed voice.

There was something approaching from the treeline, something that was not an ant: bigger, and with more legs. It was watching them; there was no other way to put it. It had enormous great dark orbs, like the eyesockets of a skull, and it approached in sudden fits of movement, a rapid scuttle, then it was still and regarding them once more.

It was a spider, a monster spider like a bristling, crooked hand. Holsten stared at its ragged, hairy body, its splayed legs, the hooked fangs curled beneath it. When his gaze strayed to the two large eyes that made up so much of its front, he felt an unbearable shock of connection, as though it was trespassing on territory he had only ever shared with another human being before.

Scoles levelled his pistol, hand shaking.

'Like on the drone recording,' Lain said slowly. 'Fuck me, it's as long as my *arm*.'

'Why is it watching us?' Nessel demanded.

Scoles swore, and then the gun boomed in his hand, and Holsten saw the crouching monster spin away in a sudden flurry of convulsing limbs. The mutineer chief's expression was slowly turning to one of despair – that of a man who, it seemed, would next turn the gun on himself.

'What am I hearing?' Nessel asked.

Holsten had somehow just thought it was a rolling echo of the gunshot, but now he realized that there was something more, something like thunder. He looked up.

He didn't quite believe what he was seeing. There was a shape in the sky. It grew larger as he watched, slowly descending towards them. A moment later a bright wash of light seared down from it, illuminating the entire crash site in its pale radiance.

'Karst's shuttle,' Lain breathed. 'Never thought I'd be glad to see him.'

Holsten looked over to Scoles. The man was staring up at the descending vehicle, and who could guess at what bitter, desperate thoughts were passing through his head?

The approaching shuttle got to about ten feet off the ground, jockeyed a little, and then picked a landing site some way back down the devastated scar that the crash-landing cabin had created. Even as it came down, the side-hatch was opening, and Holsten saw a trio of figures in security detail armour, two of them with rifles already levelled.

'Drop the weapon!' boomed Karst's amplified voice. 'Surrender and drop the weapon! Prepare to be evacuated.'

Scoles's hand was shaking, and there were tears at the corners of his eyes, but Nessel put a hand on his arm.

'It's over,' she told him. 'We're done here. There's nothing left for us. I'm sorry, Scoles.'

The mutineer chief gave a final glance around at the looming forest that no longer seemed so wonderfully vibrant and green and Earth-like. The shadows seemed to throng with unseen eyes, with chitinous motion.

He dropped the pistol disgustedly, a man whose dreams had been shattered.

'Okay, Lain, Mason, you come right over here first. I want to check you're unharmed.'

Lain did not hesitate, and Holsten shambled after her, feeling only the faintest deadened sense of pain, yet still having to labour at both breathing and walking, weirdly disconnected from his own body.

'Get in,' Karst told them.

Lain paused in the hatch. 'Thank you,' she said, without so much of her usual mockery.

'You think I'd leave you here?' Karst asked her, visor still looking outwards.

'I thought Guyen might.'

'That's what he wanted them to think.'

Lain didn't look convinced, but she helped Holsten up after her. 'Come on, get your prisoners and let's get out of here.'

'No prisoners,' Karst stated.

'What?' Holsten asked, and then Karst's men started shooting.

Both of them had taken Scoles as their first target, and the mutineer leader went down instantly with barely a yell. Then they were turning their guns on the other two – Holsten barrelled into them, shouting, demanding that they stop. 'What are you doing?'

'Orders.' Karst shoved him back. Holsten had a wheeling glimpse of Tevik and Nessel trying to put the crashed cabin between themselves and the rifles. The mutineer pilot fell, struggled to his feet clutching at his injured leg, and then jerked as one of the security men picked him off.

Nessel made it to the treeline and vanished into the deeper darkness there. Holsten stared after her, feeling a crawling horror.

Would I rather be shot? Surely I would. But it wasn't a choice anyone was asking of him.

'We have to get her back, alive,' he insisted. 'She's . . . valuable. She's a scholar, she's got—'

'No prisoners. No ringleaders for a future mutiny,' Karst told him with a shrug. 'And your woman up there doesn't care so long as there's no interference to her precious planet.'

Holsten blinked. 'Kern?'

'We're here to clear up the mess for her,' Karst confirmed. 'She's listening right now. She's got her finger on the switch of all our systems. So it's straight in, straight out.'

'You bargained with Kern to come and get us?' Lain clarified.

Karst shrugged. 'She wanted you out of the picture down here. We wanted you back. We cut a deal. But we need to get going now.'

'You can't . . .' Holsten stared out from the hatch at the deep forest beyond. *Call Nessel back just to have her executed?*

He subsided, realizing only that, at heart, he was just glad to be safe.

'So, Kern,' Karst called out, 'what now? I don't much fancy going into *that* to get her, and I reckon that would just involve more of that interference you don't want.'

The clipped, hostile tones of Avrana Kern issued from the comms panel. 'Your inefficiency is remarkable.'

'Whatever,' Karst grunted. 'We're coming back to orbit, right? Is that okay?'

'It would seem the least undesirable option at this point,' Kern agreed, still sounding disgusted. 'Leave now, and I will destroy the crashed vessel.'

'The . . . ? She can *do* that?' Lain hissed. 'You mean she could have . . .'

'It's kind of a one-shot. She's got our drone up there under her control,' Karst explained. 'She's going to stick it into the crash there and then do some kind of controlled detonation of its reactor – burn up the wreck without flattening the entire area. Doesn't want her precious monkeys playing with grown-up toys or something.'

'Yeah, well, we didn't see any fucking monkeys,' Lain muttered. 'Let's get out of here.'

3.10 GIANTS IN THE EARTH

Portia examines the creature as it sleeps.

She was not in time to see any of the momentous, inexplicable events that left a great, burning scar across the face of her world – the fires that are still burning despite the ants' best efforts to contain them. From others of her kind she has heard a garbled version of events, crippled by the tellers' inability to understand what it is they have witnessed.

It will all be remembered though, through the generations to come. This Understanding, this contact with the unknowable, will be one of the most analysed and reinterpreted events of all her species' histories.

Something fell from the sky. It was not the Messenger, which clearly retains its regular circuit of the heavens, but in the mind of Portia and her kin it seems linked to that orbiting mote. It is a promise that the skies are host to more than one mobile star, and that even stars may fall. Some hypothesize that it was a herald or forerunner, a message from the Messenger, and that if its meaning can only be interpreted, then the Messenger will have new lessons to teach. Over the generations, this view – that a test has been set beyond the simple, pure manipulation of numbers – will gain in popularity, whilst simultaneously being viewed as a kind of heresy.

The events themselves seem inarguable, however. Something fell, and now it is a blackened shell of metals and other unknown materials that defy analysis. Something else came to earth, and then returned to the sky. Most crucially, there were living things. There were giants that came from the sky.

They were fighting off scouts from the ant colony when Portia's people first saw them. Then, when the scouts had been killed or converted, the giants killed one of Portia's own people – one of Bianca's assistants. After they departed, they left some bodies of their own kind, some killed by the ants, others just dead from mysterious wounds. Swift work by Bianca's team removed these remains from the scene, with fortunate timing given the explosion that occurred soon after, ending any useful enquiry, and killing a further handful of Bianca's males.

At the time, nobody realized that one of the star-creatures had remained alive and entered the forest.

Now Portia examines the thing, as it appears to sleep. The shape of a human being sparks no ancestral recollection in her. Even had her distant antecedents any memories to pass on, their tiny keyhole's span of vision would have been unable to appreciate the scale of anything so large. Portia herself is having difficulties: the sheer size and bulk of this alien monster give her pause for thought.

The creature has already killed two of her kind, when it encountered them. They had tried to approach, and the thing had attacked them on sight. Biting it had little or no effect – being designed for use against spiders, Portia's venom has limited effect against vertebrates.

If it was just some monstrous, oversized beast, then to trap and kill it would be relatively simple, Portia decides. If the worst came to the worst, they could simply set the ants on it, as they are obviously more than equal to the task. The mystical significance of this creature is a different consideration, however. It has come from the sky: from the Messenger, ergo. It is not a threat to be confronted, but a mystery to be unravelled.

Portia feels the thrumming of destiny beneath her feet. She has a sense that everything that is past and everything that is to come are balanced at this point in time, the fulcrum resting within herself. This moment is one of divinely mandated significance. Here, in its monstrous living form, is some part of the Messenger's message.

They will trap it. They will capture it and bring it back to Great Nest, using all the artifice and guile at their command. They will find some way to unravel its secret.

Portia glances upwards – the canopy of the forest keeps the stars from her view, but she is keenly aware of them: both the fixed constellations that wheel slowly across the arch of the year and the Messenger's swift spark in the darkness. She thinks of them as her people's birthright, if her people can only understand what they are being told.

Her kind has won a great victory over the ants, turning enemies into allies, reversing the tide of the war. From here on, colony after colony will fall to them. Surely it is in recognition of this, in reward for their cleverness and endurance and success, that the Messenger has sent them this sign.

With her body twanging with manifest destiny, Portia now plans the capture of her colossal prize.

3.11 THIS ISLAND GULAG

From the comms room, Holsten watched the last shuttle depart for the moon base, carrying its oblivious human cargo.

Guyen's plan was simple. An active crew of fifty had been woken up and briefed on what was expected – or perhaps demanded – of them. The base was ready for them, everything constructed by the automatics during the *Gilgamesh's* last long sleep, and tested fit for habitation. It would be the crew's job to keep it running and operational, so as to turn it into a new home for the human race.

They would have another two hundred in suspension – ready to call on when they needed them – to replace losses or more hopefully to expand their active population when the base was ready for them. They would have children. Their children would inherit what they had built.

At some time in the future, generations later, it was anticipated that the *Gilgamesh* would return from its long voyage to the next terraforming project, hopefully carrying a cargo of pirated Old Empire technology that would, as Guyen said, make everyone's lives that much easier.

Or enable him to mount an attack on the Kern's satellite and claim her planet, Holsten thought, and surely he wasn't alone in thinking that, though nobody was voicing it.

If the *Gilgamesh* did not return – if, say, the next system had a more aggressive guardian than Kern, or some other mishap should befall the ark ship – then the moon colony would just have to . . .

'Manage' was the word that Guyen had used. Nobody was going behind that. Nobody wanted to think about the limited range of fates possible for such a speck of human dust in the vast face of the cosmos.

The newly appointed leader of the colonists was not another Scoles, certainly. That intrepid woman listened to her orders with grim acceptance. Looking into her face, Holsten told himself that he could see a terrible, bleak despair hiding in her eyes. What was she being handed, after all? At the worst a death sentence, at the best a life sentence. An undeserved penal term that her children would inherit straight from the womb.

He started when someone clapped him on the shoulder: Lain. The two of them – along with Karst and his team – had only recently got out of quarantine. The only good out of the whole of Scoles's doomed excursion planetside was that there didn't seem to be any bacteria or viruses down there that posed an immediate danger to human health. And why would there be? As Lain had pointed out, there hadn't seemed to be anything human-like down there to incubate them.

'Time for bed,' the engineer told him. 'Last shuttle's away, so we're ready to depart. You'll want to be in suspension before we stop rotation. Until we get our acceleration up, gravity's going to be all over the place.'

'What about you?'

'I'm chief engineer. I get to work through it, old man.'

'Catching up on me.'

'Shut up.'

As she helped him out of the chair, he felt his ribs complain. He had been told the suspension chamber would see him heal up nicely while he slept, and he fervently hoped it was true.

'Cheer up,' Lain told him. 'There'll be a whole treasure trove of ancient nonsense for you, when you wake up. You'll be like a kid with new toys.'

'Not if Guyen has anything to say about it,' Holsten grumbled. He spared a last look at the viewscreens, at the cold, pale orb of the prison moon – the *colony* moon, he corrected himself. His unworthy thought was, *Rather you than me.*

Leaning on Lain a little, he walked carefully off down the corridor, heading for the Key Crew sleep room.

3.12 A VOICE IN THE WILDERNESS

The fallen giant had died, of course, but not for a long time. Until then she – Portia and her kin found it difficult to conceive of this thing as anything other than a she – had dwelt in captivity, eating that limited selection of foods that she was willing to consume, staring out through the mist-coloured walls that kept her in, gazing up at the open top of her pen, where the scholars would gather to observe her.

The dead giants were dissected and found to be essentially identical to mice in almost all internal structures, save for a difference of proportion in the limbs and certain organs. Comparative study confirmed their hypothesis that the living giant was probably a female, at least by comparison to its smaller endoskeletal cousins.

The debate on its purpose and meaning – on the lesson that the arrival of such a prodigy was intended to teach – lasted for generations, over the whole span of the creature's long life and beyond. Its behaviour was strange and complex, but it seemed mute, producing no kind of gesture or vibration that could be considered an attempt at speech. Some noted that when it opened and closed its mouth, a cleverly designed web could catch a curious murmur, the same that might be felt when objects were pounded together. It was a vibration that travelled through the air, rather than across a strand or through the ground. For some time this was hypothesized as a means of communication, provoking much intelligent debate, but in the end the absurdity of such an idea won out. After all, using the same orifice for eating *and* communication was manifestly too inefficient. The spiders are not deaf, exactly, but their hearing is deeply tied into their sense of touch and vibration. The giant's utterances, all the frequencies of human speech, are not even whispers to them.

Anyway, the airborne vibrations grew fewer and fewer during the thing's captivity, and eventually it ceased to make them. Some suggested this meant the creature had grown content with its captivity.

Two generations after it was taken, when the events surrounding its arrival had already passed into something resembling theology, one attendant noticed that the giant was moving its extremities, the deft sub-legs that it used to manipulate objects, in a manner imitative of palp-signalling, as though it was trying to mimic the basic visual speech of the spiders. There was a renewed flurry of interest, and a great deal of visits from other nests and trading of Understandings to enlighten future generations. Sufficient experimentation suggested that the giant was not simply copying what it saw, but that it could associate meaning with certain symbols, allowing it to request food and water. Attempts to communicate on a more sophisticated level were frustrated by its inability to approximate or comprehend more than a few very simple symbols.

The baffled scholars, drawing on their species' accumulated years of study, concluded that the giant was a simple creature, probably designed to undertake labour suitable for a thing of its immense size and strength, but no more intelligent than a Paussid beetle or a Spitter, and perhaps less.

Shortly after, the giant died, apparently of some infirmity. Its body was dissected and studied in turn, and compared to the genetically encoded Understandings resulting from examinations of the original dead giants from generations earlier.

Speculation as to its original purpose, and connection with the Messenger, continued, with the most commonly held theory being that the Messenger was served in the sky by a species of such giants, who performed necessary tasks for it. Therefore, in sending down its dumb emissaries so many years before, some manner of approbation had been intended. The inheritance of Understandings placed something of a curb on the spiders' ability to mythologize their own history, but already the correlation of their victory over the ants and the arrival of the giants had become firmly accepted as somehow related.

However, by the time this last giant died, the world of Portian theology was already being rocked by another revelation.

There was a second Messenger.

By that time the war with the ants was long over. The Paussid strategy had been successfully prosecuted against colony after colony until the spiders had reduced the insects' influence back to its original territory, where once an ancient Portia had raided their temple, stolen their idol, and unknowingly brought the word of the Messenger to her own people.

The scholars of Portia's kind had been keen not to reprogram the ant colony, as they had done with its various limbs and expeditionary forces, because in doing so its unique abilities would be lost, and the spiders were not blind to the advances that the colony's development had unlocked. So it was that years of complex campaigning had been entered into – at some considerable cost in lives – until the ant colony was manoeuvred into a position where cooperation with its spider neighbours became the most beneficial course of action, whereupon the ant colony passed, without acrimony or resentment, from an implacable foe to an obliging ally.

The spiders were quick to experiment with the uses of metal and glass. Creatures of keen vision, their studies into light, refraction and optics followed swiftly. They learned to use carefully manufactured glass to extend the reach of their sight to the micro- and macroscopic. The older generation of scholars passed the torch seamlessly to a new generation of scientists, who turned their newly augmented eyes to the night skies and viewed the Messenger in greater detail, and looked beyond.

At first it was believed that the new message came from the Messenger itself, but the astronomers quickly dispelled that notion. Working with the temple priestesses, they found that there was now another mobile point in the sky that could speak, and that its motion was slower, and curiously irregular.

Slowly, the spiders began to build up a picture of their solar system by reference to their own home, its moon and its Messenger, the sun, and that outer planet which itself possessed an orbiting body that was sending out its own, separate signal.

The one problem with this second message was that it was incomprehensible. Unlike the regular, abstractly beautiful numerical sequences that had become the heart of their religion, the new messenger broadcast only chaos: a shifting, changing, meaningless garble. Priestesses and scientists listened to its patterns, recorded them in their complex notation of knots and nodes, but could draw no meaning from them. Years of fruitless study resulted in a feeling that this new source of signal was some antithesis of the Messenger itself, some almost malevolent source of entropy rather than order. In the absence of more information, all manner of curious intentions were credited to it.

Then, a few years later, the second signal ceased to vary and settled on a single repeated transmission, over and over, and this again led to a mass of speculation across what had by then become a loose-knit global community of priest-scientists. Again and again the signal was parsed for meaning, for surely a message repeated over and over so many times must be important.

There was one curious school of thought that detected some manner of need in the signal, and quaintly fancied that, out there through the unthinkable space between their world and the source of that second message, something lost and desperate was calling for help.

Then the day came when the signal was no more, and the baffled spiders were left staring blankly up into a heaven suddenly impoverished, but unable to understand why.

4
ENLIGHTENMENT

4.1 THE CAVE OF WONDERS

When he was a child, Holsten Mason had been mad about space. The exploration of Earth's orbit had been ongoing for a century and a half by then, and a generation of astronauts had been raiding the fallen colonies, from the lunar base to the gas giant moons. He had immersed himself in dramatic reconstructions of bold explorers entering dangerous derelict space stations, avoiding the remaining automated systems to pillage tech and data from the burnt-out old computers. He had watched actual recordings of the real-life expeditions – often disturbing, often cut off suddenly. He remembered, at no more than ten years old, seeing a helmet torch play over the vacuum-desiccated corpse of a millennia-old spaceman.

By the time he was grown up, his interest had migrated back through time from those bold scavenger pioneers to the lost civilization that they were rediscovering. Those days of discovery! So much had been hauled back down from orbit but so little of it was understood. Alas, the golden days of the classicist were already on the wane when Holsten had begun his career. He had lived to see his discipline steadily tainted by vicarious disgrace; there was less and less still to be gleaned from the scraps and splinters which the Old Empire had left behind, and it had become evident that those long-dead ancestors were still present, in a malign, intangible way. The Old Empire was reaching out of deep history to inexorably poison its children. Small wonder that the study of that intricate, murderous people gradually lost its appeal.

Now, at an inconceivable distance from his dying home, Holsten Mason had been handed the veritable grail of the classicist.

He sat in the comms room of the *Gilgamesh*, completely surrounded by the past, transmission after transmission filling the ark ship's virtual space with the wisdom of the ancients. As far as he was concerned, they had struck gold.

He was one of the few Key Crew able to participate from the comfort of the *Gilgamesh* itself. Karst and Vitas had taken a shuttle and some drones to check out the barren-looking planet below them. Lain and her engineers were out on the half-finished station itself, slowly proceeding down its compartmentalized length and recording everything they found. When they found working hardware they could access, they sent Holsten the results, and he deciphered and catalogued it wherever he could, or put it aside for further study where he could not.

Nobody had ever had access to an Old Empire terraforming station before, even an incomplete one. Nobody had ever been sure that such a thing actually existed. Here, at the wrong end of his career, and at the wrong end of the history of the human race, Holsten was finally in the undeniable position of being able to call himself the greatest expert ever on the Old Empire.

The thought was intoxicating, but its aftertaste one of bleak depression.

Holsten was now in possession of a greater trove of communications, fiction, technical manuals, announcements and trivia in several Imperial languages – but mostly Kern's Imperial C – than any scholar before him since the end of the Empire itself. All he could think was that his own people, an emergent culture that had clawed its way back to its feet after the ice, was nothing but a shadow of that former greatness. It was not simply that the *Gilgamesh* and all their current space effort was cobbled together from bastardized, half-understood pieces of the ancient world's vastly superior technology. It was *everything*: from the very beginning his people had known they were inheriting a used world. The ruins and the decayed relics of a former people had been everywhere, underfoot, underground, up mountains, immortalized in stories. Discovering such a wealth of dead metal in orbit had hardly been a surprise, when all recorded history had been a progress over a desert of broken bones. There had been no innovation that the ancients had not already achieved, and done better. How many inventors had been relegated to historical obscurity because some later treasure-hunter had unearthed the older, superior method of achieving the same end? Weapons, engines, political systems, philosophies, sources of energy . . . Holsten's people had thought themselves lucky that someone had built such a convenient flight of steps back up from the dark into the sunlight of civilization. They had never quite come to the realization that those steps led only to that one place.

Who knows what we might have achieved, had we not been so keen to recreate all their follies, he thought now. *Could we have saved the Earth? Would we be living there now on our own green planet?*

All the knowledge in the universe now at his fingertips, yet to that question he had no answer.

The *Gilgamesh* had translation algorithms now, mostly designed by Holsten himself. Previously the sum total of the ancients' written word had been so scarce that automatic deciphering had been infinitely hit-and-miss – he would still not have liked to have any conversation with Avrana Kern via a translation by the *Gilgamesh*, for example. Now, with a library of miscellanea at his fingertips the computers were working with him to turn out at least halfway comprehensible versions of Imperial C. Most of the treasure trove of knowledge remained locked within ancient languages, though. Even with electronic help, there simply wasn't time to decode it all, and most likely the bulk of it was simply of no interest to anyone but himself. The best he could do was get an idea of what each separate file represented, catalogue it for future reference, and then pass on.

Sometimes Lain or her people would contact him with questions, mostly about tech they had found but which seemed to serve no obvious purpose. They would give him vague search terms and send him digging through his own directories for something that might pertain to it. More often than not, his organization and the wealth of material eventually yielded something of use, and he would set out a working translation of it. The fact that they could have looked for themselves was something he occasionally commented on, but it was plain that the engineers felt actually skimming Holsten's catalogue was far more difficult than just pestering him about it.

To be honest, he had hoped to get some talk of a more social nature with Lain but, in the forty days he had been awake this time round, he had not so much as met her face to face. The engineers were busy, actually living out there on the great hollow cylinder of the station most of the time. They had thawed out and awoken an auxiliary crew of thirty trained people from cargo to help them, and still there was more work to be done than they could keep up with.

Six people had died: four to what had either been a working security system or a defective maintenance system, one to a suit malfunction, and one to sheer clumsiness, by managing to get their suit cut open whilst trying to hurry equipment through a jagged gap in the station infrastructure.

It was far less than those early exploration recordings would have led him to expect, but then there were no ancient dead here, no suggestion that this installation had fallen victim to the infighting that had brought down the Empire and its entire way of life. The long-ago engineers had simply departed, probably heading back for Earth when everything went wrong. This terraforming project they had begun had been left to the slow, heedless mercy of the stars.

It could have been far worse. Lain had said the place had been poisoned, infected with some kind of electronic plague that had destroyed the original life support and a great deal of the station's core systems. The *Gilgamesh* had turned out to be too much of a poor imitation of the Old Empire's elegant technology, though. Their technology had proved stony ground, the virtual attack frustrated by their primitive systems. Whether Kern had known and sent them into a trap was a subject of some debate amongst everyone except Engineering, who had been tasked with jury-rigging as much of the station's systems as possible into giving up their secrets.

A sound behind Holsten brought him abruptly out of his

reverie. It had been a quiet, stealthy sound, and for a moment he had a nightmare flash of memory of that distant green world with its giant arthropods. No monster, though: behind him was only Guyen.

'It's all going well, I trust?' the ark ship commander inquired, regarding Holsten as though suspecting him of something disloyal. He was leaner and greyer now than he had been when leaving the moon colony behind. Whilst Holsten had slumbered peacefully, the commander had been waking up, on and off, to oversee the operation of his ship. Now he looked down on his chief classicist with an actual seniority in age to match his rank.

'Steadily,' Holsten confirmed, wondering what this visit was about. Guyen wasn't a man for pleasantries.

'I've been looking over your catalogue.'

Holsten fought down the temptation to express surprise at anyone doing such a thing, let alone Guyen.

'I've a list of items I want to read,' the commander told him. 'At your earliest convenience, of course. Engineering requests take precedence.'

'Of course.' Holsten tilted his head at the screen. 'Do you want to . . . ?'

Guyen passed over a tablet displaying half a dozen numbers entered neatly there, in the format of Holsten's homegrown indexing system. 'Direct to me,' he pressed. He didn't actually say, *Don't tell anyone else about this*, but everything in his manner hinted at it.

Holsten nodded mutely. The numbers gave him no suggestion as to what it was all about, or why any of this needed to be requested in person.

'Oh, and you might want to come listen. Vitas is going to

tell us the news about the planet here, and how far along the terraforming got.'

That would be welcome, and something Holsten had been impatiently waiting for. Eagerly he got up and followed after Guyen. Enough of the secrets of the past for now. He wanted to hear a little more of the present and the future.

4.2 DEATH COMES RIDING

Portia looks out across the vast, interconnected complexity that was Great Nest and sees a city just beginning to die.

In the last few generations, Great Nest's population has swelled to somewhere near a hundred thousand adult spiders, and countless – uncounted – young. It spreads through several square miles of forest, reaching from the earth to the canopy, a true metropolis of the spider age.

The city Portia sees now is depopulated. Although the dying has only just started, hundreds of females are abandoning Great Nest for other cities. Others simply strike out into the remaining wilderness to take their chances, relying on centuries-old Understandings to recapture the lifestyle of their ancient huntress ancestors. Many males have fled too. Already the delicate structures of the city are showing some disrepair as basic maintenance is disregarded.

Plague is coming.

In the north, a handful of great cities are already in ruins. A global epidemic is leaping from community to community. Hundreds of thousands are already dead from it, and now Great Nest has seen its own first victims.

She knows this was inevitable, for this current Portia is a priestess and a scientist. She has been working to try and understand the virulent disease, and to find a cure.

She does not quite understand why this disease has had such an impact. Aside from its highly contagious nature, and its ability to spread by contact – and somewhat less reliably through the air – the sheer concentration of bodies in the cities of Portia's people have turned a minor, controllable infection into something more virulent than the Black Death. Such great concentrations of bodies have led to all manner of squalor and health problems; Portia's people were only beginning to grasp the need for collective responsibility for such issues when the spread of the plague caught them unawares. Their casual, almost anarchic form of government is not well suited to taking the sort of harsh measures that might be effective.

Another factor in the deadliness of the disease is the practice, increasingly common in the last century, of females choosing males born within their own peer group as mates, in an attempt to concentrate and control the spread of their Understandings. This practice – well meaning and enlightened in its way – has led to inbreeding that has weakened the immune systems of many powerful peer houses, meaning that those who might possess the power to take action are often first to come down with the plague when it erupts. Portia is aware of this pattern, though not the cause, and she is also aware that her own peer group fits that pattern all too well.

She is aware that there are tiny animicules associated with disease, but her magnifying lenses are not acute enough to detect the viral culprit for the plague. She has the results of experiments carried out by fellow scientists from other cities, many of whom are dead of the plague themselves, now. Some even arrived at a theory of vaccination, but the immune system of Portia's people is not the efficient and adaptive machine that humans and other mammals can boast. Exposure to a contagion simply does not prepare them for later, kindred infections in the same way.

The world is falling apart, and Portia is shocked at how little it has taken for this to occur. She had never realized that her whole civilization was such a fragile entity. She hears the news from other cities where the plague is already rife. Once the population begins to drop – from death and desertion – the whole structure of society collapses swiftly. The elegant and sophisticated way of life that the spiders have built for themselves has always been strung over a great abyss of barbarism, cannibalism and a return to primitive, savage values. After all, they are predators at heart.

She retreats to the Temple, picking her way past the mass of citizens who have taken refuge therein, seeking some certainty from beyond. There are not as many as the day before. Portia knows this is not just because there are fewer of her people left in the city: she is also aware that there is a slowly growing disillusionment with the Messenger and Her message. *What good does it do us?* they ask. *Where is the fire sent from heaven to purge the plague?*

Touching the crystal with her metal stylus, Portia dances to the music of the Messenger as it passes overhead, her complex steps describing perfectly the equations and their solutions. As always, she is filled by that measureless assurance that something is out there: that just because she cannot understand something *now* does not mean that it cannot be understood.

One day I will comprehend you, is her thought directed to

the Messenger, but it rings hollow now. Her days are num-bered. All their days are numbered.

She finds herself entertaining the heretical thought, *If only we could send our own message back to you*. The Temple acts fiercely against that sort of thinking, but it is not the first time Portia has considered the idea. She is aware that other scientists – even priestess-scientists – have been experiment-ing with some means of reproducing the invisible vibrations by which the message is spread. Publicly, the Temple cannot condone such meddling, of course, but the spiders are a curious species, and those who are drawn to the Temple are the most curious of all. It was inevitable that the hot-house flower of heresy would end up nurtured by those very guardians of the orthodox.

On this day, Portia finds that she believes that if they could somehow speak across that vast and empty space to the Messenger, then She would surely have an answer for them, a cure for the plague. Portia finds, just as inexorably, that no such dialogue is possible, no answer will come, and so she must find her own cure before it is too late.

After Temple, she returns to her peer house, a great, sprawling many-chambered affair slung between three trees, to meet with one of her males.

Since the ravages of the plague began, the role of the male in spider society has changed subtly. Traditionally the best lot in life for a male was to hitch his star to a powerful female and hope to be looked after, or else – for those born with valuable Understandings – to end up a pampered com-modity in a seraglio, ready to be traded away or mated off as part of the constantly shifting power games between peer houses. Other than that, the lot of a male came down to being a kind of underclass of urban scavengers constantly fighting each other over scraps of food, and always at risk without female patronage. However, from being a host of the useless and the unnecessary, decorative and fit for menial labour at best, a furtive meal at worst, they have become a desperate resource in time of need. Males are less independent, less able to fend for themselves out in the wilds, and so they tend to stay when females flee. That Great Nest and many other cities remain functioning at all is due to the number of males who have taken the chance to step into traditionally female roles. There are even male warriors, hunters and guards now, because someone must take up the sling and the shield and the incendiary grenade, and often there is nobody else to do so.

Females in Portia's position have long had their pick of male escorts and, whilst some keep them about merely to dance attendance – literally – and add to a female's apparent importance, others have trained them as skilled assistants. The Bianca of old, with her male laboratory assistants, had uncovered something of a truth about spider gender politics when she complained that working with females involved far too much competition for dominance, and old instincts lie shallowly under the civilized surface. This current Portia, too, has come reluctantly to trust in males.

Not long ago she sent out a band of males, a gang of adventurers that she had made frequent use of before. They were all capable, used to working together from their youngest days as abandoned spiderlings on the streets of Great Nest. Their mission was one that Portia felt no female would accept; their reward was to be the continued support of

Portia's peer group: food, protection, access to education, entertainment and culture.

One of them has returned: just the one. Call him Fabian.

He comes to her now at the peer house. Fabian is missing a leg, and he looks half-starved and exhausted. Portia's palps flick, sending one of the immature males from the crèche to find some food for them both.

Well? An impatient twitch as she watches him.

Conditions are worse than you thought. Also, I had difficulty re-entering Great Nest. Travellers suspected of coming from the north are being turned away if female, killed out of hand if male. His speech is a slow shuffle of feet, slurred and uneven.

Is that what happened to your comrades?

No. I am the only one to return. They're all dead. Such a brief eulogy this, for those that he had spent most of his life with. But then it is well known in Portia's society that males do not really feel with the same acuity as females, and certainly they cannot form the same bonds of attachment and respect.

The juvenile male returns with food: trussed live crickets and vegetable polyps gathered from the farms. Gratefully, Fabian scoops up one of the bound insects and inserts a fang. Too exhausted to bother using venom, he sucks the spasming creature dry.

There are survivors in the plague cities, as you had thought, he continues, as he eats. *But they retain nothing of our ways. They live like beasts, merely spinning and hunting. There were females and males. My companions were taken and devoured, one by one.*

Portia stamps anxiously. *But were you successful?*

Fabian's ordeal has sufficiently affected him that he does not immediately respond to her enquiry, but asks back, *Are you not worried that I might have brought the plague to Great Nest? It seems likely I must have contracted it.*

It is already here.

His palps flex slowly, in a gesture of resignation. *I have succeeded. I have brought three spiderlings taken from the plague zone. They are healthy. They are immune, as those others living there must be. You were right, for what good it may do us.*

Take them to my laboratory, she instructs him. Then, seeing his remaining limbs tremble, she continues: *After that, the peer house is yours to roam. You will be rewarded for this great service. Merely ask for whatever you wish.*

He regards her, eye to eye, a bold move – but he was always a bold male, and why else would he have made such a useful tool? *Once I have rested I would assist you in your work, if you would let me,* he tells her. *You know I have Understandings of the biochemical sciences, and I have studied also.*

The offer surprises Portia, who shows it in her posture.

Great Nest is my home, too, Fabian reminds her. *All I am is contained here. Do you truly believe that you can defeat the plague?*

I believe that I must try or we are all lost, anyway. A sombre thought, but the logic is undeniable.

4.3 NOTES FROM A GREY PLANET

Holsten was taken aback by the number of people who had gathered to hear the news. The *Gilgamesh* was short of auditoriums, so the venue was a converted shuttle bay, bare and echoing. He wondered if the absent shuttles were currently clamped to the derelict station, or whether this was where he and Lain had been kidnapped and brought to by the mutineers. All the bays looked the same, and any damage had presumably been repaired by now.

In his solitary labours he had lost track of just how many people had been woken up to assist with the reclamation effort. At least a hundred were sitting around the hangar, and he was struck with an almost phobic response to them: too many, too close, too enclosed. He ended up hovering next to the doorway, realizing that some part of his mind had resigned itself to a future of dealing only with a few other humans, and had perhaps preferred that.

And why are we all here, anyway? There was no actual requirement for physical attendance, after all. He himself could have continued his work and watched Vitas's presentation on a screen, or had her warbling away in his ear. Nobody needed to shift their pounds of flesh over here just to trust to their antiquated eyes and ears. Vitas herself had no practical need to give a presentation in person. Even back home, this sort of academic status-mongering had been conducted at a distance, most of the time.

So why? And why did I come? Looking over the crowd gathered there, hearing the murmur of their excited conversation, he could speculate that many of them must have come just to be sociable, to be with their fellows. *But that's not me, is it?*

And he realized that it was, of course. He was tethered inextricably to a social species, however much he might fancy himself as a loner. There was, even in Holsten, a desire to interact with other human beings, preserving a bond between himself and everyone else here. Even Vitas was present not for scholarly prestige or for status amongst the crew, but because she needed to reach out and know there was something she could reach out to.

Looking over the crowd, Holsten could see few familiar faces. Aside from Vitas's own science team, most of Key Crew were occupied on the station, and almost everyone here had last opened their eyes way back on Earth, so could know nothing of Kern or the green planet or its terrible inhabitants save what they were told, or from what unclassified material was available in the *Gil's* records. Whilst it was true that a lot of them were young, it was the knowledge gap that made him feel old, as though he had been awake for centuries longer than they, rather than just a few strung-out days passed in another solar system.

Guyen had found a place at the back, keeping similarly aloof, and now Vitas stepped forward, precise and fastidious, looking over her audience as though not entirely sure she had come into the right room.

The screen her team had installed, taking up much of the

wall behind her, shifted from a dead to a lambent grey. Vitas regarded it critically, and then managed a thin smile.

'As you know, I have been overseeing a survey of the planet that we are currently in orbit around. It seems unarguable now,' and she was good enough to throw a tiny nod Holsten's way, 'that we have arrived at one of a string of terraforming projects that the Old Empire was pursuing immediately before its dissolution. The previous project we saw was complete, and under a quarantine imposed for unknown purposes by an advanced satellite. As we are discovering, work at our current location appears to have been arrested during the terraforming process itself, and the control facility abandoned. I am aware that Engineering has been undertaking the formidable task of investigating that facility, whilst I have been investigating the planet itself to see if it might serve us in any fashion as a home.'

There was nothing in this clipped, dry delivery to give any clue as to her conclusions, if conclusions there were. This was not showmanship or a desire for suspense, simply that Vitas considered herself a pure scientist first and foremost, and would report positive and negative results with equal candour without judging the value or desirability of the outcome. Holsten was familiar with that particular academic school, which had grown more and more popular towards the end on Earth, as positive results became harder to find.

Vitas looked out over the gathering, and Holsten tried to interpret her expression, her body language, anything to get an idea of where this was going. *Do we stay here? Are we heading onwards? Are we going back?* That last possibility was his major concern, for he was one of the very small number who had first-hand experience of Kern's green world.

The screen brightened, grey to grey to grey, and then there was the curve of a dark horizon, and they were now looking at the grey planet.

'As you'll have remarked, the surface of this planet seems curiously uniform. Spectrographic analysis, however, shows abundant organic chemistry: all the elements we might need to survive,' Vitas told them. 'We dropped a pair of drones as soon as we had established a high orbit. The images that you will be seeing are all taken from drone camera. The colours are the true colours, with no touching-up or artistic licence.'

Holsten wasn't seeing any colours, unless grey counted, but as sunrise crept across the orb displayed before him he saw contours, shadows: indications of mountains, basins, channels.

'As you can see, this planet is geologically active, which may have been a prerequisite for the Empire's terraforming. We don't know whether this is simply because, of all the Earth-like qualities they wished to find in a new world, that would be the most difficult to fabricate – perhaps outright impossible – or alternatively that they have, indeed, instilled that quality into the planet at an early stage. Hopefully the recovered information from the station will give us an idea of how they went about the process. It is within the bounds of possibility that one day we ourselves may be able to dupli-cate the feat.' And there was at least a hint there that Vitas was feeling a little excited by the thought. Holsten was sure her voice lifted a semitone, that one of her eyebrows even twitched.

'You can see here the drone readings of the basic condi-tions planetside,' Vitas continued. 'So: gravity around eighty per cent of Earth's, a slow rotation giving around a four-hundred-hour diurnal cycle. Temperature is high, bearable around the poles, survivable in northern latitudes, but probably not within human tolerance towards the equator. You'll note that oxygen levels are only around five per cent, so no easy home here, I'm afraid. A salutary lesson nonetheless, as you will see.'

The image shifted to a much closer view of the surface, with the drones flying far lower, and a ripple went through the audience; one of bafflement, disquiet. The grey was alive.

The entire surface, as far as the drone camera could register, was covered in a dense interlaced vegetation, grey as ashes. It feathered out into fern-like fronds that arched over each other, spreading hand-like folds to catch the sunlight. It erupted into phallic towers that were warty with buds or fruiting bodies. It covered the mountains to their very tips. It formed a thick, grey fur on every visible surface. The image shifted, and shifted, and Vitas noted different locations, with an inset global map showing where the views were taken from. The details of the view, however, barely changed.

'What you are looking at is best thought of as a fungus,' the science chief explained. 'This solitary species has colonized the entire planet, pole to pole and at every altitude. Scans of the underlying ground – as overlain here – show that the actual topography of the planet is as varied as one might expect of a substitute Earth – there are sea basins but no seas, river valleys but no rivers. Investigation suggests that there is a planet's worth of water bound up in that organism you see before you. And it may even be a *single* organism. There's no obvious division observable. It appears capable of some manner of photosynthesis, despite the colour, but the low oxygen levels suggest this is chemically distinct from anything we're familiar with. It's not known whether this pervasive species is somehow an intended part of the terra-forming process, or if it was the result of an error, and its irremovable presence led the engineers to abandon their work, or whether it has arisen after that abandonment – the natural by-product of a part-completed job. In any event, I think it safe to say that the stuff is there to stay. This is now its world.'

'Can it be cleared?' someone asked. 'Can we burn it back, or something?'

Vitas's outward calm had at last been ruffled. 'Good luck burning anything with that little oxygen,' she tutted. 'Besides, I am recommending no further investigation of this planet. By the time we had established the position down there, and conducted some exploratory research, the drones were beginning to show signs of reduced functionality. We kept them going for as long as we were able, but both of them eventually ceased working altogether. The air down there is virtually a spore soup, new fungal colonies looking to sprout on any fresh surface that becomes exposed. Which reminds me, with all the excitement within this system and the last, we need to construct more drones in the workshops once the resources are available. We have very few of them left.'

'Granted,' Guyen replied, from the back. 'Get onto it. I think we can assume this place isn't going to be our home any time soon,' he added. 'But that's not going to be a prob-lem. Our priority is to gather everything we can from the station, file it, translate it, and work out what we can put into action. At the same time we're undertaking a major overhaul of the Gilgamesh's own systems, repairing and replacing where we can. There's a lot of useable tech on that station, if we can find a way to splice it to our own. And don't worry about not being able to go live on Fungus World. I have a plan. There *is* a plan. With what we've found here, we can go and take our birthright.' The speech veered into the messianic so abruptly that even Guyen himself seemed surprised for a moment, but then he turned and departed, curious conversation welling up in his wake.

The plague is insidious at first, then tyrannous, and at last truly terrifying. Its symptoms are by now well recorded, reliably predictable – everything, in fact, except preventable. The first sure signs are a feeling of heat in the joints, a rawness at the eyes, mouthparts, spinnerets, anus and book-lungs. Muscle spasms, especially in the legs, follow; at first just a few, a stammering in speech, a nervous dance not quite accounted for, then more and more the victim's limbs are not her own, leading her in babbling, staggering, whole frantic meaningless journeys. Around this time, from ten to forty days after the first involuntary twitch, the virus reaches the brain. The victim then relinquishes her grasp on who and where she is. She perceives those around her in irrational ways. Paranoia, aggression and fugue states are common during this phase. Death follows in another five to fifteen days, immediately preceded by an irresistible desire to climb as high as possible. Fabian has recounted in some detail the dead city that he has visited once more: the highest reaches of the trees and the decaying webbing were crowded with the rigid carapaces of the dead, glassy eyes fixed upwards on nothing.

Prior to those first definitive symptoms, the virus is present in the victim's system for an unknown period but often as long as two hundred days, while slowly infiltrating the patient's system without any obvious harm. The victim feels occasional periods of heat or dizziness, but there are other potential causes for this and the episodes usually go unreported; all the more so because, prior to the disease taking hold in Great Nest – as it now has – any suspected sufferers were exiled on pain of death. Those incubating the disease were part of an inadvertent conspiracy to mask the signs of outbreak for as long as possible.

During this early, innocent-seeming phase, the disease is moderately contagious. Being close to a sufferer for an extended period of time is very likely to lead to oneself contracting the disease, although bites from deranged victims in their last phases are the surest way to become infected.

There have been half a dozen late-stage victims in Great Nest. They are killed on sight, and at range. There are three times as many lingering in the mid-stage, and so far no consensus has been reached regarding them. Portia and others are insistent that a cure is possible. There is a tacit agreement amongst the temple scientists to conceal just how little idea they have of what can be done.

Portia is making the best uses of Fabian's prizes that she can. The spiderlings came from the plague city, and she can only hope that this means they are immune to the plague, and that this immunity will somehow be amenable to study.

She has tested them, and taken samples of their haemolymph – their arachnid blood – to examine, but all her lenses and analyses have so far discovered nothing. She has ordered that fluids from the spiderlings be fed or injected into mid-stage victims, a manner of transfusion having been pioneered just a few years before. The limited immune system of the spiders means that blood-type rejection is far less of an issue. In this case the attempt has had no effect.

In working with sufferers, in order to preserve herself as long as possible from the inevitable moment when she becomes her own test subject, she has used Fabian, and he has liaised with the males within those peer houses where the plague has taken hold. It is known that males are a little hardier than females where the plague is concerned. Ironically, ancient genetics link the elegance and stamina of their wooing dances with the strength of their immune systems, keeping a constant pressure on natural selection.

Everything that Portia has tried has so far failed, and none of her fellows has obtained any better results. She is beginning to drift into ever more speculative sciences, desperate for that one lateral thought that will save her civilization from a collapse into dispersed barbarism.

She has now been working in her laboratory for the best part of a day. Fabian has departed with a new batch of solutions to pass to his counterparts within the sealed lazar-houses that the dwellings of infected peer groups have become. She has no particular belief that these solutions will work. She feels she has reached the end of her capabilities, frustrated with the great void of ignorance that she has found, while standing out here at the very edge of her people's comprehension.

She now has a visitor. Under other circumstances she would turn this one away, but she is tired, so very tired, and she desperately needs some new perspective. And new – disturbingly new – perspectives are what this visitor is all about.

Her name is Bianca and she was formerly one of Portia's

peer group. She is a large, overfed spider with pale brindling all over her body, who moves with a fidgety, nervous energy that makes Portia wonder whether, if Bianca caught the disease, anyone would actually notice.

Bianca was formerly of the Temple, too, but she did not fulfil her duties with the proper respect. Her curiosity as a scientist overwhelmed her reverence as a priestess. She had begun experiments with the crystal and, when this was discovered, she came very close to being exiled for her disrespect. Portia and her other peers interceded on her behalf, but she effectively fell from those lofty levels of society, losing both her status and her friends. It was assumed that she would leave Great Nest, or perhaps die.

Instead, somehow Bianca has clung on and even thrived. She has always been a brilliant mind – perhaps that is another reason Portia, at the end of her own mental resources, lets her in – and she has bartered her skills like a male, by serving lesser peer houses, and eventually forming a new peer group of her own, drawn from other disaffected scholars. In better times, the major peer houses were always on the point of censuring or exiling the entire clutch of them, but now nobody cares. Portia's people have other matters to concern them.

They say you are close to a cure? However, Bianca's stance and the slight delay in her movements convey scepticism very neatly.

I work. We all work. Portia would normally exaggerate her prospects, but she is feeling too weary. *Why are you here?*

Bianca shuffles slyly, eyeing Portia. *Why, sister, why am I ever anywhere?*

This is not the time. So Bianca is after her usual, then.

Portia huddles miserably, the other spider stepping close to hear her muted speech.

From what I hear, there may be no other time Bianca says, half-goading. *I know what messages come down the lines from the other cities. I know how many other cities have no messages left in them. You and I both know what we are facing.*

If I had wanted to think further on that just now, I would have remained in my laboratory, Portia tells her with an angry stamp. *I will not give you access to the Messenger's crystal.*

Bianca's palps quiver. *I even had my own crystal, did you know? And the Temple found out, and took it away. I was close . . .*

Portia does not need to know what she was close to. Bianca has one obsession, and that is speaking to the Messenger, sending a message *back* to that swift-moving star. It is a subject of debate within the Temple every generation – and in every generation there is one like Bianca who will not take no for an answer. They are watched, always.

Portia's position is wretched because, left to herself, she would probably support Bianca. She is swayed by the majority, however, in the way that most large decisions fall out when the great and the good stand on the same web and debate. The Temple old guard, the priestesses of the former generation, hold the message sacrosanct and perfect. The path of Portia's people is to better appreciate it, to learn the hidden depths of the message that have yet to be unlocked. It is not for them to try and howl into the darkness to attract the Messenger's attention. Passing overhead, the Messenger observes all. There is an order to the universe, and the Messenger is proof of that.

Each generation a few more voices are raised in dispute, but so far that enduring meme has won out. After all, did the

Messenger not intervene during the great war with the ants, with no need for anyone to *ask* for help? *If it is within the Messenger's plan to help Portia's kind, then such help will come without being solicited.*

Why come to me? I will not go against Temple, Portia tells her as dismissively as she can manage.

Because I remember you from when we were still truly sisters. You want the same thing as me, only not quite enough.

I will not help you, Portia declares, her weariness adding a finality to the phrase. *There is no speaking back to the Messenger anyway. Our people need the Temple as a source of reassurance. Your experiments would likely take that from them, and for what? You cannot achieve what you wish, nor is it a thing to be achieved.*

I have something to show you. Suddenly Bianca is signalling and some males are bringing in a heavy device slung between them, stepping in sideways to lower it to the taut floor, which stretches a little more to take the weight.

It has long been known that certain chemicals react with metals in curious ways, Bianca noted. *When combined, linked properly, there is a force that passes along the metals and through the liquids. You remember such experiments from when we were learning together.*

A curiosity, nothing more, Portia recalled. *It is used for coating metals with other metals. I recall there was an ant colony induced to make the task work, and they produced remarkable goods.* This memory from her comparatively innocent youth lends her a little strength. *Many noxious fumes, though. Work fit for ants only. What of it?*

Bianca is attending to her device, which resembles the experiments that Portia recalls in that it has compartments of chemicals within other chemicals, linked by rods of metal, but it has other metal parts too: metal painstakingly teased out until it is as fine as thick silk, coiled densely in a column. Something changes in the air and Portia feels her hair prickle, as though a storm is coming – an event that always inspires a very reasonable fear because of the damage that natural fires can cause to a city.

This toy of mine is at the heart of an invisible web, Bianca tells her. *By careful adjustment, I can use it to pluck the strands of that web. Is that not remarkable?*

Portia wants to say that it is nonsensical, but she is intrigued, and the idea of some all-encompassing web is attractive, intuitive. How else could they be connected with . . . ?

What you say is that this web is what the Messenger speaks to us through?

Bianca skitters about her novel device. *Well, there must be some connection or how could we receive the message? And yet the Temple does not speculate. The message simply 'is'. Yes, I have found the great web of the universe, the web that the Messenger plucks its message upon. Yes, I can send our reply.*

Even for Bianca this is a bold and fearful boast.

I do not believe you, Portia decides. *You would have done it already, if it could be done.*

Bianca stamps angrily. *What point in calling to the Messenger if I cannot hear her words? I need access to the temple.*

You wish the Messenger to recognize you, to speak to you. So it is Bianca's ego that really drives this experiment. She was always thus: always ready to measure legs with the whole of creation. *This is not the time.* Portia feels exhausted once more.

Sister, we have no more time. You know that, Bianca wheedles.

Let me fulfil my plan. I cannot leave this to future generations. Even if I could pass the Understanding on, there will be no future generations worth speaking of. Now is the only time.

There will be future generations. Portia does not step out those words, only thinks them. *Fabian has seen them: living like beasts in the ruins of our cities, heads crowded with Understandings that they cannot use, because all the architecture of their mothers' world has gone. What use is science then? What use the Temple? What use art when there are so few left that all they can do is feed and mate? Our great Understandings will die off, generation to generation, until none of those left alive will remember who we were.* But the thought is incomplete, something nagging at her. She finds herself thinking of the selection of Understandings – those lost survivors will presumably have some long-ago Understandings to assist them in their hunting, and those offspring that inherit such primal Understandings would become the new lords of the world. But that will not be all that they inherit . . .

Portia leaps up, electrified into wakefulness as though she had inadvertently touched the wrong end of Bianca's machine. A mad thought has come to her. An impossible thought. A thought of science.

She signals one of her attendant males and demands to know if Fabian has returned. He has, and she has him sent for.

I must work in my laboratory, she tells Bianca, and then hesitates. Bianca is half-mad already, a dangerous maverick, a potential revolutionary, but her brilliant intellect was never in doubt. *Will you assist me? I need all the help I can get.*

Bianca's surprise is evident. *It would be an honour to work with my sisters once more, but . . .* She does not quite articulate the thought, but she tilts her eyes over towards her machine, now inactive and no longer stressing the air with its invisible web.

If we succeed, if we survive, I will do all I can to take your plea to Temple. And a rebellious thought of Portia's own. *If we survive, it will be by our own merits, not because of the Messenger's aid. We are now on our own.*

4.5 DREAMS OF THE ANCIENTS

'Mason.'

Holsten started, half asleep over his work, and almost fell off his chair. Guyen was standing right behind him.

'I – ah – was there something?' For a moment he was racking his brains to remember whether he had already finished the translations that the commander had been asking after. But yes, he'd sent those over for Guyen's personal inspection yesterday, hadn't he. Had the man read them *already*?

Guyen's face gave no clues. 'I need you to come with me.' The tone could quite easily have accommodated the inference that Holsten was about to be shot for some treason committed against Guyen's one-man regime. Only the lack of an accompanying security detail was reassuring.

'Well, I . . .' Holsten made a vague gesture towards the console before him but, in truth, the work had lost much of its interest for him over the last few days. It was repetitive, it was gruelling, and in a curiously personal way it was depressing. The chance to get a break from it, even in Guyen's company, was inexpressibly attractive. 'What do you need, chief?'

Guyen motioned for him to follow and, after a few turns along the *Gilgamesh*'s corridors, Holsten could guess that they were heading for the shuttle bays. This was not exactly a path that he remembered fondly. Here and there he even saw the odd bullet scar that the maintenance crews had yet to get around to dealing with.

He almost resurrected those long ago/recent days then, almost made the mistake of talking about old times with Guyen. He restrained himself just in time. Odds on, Guyen would just have stared at him blankly, but there was an out-side chance that he actually *would* want to talk about the failed mutiny, and where would that leave Holsten? With that one question that had obsessed his thoughts for those long days after he and Lain were brought back to the *Gil*. As he sat in solitary decontamination – just like Lain and all of Karst's crew – he had turned those events over and over, trying to work out which of Guyen's words and deeds had been bluff, and what had been cold-heartedly meant. He had wanted to talk to Karst about it at the time, but had not been given the chance. How much of the way that desperate rescue mission had gone was Guyen's plan; how much was Karst's improvisation? He had always thought the security chief was a thug and yet, in the end, the man had gone to ridiculous lengths to get the hostages back alive.

I owe you, Karst, Holsten acknowledged, but he did not know whether he owed Guyen.

'Are we . . . ?' he asked the commander's back.

'We are going to the station,' Guyen confirmed. 'I need you to look at something.'

'Some text there, or . . . ?' He envisaged spending the day translating warning notices and labels for an increasingly opaque Guyen.

'You're a classicist. You do more than translations, don't you?' Guyen rounded on him. 'Artefacts, yes?'

'Well, yes, but surely Engineering . . .' Holsten was aware that Guyen had wrong-footed him often enough that he hadn't really finished voicing a properly articulated thought since the man arrived.

'Engineering want a second opinion. I want a second opinion.' They came out into a shuttle bay to find a craft ready and waiting, with open hatch and a pilot kicking her heels beside it, reading something on a pad. Holsten guessed it was one of those approved works that Guyen had released from the *Gil's* capacious library, although there was also a brisk trade in covert copies of unauthorized books – writing and footage supposedly locked down in the system. Guyen would get angry over it, but never seemed able to stem it, and Holsten privately suspected that was because the censorship he had ordered Lain to put in place was never going to be able to keep out the chief culprit – to wit, Lain herself.

'You must be grateful for a chance to actually walk the satellite yourself,' Guyen suggested, as the two of them took their seats and strapped in. 'Footsteps of the ancients and all. A classicist's dream, I'd have thought.'

In Holsten's experience, a classicist's dream was far more about letting someone else do the dangerous work, and then sitting back to write erudite analyses of the works of the ancients or, increasingly as his career had progressed, of other academics' writings. Beyond that, and far beyond anything he might tell Guyen, he had come to a depressing realization: he did not like the ancients any more.

The more he learned of them, the more he saw them not as spacefaring godlike exemplars, as his culture had

275

originally cast them, but as monsters: clumsy, bickering, short-sighted monsters. Yes, they had developed a technology that was still beyond anything Holsten's people had achieved, but it was just as he had already known: the shining example of the Old Empire had tricked Holsten's entire civilization into the error of mimicry. In trying to *be* the ancients, they had sealed their own fate – neither to reach those heights, nor any others, doomed instead to a history of mediocrity and envy.

Their flight to the station was brief, moving from acceleration to deceleration almost immediately, the pilot jockeying with physics as she liaised with the *Gil* and whatever impromptu docking control had been set up on the station.

The station was a series of rings about a gravity-less central cylinder that still housed the most complete Old Empire fusion reactor that anyone had ever seen. Lain's team had managed to restore power to the station with remarkably little difficulty, finding the ancient machines still ready to resume functioning after their millennia-long sleep. It was this seamless and elegant technology that had, by imitation and iteration, spawned the systems of the *Gilgamesh* which had got them this far into space at the cost of only a few per cent of their human cargo.

With some ring sections rotating again, there was something approaching normal gravity within parts of the station, for which Holsten was profoundly grateful. He had not been sure what he would find on stepping out of the shuttle, but this first ring of the station had been thoroughly explored and catalogued, and subsequently colonized by Lain's greatly expanded team of engineers. He and Guyen came out into a wave of energy, bustle and noise, to see the corridors and rooms crowded with off-duty engineers. There was an impromptu canteen serving food, rec rooms where screens had been rigged up to show footage from the *Gil's* archives. Holsten saw games being played, intimate embraces, and even what might have been some sort of dramatic rendition that was cut very short when Guyen was sighted. Under Lain's custodianship the engineers had become a hard-working but irreverent bunch, and Holsten suspected that their Great Leader was not universally respected.

'So where's this thing of yours?' Holsten asked. He was increasingly curious about Guyen's motivations, because it seemed that there was surely nothing a classicist could advise upon that could not have been dealt with just as easily over a remote link. *So why has Guyen hauled me all the way over here?* There were some possible answers, but none he liked. Chief amongst them was the idea that no communications between the station and the *Gilgamesh* were particularly secure. Anyone with a little savvy could theoretically be listening in. Of course, nobody was likely to have anything to say that was of a sensitive nature, were they?

Perhaps they were.

A shiver ran through Holsten as he dogged Guyen's heels through that first ring section, until they arrived at a hatch linking to the next.

Has he found something? He imagined the commander piecing through reports with an eye for who-knew-what. Something had caught his eye, though, surely – something that perhaps nobody else had perceived in quite the same way. And now it was evident that Guyen was keen on keeping it this way.

Which makes me his confidant? It was not a comfortable thought.

They progressed further through the station, from ring to ring, airlock to airlock, the bustle of relaxing engineers giving place to a different, more focused flurry of activity. They were now stepping carefully through those areas of the station that were still being thoroughly investigated. The first sections were reckoned safe now, therefore left to the most junior of Lain's people – often recent awakenees of limited experience – to restore a few final systems or finish the last of the cataloguing. After that, Guyen directed Holsten to get himself into an environment suit, and to keep his helmet on at all times. They would be entering parts of the station where air and gravity were not necessarily guaranteed commodities.

From that point on, everyone they passed was similarly suited up, and Holsten knew that the pace of breaking new ground was limited by the reserves of such equipment that the *Gilgamesh* carried or could manufacture. He and Guyen passed a dwindling number of engineers working on key systems, trying to restore the station's basic life-support to the extent where they could declare this ring section safe for unprotected work. The banter and easy nature of the previous sections were gone, the work efficient and focused.

The next section they reached had gravity but no air, and they walked through a nightmare of intermittent lights and flashing warnings that threatened dire consequences in Imperial C. Engineers, faceless in their environment suits, fought to cure the ravages of time and work out where the old systems had failed, and how to work a repair around the ancient and intimidatingly advanced technology.

We're walking back in time, Holsten thought. Not back to

the days of the Old Empire, but back through the engineers' efforts to restore the station. Once there would have been nothing here, no light, no atmosphere, no power, no gravity at all. Then came Lain, mother goddess in miniature, to bring definition to the void.

'We're crossing to the next ring. It has some power, but they've not got the section rotating,' Guyen cautioned, his voice crisp over the helmet radio.

Holsten fumbled for a moment before remembering how to transmit. 'That's where we're going?'

'Indeed. Lain?'

Holsten started, wondering which of the three suited figures now in sight was the chief engineer. When Lain's voice came over the com, though, it seemed to sync with none of their movements, and he guessed that she was probably elsewhere on the station.

'Hola, chief. You're sure you want to do this?'

'You've already had people go over the section for active dangers,' Guyen pointed out. That would be the first step, Holsten knew – the step he himself would never witness first-hand. Before anyone could start patching up the key systems, a crew would have to go into that lightless, airless place and check to make sure that nothing the ancients had left behind was going to try and kill them.

At least the station hasn't been deliberately rigged to be like that. That had been the bane of the old astronaut-explorers of the past, of course. The ancients had gone down fighting – fighting each other. They had not been idle when it came to making their orbital installations difficult to get into, and often the traps were the last things still functioning on an otherwise dead hunk of spinning metal.

'Chief, you're going somewhere without basic life-support. It doesn't *need* to be actively dangerous,' Lain replied. 'No end of things can go wrong. Who's that with you, anyway? He's not one of mine, is he?'

Holsten wondered where she was observing him from, but then presumably the internal surveillance had proved easier to restore than breathable air.

'Mason, the classicist.'

A pause, then: 'Oh. Hi, Holsten.'

'Hello, Isa.'

'Look, chief,' Lain sounded bothered. 'I said you needed someone to go with you, but I assumed you'd be taking someone who was trained for it.'

'I'm trained for it,' Guyen pointed out.

'*He's* not. I've seen him in zero-G. Look, sit tight and I'll come over—'

'You will not,' Guyen snapped angrily. 'Stick by your post. I know you've got half a dozen people in the next section. Any difficulties and we'll signal them.' He sounded a little too insistent to Holsten.

'Chief—'

'That's an order.'

'Right,' came Lain's voice, and then, 'Fuck, I don't know what the bastard's up to, but you look after yourself.' It took Holsten a startled moment to work out that she must be transmitting only to him. 'Look, I'll send to the tripwire crew and tell them to keep an eye out. Call out if there's any trouble, all right? Yes, the place has been gone over, and they're working to restore full power and all the rest. But just be careful – and whatever you do don't turn anything *on*. We've sent in a team for a first-stage survey of it, but we don't know what most of it actually does. That ring looks like it's set up for some sort of command-and-control, or maybe it's just terraforming central. Either way, no pressing buttons – and you warn me if Guyen looks like he's about to. You remember how to get a dedicated channel?'

To his surprise, Holsten found that he did, prodding at tongue controls that worked just like those in the mask the mutineers had put on him. 'Testing?'

'Good man. Now, you look after yourself, right?'

'I'll try to.'

It did not take long for the classicist's dreams of becoming a space explorer to be cruelly dashed. The environment suits had magnetic boots, which was an idea that Holsten had just sort of accepted when he was a child watching films of bold space explorers, but which proved frustrating and exhausting to actually use. Simply gliding through the chambers of the station like a diver in the ocean also proved considerably more difficult than he had anticipated. In the end, Guyen – who could apparently clamber about the depthless spaces like a monkey – had to run a lanyard from belt to belt so that he could haul Holsten back when the classicist drifted helplessly away.

The interior of that ring – the furthest limit of their expansion through the station – was not properly lit up yet, but there were countless dormant panels and slumbering banks of readouts that glowed their dormancy softly to themselves, and the suit lights were enough to navigate by. Guyen was setting as swift a pace as he could, plainly knowing just where he was going. Holsten's own ignorance in that regard was never far from his mind.

'I have hijacked your suit camera,' came Lain's voice inside his helmet, 'because I want to know what the old man is after.'

At that point Holsten was dangling after Guyen like a balloon, and so he felt he could spare some time for conversation. 'I thought *I* was the old man.'

'Not any more. You've seen him. I don't know what he was doing on the way here, but it looks like he's been around for years more than us.' He heard her draw breath to say more, but then Guyen was slowing down, hauling Holsten closer and then touching him down to the wall so that his boots could get purchase; Lain's voice said, 'Oh, it's *that* thing he likes, is it?'

There was a coffin there – like a suspension chamber with its head end built into the wall. Holsten knew that the station had come with a very limited suspension facility – as far as they had explored it – so it had not been intended for anyone to spend a few lifetimes here. Besides, what would be the point of all this room, all of the complex, sleeping machinery, just to preserve a single human body for posterity?

The pad on Holsten's suit signalled that it had received new information, so he took it out, fumbling in his gloves, and managed to get the data up, seeing the first-pass survey of this room and its contents. The engineers had not known what it was, therefore had noted its basic features, recorded pictures, and moved on. They had also activated some of the consoles in the room, dumped some data for later analysis by someone like Holsten, then thought no more about it. These had been some of the files Guyen had wanted translated. Holsten called them up now, wondering how good his work on them had been. It had been complex technical stuff, even though it had been just a surface fragment of the knowledge locked in here.

Now he scanned those files again, the dense originals and his own computer-assisted translations, along with everything else the original cursory survey had recorded about this room. Guyen was looking at him expectantly.

'I . . . what am I supposed to be doing?'

'You're supposed to be telling me what this thing is.'

'For this, you need me *here*?' Holsten's rare temper sparked a little. 'Chief, I could just—'

'Your translation is mostly incomprehensible,' Guyen began.

'Well, technical details—'

'No, that's all to the good. This way it can be just between you and me. So I want you to go through this again and confirm – tell me just what this is. And we're here specifically so the device can help you understand it.'

Guyen turned back to the coffin and hunched over it, reaching into the toolbelt that he had slung from his suit harness. Holsten's anxiety spiked and he very nearly broadcast his worries directly to Guyen, before remembering to switch channel over to Lain.

'He's turning something on,' he got out, and then the whole array around the coffin lit up like a festival: screens and panels flaring and stuttering into life, and the humanoid space at its heart ghosting with a pale blue glow.

'I see it.' Lain's voice blurred with static, then stabilized. 'Look, I've got my people right outside. Any trouble they'll be all over you. But I want to see.'

So do I, Holsten realized, leaning closer to the displays.

'These are . . . error messages?' Guyen murmured.

'Missing connections . . . The engineers think the main computer was gutted by the virus,' Holsten speculated, 'so all we've got are isolated systems.' And that *all we've got* was still an overstuffed library of esoteric knowledge. 'It looks like it's trying to link up to something that's not there. It's basically listing a whole load of . . . somethings that it can't find.'

Guyen examined the control panels, his bulky, gloved hands approaching the surfaces occasionally but not committing to a touch. 'Get it to tell me what it is,' he said. He had left the channel open, and Holsten was not sure whether those words had been intended for export.

'Listen carefully,' Lain said clearly in Holsten's ear. 'I want you to try something with the panel. It's a routine we developed, when we started up here, for cutting through this sort of shit. Seems to work on most of the kit here. You'll have to blag it to Guyen that it's your idea, or that you read it somewhere on our reports or something.'

'Sure.'

Guyen let him take over at the panel, bathed in the pale illumination from the coffin, and he followed each of Lain's commands carefully, hesitating every time to let her correct him where necessary. The sequence was only fifteen steps, touching the screen carefully to unlock new cascades of options and complaints until he had somehow stripped away all of the device's plaintive demands for its lost links and pared it down to what was left.

Which was . . .

'Emergency upload facility,' Holsten translated, a little uncertainly. He stared at that human-shaped absence at the heart of the machine. 'Upload of what?'

He glanced at Guyen then and saw a swiftly hidden expression on the man's face, clear even within the gloom of his helmet. The commander's face had been all triumph and hunger. Whatever he was really looking for, he had found it here.

4.6 THE MESSENGER WITHIN

Plague has worked its way thoroughly into the heart of Great Nest until physical contact between peer houses has almost ceased. Only the desperate and the starving roam the streets. There have been attacks – the healthy assaulting those they believe to be sick, the hungry stealing food, the incurably deranged attacking whatever their inner demons prompt them to.

And yet the straining strands of the community have not quite parted, the trickling exodus has not become a flood – due in no small part to Portia and her peers. They are working on a cure. They can save Great Nest and, by extension, civilization itself.

Portia has enlisted not only Bianca but every scientist – Temple and otherwise – that she has faith in. This is no time for reserving the glory to her peer group, after all.

And, in contacting them all, she has made sure that they all know who she is, and that she, as instigator, is their leader. Her dictates twang out across Great Nest on taut wires, received and relayed by diligent male attendants. Normally cooperation between peer houses does not work smoothly at this level: too many egos, too many females vying for dominance. The emergency has focused them wonderfully.

This is my new Understanding, Portia had explained to them. *There is a quality that these immune children have that marks them out from their fallen peers. They were born into a plagued city, but they survived. It seems likely, given how long the plague had been rife in their home, that they must have been born from eggs laid by progenitors likewise resistant to the infection. In short, it is a resistance that they inherited. It is an Understanding.*

This prompted a storm of objection. The process by which new Understandings were laid down was not fully understood, but those Understandings related only to knowledge – a recollection of how to do things, or how things were. Where was the evidence that a reaction to a disease could also be passed on to offspring?

These spiderlings are the evidence, Portia had informed them. *If you doubt that, then I have no use for you. Reply to me only if you will help.*

She lost perhaps a third of her correspondents, who have since sought answers elsewhere, and with no success. Portia herself, however, whilst having made advances enough to justify her area of research, is running into the very limits of her people's technology and also the boundaries of their comprehension.

One of the other scientists who chose to support Portia – call her Viola – has studied the mechanism of Understandings for years, and passed on to Portia all she knew: great tangled nets of notes setting out her procedures and results. The spiders are very reliant on the effortless generational spread of knowledge that their Understandings produce. Their written language, a system of knots and ties, is awkward, long-winded and hard to preserve and store, and this has slowed Portia's progress greatly. She cannot wait for off-spring to inherit her colleague's grasp of the subject; she needs that acumen now. Viola herself was initially unwilling to even cross the city, for fear of infection.

Today, confirmation arrived that Viola has entered the second stage of the plague, and knowing that is a keen incentive in Portia's mind: her colleagues are falling one by one to the enemy they seek to defeat. It can only be a matter of time before Portia feels the stirring of it within her own joints.

Bianca is already infected, she believes. In private the maverick scientist has confessed to Portia that she is feeling those elusive first-stage symptoms. Portia has kept her close anyway, knowing that by now there may be no spider in the whole of Great Nest that is not incubating the same disease.

Except for those maddeningly few who are somehow immune.

Thanks to her failing colleague, however, she has a tool formerly denied her. Viola's peer group operates an ant colony that has been nurtured to the task of analysing the physiological stigmata of Understandings.

This is another great advance that Portia's society is built on, and yet one that has become a serious limiter of their further advancement. There are hundreds of tamed ant colonies within Great Nest, not counting those in the surrounds that undertake the day-to-day business of producing food, clearing ground or fending off incursions of wild species. Each colony has been carefully trained, by subtle manipulation of punishment, reward and chemical stimulus, to perform a specific service, giving the great minds of the spiders access to a curious kind of analytical engine, using the cascading decision trees of the colony's own governance as gearing. Each colony is good for a very limited set of related calculations – a vastly skilled yet vastly specialized *idiot savant* – and retraining a community of ants is a long and painstaking task.

However, Viola has already put in the work, and Portia sent her samples from the three captive spiderlings for comparison to the studies Viola had already undertaken of other members of their species. The results were delivered in a veritable rolled carpet of writing, along with Viola's admission of her own infirmity.

Since then, Portia and Bianca have been poring over her copious reasoning, stopping frequently to confer over what Viola may or may not have meant. Their system of writing was originally brought into being to express transient, artistic thoughts – elegant, elaborate and pictorial. It is not ideal for setting down empirical scientific ideas.

Fabian is often in evidence, bringing food and drink and offering his own interpretations when asked. He has a keen mind, for a male, and brings a different perspective. Moreover, he seems to have lost nothing of his vigour and dedication, despite showing a few first-stage symptoms himself. Usually, when any spider comes to believe that she or he is infected, the quality of their service steadily erodes. The problem is so great that even the most undesirable male can find patronage if he has the will to work. Great Nest's society is undergoing curious, painful shifts.

Viola's studies are in another language still, inexpertly rendered in that knotwork script. In her writings, she calls it the language of the body. She explains that every spider's body contains this writing, and that it varies from individual to individual, but not randomly. Viola has experimented on spiderlings out of eggs isolated from clutches where the parentage is known, and has discovered that their internal language is closely related to the parents. This was to have been her grand revelation, in the looked-for years to come, when the completed study would allow her to dominate Great Nest's intellectual life. Portia herself is quite aware of the humbling genius that she is looking at. Viola has uncovered the secret language of Understandings – if it could only be translated.

That is the sticking point. Viola knows enough to state confidently that what her ants can sequence from biopsy samples is the hidden book that resides within each and every spider, but she cannot read it.

However, her ants have a final gift for Portia. There is a passage, in the book of the spiderlings retrieved by Fabian, which is new. Ants of another of Viola's colonies have been trained to compare these hidden books and highlight differences. The same paragraph, never before seen, turns up in each of the three immune infants. This, Viola hypothesizes, may represent their Understanding of how to ward off the plague.

Portia and her fellows are briefly ecstatic, finding themselves on the very brink of success, the epidemic as good as beaten. Viola has one last comment, though, and her spinning is noticeably harder to read by this point.

She points out that, just as she has no way of reading the inner book, so she has no means by which to write on it. Other than allowing the spiderlings to grow and breed a new generation that will grow into a wild and barbaric immunity, this new knowledge is theoretically fascinating, yet practically useless.

There follow some days while the city decays about them, each hour sending the communication strands dancing with the grim news of yet more victims, of peer houses sealed, of the esteemed names of Great Nest who have gone mad and been put down, or who have taken their own lives by poison because to surrender that hard-earned gift of intelligence is worse still. Portia and Bianca are in shock, as if the plague has come early to cripple their minds. They were so close.

It is Bianca who returns to the work first. Her steps stutter and shudder with uncontrollable utterance. She is closer to death, therefore she has less to lose. She pores over Viola's notes while Portia regains her mental fortitude, and then one morning Bianca is gone.

She returns late that night, and has a brief, trembling stand-off with the guardians of the peer house before Portia convinces them to let her back in.

How is it out there? Portia herself does not venture forth any more.

Madness, is Bianca's brief reply. *I saw Viola. She will not last much longer, bbbbbut she was able to tell me. I must show you, while I sssssstill can.* The disease is jumping from leg to leg, sending her speech into sudden, involuntary repeats. She is never still, prowling about the peer house while she fights to form the words, as though trying to escape the thing that is killing her. She claws her way up the taut silk of the walls, and somewhere within her body lies that keening desire to climb, to climb and then to die.

Tell me, Portia insists, following her meandering trail. She sees Fabian following at a respectful distance, and signals him closer because another perspective on whatever Bianca will say can only be useful.

What comes out is pared down to the minimal, the essential, and Portia thinks Bianca has been pondering it on her return journey through the city, knowing that her ability to describe is constantly being eroded by a pestilential tide.

There is a deeper book, she hammers out, stamping each word on to the yielding floor in a shout of footwork. *Viola identifies it. There is a second book in a second code, short and yet full of information, and different, so different. I asked Viola what it was. She says it is the Messenger within us. She says the Messenger is always to be found when new Understandings are laid down. She says it dwells with us in the egg, and grows with us, our invisible guardian, each one of us, she says, she says.* Bianca turns on the spot, her wide, round eyes staring at everything around her, palps trembling in a frenzy of broken ideas. *Where is Viola's treatise?*

Portia guides her to the great unrolled skein that is Viola's life's work, and Bianca, after several false starts, finds this 'deeper book'. It is barely an appendix, a complex tangle of material that Viola has been unable to unravel, because it is written within the body in a wholly alien manner, far more compact, efficient and densely organized than the rest. The spiders cannot know, but there are good reasons for the contrast. This is not the product of natural evolution, or even evolution assisted: this is that which assists. Viola and her ant farm have isolated the nanovirus.

Portia spends a long time, after Bianca has staggered away, in reading and re-reading and doing what her kind have always done best: making a plan.

The next day she sends word to Viola's peer house: she needs the use of their specialized colonies. At the same time she is begging and borrowing the expertise of another half-dozen scientists still willing and able to assist her. She sends Fabian with instructions to her own colonies as well, those that can perform a range of functions, including doing their level best to duplicate any chemicals that they are given a sample of.

Viola's peer house – though their erudite mistress is past helping now – isolate the fragment of the body's book unique to the immune spiderlings, but they do more than this. They isolate the nanovirus as well: the Messenger Within. Precious days later, their males stagger across to Portia's peer house with vats of the stuff – or at least some do. Others are killed on the streets, or simply flee. Great Nest's survival stands on a knife edge.

Portia spends her time in the temple, hearing the voice of the Messenger above, and trying to listen to the Messenger that is within herself. Was it just a conceit of Viola's to use that term? No, she had her reasons. She grasped that what- ever that alien, artificial tangle of language is doing, it has a divine function: drawing them out of the bestial and into the sublime. It is the hand that places Understandings within the mind and tissue of life, so that each generation may become greater than the last. *So that we may know you*, Portia reflects, as she watches that far away light arc across the sky. It seems self-evident now that Bianca has been right all this time. Of course the Messenger is waiting for their reply. This was heresy such a short time ago, but Portia has since looked within herself. *Why should we be made thus, to improve and improve, unless it is to aspire?*

To Portia, as always with her species, her conclusions are a matter of extrapolated logic based on her best comprehen- sion of the principles the universe has revealed to her.

Days later, the ants have produced the first batch of her serum, a complex mixture of the immune spiderlings' genetic fragment and the nanovirus: Messenger and Message circling and circling within that solution.

By this time, over half of Portia's peer house are well into the second stage. Bianca and several others have entered the third, and are confined, each to a separate cell, where they will starve. What else is to be done with them?

Portia knows what else.

Fabian offers to go in her place, but she knows that the late-stage infected will kill a little male like him effortlessly. She rounds up a handful of desperate, determined females, and she takes up her artificial fang with which she will inject her serum at the point where the patient's legs meet the body, close to the brain.

Bianca fights against them. She bites one of Portia's orderlies and injects two full fangs of venom, paralysing her victim instantly. She kicks and staggers and rears up, challenging them all. They rope her and bind her un-gently, turning her on to her back even as her mouthparts flex furiously at them. All language is gone from her, and Portia acknowledges that she does not know if this stage of the plague can even be reversed.

Still, Bianca will be the proof or disproof of that. Portia drives her syringe in.

4.7 NOT PRINCE HAMLET

The influx of new material from the abandoned station had slowed dramatically, every database and store having been raided and transferred over to the *Gilgamesh*. Holsten's cataloguing duties were mostly done, and now he was merely an on-call translator for when the engineers needed help in getting something working.

Most of his time he spent on Vrie Guyen's private project, and if he didn't, Guyen would soon be round wanting to know why.

The ark ship was crawling with unaccustomed life, given that several hundred of its cargo had found themselves prodded back into a waking state light years away from their last memories, given hasty, unsatisfactory explanations of where they were and what needed doing, and then set to work. The ship was *noisy*, and Holsten found himself constantly baffled by the din. Not only was there the shudder and bang of the actual works, but there was the unceasing murmur of *people* doing things like *living* and *talking* and, not to put too fine a point on it, having a good time in a variety of ways. It seemed that everywhere Holsten went he saw impromptu couples – could they be anything *but* impromptu, given their circumstances? – clinched in some manner of embrace.

They made him feel very old, sometimes. They were all so

young, just like all the *Gil's* cargo, save for a few tired old specialists like himself.

They were refitting the ark ship – *and if I feel like this, how old does the* Gilgamesh *feel, eh?* – with all manner of toys ripped out of the station. Not least was a new fusion reactor, which Vitas reckoned would prove more than twice as efficient as the far more recently built original, and be able to sustain economic acceleration for far longer with the fuel available. Other technology was merely being extrapolated, the *Gil's* systems being fine-tuned after the ancient model.

In Holsten's mind ran that same litany: *Coat-tails, coat-tails*. They were still clutching at the receding train of the Old Empire, still twisting themselves into knots to stay securely in its shadow. Even as his compatriots celebrated their newfound bounty, all he saw was a people condemning their descendants to evermore be less than they might have been.

Then the message came from Lain: she wanted him over on the satellite. 'Some sort of dangerous translation or something', to be precise.

Between Guyen's constant pressure and the aggressively exclusive youth of the rest of the human race, Holsten was feeling quite sorry for himself by that time. He was not particularly looking forward to being made fun of, which was apparently what Engineering thought he was there for. He seriously considered ignoring Lain if she wasn't even prepared to ask him properly. In the end it was Guyen that decided him, because a trip to the station would give Holsten some blessed relief from the commander's vulture-like presence.

He signalled to her that he was coming, and found a

shuttle and pilot were ready for him in the bay. On the journey over, he turned the external cameras towards the planet and stared moodily at the fungal grey orb, imagining it reaching upwards, vast building-sized towers of fruiting bodies bloating into the upper atmosphere to seize the tiny intruders that had dared to dispute its complete mastery of the world.

A pair of engineers – from Lain's original Key Crew, he reckoned – were waiting for him at the station end, assuring him that he wouldn't need to suit up.

'All the parts we're still bothered about are stable,' they explained. When Holsten asked them what the problem actually was, they just shrugged, blithely unconcerned.

'Chief'll tell you herself,' was all he got from them.

And finally he was almost unceremoniously shoved into a chamber in the second rotating ring segment, where Lain was waiting.

She was sitting at a table, apparently about to start on a meal, and for a moment he hovered in the hatchway, assuming that his timing was off as usual, before noticing that there were utensils for two.

She raised her eyebrows challengingly. 'Come on in, old man. Got some tens-of-thousands-of-years-old food here. Come and do history to it.'

That actually got him into the room, staring at the unfamiliar food: thick soups or sauces, and greyish chunks that looked uncomfortably as if they might have been hacked from the planet below them. 'You're joking.'

'Nope, food of the ancients, Holsten. Food of the gods.'

'But that's . . . surely it can't still be edible.' He sat himself across from her, staring down in fascination.

'We've been living on it for almost a month now, over here,' she told him. 'Better than the pap the *Gil* churns out.'

A loaded pause came and went, and Holsten looked up sharply as she gave a bitter little laugh.

'My starter gambit worked too well. You're not supposed to actually *be* that interested in the food, old man.'

He blinked at her, studying her face, seeing in it the extra hours she had put in, both here on the station, and in sporadic waking days during the journey from Kern's World, while making sure the ship didn't consume more of its precious cargo by malfunction and error. *We're a good match now*, Holsten realized. *Look at the two of us.*

'So this is . . .' He made a gesture at the assortment of bowls on the table and ended up getting some sort of orange goo on his finger.

'What?' Lain demanded. 'It's nice here, isn't it? All the conveniences: light, heat, air and rotational gravity. This is the lap of luxury, believe me. Hold on, wait a moment.' She fiddled with something at the table edge, and the wall to Holsten's left began to fall away. For a heart-stopping moment he had no idea what was happening, save that the dissolution of the entire station appeared to be imminent. But there was a somewhat clouded transparency left behind after the outer shutters groaned open and, beyond it, the vastness of the rest of creation. And one more thing.

Holsten was staring out at the *Gilgamesh*. He had not seen it from the outside before, not properly. Even when being returned to it after the mutiny, he had passed from shuttle interior to ark ship interior without even thinking about the great outdoors. After all, in space the great outdoors existed mostly to kill you.

'Look, you can see where we're putting the new stuff in. All looks a bit tatty, doesn't it? All those micro-impacts on the way, all that vacuum erosion. The old boy's certainly not what he was,' Lain remarked softly.

Holsten said nothing.

'I thought it would be . . .' Lain started. She tried a smile, then began another one. He realized that she was unsure of him, nervous even.

He navigated his way across the table to touch her hand, because frankly neither of them was good with those sort of words, nor were they young enough to have the patience to fumble through them.

'I can't believe how fragile he looks.' The future, or lack of it, decided by the fate of that metal egg – tatty, patched and, from this vantage point, how *small* the *Gilgamesh* looked.

They ate thoughtfully, Lain progressing from brief moments where she talked far too fast, trying to force on a conversation for the patent reason that she felt they should be having one, then subsiding into longer stretches of companionable quiet.

At last, Holsten grinned at her, out of one of those periodic silences, feeling the youth of the expression stretch his face. 'This is good.'

'I hope it is. We're shipping tons of the stuff over to the *Gil*.'

'I don't mean the food. Not just that. Thank you.'

After they had eaten, and with the rest of Lain's crew tactfully out of sight and out of mind, they retired to another room she had carefully prepared. It had been a long time since their previous liaison on the *Gilgamesh*. It had been centuries, of course – long, cold spacefaring centuries. But it *seemed* a long time, also. They were part of a species that had become unmoored from time, only their personal clocks left with any meaning for them while the rest of the universe turned to its own rhythms and cared nothing for whether they lived or died.

There had been those back on Earth who claimed the universe cared, and that the survival of humanity was important, destined, *meant*. They had mostly stayed behind, holding to their corroding faith that some great power would weigh in on their behalf if only things became so very bad. Perhaps it had: those on the ark ship could never know for sure. Holsten had his own beliefs, though, and they did not encompass salvation by any means other than the hand of mankind itself.

'What's he after?' Lain asked him later, as they lay side by side beneath a coverlet that had perhaps been some ancient terraformer's counterpane thousands of years before.

'I don't know.'

'I don't know either.' She frowned. 'That worries me, Holsten. He's even got his own engineers doing all the work, you know that? He took his pick from the cargo, woke up a bunch of second-stringers and made them his own personal tech crew. Now they're installing all that stuff you're helping him with, fitting the *Gil* with it. And I don't know what it does. I don't like having things on my ship that do things I don't know about.'

'Are you asking me to betray the commander's trust?' Holsten was joking as he said it, but then he was suddenly stung by the thought, 'Is that what this is about?'

Lain stared at him. 'Do you think that?'

'I don't know what to think.'

'What this is *about*, old man, is me wanting to scratch an itch without messing up the way my crew works and . . .' He could hear her trying to harden the edge in her voice, and hear it crack a little, even as she did so. 'And you know what? I've been on my own a lot over the last . . . what? Two hundred fucking years, is what. I've been on my own, walking around the *Gil* and keeping him together. Or with some of my crew, sometimes, to fix stuff. Or sometimes Guyen was there, like that's better than being on your own. And there was all that mad stuff . . . the mutiny, the planet . . . and I feel like I forget how to talk to people, sometimes, when it's not – not the job. But you . . .'

Holsten raised an eyebrow.

'You're fucking awful at talking to people too,' she finished viciously. 'So maybe when you're around it doesn't feel so bad.'

'Thank you very much.'

'You're welcome.'

'Guyen's thing, it's for uploading people's brains into a computer.' It felt oddly good for him to no longer be the sole custodian of that information. Otherwise, only Guyen knew, as far as Holsten was aware. Even his tame engineers were just working to rote, each on their own piece.

Lain considered that. 'I'm not sure if that's a great thing.'

'It could be very useful.' Holsten's tone of voice did not even convince himself.

Lain merely made a sound – not a word, not anything really – just to show him she'd heard him. It left Holsten turning over in his mind what little he had learned about the device from the technical manuals Guyen had set him to work on. They had all been written for people who already *knew* what the device did, of course. There was no handy moment when the authors had stopped and gone back to explain the basics for their unthinkably distant monkey descendants.

Holsten was becoming sure that he now knew what the upload facility was, though. More, he thought that he might have seen the result of one, and what happened when someone was mad enough to make themselves its subject.

For out there, in the distant dark around another world, in her silent metal coffin, was Doctor Avrana Kern.

4.8 AGE OF PROGRESS

Ever afterwards, Bianca has suffered from momentary fits, stumblings in speech and gait, sudden epilepsies when she is cut adrift from her surroundings for varying periods of time, her legs drumming and spasming as if trying urgently to impart a message in some idiolectic code.

But she has survived the plague and, when a fit is not upon her, retained her mind. For Viola, whose biochemical genius furnished the means, the cure came too late. Many others, great minds, great warriors, leading females of peer houses, starving males in the gutter, all have been struck down. Great Nest has been saved, but thousands of its inhabitants were not so lucky. Other cities were similarly affected, even with production of the cure taking over the work of every suitable ant colony, and the theoretical basis being sung down the lines that link the spider communities together. The disaster has been averted, but narrowly. It is now a new world, and Portia's people recognize the fragility of their place in it. A great many things are poised on the point of change.

It is not Portia herself who first grasps the wider import of her cure. It is hard to say which scientist was first to the mark: it is one of those ideas that seems simultaneously to be everywhere, exciting every enquiring mind. Portia's treatment has allowed living adult spiders to benefit from a foreign Understanding. Yes, what was transferred was an immunity, but surely the process would work with other Understandings, if they can only be separated out and their page noted in Viola's great book of the body. No longer will the spread of knowledge be held down by the slow march of generations or by laborious teaching.

The need for this technology is great. The depredations of the plague have made Understandings hard to find: where once a given idea might be held within scores of minds, now there are just a handful at best. Knowledge has become more precious than ever.

It is only a few years after the plague that the first idea is transferred between adults. A somewhat garbled Understanding of astronomy is imparted to a male test subject (as are all such, given some failures in earlier experiments). From there on, any spider may learn anything. Every scientist of Portia's generation and beyond will stand on the shoulders of the giants that she chooses to reside within her. What one knows, any can know, for a price. An economy of modular, tradable knowledge will swiftly develop.

But that is not all.

After she is recovered, Portia presents Bianca to the Temple. She explains about her fellow's contribution to the cure. Bianca is permitted to address the assembled priestesses.

There has been a shift of orthodoxy in the wake of the plague. Everyone is having to stretch their minds to fill the gaping void left by all those who did not survive. Old ideas are being revisited, old prohibitions reconsidered. There is a great feeling of destiny, but it is a self-made destiny. They have passed the test. They are their own saviours. They wish to communicate something to that one point of intellect outside their sphere: the most basic, essential signal.

They wish to tell the Messenger, *We are here*.

Bianca's battery, in and of itself, does not make a radio transmitter. Whilst the experiments with the transmission of Understandings between spiders progress, so does the investigation into the transmission of vibrations across the invisible web that is strung from their world to the distant satellite and beyond.

Years later, an ageing Bianca and Portia are amongst a crowd of the intimates of the temple, now ready to speak to the unknown, to cast their electromagnetic voice into the ether. The replies to the Messenger's mathematical problems – that every spider knows and understands – are ready for transmission. They wait for the Messenger to appear in the night sky above, and then they send that unequivocal first transmission.

We are here.

Within a second of the last solution being sent, the Messenger ceases its own transmissions, throwing the whole of Portia's civilization into a panic that their hubris has angered the universe.

Several fraught days later, the Messenger speaks again.

4.9 EX MACHINA

The signal from the green planet resonated through the Brin 2's Sentry Pod like an earthquake. The ancient systems had been waiting for just this moment – it seemed forever. Protocols laid down in the days of the Old Empire had gathered dust through the ages, through the entire lifespan of the new species that was even now announcing its presence. They had grown corrupted. They had lost their relevance, been overwritten, been infiltrated by the diseased spread of the uploaded Kern persona that the Sentry Pod had been incubating like a culture all these years.

The systems received the signal, checked over the sums and found them within tolerance, recognized that a critical threshold had been passed with respect to the planet below. Its purpose, rusty with aeons-long disuse, was abruptly relevant again.

For a recursive, untimed moment, the systems of the Sentry Pod – the sea of calculation that boiled behind the human mask of Eliza – were unable to make a decision. Too much had been lost, misfiled, edited out of existence within its mind.

It attacked the discontinuities within its own systems. Whilst it was not truly a self-aware artificial intelligence, it nevertheless knew itself. It restored itself, worked around insoluble problems, reached the right conclusion by estimate and circuitous logic.

It did its best to awaken Avrana Kern.

The distinction between living woman, uploaded personality construct and pod systems was not finely drawn. They bled into one another, so that the frozen sleep of the one leaked nightmarish dreams into the cold logic of the others. A lot of time had passed. Not all of Avrana Kern remained viable. Still, the pod did its best.

Doctor Kern awoke, or she dreamt of waking, and in her dream Eliza hovered at her bedside like an angel and provided a miraculous annunciation.

This day is a new star seen in the heavens. This day is born a saviour of life on Earth.

Avrana fought with the trailing weeds of her horrors, struggling to resurface enough to understand what was really being told to her. She had not been truly conscious for some time – had she ever been? She had confused recollections of some dark presence, intruders attacking her charge, the planet below that had become her purpose, the sum total of her legacy. A traveller had come to steal the secret of her project – to rob her of the immortality represented by her new life, by her progeny, by her monkey-children. Had it? Or had she dreamed it? She could not separate the fact from the long cold years of sleep.

'I was supposed to be dead,' she told the watchful pod. 'I was supposed to be locked away, oblivious. I was never supposed to dream.'

'Doctor, the passage of time appears to have led to a homogenization of information systems within the Sentry

Pod. I apologize for this, but we are operating beyond our intended parameters.'

The Sentry Pod was designed to lie dormant for centuries. Avrana remembered that much. How long would it take the virus to spark intellect into generations of monkeys? Did that mean that her experiment was a failure?

No, they had signalled at last. They had reached out and touched the ineffable. And time was suddenly no longer the currency it once had been. She remembered now why she was in the Sentry Pod at all, performing this function that had been meant for someone far more disposable. Time didn't matter. Only the monkeys mattered, because the future was theirs now.

Yet those troubling half-dreams recurred to her. In her dream there had come a primitive boat of travellers claiming to be her kin, but she had looked at them and seen them for what they truly were. She had scanned through their histories and their understandings. They were the mould that had grown on the corpse of her own people. They were hopelessly corrupted with the same sickness that had killed Kern's own civilization. Better to start anew with monkeys.

'What do you want of me?' she demanded of the entity/ entities that surrounded her. She looked into their faces and saw an infinite progression of stages between her and the cold logic of the pod systems, and nowhere could she say where she herself ended and where the machine began.

'Phase two of the uplift project is now ready,' Eliza explained. 'Your authority is required to commence.'

'What if I'd died?' Avrana choked out. 'What if I'd rotted? What if you couldn't wake me?'

'Then your uploaded persona would inherit your responsibilities and authority,' Eliza replied, and then, as if remembering that it was supposed to show a human face, 'but I am glad that has not occurred.'

'You don't know what "glad" means,' but, even as she said this, Kern was not sure that it was true. There was enough of her smeared up that continuum towards the life electronic that perhaps Eliza knew more of human emotion than Kern herself was now left with.

'Proceed with the next phase. Of course, proceed with the next phase,' she snapped into the silence that followed. 'What else are we here for? What else is there?' *In a very real sense, indeed, what else is there?*

She remembered when the false humans, that disease that had outlived her people, had approached the planet. Had they? Had that actually happened? She had spoken to them. The *her* that had interacted with them must have recognized enough humanity in them to bargain, to spare them, to allow them to rescue their own. Each time she was awoken, it seemed some different assortment of thoughts took the helm of her mind. She had been in a giving vein, then. She had recognized them to be human enough to show mercy to.

She had been sentimental that day. Thinking back on it, she regained those memories of how it had felt. And they had been as good as their word, she assumed, and they had gone. There was no sign of them, or of any transmissions, within the solar system.

She had an uncomfortable feeling that it was not that simple. She had a feeling that they would be back. And now she had so much more to lose. What devastation would those false humans wreak on her nascent monkey civilization?

She would have to harden her heart.

Phase two of the uplift program was a contact exercise. Once the monkeys had developed their own singular culture to the extent that they could send radio transmissions, they were ready for contact with the wider universe. *And now I am the wider universe.* The Sentry Pod would begin developing a means of communication, starting with the simplest binary notation and using each stage to bootstrap up to a more complex language, just as if a computer was being programmed from scratch. It would take time, depending on the willingness and ability of the monkeys to learn, generation to generation.

'But first send them a message,' Avrana decided. For all that the inhabitants of the planet could not possible understand her, right now, she wanted to set the tone. She wanted them to understand what they were in for when she and they could finally communicate.

'Awaiting your message,' Eliza prompted.

'Tell them this,' Avrana declared. Perhaps, in their simian ignorance, they would record it and later re-read it, and understand it all.

Tell them this: I am your creator. I am your god.

5
SCHISM

5.1 THE PRISONER

Holsten was pondering his relationship with time.

Not long ago, it seemed that time was becoming something that happened to other people – or, as other people had then been in short supply, to other parts of the universe. Time was a weight that he seemed to have been cut free from. He stepped in and out of the forward path of its arrow, and was somehow never struck down. Lain might call him 'old man' but in truth the span of objective time that had passed between his nativity and this present moment was ridiculous, unreal. No human ever bestrode time as he had done, in his journey of thousands of years.

Now, in his cell, time weighed him down and dragged at his heels, chaining him to the grindingly slow pace of the cosmos where before he had leapt ahead across the centuries, skipping between the bright points of human history.

They had hauled him from the suspension chamber and thrown him in this cage. It had been twenty-seven days before anyone gave him even an indication of what was going on.

At first, he'd thought it was a dream of the mutineers kidnapping him. He had been quite sanguine before he realized that the people dragging him through the *Gilgamesh* were not the long-dead Scoles and company, but total strangers. Then he had entered the living quarters.

The smell had assailed him – an utterly unfamiliar, sick reek that even the *Gil's* ventilation had not been able to purge. It was the scent of close-packed human habitation.

He had a blurred recollection of a former operations room now festooned with grey cloth, a veritable shanty town of makeshift drapes and hangings and close partitions – and people, lots of people.

The sight had shocked him. Some part of him had grown comfortably used to being part of a small and select population, but he registered at least a hundred unfamiliar faces in that brief moment. The press of them, the closeness of their living conditions, the smell, the sheer raucous noise, all of it merged into the sense of confronting a hostile creature, something fierce and inimical and all-consuming.

There had been children.

His wits had started to come to him by then, with the thought: *The cargo's got loose!*

His captors all wore robes of the same sheer, grey material that the squatters were also using for their amateurish tents – something that the *Gilgamesh* had presumably been storing for some other purpose entirely, or that had been synthesized in the workshops. Holsten had spotted a few shipsuits during his hurried passage through the living quarters, but most of the strangers had been wearing these shapeless, sagging garments. They were all thin, malnourished, underdeveloped. They wore their hair long, very long, past the shoulders. The whole scene had a weirdly primal feel to it, a resurgence of the primitive days of mankind.

They had seized him, locked him up. This was not just some room in the *Gil* that they had secured. Within one of the shuttle bays they had welded together a cage, and this had become his home. His captors had fed him and sporadically removed the pail provided for his other functions, but for twenty-seven days that was all he had. They seemed to be waiting for something.

For his part, Holsten had eyed the shuttle airlock and begun to wonder if his future did not include some kind of space-god sacrifice. Certainly the manner of his captors was not simply that of oppressors or kidnappers. There was a curious respect, almost reverence to be observed amongst some of them. They did not like to touch him – those who had manhandled him to the cage had worn gloves – and they refused to meet his eyes. All this reinforced his growing belief that they were a cult and he was some sort of sacred offering, and that the last hope for humanity was even now vanishing away beneath a tide of superstition.

Then they set him to work, and he realized that he must surely be dreaming.

One day he woke up in his cell to find that his captors had brought in a mobile terminal: a poor, lobotomized sort of a thing, but at least a computer of sorts. He leapt on it eagerly, only to find it linked with nothing, entirely self-contained. There was data there, though, files of familiar proportions written in a dead language that he was frankly coming to loathe.

He looked up to find one of his captors peering in – a thin-faced man, at least a decade younger than Holsten but small-framed like most of them and with pockmarked skin suggesting the aftermath of some manner of disease. As with all these bizarre strangers, he had long hair, but it was carefully plaited and then coiled at the back of his neck in an intricate knot.

'You must explain it.'

It was the first time any of them had spoken to Holsten. He had begun to think that he and they shared no common language.

'Explain it,' Holsten repeated neutrally.

'Explain it so it can be understood. Make it into words. This is your gift.'

'Oh, for . . . you want me to translate it?'

'Even so.'

'I need access to the *Gil*'s main systems,' Holsten stated.

'No.'

'There are translation algorithms I wrote. There are my earlier transcriptions I'll need to refer to.'

'No, you have all you need in *here*.' With great ceremony the robed man pointed at Holsten's head. 'Work. It is commanded.'

'Commanded by whom?' Holsten demanded.

'Your master.' The robed man stared coldly at Holsten for a moment, then suddenly broke off his gaze, as though embarrassed. 'You will work or you shall not eat. This is commanded,' he muttered. 'There is no other way.'

Holsten had sat down at the terminal and looked at what they wanted from him.

That was the beginning of his understanding. Obviously he *was* dreaming. He was trapped within a dream. Here was a nightmarish environment, both familiar and unfamiliar. Here was a task without logic that was nonetheless the cracked mirror of what he had undertaken when last awake, when the *Gilgamesh* had been in orbit over the grey planet. He was in the suspension chamber still, and dreaming.

But of course one did not dream in suspension. Even Holsten remembered enough about the science to know that. One did not dream because the cooling process brought brain activity to an absolute minimum, a suspension of even the subconscious movements of the mind. This was necessary because unchecked brain activity during the enforced idleness of a long sleep would drive the sleeper insane. Such a situation arose out of faulty machinery. Holsten remembered clearly that they had lost human cargo already: perhaps this is how it had been for those martyrs.

It was a strangely calming revelation to know that his suspension capsule must be failing at some deep, mechanical level, and that he was lost inside his own mind. He tried to imagine himself fighting with the sleeping-chamber, crawling up the steep incline of ice and medication so as to wake up, beating on the unyielding inside of the coffin, buried alive within a ship-shaped monument to mankind's absurd refusal to give up.

None of it got the adrenaline going. His mind stubbornly refused to leave that makeshift cell in the shuttle bay, as he worked slowly through the files he had been left with. And of course it was a dream, because they were more of the same: more information about Guyen's machine, the upload facility the man had wrenched whole from the abandoned terraform station. Holsten was dreaming an administrative purgatory for himself.

Days went by, or at least he ate and slept and they slopped out his pail. He had no sense of anything functional happening outside the cage. He could not see what these people were *for*, save living day to day and forcing him to translate, and producing more of themselves. They seemed a weirdly orphan population: like lice infesting the ark ship, that the *Gil* might any moment purge from its interiors. They must have begun life as cargo, but how long ago? How many generations?

They continued to regard him with that curious reverence, as though they had caged a demigod. It was only when they came to shave his head that he fully understood that. They, none of them, seemed to cut their hair, but it was important to them that his scalp was cropped back to fuzz. It was a sign of his status, his difference. He was a man of an earlier time, one of the originals.

As is Vrie Guyen. The unhappy thought finally dispelled his somewhat fond thought that this might all be some hibernation nightmare. Wading his way through tangled philosophical treatises concerning the implications of the upload process, he had a window into Guyen's tightly clenched, control-hungry mind. He began to assemble the sketchiest possible picture of what might be going on; of what might have *gone wrong*, therefore.

Then one day they opened his cage, a handful of robed figures, and led him out. He was not finished on his current project, and there was a tension about his keepers that was new. His mind immediately boiled with all manner of potential fates they could be intending for him.

They moved him out of the hangar and into the corridors of the *Gilgamesh*, still not speaking. They seemed to lack the show of reverence in which they had previously held him, which he reckoned could not bode well.

Then he saw the first bodies: a man and a woman collapsed in their path like string-cut marionettes, the textured flooring sticky with a slick of blood. They had been hacked at with knives, or at least that was Holsten's impression. He was hurried on past them, his escorts – captors – paying no obvious heed to the dead. He tried to question them, but they just hauled him along quicker.

He considered struggling, shouting, protesting, but he was scared. They were all solidly made people, bigger than most of the grey ship-lice he had observed so far. They had knives in their belts, and one had a long plastic rod with a blade melted into the end: these were the ancient tools of the hunter-gatherers remade from components torn from a spaceship.

It had all been handled so swiftly and confidently that only right at the end did he realize that he had been kidnapped: wrested from one faction by another. At once, everything became worse than he had thought. The *Gilgamesh* was not just crawling with crazy descendants of awoken cargo, but they had already begun fighting each other. It was the curse of the Old Empire, that division of man against man that was the continual brake on human progress.

He was hustled past sentries and guards, or so he took them to be: men and women, some in shipsuits, some in makeshift robes, others in piecemeal home-made armour, as though at any moment someone would be arriving to judge the world's least impressive costume competition. It should have been ridiculous. It should have been pathetic. But, looking into their eyes, Holsten was chilled by their steely purpose.

They brought him into one of the ship's workshop rooms, housing a score of terminals, half of them dead, the rest flickering fitfully. There were people working on them – real technical work befitting real civilized people – and it looked to Holsten as though they were fighting for control, engaged in some colossal virtual battle on an invisible plane.

At the far end of the room was a woman with short-cut hair, a little older than Holsten. She wore a shipsuit that had been fitted out with plastic scales and plates, like somebody's joke idea of a warrior queen, if only she had not looked so very serious. There was a ragged, healed scar about her chin, and a long pistol was thrust through her belt, the first modern weapon Holsten had seen.

'Hello, Holsten,' she said, and his interpretation of what he was seeing suddenly flipped like a card turning over.

'Lain?' he demanded.

'Now you've got that look on your face,' she observed, after giving him enough time to get over his surprise. 'That one that's sort of "I have no idea what's going on", and frankly I can't seriously believe that. You're supposed to be the smart guy, after all. So how about you tell me what you know, Holsten.' She sounded partly like the woman Holsten remembered, but only if that woman had been living hard and rough for some time.

He gave the request due consideration. A lot of him genuinely wanted to disavow any knowledge, but she was right: that would be self-serving mendacity. *I'm just a poor academic doing what I'm told. I'm not responsible.* He was beginning to think that he was indeed, in part, responsible. Responsible for whatever was happening now.

'Guyen's taken over,' he hazarded.

'Guyen's the commander. He's already, what, *over*. Come on, Holsten.'

'He's woken up a whole load of cargo.' Holsten glanced at Lain's villainous-looking crew. Some of them he thought he recognized as her engineers. Others could well be more of the same cargo that Guyen had apparently now pressed into service. 'I'd guess he started on that a while ago – looks like they're maybe two, three generations down the line? Is that even possible?'

'People are good at making more people,' Lain confirmed. 'Fuckwit never thought that one through, or maybe he did. They're like a cult he's got. They know fuck all but what he's told them, yeah? Any of the originals from cargo who might have argued, they're long gone. These skinny little creeps were basically raised on stories of Guyen. I've heard some of them talking, and they're fucked up, seriously. He's their saviour. Every time he went back into suspension, they had a legend about his return. It's all kinds of messianic shit with them.' She spat disgustedly. 'So tell me for why, Holsten.'

'He had me working on the upload facility taken from the station.' A little of the academic crept back into Holsten's unsteady tones. 'There was always a suggestion that the ancients had found out how to store their minds electronically, but the EMP phase of their war must have wiped the caches out, or at least we never found any of them. It's not clear what they actually used it for, though. There's very little that's even peripheral reference. It didn't seem to be a standard immortality trick—'

'Spare us!' Lain broke in. 'So, yes, Guyen wants to live forever.'

Holsten nodded. 'I take it you're not in favour.'

'Holsten: it's Guyen. Forever. Guyen forever. Two words that do not sit well together.'

He glanced at her confederates, wondering if things here in Lain's camp had got to the point where dissent was punishable. 'Look, I understand it's not the most pleasant idea, but he's got us this far. If he wants to load his mind into some piece of ancient computing, then are we definitely sure that's something worth, you know, *killing* people over?' Because Holsten was still thinking a little about those crumpled bodies he had seen, the price of his freedom.

Lain put on an expression to show that she was considering this viewpoint. 'Sure, fine, right. Except two things. One, I only got one look at his new toy before he and I had our falling out, but I don't reckon that thing's a receptacle for minds: it's just the translator. The only place he can *go* is the *Gilgamesh*'s main system, and I seriously do not think that it's set up to keep doing all of its ship-running with a human mind shoved into it. Right?'

Holsten considered his relatively extensive understanding of the upload facility. 'Actually, yes. It's not a storage device, the thing we took from the station. But I'd thought he'd got something else from there . . . ?'

'And have you seen any of your old files that suggest he has?'

A grimace. 'No.'

'Right.' Lain shook her head. 'Seriously, old man, did you not think about what it was all meant for, when you were doing his work?'

Holsten spread his hands. 'That's unfair. It was all . . . I had no reason to think that there was anything *wrong*. Anyway, what's your second thing?'

'What?'

'Two things, you said. Two reasons.'

'Oh, yes, he's completely nut-bucket crazy. So that's what you're diligently working to preserve. An utter god-complex lunatic.'

Guyen? Yes, a bit of a tyrant, but he had the whole human race in his hands. Yes, not an easy man to work with, someone who kept his plans to himself. 'Lain, I know that you and he . . .'

'Don't get on?'

'Well . . .'

'Holsten, he's been busy. He's been busy for a very long time since we left the grey planet. He's set up his fucking cult and brainwashed them into believing he's the great hope of the universe. He's got this machine mostly up and running. He's tested it on his own people – and believe me that's not gone well, which is why it's still only *mostly* up and running. But he's close now. He has to be.'

'Why *has* to be?'

'Because he looks like he's a fucking *hundred*, Holsten. He's been up and about for maybe fifty years, on and off. He told his cultists he was God, and when he woke up next time they told him he was God, and that little loop has gone round and round until he himself believes it. You see him, after they woke you?'

'Just his people.'

'Well, believe me, any part of his brain that you might recognize abandoned ship a long time ago.' Lain looked into Holsten's face, hunting out any residual sympathy there for the commander. 'Seriously, Holsten, this is his plan: he wants to put a copy of his brain into the *Gil*. He wants to *become* the *Gil*. And you know what? When he's done it, he won't need the cargo. He won't need most of the ship. He won't need life-support or anything like that.'

'He's always had the best interests of the ship at heart,' said Holsten defensively. 'How do you know—?'

'Because it's already *happening*. Do you know what this ship was *not* designed for? Several hundred people living on it for about a century. Wear and tear, Holsten, like you wouldn't believe. A *tribe* of people who don't know how anything actually works getting into places they're not supposed to be, buoyed up by their sincere belief that they're doing God's work. Things are falling apart. We're running out of supplies even with what we took from the station. And they just go on eating and fucking, because they *believe* Guyen will lead them to the promised land.'

'The green planet?' Holsten said softly. 'Maybe he will.'

'Oh, sure,' Lain scoffed. 'And that's where we're heading all right. But, unless things get back under control and people go back to the freezer, Guyen'll be the only one to get there – him and a shipful of corpses.'

'Even if he does manage to upload himself, he'll need people to fix him.' Holsten wasn't sure precisely why he was defending Guyen, unless it was that he had long made a profession out of disagreeing with just about every proposition put in front of him.

'Yeah, well.' Lain rubbed at the back of her neck. 'There was all that auto-repair system business we took from the station.'

'I didn't know about that.'

'It was priority for my team. Seemed like a good idea at the time. I know, I know – conniving at our own obsolescence. It's up and running, too, or looks like it. But, from what I saw, it's not dealing with the cargo or even most of the systems we need. It's only set up for those parts of the ship Guyen's interested in. The non-living parts. Or that's the best impression I got, before I took my leave.'

'After Guyen woke you.'

'He wanted me to be part of his grand plan. Only, when he gave me access to the *Gilgamesh*, I found out too much way too fast. Some seriously cold stuff, Holsten. I'll show you.'

'You're still in the system?'

'It's all over the ship, and Guyen's not good enough to lock me out . . . Now you're wondering why I haven't screwed him over from inside the computer.'

Holsten shrugged. 'Well, I was, yes, actually.'

'I told you he's been testing the upload thing? Well, he's had some partial successes. There are . . . *things* in the system. When I try and cut Guyen out, or fuck with him, they notice me. They come and start fucking right back. Guyen, I could handle, but these are like . . . retarded little AI programs that think they're still people. And they're Guyen's, most of them.'

'Most of them?'

Lain looked unhappy – or rather, unhappier. 'Everything's going to crap, Holsten. The *Gil*'s already starting to come apart at the system level. We're on a spaceship, Holsten. Have you any idea how fucking *complex* that is? How many different subsystems need to work properly just to keep us alive? At the moment, it's actually the auto-repair that's keeping everything ticking over, rerouting around the cor-rupted parts, patching what it can – but it's got limits.

Guyen's pushing those limits, diverting resources to his grand immortality project. So we're going to stop him.'

'So . . .' Holsten looked from Lain to her crew, the old faces and the new. 'So I know about the upload facility. So you got me out.'

Lain just looked at him for a long moment, fragments of expression burning fitfully across her face. 'What?' she said at last. 'I'm not allowed to just rescue you, because you're my friend?' She held his gaze long enough that he had to look away, obscurely ashamed of what was objectively an entirely reasonable paranoia he felt about her, about Guyen, and about near enough everything else.

'Anyway, get yourself cleaned up. Get yourself fed,' she instructed him. 'Then you and I have an appointment.'

Holsten's eyebrows went up. 'With who?'

'Old friends.' Lain smiled sourly. 'The whole gang's together again, old man. How about that?'

5.2 IN GOD'S COUNTRY

Portia stretches and flexes her limbs, feeling the newly hardened sheen of her exoskeleton and the constricting net of the cocoon she has woven about herself. The urge came at an inconvenient time, and she put it off as long as she could, but the cramping tightness at every joint had eventually became unbearable and she was forced to go into retirement: a moon's-span of days out of the public eye, fretting and fidgeting as she split her way out of her cramped old skin and let her new skeleton dry out and find its shape.

During her lying-in she has been attended by various members of her peer house, which is a dominant force now in Great Nest. There are two or three others who, as a union, could challenge the hold of Portia's family, but they are seldom friends with one another. Portia's *agents provocateurs* ensure that they are kept constantly fighting over second place.

The political realities of Great Nest are finely balanced just now, however. Despite the reports brought to her daily during her lying-in, Portia knows there will be dozens of key pieces of information that she will have to catch up with. Thankfully, there is a ready mechanism for doing that.

Portia is the greatest priestess of the Messenger that Great Nest has, but a month out of circulation will have given many of her sisters ideas. They will have been talking to that fleet, all-important light in the sky, receiving the bizarre, garbled wisdom of the universe, and using it for their own benefit. They will have been taking over the grand, often incomprehensible projects ordered by the voice of God. Portia will have to jostle to recover her old prominence.

She descends to the next chamber, a gaggle of younger females attending her. A flicker of her palps and a male is brought in. He has lived a busy month, and been present at gatherings that his gender are usually banned from. Everywhere that Portia might have gone, he was brought by her adherents. He has had every missive, every discovery and reversal, every proclamation of God patiently explained to him. He has been well fed, pampered; he has wanted for nothing.

Now, one of the females brings forward a bulging bulb of silk. Within is the distilled Understanding that the last month has added to this male. It comprises an intelligence report which, if delivered in any conventional way, would be interminable in its detail. That single draught contains enough secrets of Portia's peer house to hand Great Nest on a platter to any of her enemies.

She drinks, the fluid thick with learning, the bulb held within her palps as she carefully drains its contents, before passing it to her subordinates to be destroyed. Already she feels a flutter of discord inside her as the nanovirus she has just ingested begins to fit the purloined knowledge into place within her own mind, accessing the structure of her brain and copying in the male's memories. Within a day and a night she will know all that he knows, and likely she will have lost some unfrequented mental pathways too, some obsolete skill or distant recollection reconfigured into the new and the necessary.

I will send word about him. She indicates the male. Once she is sure that the new Understandings have taken, the male will be disposed of – killed and eaten by one of Portia's clique. He knows too much, quite literally.

Portia's society has come some way since the primitive days when the females ate their mates as often as not, but perhaps not so very far. The killing of males under the protection of another peer house is a crime that demands restitution; the needless killing of any male garners sufficient social disapprobation that it is seldom practised, and the culprits usually shunned as wasteful and lacking that golden virtue of self-control. However, to kill a male for a good reason, or after coitus, remains acceptable, despite occasional debates on the subject. This is simply the way things are, and the conservation of tradition is important in Great Nest these days.

Great Nest is a vast forest metropolis. Hundreds of square kilometres of great trees are festooned with the angled silk dwellings of Portia's kin, constantly being added to and remodelled as each peer house's fortunes advance or decline. The greatest of the spider clans dwell in the mid-level – shielded from the extremes of weather, but suitably distant from the lowly ground where those females without a peer group must fight for leg-room with a swarm of half-savage feral males. In between the peer houses are the workshops of artisans who produce that dwindling stock of items that ants cannot be bred to manufacture, the studios of artists who weave and craft and construct elegant knot-script, and the laboratories of scientists of a score of disciplines. Beneath the ground, amongst the roots, crawl the interlocking networks of ants, each nest to its own specialized task. Other, larger, nests radiate out from the metropolis's limits, engaged in lumberjacking, mining, smelting and industrial manufacture. And, on occasion, war. To fight the *other* is something that every ant colony can remember how to do, if the need arises, although Great Nest, like its rivals, has specialist soldiers as well.

Portia, on her way to temple, feels fragments of current affairs falling into place within her. Yes, there have been further troubles with Great Nest's neighbours: the lesser nests – Seven Trees, River Chasm, Burning Mountain – they are testing the boundaries of territory once again, jealous of the supremacy of Portia's home. It is likely that there will be a new war, but Portia is not concerned about the result. Her people can muster far more ants – and far better designed ants – for the fight ahead.

The sheer size of Great Nest necessitates a public transport system in the higher reaches. The central temple where Portia holds sway is some distance from the site of her lying-in. She is aware that the transporting of things is the province of God, and among God's troubling, hard-to-understand plans are various means of moving from place to place at great speed, but so far no peer house, no city, has succeeded in realizing any of them. The spiders have made their own arrangements in the interim, albeit with a cringing awareness that they are inadequate compared to the Divine Plan.

Portia boards a cylindrical capsule that is strung along a thick, braided strand, and lets it carry her at a rushing speed through the arboreal glory that is her home. The motive power is partly stored energy in silk springs, a macro-engineered development drawn from the structure of spider-silk itself, and partly cultured muscle: a mindless slab of contracting tissue running along the dorsal rib of the capsule, obliviously hauling itself over and over – efficient, self-repairing and easy to feed. Great Nest is a complex inter-connecting web of such capsule-runs, a network amongst networks, like the vibrational communications strands that go everywhere, since the temple maintains a rigorous monopoly on the invisible traces of radio waves.

Shortly thereafter she steps into the temple, carefully marking the reactions of those she finds there, sniffing out potential challengers.

What is the position of the Messenger? she asks, and is told that the voice of God is in the skies, invisible against the daylight.

Let me speak to Her.

The lesser priestesses clear out of her way somewhat resentfully, having had the run of this place for a month. The old crystal receiver has been improved steadily since the messages of God became comprehensible – that being the first lesson of God, and one of the most successful. Now there is a whole machine of metal and wood and silk that acts as a terminus for a sightless strand of the great and unseen web of the universe that links all such termini, allowing Portia to speak direct to other temples across half the world, and to speak to and hear the words of God.

After God originally began speaking, it took the combined great minds of several generations to finally learn the divine language, or perhaps to negotiate that language, meeting the comprehension of God halfway. Even now, a certain amount of what God has to say is simply not something that Portia or anyone can understand. It is all set down, though, and sometimes a particularly knotted piece of scripture will yield to the teasing of later theologians.

Slowly, however, a rapport with the godhead was established by Portia's forebears, and a story was thus told. Late in the development of their culture therefore, Portia's people inherited a creation myth, and had their destiny dictated to them by a being of a power and an origin that passed all their understandings.

The Messenger was the last survivor of an earlier age of the universe, they were told. In the final throes of that age, it was the Messenger who was chosen to come to this world and engender life out of the barren earth. The Messenger – the Goddess of the green planet – remade the world so that it would give rise to that life, next seeded it with plants and trees, and then with the lesser animals. On the last day of the previous age, at the apex of creation, the Messenger dispatched Portia's distant ancestors to this world, and settled back to await their voices.

And, after so many generations of silence in which the Messenger's voice alone touched the strands of that invisible world-spanning web, the temples now sing back, and the balance of God's plan is parcelled out in piecemeal revelations that almost nobody can yet understand. The Messenger is trying to teach them how to live, and this involves building machines to accomplish purposes that Portia's people can hardly grasp. It involves dangerous forces – such as the spark that sends signals up the strands of the ether to the Messenger, but of a vastly greater power. It involves bizarre, mind-hurting concepts of nested wheels and eyes, fires and channelled lightning. The Messenger is trying to help them, but its people are unworthy, so preaches the Temple – why else would they fail their God so often? They must improve and become what God has planned for them, but their manner of life and building and invention is wholly at odds with the vision that the Messenger relates to them.

Portia and her sisters are often in contact with the temples of other cities, but they are nevertheless drawing apart. God speaks to each of them, each temple being assigned its own frequency, but the message substantially the same – for Portia has eavesdropped on God's dictates to others before. Each temple translates the good news differently; interprets the words and co-opts them to fit with existing mental structures. Worse, some temples are losing their faith entirely, beginning to recast the words of the Messenger as something other than divine. This is a heresy, and already there has been conflict. After all, that tiny point of moving light is their only connection to a greater universe which – they are told – they are destined to inherit. To question and alienate that swift star could leave them abandoned and alone in the cosmos.

By the end of the day, between reports and the Understanding the male has just gifted to her, she has caught up with what has transpired in her absence. Friction with the apostate Seven Trees temple is high, and there has been serious infringement at the mine sites. The demands of God mean that raw materials – metals especially – are in high demand. Great Nest has maintained a monopoly of all good veins of iron and copper, gold and silver anywhere near its ever-extending reach, but other cities constantly dispute this, by sending their own ant colonies out in column to raid the workings. It is a war where the weapons, so far, have been more efficiently bred miners rather than fiercer warriors, but Portia is aware that this cannot continue. God herself has stated, in one of those long philosophical diatribes She is partial to, that there is always a single end-point to conflict if neither side will pull back from the brink.

Spider has always killed spider. From the start, the species has had a streak of cannibalism, especially female against male, and they have often struggled for territory, for local dominance. Such killings have never been casual or common, however. The nanovirus that runs through each of them forms another web of connections, reminding each of the sentience of the other. Even males partake: even their little deaths have a meaning and a significance that cannot be denied. Certainly the spiders have never fallen so far as to practise widespread slaughter. They have reserved their wars for defending themselves against extra-species threats, such as that long-ago war against the ant super-colony that in the end proved such a boost for their technology. For a species that thinks naturally in terms of interconnected networks and systems, the idea of a war of conquest and extermination – rather than a campaign of conversion, subversion and co-option – does not come easily.

God has other ideas, however, and the superiority of God's ideas has become a major point of dogma for the Temple – after all, why would anyone need a temple otherwise?

When she is finally on top of developments both theological and political; when she has been capsuled out of the city limits to visit the divine workshops where her priest-engineers labour to try and make real something – anything – from God's perplexing designs, only then does she find time for a personal errand. For Portia, personal and priestly are almost always interwoven, but in this she is indulging herself: finding time to meet with one little mind amongst so many, and yet such a jewel of clarity. Several of the key moments of epiphany, in which God's message was untangled even slightly, have originated with this remarkable brain. And yet she feels a tug of shame in spending her time in travelling to this little-remarked laboratory where her unacknowledged protégé is given the chance to experiment and build without the rigid control that the Temple traditionally exerts.

She enters without fanfare, finding the object of her curiosity studying the latest results, a complex notation of chemical analysis woven automatically by one of the ant colonies of the city. Interrupted by her presence, the scientist turns and waves palps in complex genuflection, a dance of respect, subservience and pleading.

Fabian, she addresses him, and the male shivers and bobs.

Before coming here, Portia has been to the outer laboratories to view the progress on God's plan, and she is not heartened.

The history of the Messenger's contact with Her chosen is the enactment of a plan. Once the language barrier was breached – as it is still being breached, missive to missive – God wasted no time in establishing Her place in the cosmos. There was, at the time, some debate amongst the scholars, but against a voice from the stars that promised them a universe grander than anything they had imagined, what could the sceptics suggest? The fact of God was inarguable.

That it served the Temple to argue God's corner is something Portia is aware of. She is aware that the first reaching out to God was a defying of Temple edicts of the time. Now she finds herself wondering what might happen if the Great Nest temple itself once again defied God.

Unfortunately the most obvious answer is that God would simply gift more of Her message to other temples and not to Great Nest. A unity of religion has led to a rivalry and factionalism between the nests. In all their long histories they have worked together, kindred nodes on a world-spanning continuum. Now divine attention has become a resource that they must squabble for. Of course Great Nest is pre-eminent amongst the foremost favourites of God, with its own knot of frequencies with which it monopolizes much of the message. Pilgrims of other nests must come begging for word of what it is that God wants.

Only those of the inner temple are uncomfortably aware that the message they distribute to those petitioners is merely a best guess. God is at once specific and obscure.

Portia has viewed the best efforts in those high-risk laboratories outside the city. They are distant because they must be surrounded by a firebreak. God is in love with the same force that burns in the radios. The ants there smelt vast lengths of copper that carry pulses of that tame lightning just as silk can carry simple speech. Except that the lightning is not so easily tamed. A spark is often all it takes to birth a conflagration.

The temple scientists try to build a network of lightning according to God's designs, but it achieves nothing, save occasionally to destroy its own creators. Somewhere out there, Portia fears, some other community may be closer than Great Nest to achieving God's intent.

God's work is not to be entrusted to males, but Fabian is special. Over the last few years, Portia has become curiously reliant on his abilities. He is a chemical architect of surpassing skill.

It is the age-old limiting factor: the ants are slow. The scientific endeavour of each spider nest rests on its ability to train its ant colonies to perform needed tasks: manufacturing, engineering, analysis. Whilst each generation has become more adept, pushing the boundaries of their organic technology, each fresh task requires a new colony, or else for a colony's existing behaviour to be overwritten. Spiders like Fabian create chemical texts that give an ant colony its purpose, its complex cascade of instinct that allows it to perform the given task. Although in truth there are few like Fabian, who accomplishes more, more elegantly and in less time, than any other.

Fabian possesses everything a male might desire, and yet he is unhappy. Portia finds him a bizarre mix: a male whose value has made him forthright enough that she sometimes feels she is dealing with a competing female.

Before she retired to moult, he was hinting that he was on the brink of a great advance, and yet a month later he has not broached the subject further with any of her subordinates. She wonders if he has saved it all for her. They have a complex relationship, she and Fabian. He danced for her once, and she took the gift of his genetic material to add to her own, so as to gift their combined genius to posterity. He has learned a great deal more, since then, that he has not passed on. In truth she should wait for him to petition her but, now she is here, the subject has come up.

I am not ready, he replies dismissively. *There is more to learn.*

Your great discovery, she prompts. Fabian is a volatile genius. He must be handled with a care normally unbecoming in dealing with a male.

Later. It is not ready. He is agitated, twitchy in her presence. Her scent receptors suggest that he is quite ready to mate, so it is his mind that is holding him back. *Let us get it over with now*, she suggests. *Or perhaps simply distil your new Understandings? Whilst I do not want anything to happen to you, there are always accidents.*

She had not intended a threat, but males are always cautious around females. He becomes quite still for a moment save for a nervous fidgeting of his palps, an unconscious plea for his life that goes back through the generations to before their kind ever developed language.

Osric is dead, he tells her, which she was not expecting. She cannot place the name and so he adds, *He was one of my assistants. He was killed after a mating.*

Tell me who was involved and I shall reprimand her. Your people are too precious to consume in such a way. And Portia is genuinely displeased. There remains a tight faction of ultra-conservatives in Great Nest that believe males can have no genuine qualities that are not simply a reflection of the females around them, but that hard-line philosophy has been dying out ever since the plague, when a simple lack of numbers saw males assume all manner of roles normally reserved for the stronger sex. Other city states, like Seven Trees, have gone even further, given the far greater ravages of plague there. Great Nest, originator of the cure, has combined cultural dominance with a greater social rigidity than many of its peers.

The improved mining architecture has been completed, Fabian drums out distractedly. *You are aware that I myself may be killed any day?*

Portia freezes. *Who would dare so tempt my disapproval?*

I don't know, but it may happen. If the meanest female is killed, that is a matter for investigation and punishment, just as if someone were to damage the common ground of the city or to speak out against the temple. If I am killed, then the only crime the perpetrator commits is to displease you.

And I would be displeased greatly, and that is why it will not happen. You need not fear, Portia explains patiently, thinking: *Males can be so highly strung!*

But Fabian seems oddly calm. *I know it will not happen, so long as I retain your favour. But I am concerned that it can happen, that such things are permitted. Do you know how many males are killed every month in Great Nest?*

They die like animals down in the lower reaches, Portia tells him. *They are of no use to anyone save as mates, and not even as mates of any substance most of the time. That is not something you need to concern yourself with.*

And yet I do. Fabian has more he wants to communicate, she can tell, but he stills his feet.

You are worried that you may lose my favour? Keep working as you are, and there is nothing in Great Nest you will not have, Portia assures the fragile male. *No comfort and no delicacy shall be denied you. You know this.*

He starts to phrase a response – she sees the emerging concepts strangled, stillborn, as he overrides the trembling of his palps. For a moment she thinks he will enumerate the things he *cannot* have, no matter how favoured, or that he will raise the point (again!) that all he *can* have, he can attain only through her or some other dominant female. She feels frustrated with him: what does he *want* exactly? Does he not realize how fortunate he is compared to so many of his brothers?

If only he was not so *useful* . . . but it is more than that. Fabian is a curiously appealing little creature, even aside from his concrete achievements. That combination of Understandings, impudence and vulnerability makes him a knot that she cannot stop pondering. She must some day tease him out straight or cut him through.

After that unsatisfactory confrontation with Fabian, she returns to her official duties. As a senior priestess, she has been asked to examine a heretic.

From radio communications with other temples, she is aware that other nests display varying tolerances for outspoken heresy, depending on the strength of the local priesthood. There are even those nests – some worryingly close – where the Temple is a shadow of its former strength, so that the city's governance depends on a collusion of heretics, lapsed priests and maverick scholars. Great Nest itself remains a cornerstone of orthodoxy, and Portia is aware that even now there are plans to exert some measure of forceful persuasion on its recusant neighbours. This is a new thing, but God's message can be interpreted as supporting it. The Messenger grows frustrated when Her words are ignored.

Within Great Nest itself, the seed of heresy has recently taken root within the very scientists the temple relies on. The mutterings of artisan females who have lost Temple favour, or vagrant males fearful for their worthless lives, are easy to ignore. When Great Nest's great minds start to question the dictates of Temple, important magnates such as Portia must become involved.

Bianca is one such: a scientist, a member of Portia's peer group, a former ally. She has probably entertained heretical views for a long time. Implicated by another wayward scholar, an unannounced search of Bianca's laboratories demonstrated how her personal studies had veered on to astronomy, a science particularly prone to breeding heretics.

Portia's kind are hard to imprison, but Bianca is currently confined to a chamber within the tunnels of a specialist ant colony bred for this purpose. There is no lock or key but, without adopting a certain scent, changed daily, she would be torn apart by the insects if she tried to leave.

The ant gatekeepers of the colony receive the correct code-pheromone from Portia, and douse her with today's pass-scent. She has a certain period of time in which to conduct her business, after which she will become as much a prisoner as Bianca.

She feels a stab of guilt over what she is about. Bianca should have been sentenced by now, but Portia is steeped in memories of her sister's company and assistance. To lose Bianca would be to lose a part of her own world. Portia has abused her authority just to gain this chance to redeem the heretic.

Bianca is a large spider, her palps and forelegs dyed in abstract patterns of blue and ultraviolet. The pigments are rare, slow and expensive to fashion, so to sport them displays the considerable influence – an intangible but unarguable currency – that Bianca until recently could muster.

Hail, sister. Bianca's stance and precise footwork give the message a barbed emphasis. *Here to bid me farewell?*

Portia, already ground down by the vicissitudes of the day so far, hunches low, foregoing all the usual physical posturing and bluster. *Don't drive me away. You have few allies in Great Nest now.*

Only you?

Only me. Portia studies Bianca's body language, seeing the larger female change stance slightly, reconsidering.

I have no names to reveal, no others to betray to you, the accused warns the inquisitor. *My beliefs are my own. I do not need a brood around me to tell me how right I am.*

Leaving aside the fact that many of Bianca's accomplices have already been seized and sentenced under the Temple's authority, Portia has already decided to abandon that line of enquiry. There remains only one thing at stake. *I am here to save you. Only you, sister.*

Bianca's palps move slightly, an unconscious expression of interest, but she says nothing.

I do not wish a home that I cannot share with you, Portia tells her, her steps and gestures careful, weighty with consideration. *If you are gone, there will be a hole torn in my world, so that all else falls out of shape. If you recant, I will go to my fellows at Temple, and they will listen to me. You will fall from favour, but you will remain free.*

Recant? Bianca echoes.

If you explain to Temple that you were mistaken or misled, then I can spare you. I shall have you for my own, to work alongside me.

But I am not *mistaken.* Bianca's movements were categorical and firm.

You must be.

If you turn lenses on the night sky, lenses of the strength and purity that we can now produce, you will see it too, Bianca explains calmly.

That is a mystery that cannot be comprehended by those outside Temple, Portia reprimands her.

So say those inside Temple. But I have looked; I have seen the face of the Messenger, and measured and studied it as it passes above. I have set out my plates and analysed the light that it seems to shed. Light reflected from the sun only. And the mystery is that there is no mystery. I can tell you the size and speed of the Messenger. I can even guess at what it is constructed from. The Messenger is a rock of metal, no more.

They will exile you, Portia tells her. *You know what that means?* For females do not kill other females any more, and the harshest sentence of Great Nest is to deny the accused that metropolis's wonders. Such felons receive a chemical branding that marks them out for death if they approach any of the city's ant colonies – and many other colonies beyond, as the mark does not discriminate. To be exiled all too often means a return to solitary barbarism in the depths of the wilds, forever retreating before civilization's steady spread.

I have taken on many Understandings in my life, Bianca clearly might as well not have heard. *I have listened to another Messenger's incomprehensible signals in the night. The thing you call God is not even alone in the sky. It is a thing of metal that demands we make more things of metal – and I have seen it, how small it is.*

Portia skitters nervously, if only because, in her lowest hours, she herself has played host to similar thoughts. *Bianca, you cannot turn away from Temple. Our people have followed the words of the Messenger since our earliest days – from long before we could understand Her purpose. Even if you have your personal doubts, you cannot deny that the traditions that have* built Great Nest have allowed us to survive many threats. *They have made us what we are.*

Bianca seems sad. *And now they prevent us from being all that we could be*, she suggests. *And that is at the heart of me. If I were to cut myself away from it, there would be nothing left of me. I do not just feel Temple is mistaken, I believe that Temple has become a burden. And you know that I am not alone. You will have spoken with the temples in other cities – even those cities that Great Nest is hostile to. You know that others feel as I do.*

And they will be punished, in turn, Portia tells her. *As will you.*

5.3 OLD FRIENDS

Four of them met in an old service room that seemed to represent neutral ground in the midst of those parts of the ship claimed by the various cliques. Lain and the other two all had retinues who waited outside, eyeing each other nervously like hostile soldiers in a cold war.

Inside, it was a reunion.

Vitas hadn't changed – Holsten suspected that overall she had not been out of the freezer much longer than he had, or perhaps she just wore the extra time well: a neat, trim woman with her feelings buried sufficiently deep that her face remained a cypher. She wore a shipsuit, still, as though she had stepped straight from Holsten's memories without being touched by the chaos that the *Gilgamesh* was apparently falling into. Lain had already explained how Vitas had been enlisted by Guyen to help with the uploader. The woman's thoughts on this were unknown, but she had come when Lain got a message to her, slipping through the circles of Guyen's cult like smoke, shadowed by a handful of her assistants.

Karst looked older, closing in on Holsten's age. His beard had returned – patchy, greying in uneven degrees – and he wore his hair tied back. A rifle was slung over his shoulder, barrel downwards, and he had come in armour, a full suit of the kind that Holsten remembered him favouring before – good against Lain's gun, perhaps not so much against a knife. His technological advantage was being eroded by the backwards nature of the times.

He was also working with Guyen, but Lain had explained that Karst was something of a law unto himself these days. He controlled the ship's armoury and only he had ready access to firearms in any quantity; his security detail, and whatever conscripts he had enlisted, were loyal to him first and foremost. And so was he, of course: Karst was Karst's chief priority, or so Lain believed.

Now the security chief let out a loud bark of what sounded like derision. 'You even broke the old man out of his grave for us! That sick for nostalgia, Lain? Or maybe for something else?'

'I broke him from a cage in Guyen's sector,' Lain stated. 'He's been there for days. I guess you didn't know.'

Karst glowered at her, then at Holsten himself, who confirmed it with a nod. Even Vitas seemed to be unsurprised, and the security chief threw up his hands.

'Nobody tells me fucking *anything*,' he spat. 'Well, well, here we all are. How fucking *pleasant*. So how about you speak your piece.'

'How've you been, Karst?' Holsten asked quietly, wrong-footing everyone, including Lain.

'Seriously?' The security chief's eyebrows disappeared into his shaggy hairline. 'You actually want to do the small-talk thing?'

'I want to know how this can possibly work, this . . . what Lain's told me is going on.' Holsten had decided, on the way over, that he was not merely going to be the engineer's yes-man. 'I mean . . . how long's this been going on for? It just seems . . . insane. Guyen's got a cult? He's been futtering with this upload thing for, what, decades? Generations? Why? He could just have brought this business before the Key Crew and talked it over.' He caught an awkward look shared between the three others. 'Or . . . right, ok. So maybe that did happen. I suppose I wasn't Key Crew enough to be invited.'

'It wasn't as though anyone needed anything translated,' Karst said, with a shrug.

'At the time there was some considerable debate,' Vitas added crisply. 'However, on balance it was decided that there was too much unknown about the process, especially its effect on the *Gilgamesh*'s systems. Personally I was in favour of experimentation and trial.'

'So, what, Guyen just set himself to wake early, got a replacement tech crew out of cargo, and started work?' Holsten hazarded.

'All in place when he woke me. And frankly, I don't pretend to understand the technical arguments.' Karst shrugged. 'So he needed me to track down people who were escaping from his little prison-camp cult thing. I figured the best thing I could do was look after my own people and make sure nobody else got hold of the guns. So, Lain, you want the guns now? Is that it?'

Lain cast a glance at Holsten to see if he was about to go off on another tangent, then nodded shortly. 'I want the help of your people. I want to stop Guyen. The ship's falling apart – any more and the main systems are going to be irretrievably compromised.'

'Says you,' Karst replied. 'Guyen says that once he actually does the . . . does the *thing*, then everything goes back to normal – that he'll be in the computer, or some copy of him, and everything'll run as sweet as you like.'

'And this is possible,' Vitas added. 'Not certain, but possible. So we must compare the potential danger of Guyen completing his project with that of an attempt to interrupt him. It is not an easy judgement to make.'

Lain looked from face to face. 'And yet here you both are, and I'll bet Guyen doesn't know.'

'Knowledge is never wasted,' Vitas observed calmly.

'And what if I told you that Guyen's withholding knowledge from you?' Lain pressed. 'How about transmissions from the moon colony we left behind? Heard any of those lately?'

Karst looked sidelong at Vitas. 'Yeah? What've they got to say?'

'Fucking little. They're all dead.'

Lain smiled grimly into the silence that generated. 'They died while we were still on our way to the grey planet system. They called the ship; Guyen intercepted their messages. Did he tell any of you? He certainly didn't tell me. I found the signals archived, by chance.'

'What happened to them?' Karst said reluctantly.

'I've put the messages up on the system, where you can both access them. I'll direct you to them. Be quick, though. Unprotected data gets corrupted quickly nowadays, thanks to Guyen's leftovers.'

'Yeah, well, he blames *you* for that. Or Kern sometimes,' Karst pointed out.

'Kern?' Holsten demanded. 'The satellite thing?'

'It was in our systems,' Vitas remarked. 'It's possible it left some sort of ghost construct to monitor us. Guyen believes so.' Her face wrinkled up, just a little. 'Guyen has become somewhat obsessed. He believes that Kern is trying to stop him.' She nodded cordially to Lain. 'Kern and you.'

Lain folded her arms. 'Cards on the table. I see no fucking benefit to Guyen becoming an immortal presence in our computer system. In fact, I see all manner of possible drawbacks, some of them fatal for us, the ship and the entire human race. Ergo: we stop him. Who's in? Holsten's with me.'

'Well, shit, if you've got *him*, why'd you need the rest of us?' Karst drawled.

'He's Key Crew.'

Karst's expression was eloquent as to his opinion of that.

And is that it, for me? I'm just here to add my miniscule weight – unasked! – to Lain's argument? Holsten considered morosely.

'I confess that I am curious as to the result of the commander's experiment. The ability to preserve human minds electronically would certainly be advantageous,' Vitas stated.

'Planning to become Bride of Guyen?' Karst asked, startling a glare from her.

'Karst?' Lain prompted.

The security chief threw his hands up. 'Nobody tells me anything, not really. People just want me to do stuff and they're never straight with me. Me? I'm for my people. Right now, Guyen's got a whole bunch of weirdos who have been raised from the cradle on him being the fucking messiah. You've got a handful of decently tooled and trained lads and lasses here, but you're not exactly the fighting elite. Take on

Guyen and you'll lose. Now I'm not a fucking *scientist* or anything, but my maths says why should I help you when I'll likely just get my people hurt?'

'Because you've got the guns to counter Guyen's numbers.'

'Not a good reason,' Karst stated.

'Because I'm right, and Guyen's going to wreck the ship's systems by trying to force his fucking ego into our computers.'

'Says you. He says differently,' Karst replied stubbornly. 'Look, you reckon you've got an actual plan, as in an actual plan that would have a chance of success and not just "let Karst do all the work"? Come to me with that, and maybe I'll listen. Until then . . .' He made a dismissive gesture. 'You've not got enough, Lain. Not chances, nor arguments either.'

'Then just give me enough guns,' Lain insisted.

Karst sighed massively. 'I only really got as far as making one rule: nobody gets the guns. You're worried about the damage Guyen'll do with this thing he wants to do? Well, I don't get any of that. But the damage when everyone starts shooting everyone else – and all sorts of bits of the ship, too? Yeah, that I understand. The mutiny was bad enough. Like I say, come back when you've got more.'

'Give me disruptors, then.'

The security chief shook his head. 'Look, sorry to say it, but I still don't think that'll even the odds enough for you to actually *win*, and then Guyen's not exactly going to be scratching his head about where all your dead people got their toys from, eh? Get me a proper idea. Show me you can actually pull it off.'

'So you'll help me if I can show I don't actually need you?'

He shrugged. 'We're done here, aren't we? Let me know when you've got a plan, Lain.' He turned and lumbered off, the plates of his armoured suit scraping together slightly.

Lain was icily furious as Karst and Vitas left, fists clenching and re-clenching.

'Pair of self-deluding fuckwits!' she spat. 'They know I'm right, but it's Guyen – they're so used to doing what that mad son of a bitch says.'

She glared at Holsten as if daring him to gainsay her. In fact, the historian had felt a certain sympathy with Karst's position, but plainly that was not what Lain wanted to hear.

'So what will you do?' he asked.

'Oh, we'll act,' Lain swore. 'Let Karst keep his precious guns locked up. We've got one workshop up and running, and I've already started weapons production. They won't be pretty, but they're better than knives and clubs.'

'And Guyen?'

'If he's got any sense, he's doing the same, but I'm better at it. I'm Engineering, after all.'

'Lain, are you sure you want a war?'

She stopped. The regard she turned on Holsten was a look from another time – that of a martyr, a warrior queen of legend.

'Holsten, this isn't just about me not liking Guyen. It isn't because I want his job or I think he's a bad person. I have taken my own best professional judgement, and I believe that if he goes ahead with uploading his mind, then he will overload the *Gilgamesh*'s system, causing a fatal clash of both our tech and the Empire stuff we've salvaged. And when that happens, everyone dies. And I mean everyone. I don't care if

Vitas wants to make notes for some non-existent posterity, or if Karst won't get off the fucking fence. It's up to me – it's up to me and my crew. You're lucky. You woke late, and then you got to sit in a box for a bit. Some of us have been pushing every which way for a long time, trying to turn this around. And now I'm basically an outlaw on my own ship, at open war with my commander, whose crazy fanatic followers will kill me on sight. And I'm going to lead my engineers into fucking *battle* and actually *kill* people, because if someone doesn't, then Guyen kills everyone. Now are you with me?'

'You know I am.' The words sounded tremulous and hollow to Holsten himself, but Lain seemed to accept them.

They were attacked as they were crossing into what Lain seemed to consider her territory. The interior of the *Gilgamesh* made for odd tactics: a network of small chambers and passages fitted into the torus of the crew area, bent and twisted like an afterthought around the essential machinery that had been put in first. They had just reached a heavy safety door that Lain – in the lead – obviously expected to open automatically. When it slid a shuddering inch, then stopped, there was no obvious suspicion amongst the engineers. It seemed to Holsten that, under the present regime, little things must be going wrong all the time.

With a tool case already in hand, one of them pried off a service plate, and Holsten heard the words, 'Chief, this has been tampered with,' before a hatch above them was kicked open and three ragged figures dropped upon them with ear-splitting howls.

They had long knives – surely nothing from the armoury,

so Guyen's people had been improvising – and they were absolutely berserk. Holsten saw one of Lain's people reel back, blood spitting from a broad wound across her body, and the rest were down to grappling hand-to-hand almost immediately.

Lain had her gun out but was denied a target, a lack that was rectified when another half-dozen appeared, running full-tilt from the direction they had come. The weapon barked three times, colossally loud in the confined space. One of the robed figures spun away, his battle-cry abruptly turning into a scream.

Holsten just ducked, hands over his head, his view of the fight reduced to a chaos of knees and feet. Historian to the last, his thought was: *This is what it must have been like on Earth at the very end, when all else was lost. This is what we left Earth to avoid. It's been following after us all this time.* Then someone kicked him in the chin, probably entirely without malice, and he was sent sprawling, trampled and stamped on, under the thrashing feet of the melee. He saw Lain's gun smashed from her hand.

Someone fell across his legs heavily, and he felt one knee being wrenched as far as it would go, a shockingly distinct and insistent pain amidst all the confusion. He struggled to get free and found himself furiously kicking at the expiring weight of one of Guyen's mad monks. His mind, which had temporarily given up any illusion of control, was wondering whether the commander had promised some sort of posthumous reward for his minions, and whether that promise was any consolation with a torn-open stomach.

Suddenly he was clear, and scrabbling at the wall to regain his feet. His twisted knee savagely resisted bearing any of his weight, but he was adrenalined to the eyeballs right then, and overrode it. That got him all of two steps away from the skirmish, whereupon he was grabbed. Without warning, two of Guyen's bigger goons were on him, and he saw a knife glinting in one hand. He screamed, something to the tune of begging for his life, and then they bounced him off the wall for good measure. He was convinced he was about to die, his imagination leaping ahead, trying to brace him against the coming thrust by picturing the blade already in him in agonizing detail. He lived through the sickening lurch of impact, the cold keening of the knife, the warm upsurge of blood as those parts of him that his skin had kept imprisoned for so very, very long finally took their chance at freedom.

He was living it, in his head. Only belatedly did he realize that they had not stabbed him at all. Instead, the two of them were hurrying him away from the fight, heedless of his staggering, limping gait. With a start of horror – as though this was worse than a stabbing – he realized that this was not just random gang warfare, Guyen vs. Lain.

This was the high priest of the *Gilgamesh* recovering his property.

Fabian is brought into Portia's presence after his escorts return him to the peer house. Her reaction on seeing him is a mixture of relief and frustration. He has been missing for most of the day. Now he is brought into a room of angled sides deep within the peer group's domain, where Portia hangs from the ceiling and frets.

This is not the first time that he has evaded his custodians and gone walkabout, but today he was retrieved from the lower reaches of Great Nest, closest to the ground, a haunt of hungry females who either lack or have left their peer groups; the habitat of the busy multitudes of maintenance colonies whose insect bodies keep the city free from refuse; an abode of the numberless, hopeless, unwanted males.

For someone like Fabian, it is a good place to go to die.

Portia is furious, but there is a genuine streak of fear for his wellbeing that he can read in her jittery body language. *You could have been killed!*

Fabian himself is very calm. *Yes, I could.*

Why would you do such a thing? she demands.

Have you ever been there? He is crouching by the room's entrance, his round eyes staring up at her, still as stones when he is not actually speaking. With her elevated stance that would let her leap on him and pin him in an instant, there is a curious tension between them: hunter and prey; female and male.

The ground down there is a tattered mess of broken silk, he tells her; *of hastily built shacks where dozens of males sleep each night. They live like animals, day to day. They prey on the ants and are preyed on in turn. The ground is littered with the drained husks where the females have made meals of them.*

Portia's words thrum towards him through the boundaries of the room. *All the more reason to be grateful for what you have, and not risk yourself.* Her palps flash white anger.

I could have been killed, he echoes, matching her stance, and therefore her intonation, perfectly. *I could have lived my entire life there, and died without memory or achievement. What separates me from them?*

You are of value, Portia insists. *You are a male of exceptional ability, one to be celebrated, to be protected and encouraged to prosper. What have you ever been denied that you have asked for?*

Only one thing. He walks forwards a few careful steps, as though he is feeling out the strands of a web that only he can see. His palps move lazily. His progress is almost a dance, something of the courtship but laced with bitterness. Theirs is a voiceless language of many subtle shades. *They are like us, and you know it. You cannot know what they might have achieved if they had been allowed to live and to prosper.*

For a moment she does not even know what he means, but she sees his mind is still focused on that detritus of doomed males whose lives will take them no further than the foot of the trees.

They are of no value or worth.

But you cannot know that. There could be a dozen geniuses dying every day, who have never had an opportunity to demon-

strate their aptitude. *They think, as we do. They plan and hope and fear. Merely see them and that connection would strum between you. They are my brothers. No less so, they are yours.*

Portia disagrees vehemently. *If they were of any quality or calibre, then they would ascend by their own virtues.*

Not if there was no structure that they could possibly climb. Not if all the structure that exists was designed to disenfranchise them. Portia, I could have been killed. You yourself said it. I could have been taken by some starving female, and nothing in that would be seen as wrong, save that it might anger you. He has stepped closer, and she feels the predator in her twitch, as if he were some blind insect blundering too close, inviting the strike.

Portia's rear legs close up, building muscle tension for the spring that she is fighting against. *And still you are not grateful that I think enough of you that your life is preserved.*

His palps twitch with frustration. *You know how many males busy themselves around Great Nest. You know that we fulfil thousands of small roles, and even some few great ones. If we were to leave the city all at once, or if some plague were to rid you of all your males, the nest would collapse. And yet every one of us has nothing more than we are given, and that can be taken away from us just as swiftly. Each one of us lives in constant fear that our usefulness will come to an end and that we will be replaced by some more elegant dancer, some new favourite, or that we will please too much and mate, and then be too slow to escape the throes of your passion.*

That is the way things are. Following her argument with Bianca, Portia is finding this polemic too much to deal with. She feels as though her beloved Great Nest is under assault from all sides, and most from those who ought to be her allies.

Things are the way we make them. Abruptly his pose changes, and he is stepping sideways, away from her, loosening that taut bond of predation that was building between them. *You asked about my discovery, before. My grand project.*

Playing his game, Portia comes down from her roost, one leg at a time, while still keeping that careful distance. *Yes?* she signals with her palps.

I have devised a new form of chemical architecture. His manner has changed completely from the intensity of a moment before. Now he seems disinterested, cerebral.

To what end? She creeps closer, and he steps away again, not fleeing her but following that unseen web of his own invention.

To any end. To no end. In and of itself, my new architecture carries no instructions, no commands. It sets the ants no tasks or behaviours.

Then what good is it?

He stops, looking up at her again, having lured her this close. *It can do anything. A secondary architecture can be distributed to the colony, to work within the primary. And another, and another. A colony could be given a new task instantly, and its members would change with the speed of the scent, as it passes from ant to ant. Different castes could be made receptive to different instructions, allowing the colony to pursue multiple tasks all at once. A single colony could follow sequences of separate tasks without the need for lengthy reconditioning. Once my base architecture is in place, every colony can be reconfigured for every new task, as often as needed. The efficiency of mechanical tasks would increase tenfold. Our ability to undertake calculations would increase at least a hundredfold, perhaps a thousandfold, depending on the economy of the secondary architecture.*

Portia has stopped still, stunned. She understands enough of how her kind's organic technology works to grasp the magnitude of what he is proposing. If it can be done, then Fabian will have surpassed the chief limiting factor that is frustrating the Temple even now, and that is preventing them from giving true reality to the Messenger's plan. The brake will come off the advancement of their species. *You have this Understanding, now?*

I do. The primary architecture is actually surprisingly simple. Building complex things out of simple things is the basis of the idea. It's like building a web. I also have a system for constructing any secondary architecture, fit for any task required. It is like a language, a concise mathematical language. He stalks forwards a few steps, as if teasing her. *You will appreciate it. It is as beautiful as the first Message.*

You must pass this Understanding to me immediately. For a moment Portia feels the strong desire to mate with him, to take his genetic material into herself, with its newfound Understanding, to set down immediately the first of the next generation who will rule the world. Perhaps she should instead have him distil his new knowledge so that she can drink it and Understand it herself, rather than leave it to her offspring, but the thought seems intimidating. How will the world look, when he gives her the secret of unlocking the future?

He does not speak. His shuffling feet and trembling palps suggest an odd coyness.

Fabian, you must pass on this Understanding, she repeats. *I cannot imagine how you thought risking yourself could be acceptable, if you hold this knowledge.*

He has ventured quite close, almost within the span of her forelegs. He is a little more than half her size: weaker, slower, more fragile and yet so valuable!

So unlike the rest of my kind? It is as if he has read her mind. *But I am not, or you cannot know if I am or am not. How many Understandings are extinguished every day?*

None like yours, she tells him promptly.

You can never know. That is the problem with ignorance. You can never truly know the extent of what you are ignorant about. I will not do it.

She physically recoils. *Explain yourself.*

It dies with me. I will not distil this Understanding. I will take steps to prevent it being taken by force. For, of course, there were chemical countermeasures for *that* now as well.

Why would you do such a thing?

Fabian looks direct into her eyes. *Unless.*

Unless? she prompts.

You are the pre-eminent priestess of Great Nest. I think there is no female more influential than you, Fabian observes, still watching her intently.

You wish to mate . . . ? she begins tentatively, because Portia is finding some difficulty in knowing what he, a pampered male, can really want that he does not already have for the asking.

No. I wish you to go to your peer group, and to Temple, and to the other great matriarchs of Great Nest, and tell them that there will be a new law. Tell them that to kill a male shall be as abhorrent to them as to kill another female. Tell them that my brothers deserve to live.

She freezes because, yes, there have been deranged philosophers in the past who might put up such an idea as an intellectual exercise, and there are those other cities where the males assumed more of the work after the ravages of the plague, and have never quite let go. But that is not Great Nest – and Great Nest's way is the true way, the preferred path of the Messenger.

Within her, biology and custom are at war. There is a place in her mind where the nanovirus lurks and it tells her that all her species are kin, are *like* her in a way that other creatures are not, and yet the weight of society crushes its voice. Males have their place; she knows this.

Don't be foolish. You cannot equate every ignorant, crawling male with one such as yourself. Of course you are protected and valued for your accomplishments. That is only natural, that merit be rewarded. The great host of males beneath us, though, the surplus, what use are they? What good are they? You are an exceptional male. Something female got into you in the egg, to make you thus. But you cannot expect my sisters to blindly extend such consideration to every male in the city just because of you. What would we do with them?

Put them to work. Find their strengths. Train them. Use them. Apparently Fabian has given this matter some thought.

Use them as what? What use can they be?

You can never know, because you do not try.

She rears up in frustration, sending him scuttling back, momentarily terrified. She would not have struck, but for a moment she wonders if that sudden injection of fear might assist her argument. When he settles himself across the chamber from her, though, he seems even more resolved.

What you ask is unnatural, she tells him sternly, controlling herself.

There is nothing about what we do that is natural. If we prized the natural we would still be hunting Spitters in the wilderness, or falling prey to the jaws of ants, instead of mastering our world. We have made a virtue of the unnatural.

She does not trust herself to answer, so she scurries past him, almost knocking him aside. *You will reconsider*, she tells him, pausing in the doorway to beat out the rhythms of her anger. *You will give up this foolish dream.*

Fabian watches her go, eyes glinting with rebellion.

He cannot simply walk out of the peer house. From a genuine concern for his safety, Portia has given instructions that Fabian is not to leave. She does not see it as an imprisonment; it is simply not fitting for any male to wander freely. Valued males who have secured the patronage of powerful females are expected to be at their beck and call, or to labour out of sight for their betters. Other males are preferably out of sight as well as out of mind.

Fabian paces the boundaries of his laboratory chamber, knowing that he must manufacture an exit, but fearful of taking that irreversible step. If he leaves *now*, after that confrontation with Portia, he will be leaving behind everything he has known. Curiosity is built into the spider genome, but in males it is not encouraged. Fabian is fighting centuries of conditioning.

Finally he conquers his timidity and sends out a chemical signal. Shortly afterwards, the scent is picked up by a handful of ants from the city maintenance colonies, passing nearby on their endless round of duties. Their entire colony has been reprogrammed by Fabian, his master-architecture already set in place. Nobody has noticed, because the secondary structures that guide the colony about its task are functionally identical to those that were originally bred into the ants generations before – if a little more elegantly designed. Now, though, the pheromones that Fabian has released instil new behaviours in these individuals, bringing them to the silk side of his chamber, where they cut a neat exit wound for him to depart through. After they are done, he resets them, and they go about their duties with no sign that they were ever subverted. Fabian has been busy these last months in testing his discovery, with the whole of Great Nest as his experimental subject.

He has listened to the news constantly recycled by the peer group. He knows who is causing Portia distress, who has tried to challenge the order of the world – other than himself. He is a male, vulnerable from the moment he slips from the peer house. He knows where he needs to go, but he fears journeying alone. He needs a guardian. He needs a female, in fact, however much he might regret that.

Fabian's ideal female has three characteristics: she must be intellectually useful, so a commodity in her own right; she must be in a position of weakness that will allow even a male to bargain with her; she must have no interest in mating with him, or otherwise harming him. Regarding the last, he knows he must trust to chance. The first two criteria have already suggested a travelling companion. He knows who has caused Portia to fret most.

Fabian is going to see Bianca.

He pauses halfway down the tree trunk from the peer house, gazing back up at its complex collection of suspended chambers and tents. For a moment he is uncertain – should he not trust the safety of its walls, and give up his ambitions?

And what will Portia think, once she finds him gone? She represents all that he intends to overthrow, and yet he likes and respects her, and she has always done her best for him. Everything he has accomplished has been made possible only by what Portia has given him.

But no, it is that kind of gifting that he must break away from. A life lived entirely at the whim of another is no life at all. He has always been surprised at the large number of other males who see matters differently, revelling in their own cosseted captivity.

Previous excursions outside have given him the opportunity to lay groundwork, and where he has not travelled himself, he has sent his proxies instead. His new chemical architecture allows him to use ants as the delivery agent of his instructions, with colonies programming other colonies. Nobody suspects just how far this has all gone.

He suborned the prison colony relatively recently, paving the way for his insurrection. When he arrives, the ants at the tunnel mouth start forwards, antennae waving, mandibles wide in challenge. He releases a distinct, simple scent, a back door into their societal structures, and they are instantly his. With a rapid cycling of olfactory clues he alters their behaviour in specific, precise ways. The tunnel guards turn and enter their colony, unleashing a cascade of his amended architecture throughout their fellows. Fabian follows them in, as though they are his honour guard.

It takes him time to find Bianca's chamber amongst all the others held in custody. Great Nest holds no prisoners for long, executing the males and exiling females but, as the Temple tightens its dogmatic grip, the number of those crushed within its grasp only increases. With no way of getting the ants to locate an individual, Fabian is aware of time passing – already he will have been missed, but nobody should guess that here would be his destination.

Part of his mind is already considering that he should have arranged for a tissue sample somehow, with which he could program an ant to track its original. Fabian often thinks about more than one thing at once, just to save time.

Then he stumbles into Bianca's cell, and for a moment she rears up, frightened and angry, and he thinks she might strike him down without even hearing what he has to say.

I am here with an offer, he hammers out hurriedly.

Portia sent you? Bianca is suspicious.

Portia and I have taken different paths.

I know you. You are her creature, one of her males.

Fabian gathers his courage. He must say it, so as to make it real. *I am not hers. I am my own.*

Bianca watches him carefully, as though he is some prey animal behaving in an unexpected way. *Is that so?*

I am intending to leave Great Nest tonight, he tells her. *I will travel to Seven Trees.*

Why? But she is interested, inching closer.

He is very aware of her fangs, in this confined space. He does not know Bianca like he knows Portia; he cannot judge her limits and tolerances so well. *Because Seven Trees was rebuilt by males. Because they have been forced to accord males a value there.*

The flurry of her palps is a gesture of cynicism. *Seven Trees is a poor city. The males there would give all the value they are held in to be looked after by a strong Great Nest peer house, just as you have been. Life is hard there, I have heard.*

Yes, you have heard, he echoes. *And yet I would make the opposite exchange. I would have my own peer house, however poor. I would give away all of Portia's in exchange for some small territory of my own.*

She makes a disgusted gesture. *How happy I am that you came here merely to tell me this. I wish you a swift journey.*

Perhaps you will accompany me?

You will have to wait until Portia exiles me then, and hope that whatever they taint me with will not see the ants of Seven Trees becoming as hostile to me as those of our home, Bianca taps out bitterly.

You have been in communication with Seven Trees already. Fabian feels he must come out and say it.

For a moment, Bianca is still. Then a short gesture prompts him to continue.

I went to your chambers after you were exposed as a heretic, after they took you captive. I read some of the knot-books you had made your notes in. They fit with philosophies and ideas that Portia's agents report are current in Seven Trees. I saw many parts and pieces in your workshop. It occurred to me that one could construct many useful things with them, and not just the telescopes that you were known for. A radio, perhaps?

Bianca regards him stonily. Her words are stepped out stiffly. *You are a dangerous little monster.*

I am just a male who has been allowed to use his brain. Will you come with me?

You have some trick to come and go, if you are not here at Portia's orders, Bianca understands.

I have some tricks, yes. I have some tricks that Seven Trees may be glad of, if we reach there.

Seven Trees, Bianca considers. *Seven Trees will be the first city to feel the bite of Great Nest. I know what Portia has been planning, even down here. You may not enjoy your new home long.*

Then I will go somewhere else. Anywhere else but here. Fabian skips a little dance at the time-wasting, feeling that eventually someone will come to look for him, or simply to look in on Bianca. Perhaps it will even be Portia. What would she make of these two conspirators together?

Come, then, Bianca confirms. *Great Nest has lost its appeal for me now it has shrunk to the confines of this chamber. Show me your trick.*

He shows her more than that, for rather than exit upwards into Great Nest he reprograms twenty of the guards into miners. Bianca's own insect custodians dig her escape tunnel, and by morning the two of them are well on the way to Seven Trees.

5.5 THE OLDEST MAN IN THE UNIVERSE

Holsten had assumed it would be the cage for him, but apparently things had moved on somewhat in Crazyville. The weird shanty town of makeshift partitions and tents that he had glimpsed briefly before was now all around him. It baffled him really. There was no weather in the *Gilgamesh*, and any extremes of temperature were likely to prove fatal. And yet everywhere people here had put up makeshift cover against the non-existent elements, draped lines and blankets and cannibalized wall panels to demarcate personal territories that were barely big enough to lie down in. It was as if, after so many centuries spent in cold coffins, the human race was unwilling to be freed from their confines.

He had previously only got a decent look at those votaries who had overseen his captivity. Now he was being held, under guard, in what he recognized as the Communications suite. How long ago – how short a remembered time ago – he had sat here trying to initiate contact with the Brin Sentry Habitat. Now the consoles were folded away – or ripped out – and the very walls were invisible beneath layers of encrusting humanity. They peered out at him, these long-haired, grimy inheritors of the ark. They talked to one another. They stank. He was ready to loathe them, and be loathed right back, observing these degenerate savages locked in the bowels of a ship that they were slowly destroying. He could not do it, though. It was the children that dissuaded him. He had almost forgotten children.

The adults all seemed to possess some disconcerting quality, people who had been fed a narrow range of lies that had slowly locked their faces into expressions of desperate tranquillity, as though to admit to the despair and deprivation that so clearly weighed on them would risk losing them the favour of God. The children, though – the children were still children. They fought and chased each other and shouted and behaved in all the ways he remembered children doing, even back on toxic Earth where their generation had no future but a slow death.

Sitting there, he watched them peeping out, running at the sight of him, then creeping back. He saw them fabricate their little half-worlds between them, malnourished and frail and *human* in a way that Holsten felt neither their parents nor he himself still were.

It had been a long road to here from Earth, but not as far as he himself had travelled from their state of innocence. The burden of knowledge in his head burned like an intolerable coal: the certainty of dead Earth, of frozen colonies, a star-spanning empire shrunk to one mad brain in a cold satellite . . . and the ark overrun by the monkeys.

Holsten felt himself coming adrift, cut loose from any emotional anchor. He had found a point where he could look forward – future-wards – and see nothing that he could possibly want, no hoped-for outcome that was remotely conceivable. He felt as though he had reached the end of all useful time.

When the tears came, when his shoulders unexpectedly

began shaking and he could not stop himself, it felt like two thousand years of grief taking hold of him and twisting at him, wringing out his exhausted body over and over until there was nothing left.

When two large men eventually came for him, one of them touched his shoulder almost gently, to get his attention. That same reverence he had noticed when he had been their caged pet was still present, and his outburst seemed only to have deepened it, as though his tears and his misery were worth vastly more than any of theirs.

I should make a speech, he thought wryly. *I should stand up and urge them: Throw off your chains! You don't have to live like this! Except what do I know about it? They shouldn't be here at all, not three generations of ship-rats living in all the spare space of the ship, breathing all the air, eating all the food.* He had no promised land he could lead them to, not even the green planet. *Full of spiders and monsters, and would the ship even survive the journey there? Not according to Lain.* He wondered whether Guyen had thought past the point of his own ascension. Once some corrupted, half-demented copy of his mind was uploaded into the *Gilgamesh*'s systems, would he watch the suffering and death of his grey followers with equanimity? Had he promised that he would take them along with him to life everlasting? Would he care when the adults that these children grew into starved, or were cut short by the failure of the *Gil*'s life-support?

'Take me to him,' he said, and they helped him hobble away. The denizens of the tent city watched him as though he was going to intercede for them with a malign deity, perhaps one whose supplicants could only carry the messages of the faithful after their hearts had been torn out.

Shuttle bays were some of the largest accessible spaces on board. His cage had been in one, and now here was another. The shuttle was missing, again, but more than half the space was cluttered with a vast bank of machinery, a bastard chimera comprised of salvage from the *Gil* and ancient relics from the terraform station. At least half of what Holsten was looking at did not seem to be connected to anything or fulfilling any purpose – just scrap that had been superseded but not disposed of. At the heart of it, actually up on a stepped dais constructed unevenly of metal and plastic, was the upload facility, the centre of a web of cables and ducts that spilled from its coffin space, and the focus of a great deal of the supporting machinery.

But not all of it. Some of it appeared now to be keeping Guyen alive.

He sat on the steps before the uploader, as though he was a steward awaiting a vanished king, or a priest before a throne fit only for the celestial. But he was steward and king both, minister of his own divinity.

His appearance was plain proof that the ragged cult he had surrounded himself with was still capable of working with the *Gil*'s technology, most especially the medical bay. Guyen sat there quite naturally, as though at any moment he might get up and go off for a stroll. But just as the upload facility was threaded through with connections to the ship, so was Guyen. He wore robes that lay open over a shipsuit that seemed to have been patched together from several older garments, but none of it hid the fact that two thick, ridged tubes had been shunted up under his ribs, and that one of the machines beside him seemed to be doing his breathing for him, its flaccid, rubbery sacs rising and falling calmly. A handful of thinner pipes issued from just past his left collarbone, like the flowering bodies of some fungal infection, before running into the mess of medical devices, and presumably cleansing his blood. It was all familiar to Holsten from back home, and he was aware that the *Gil* must store equipment like this for the extension of life in extreme cases. He had not expected to witness an extreme case, though. He was the oldest man in existence, after all, and if anyone was going to need this stuff, it would be *him*.

Guyen was an extreme case. Guyen had beaten him to that title by a comfortable margin. Lain had said he was old, but Holsten had not really processed the concept. He had thought he knew what 'old' meant. Guyen was *old*.

The commander's skin was a shade of grey Holsten had never seen before, bagged and wrinkled about his face where his cheeks and eye sockets had sunk in. Those almost-hidden eyes did not seem to focus, and Holsten was suddenly sure that somewhere there was a machine that was seeing for Guyen as well, as though the man had just started outsourcing his biology wholesale.

'Commander.' Absurdly, Holsten felt a curious reverence creeping in on him as he spoke, as though he was about to be born again into Guyen's ridiculous cult. The man's sheer antiquity placed him beyond the realm of human affairs, and instead into that of the classicist.

Guyen's lips twitched, and a voice came from somewhere amid that nest of botched technology.

'Who is it? Is it Mason?' It was not Guyen's voice, particularly. It was not really anyone's voice, but something dreamt up by a computer that thought it was being clever.

'Commander, it's me, Holsten Mason.'

The mechanical sound that followed was not encouraging, as though Guyen's reaction was too foul-minded for his mechanical translator to pass on. Holsten was suddenly reminded that the commander had never particularly liked him.

'I see you've got the uploader . . .' Holsten petered out. He had no idea what the uploader was doing.

'No thanks to you,' Guyen croaked. Abruptly he stood up, some sort of servos or exoskeleton lifting him bonelessly to his feet and perching him there incongruously, almost on his toes. 'Running off with your slut. I might have known I couldn't depend on you.'

'All the travelling I've been doing since your clowns woke me up has been entirely the idea of other people,' Holsten shot back hotly. 'But, seriously, you don't expect me to ask questions, given what I've seen here? You've had people just . . . what, living out their lives here over the last hundred years? You've set yourself up like some kind of crazy god-emperor and conned all those poor bastards into being your slaves.'

'Crazy, is it?' For a moment Holsten thought Guyen would rush at him, pulling all those tubes out of himself on the way, but then the old man seemed to deflate a little. 'Yes, well, I can see how it might look crazy. It was the only way, though. There was so much work. I couldn't just burn through Science and Engineering, using up their lives like I've used up my own.'

'But . . .' Holsten waved a hand towards the cluttered mass of machinery at Guyen's back. 'How can this even happen? Okay, the uploader, it's old tech. It's going to need fixing up, troubleshooting, testing – that much I understand. But not a century of it, Guyen. How can you have been doing this for so long, and got nowhere?'

'This?' Guyen spluttered. 'You think the *uploader* took all that time?'

'Well, no I . . . yes . . .' Holsten frowned, wrong-footed. 'What did, then?'

'I've gone over the whole damn *ship*, Holsten. The drive's been upgraded, the system security, the hull shielding. I'd say you'd not recognize the specs of the *Gilgamesh* – if I thought you had any idea what they looked like before.'

'But . . .' Holsten waved his hands as if trying to encompass the magnitude of what the other man was saying. 'Why?'

'Because we're going to war, and it's important that we are ready for it when we arrive.'

'To war with . . .' sudden understanding struck. 'With Kern? With the satellite?'

'Yes!' spat Guyen, his lips quivering, the artificial sound of the single word far grander than anything he could surely make on his own. 'Because we've seen it now: the ice worlds, and that grey abomination we've left behind. And then there's the green planet, the life planet, the planet our ancestors made for us, and we all thought the same when we saw that: we thought: "That's going to be our home." And it is! We'll go back and take out the satellite, and we'll finally be able to stop journeying. And then what you see here, that so *offends* you with how unnatural it is, all these people living and breeding, that will be *right* again. Normal service will resume. The human race can pick up at last, after a hiatus of two thousand years. Isn't that something to strive for?'

Holsten nodded slowly. 'Yes, I . . . I suppose it is.'

'And when that's all done – after I've worked a generation of specialists from cargo to *death*, Mason! To death from sheer old age! After I've taken their descendants and had them taught, and brought them in on my vision – brought them *up* on it! – and then prepared ourselves to defend against the satellite's weapons and its attacks, why would I not go back to the upload facility and try to get it to work? Do you think any of this would have happened without me? Do you understand how important having a single vision is? This isn't something to delegate to some committee; this is the survival of the human race. And I'm old, Mason. I've worked nobody harder than I've worked myself, and I'm on the brink of collapse, every scrap of medicine we have is needed just to keep my organs working, and it's still not *done*, it's not finished. I need to see it through. I'm going to upload myself into the machine, Mason. It's the only way I have of being sure.'

'You want to be immortal.' It had been intended as an accusation but it came out as something else, something with a hint of respect.

There was a ghastly choking sound, and for a moment Holsten thought that Guyen was actually dying. But no: he was laughing.

'You think that's what this is? Mason, I'm *dying*. The uploader doesn't change that. The "me" I live inside will die. And *soon* – before we see the green planet again. I can't even go back to the coffins now. There's no way I'd ever wake up. But now that I've got the uploader working, I can preserve a copy of me, to make sure things work out. I'm not some mad dictator, Holsten. I'm not some crazy man with delusions of divinity. I was given this task: to shepherd humanity to its new home. There's nothing more important than that. Not my life, not yours.'

Holsten realized unhappily that his own moral compass was spinning by now. 'Lain thinks you'll wreck the *Gil*'s systems, if you try that. She says there are copies of your test subjects running riot through the software.'

'*I'm* my own test subject,' Guyen growled. 'Anything in the system is just cast-offs of *me*. But none of them worked. None of them *were* me – not enough of me. But what little work I could squeeze out of you before you went gallivanting has served. Perhaps that's irony. It's ready now. I can complete an upload, and then it doesn't matter if I die. *When* I die, it won't matter. And as for Lain, Vitas doesn't think it'll destroy the computer. Vitas *wants* me to do it.'

On Holsten's list of reassuring things to say, that phrase did not feature. 'Lain seems pretty sure it's going to be a bad thing.'

'Lain doesn't know. Lain thinks small; she lacks dedication.' Guyen glowered, his face screwing up like a piece of paper. 'Only I can plan long enough to save us, Mason. That's why they chose me.'

Holsten stared up at him. The guards were some distance back, and it came to him that he could leap on decrepit old Guyen and just start pulling things out until nature took its course. And also that he had no intention of doing so.

'Then why did you grab me back, if you didn't need me?'

Guyen took a few stalking, mechanical steps, pulled up by the leash of his life-support. 'You're our star historian, aren't you? Well, now you get to do the other part of your job, Mason. You get to write the histories. When they tell each other how we came to live on that green world, that other Earth, I want them to tell it right. So tell it *right*. Tell them what we did, Mason. Write it down. What we do here creates the future, the only possible future that will see our species survive.'

5.6 RESOURCE WAR

The spider city states operate a variety of mining concerns, but they themselves do not dig. They have insects for that: one of the tasks that comes more naturally to the ant colonies they use in so many different ways. For centuries there has been enough for all, since spider technology is not metal-heavy, and the organic chemicals more important to them are fabricated from the common building blocks of life itself.

This is where it starts.

An ant from a colony run by Seven Trees is now making its way deeper into a set of galleries at some distance from the city itself. Its colony extends all around it – the mine workings are its home, and its siblings' excavations just a modified form of the same tunnelling they would use to expand their nest. True, much of the colony extends into solid rock, and the ants use modern techniques to conquer that element. Their mandibles are fitted with metal picks, assisted by a selection of acids and other substances to weaken the stone. The colony plans its own mine, including drainage and ventilation to make the place a conducive workplace for the hundreds of blind miners who toil there.

This particular ant is exploring for new seams of copper within the rock. The metal ore leaves traces that its sensitive antennae can detect, and it gnaws and works patiently where a trace is strongest, digging inch by inch towards the next deposit.

This time, instead, it suddenly breaks through into another tunnel.

There is a moment of baffled indecision as the digger teeters on the brink, trying to process this new and unexpected information. After that, scent and touch have built up a sufficient picture of its surroundings. The message is clear: other ants have been here recently, ants belonging to an unknown colony. Barring other conditioning, unknown colonies are enemies by default. The ant spreads the alarm immediately, and then goes forth to investigate. Soon enough it encounters the miners of the other colony and, outnumbered, is swiftly killed. No matter: its siblings are right behind it, summoned by its alert. A cramped, vicious fight takes place, with no quarter given by either side. Neither colony has received instructions from its spider masters to cross this particular line in the sand, but nature will take its course.

The second colony, that had literally undermined the Seven Trees workings, has been sent out by Great Nest to seek for new sources of copper. Shortly thereafter, centuries of diplomacy begin to break down.

Since contact with the Messenger was first established, metals consumption has increased exponentially in an attempt to keep up with the complex blueprints that form the Divine Plan. Those cities like Great Nest that are most fervent in pursuing God's design must push outwards constantly. Supply cannot keep up with demand unless new mines are opened – or appropriated.

Consequently, more mining works are being contested between rival colonies. Elsewhere, caravans of mineral wealth fail to reach their proper destination. In a few cases entire mining colonies are uprooted, driven away or suborned. Those who lose out are all relatively small cities, and none of them strong adherents of the message. A storm of diplomacy follows, amidst considerable uncertainty as to what has actually happened. Open conflict between spider cities is almost unknown, since every city is bound to its neighbours by hundreds of ties. There are struggles for dominance but thus far in their history, the point has always been that there must be something to be dominant over. Perhaps it is due to the nanovirus still working towards unity between those that bear its particular mark of Cain. Perhaps it is simply that the descendants of *Portia labiata* have developed a worldview in which open brute conflict is best avoided.

All this will change.

Eventually, when the truth becomes sufficiently evident to all parties, the transmitters of Great Nest issue an ultimatum to its weaker neighbours. It denounces them as straying from the purity of the message, and claims for itself the right to take whatever steps it must, to put into effect the will of God. Transmissions from the Messenger, though always obscure and open to interpretation, are taken to endorse Great Nest's proclamation. Slowly at first, and then more and more rapidly, this outright division spreads from local differences into a global fragmentation of ideology. Some faithful cities have thrown in their lot with Great Nest's vision, whilst others – distant others – have set up rival claims based on different interpretations of the Messenger's commands. Certain cities that had already begun to turn away from the message have pledged support to those cities that Great Nest has threatened, but those cities themselves are not united in their response. Other cities have declared independence and neutrality, some even severing all contact with the outside world. Sister conflicts have sparked up between states which perhaps have always rubbed along with a little too much friction, always jostling for leg room, for food, for living space.

At the disputed mining sites, many of which have changed hands several times by this point, Great Nest sends in dedicated troops. Another task that ant colonies will perform without special conditioning is to fight unfamiliar ants, and a mining colony is no match for an invading army column equipped with special castes and technologies. In two months of hard warfare, not a spider has died, but their insect servants have been slaughtered in their thousands.

Great Nest can draw upon a vastly larger and more coordinated army than its opponents and one that is better designed and bred for war, but those first months are still inconclusive. When Portia and her fellows gather together to review their progress, they are faced with an unwanted revelation.

We had thought to find matters settled, Portia considers, listening to her peers weave together their next moves: a sequence of steps that will lead them to ... where? When the original actions over the disputed mining sites were agreed, their purpose had seemed very plain. They all knew they were in the right. The Messenger's will must be done, and they needed copper in great quantities – copper that Seven Trees and the other apostate cities would have little use for, save to trade to Great Nest at a ruinous cost. So: seize the mines; that had been a simple aim in itself, and it has been accomplished relatively quickly and efficiently, all things considered.

And yet it seems that building the future is never so simple. Each thread always leads to another, and there is no easy way to stop spinning. Already Portia's agents in Seven Trees and the other cities know that Great Nest's enemies are building and training forces to take back the mines, and perhaps to do even more. Meanwhile, the peer group magnates of her enemies are engaging in similar debates over what is to be done. Every council has its extremists who push for more than mere restitution. Abruptly, to call for moderation is to seem weak.

All around Portia, there are those saying that more must be done to secure Great Nest from its new-minted enemies, and thereby to secure the will of their divine creator. They are performing that oldest of tricks: constructing a path by which to reach a destination, only in this case the destination is permanent security. With each step they take towards it, that security recedes. And, with each step they take, the cost of progressing towards such security grows, and the actions required to move forward become more and more extreme.

Where will it end? Portia wonders, but she cannot bring herself to voice her doubts. An ugly mood has come to the web-walled chamber. Great Nest has its spies in other cities, individuals and whole peer groups who have been bought or who are sympathetic to the dominant city's ideology. Equally, those other cities will have their agents in Great Nest. Previously, this interconnectedness of cities has always been a virtue, a way of life. Now it is a cause for suspicion, straining the bonds between peer groups, awakening division and distrust.

Nothing is being decided here, so she heads for Temple. It seems plain to her that guidance is needed.

She transmits as good a report of the situation, and her concerns, as she can, knowing that, while her speech to the Messenger will be private, God's response will be received by anyone listening on Great Nest's frequency – which will certainly include some residing in Seven Trees.

The record of the Messenger in dispensing practical advice is not good, as Portia is painfully aware. She knows she cannot expect something so much grander than her to spare much consideration for the lowly affairs of Her creations. God is intent on Her machines that will apparently solve many problems, not least that of the maddeningly imperfect communication between the Messenger and those She has set below Her.

Portia is not expecting a clear response therefore, but the Messenger seems to understand her better than she realized. The intended meaning is not precisely clear, for despite a painstakingly negotiated common language, the Messenger and Her congregation are separated by a gulf of common ground and concepts that is only slowly being filled. However, Portia understands enough.

The Messenger is aware that there are differences of opinion amongst Her creation.

She knows that some, like Portia, work hard to fulfil Her directives.

She knows that others, such as the Temple in Seven Trees, do not, and indeed have lost much of their reverence for the Messenger and Her message.

She instructs Portia now that the very future of her people is dependent on Her will being executed precisely and promptly. She states that a time of great danger is coming, and only by obeying Her will may this be averted.

She says, in words clear enough for Portia to understand without a trace of uncertainty, that Portia should take any and all steps to reach Her goal, and that there is no higher goal than this.

Portia retreats from the temple, prey to a whirl of mixed emotions. Spider feelings are not human feelings, but there is something in her of shock, also something of elation. Never before has the Messenger spoken so clearly.

Great Nest's hand has now been forced. Not only has their duty to God been personally reaffirmed, but spies in Seven Trees and the other enemy cities will also have heard God's latest words, and they will hardly have to wonder hard about what question could have yielded that dogmatic answer.

Life in Seven Trees has not turned out to be as free and effortless as Fabian hoped.

Bianca, at least, has fitted in well enough. Her contacts amongst the astronomical sorority have seen her installed comfortably into a respected peer group, although a powerful peer house in Seven Trees is still considerably smaller and poorer than even a mediocre house in Great Nest. She did offer to find Fabian a favoured position there, and indeed worked quite hard to import him with her – perhaps to quit a debt of gratitude or perhaps because she has seen how useful that dangerous little mind of his can be. He refused.

Life has been difficult for Fabian during the months since, but he has a plan. He has begun to ascend the thread of life, and this time as nobody's pet or favourite, acting without patronage and without sacrificing his vaunted freedoms.

Males in Seven Trees may have more freedom and influence than in Great Nest, but they can still be killed out of hand. They still have no more rights than any momentary usefulness grants them.

Seven Trees also has its gutters, though there is less of an underclass than Great Nest – just as there is less of everything else – but there are still surplus males and females down on their luck; each prey for another, just fallen corpses to be cleared away by the maintenance ants.

Fabian was nearly killed several times before he was able to take the first steps in establishing himself as a diminutive power within Seven Trees. Hungry females stalked him, delinquent males chased him from their territories, and he grew shrunken from starvation and exposure. At last, though, he was able to make contact with some females who had lost everything, yet had not quite descended into unthinking cannibalism. He managed to catch them on the very cusp of savagery.

They are three haggard sisters, ageing scions of a peer group that is now nothing but a memory in the higher reaches of the city. When Fabian found them they still kept a little tent of a peer house in good repair, at the very base of one of the trees that regrew here after that great and ancient war when the ants burned down the originals. They listened to him speak, taking turns to vanish from his sight purportedly to instruct the house males concerning his meagre entertainment. He knew there were no males, and what hospitality they could muster was mere crumbs: tiny insects and an old, half-mummified mouse that they had been feeding off for days.

I will reverse your fortunes, he told them. *But you must do what I say.*

He needed them. It was a bitter admission, but any social group must be fronted by females. *For now.*

What must we do? they had asked him. Any flavour of hope was nectar to them, even that offered by a scruffy foreign male.

Just be yourselves, he had assured them. *I will do the rest.*

Having attached himself to them, he had gone out with more confidence to begin recruiting.

There were hundreds of abandoned males scratching a living on the ground level around Seven Trees. They lacked training, education or useful experience, but they all had inherited Understandings of one kind or another. Now Fabian sought them out, interviewed them, adopting those who had abilities he could use.

Acting as merely the servant of one of the old crones he ostensibly worked for, he began to undertake jobs for more powerful peer houses, employing the chemical architecture of the ant colonies. With his unique system, it was not long before word of his prowess began to spread. The peer house of the three old females accumulated favours and barter. Soon they were spinning themselves a new house higher up on the tree, reaching for the same dizzying heights they had once known.

When they tried to take it all away from him, as Fabian had known they would, he had simply stopped working. By then the other males had grown to understand his ambition and they downed tools as well. A new arrangement was reached. The females were free to enjoy the status that Fabian's work brought them, but his would be the mind that directed the house, and – most importantly – his people were to be sacrosanct. The males of his house must not be touched.

Still, it has been a long, slow road to get anywhere. As a result, Fabian's unorthodox methods have just begun to bear fruit within the social network of Seven Trees at around the time that the mining skirmishes erupt.

Once the rumours reach him, he is quick to re-establish contact with Bianca. Her position has shifted from independent scientist to political advisor, as the major peer houses of Seven Trees and its neighbours try to come up with a suitable response. Great Nest has almost contemptuously stripped them of all their mines, but nobody is keen to be the first to suggest a straight-out violent response.

When diplomats contact Great Nest to try and negotiate, however, they come up against the new world that Portia has constructed after talking to God. Instead of simply beginning to exploit its own strength in return for concessions, as is traditional, Great Nest's position is uncompromising. Demands are made for other resources belonging to Seven Trees and the allied cities: farms, colonies, laboratories. When Seven Trees protests, the speakers for Great Nest label them heretics. The Messenger has spoken. She has chosen Her champions. This is not war: it is a crusade.

Then, and only then, does Seven Trees send out a large force of fighting ants to retake the mines. They are met by a similar force from Great Nest, and a battle ensues that is only a faint echo of the tumult promised for the future. The ants fight with mandibles, with blades, with acids and fire. They fight with chemicals that confuse the enemy, drive them berserk, attack their respiratory surfaces, suborn them and change their allegiance. The force sent from Great Nest readily obliterates the attackers.

A simple radio message is received in Seven Trees – and in all of its allies' cities – the next day.

Now we will come for you. Surrender yourselves to our Understandings or we will do what we must. The Messenger wills it.

There is chaos then, with the loose-knit, non-hierarchical spider society threatening to tear itself apart, as it has before under intense pressure. Ruling councils rise and fall. Some advocate surrender and appeasement, others outright resistance, others simply suggest flight. None of these carries the majority, instead each fragments and factionalizes in turn. The stakes are higher every day.

Then, one day, with an army from Great Nest already dispatched and on its way, Bianca asks to be allowed to address the great and the good of the city.

She finds herself positioned in the centre of a web with almost forty powerful females crouching at its edges, legs forward attentively to catch her words as the individual strands relay them. They listen intently. Everyone knows that they need a masterstroke now, to save themselves, but nobody can agree on what it might be.

But Bianca herself has nothing to say. Instead, she tells them, *I will bring one to you now who has found a way to combat this threat. You must listen until the end. You must hear what he has to say.*

The reaction is instant derision, shock and anger. The powers-that-be of Seven Trees do not have time for such foolishness. There is nothing a male could have to say that they themselves have not already considered a dozen times over.

Bianca presses on. *This male is from Great Nest*, she explains. *It is only through his assistance that I was able to escape from there. He possesses a curious facility with ants. Even in Great Nest his work was highly respected, but I believe he has discovered something secret, something new. Something Great Nest does not yet have.*

At last, by such means, she is able to gather their attention, soothe them, persuade them to hear Fabian out.

The male creeps out, to be pinned by their collective gaze. Fabian has given this moment some thought, based on his earlier failure with Portia. He will not ask for too much. He will show, rather than tell. He will woo them, but as a female does, with success, rather than as a male, with flattery.

Give me a force of ants and I shall defeat their army, he declares.

Their response is not as negative as he had expected. They know he is a turncoat from Great Nest, after all. They question him carefully, whilst he gives evasive, cautious answers, in a fencing match of subtle vibration and noncommittal gesture. He hints at having some secret knowledge of the Great Nest ant colonies, but he gives them nothing more. He watches them confer, plucking discreetly the radial strands of the web to send messages around their circle without their conference reaching the centre where he crouches.

How many ants? one asks him at last.

Just a few hundred. He only hopes that this will be sufficient. He is risking everything on this one venture, but the smaller the force he takes with him, the more valuable will seem his victory.

It is a ridiculously small force compared to the army that is encroaching on Seven Trees' territory, and in the end the females feel that there is little to lose. The only other serious alternative is to surrender and give up all they own to the peer groups of Great Nest.

Fabian heads with all speed back to his own peer house and chooses a score of his most able assistants, all males. They know much of his secret: the new architecture. He and they set at once to the most laborious task, reconditioning the ants he has been gifted with to obey his primary architecture, so that they can be given instructions while on the run.

The next day they leave Seven Trees for, Fabian hopes, the annals of history. He travels with his cadre of apprentices, with his meagre force of insect soldiers – and with Bianca. The leaders of Seven Trees could not countenance a force devoid of any female guidance, and so she is its figurehead, the respectable face of Fabianism.

For her part, Bianca has not been let in on Fabian's secret, but she remembers their miraculous escape from Great Nest and knows his reputation as a chemical architect. She has yoked her future to his, and now must hope that he is as good as he thinks he is.

The old weapons that allowed their species to fully dominate the ants – and thereby vastly enrich and complicate their society – are no longer viable weapons of war. The deconditioning effect of the Paussid beetle master-scent is something that most ants are now conditioned to resist, both because of inter-spider rivalries, and simply because the Paussid beetles themselves are constantly hacking colony architecture for their own purposes, remaining a persistent ghost in the organic machine. The spiders can only strive to minimize their effects.

Fabian's plan is more complex, therefore more risky. The first phase is a frontal assault.

The path that the Great Nest column is likely to take has already been densely strewn with a complex maze of dead-falls, spring-traps, webs and fire-traps. No spider would be fooled by them, but ant senses are easier to deceive, especially as they have little ability to sense anything at a distance. The Great Nest force is screened by a large, dispersed cloud of scouts to find and trigger these traps, and it is on to these that Fabian sets his own troops.

The response is immediate, alarm scents drawing more and more of the invaders. Positioned upwind of the skirmish, Fabian releases scent after scent into the air. Each one contains a fresh set of instructions, chemically encoded, allowing his small force to react swiftly, to change tactics and outmanoeuvre the enemy, whilst the Great Nest ants are simply following a basic battle architecture little changed from the insects' ancient fighting instincts.

Within minutes Fabian's forces have pulled out with minimal losses, and with prisoners, a handful of scouts cut off, immobilized and carried away.

Fabian and his fellows retreat, and keep retreating until the pursuing scouts from Great Nest break off and follow their own scent trails back to the advancing column. Left in peace, Fabian's team set up their laboratory and use samples from the captured scouts to brew up a fresh set of instructions for their soldiers.

Their ants are given their initial orders. Their little force splits up, each ant to its own, and heads for the enemy.

What are you doing? Bianca demands. *You have thrown away your army.* Everyone knows that ants are only effective in force. A lone ant counts for nothing.

We must move, is all Fabian will say. *We must be upwind of them.* It is an annoying limitation of his technique, but one he will solve in time. He is already working out systems in his head, using Paussid beetles as carriers of new information, or somehow triggering chemical releases by distant visual cues . . . but for now he must work with what he has.

The host of individual ants reach the enemy column, and pass through the far-flung screen of scouts without any alarm being raised. They touch antennae with the invaders, a quick fidget of appendages, and are let through, recognized as friends.

From a viewpoint in the branches, Fabian tensely watches his ants accumulating unnoticed within the Great Nest ranks. Now comes the hardest step for Fabian himself. He has never been responsible for the death of another of his species. He knows that there are those who live lives of deprivation where to fight, kill and even consume another spider is simple survival, but he feels strongly that he is working directly against such deprivation, and that to kill one's own belongs in the past. The nanovirus in him resists the necessity of what he intends, recognizing the sibling strains in his potential victims.

His plan is delicately balanced, however, and he cannot let anything endanger it.

There are a dozen or so observers from Great Nest moving amidst the thousands-strong column. Surely they will notice the foreign ants amongst their ranks? Although the Great Nest army will already have its rigid architecture in place, there will be a series of pre-set protocols that the spider officers will trigger, no doubt including one to order the attack on Seven Trees itself. It is possible that one of these pre-prepared positions will be some manner of emergency response.

Fabian releases his next set of instructions with some foreboding.

His infiltrators systematically seek out and murder the Great Nest spiders accompanying the army. They attack fearlessly, releasing alarm scents that throw the nearby loyalist ants into a frenzy. It is a calculated, merciless act painstakingly planned out in advance. Watching the result, which leaves knots of ants grappling over loose limbs and scraps of carapace, Fabian's people and Bianca are quiet and subdued. Of course it is not the first time that spider has killed spider, or even that male has killed female, but this is different. It represents a gateway to a new war.

From there on, the Great Nest column is doomed. Fabian's soldiers eat it from the inside out. The invading army has some defences, pre-set conditioning to defend itself against unexpected attack, plus shifting scent codes that change in a prearranged sequence over time. But Fabian's new architecture allows him to shift swiftly to adapt. The lumbering composite engine that is the Great Nest army has detected that something is going wrong, but it simply cannot adjust quickly enough to understand the threat. A trail of dead ants stretches for kilometres, by the time Fabian is through. His own losses are less than a dozen. His Thermopylae has been not a physical but a mental constriction that the enemy simply could not pass through while he held it against them.

Great Nest is not defeated yet. The column Fabian has

destroyed is merely a fraction of the military machine that the Temple there can set in motion. Seven Trees' victory will be answered by further aggression, no doubt. Fabian returns home and presents himself to the ruling females.

They demand to know his secret. He will not tell them, and he confirms that he and all of his peer group have taken precautions to ensure that their new Understandings cannot be extracted by force from their dead bodies.

One of the females – call her Viola – takes the lead. *So what will you do?*

Fabian suspects that she has thought further ahead than her sisters, having used his services before the war came. She has some idea how he thinks.

I will defeat Great Nest and its allies, he declares. *If necessary I will take an army from Seven Trees all the way to their city, and show them the error of their ways.*

The reactions he sees are a fascinating mix: horror that a male can speak so boldly of such large matters; ambition to see their stronger rival humbled; desperation – because what option do they have?

Viola prompts him to go on: she knows there is more.

I have a condition, he admits. Before that massed and hostile gaze, he outlines for them what he wants, what he wishes them to commit Seven Trees to, in return for its survival. It is the same deal he put before Portia. They are scarcely more inclined towards it, but then Portia was not in their current precarious position.

I want the right to live, he tells them, as firmly as he dares. *I want the death of a male to be punishable, just as the death of a female is – even a death after mating. I want the right to build my own peer house, and to speak for it.*

A million-year prejudice stares back at him. The ancient cannibal spider, whose old instincts still form the shell within which their culture is nestled, recoils in horror. He sees the conflict within them: tradition against progress, the known past against the unknown future. They have come so far, as a species; they have the intellect to break from the shackles of yesterday. But it will be hard.

He turns slowly on the spot in a series of short, jerky moves, looking from eye to eye to eye. They weigh him up, and they weigh the cost of his demands against the cost of having to acquiesce to Great Nest. They consider what his victory has bought them, and how it has improved their bargaining position. They ponder what Great Nest will exact from them if they surrender – certainly the temple at Seven Trees will be emptied and filled with foreign priestesses, all enforcing their orthodox vision of the Messenger's will. Control of Seven Trees will be removed from these females here. Their city will become a puppet worked by strings from afar, dancing to the pulse of Great Nest's radioed instructions.

They confer, they agonize, they threaten each other and scuffle for dominance.

At last they formulate their answer.

'It wasn't meant to happen like this. It wasn't meant to take so much *time.*'

Holsten was dining with Guyen. The commander's cultists, or highly trained engineers or whatever they really were, had brought him some of the rations that he remembered being pillaged wholesale from the terraforming station. It was heated and thawed to a warm slurry, and he spooned this slop unenthusiastically into his mouth as the old man talked. What Guyen ate these days was unclear, but he probably had a tube for that – and another one at the other end to deal with what his desiccated insides couldn't process.

'I woke up a crew that looked good, according to the records. They all had tech experience,' Guyen went on, or at least the machines that spoke for him did. 'We had all the kit we'd taken from the station. Preparing the ship was supposed to be *quick*. Just another few days. Just another few months. Just another year. Always just another year. And then I'd go to sleep for a bit, and wake up, and they'd still be at work . . .' His withered face went slack with remembering. 'And you know what? One day I woke up, and all those young faces . . . I realized that half the people doing the work had been born *outside* suspension. I'd taken up peoples' whole lives, Mason – they'd been trying to make it work for that long. And the new generation . . . they didn't know as much. They had learned what they could but . . . and then came another generation, devolving, understanding less than before. Everyone was too busy *doing* the work to pass on the knowledge. They knew nothing but the ship, and me. I had to lead them because they had work to do, no matter how inferior they were, how much longer it would take.'

'Because you need to fight the Kern satellite, the Brin habitat thing?' Holsten filled in for him, between mouthfuls.

'I have to save the species,' Guyen confirmed, as though that meant the same thing. 'And we did it. We did it, all of us. All those lives weren't wasted, after all. We have Empire tech defences, physical and electronic. There's not a weak point left where Kern can sneak in and switch us all off. But by then I realized that I was *old*, and I realized how much the ship needed me, and so we got the upload facility and started work on that. I've given everything, Mason. I've given so many years to the *Gilgamesh* project. I want . . . I really want to just close my eyes and let go.' The artificial voice fell to a static whisper. Holsten recognized this as a sacrosanct pause, and he didn't try to insert any words.

'If I thought there was no need of me,' Guyen murmured. 'If I thought they – you – could manage without my guidance, then I would go. I don't *want* to be here. Who would want to be this dying, intubated thing? But there's nobody else. The human race stands on my shoulders, Mason. I am the shepherd. Only through me will our people find their true home.'

Mason nodded, and nodded, and thought that Guyen might or might not believe all of that, but knew that he detected a thread of mendacity nonetheless. Guyen had never been a man to take advice or to share command. Why should he now be a man who would hand it over, especially when a kind of immortality was his for the taking if this upload business worked?

If the uploader didn't wreck the *Gilgamesh*'s systems.

'Why not Lain?' he asked Guyen.

The old man twitched at the name. 'What about Lain?'

'She's chief engineer. You wanted all this work doing, so why not pop her out sooner? I've seen her. She's older, but not . . .' *not as much as you,* 'not that much older. You can't have sprung her from the chambers that long ago. Why not start with her?'

Guyen glowered at him for a moment, or perhaps some machine glowered at him on Guyen's blind behalf. 'I don't trust Lain,' he snapped. 'She has ideas.'

There was no real answer to that. By now Holsten had already formed distinct ideas about whether Guyen was crazy, and whether Lain was sane. Unfortunately that did not seem to translate into an equal certainty about which of them was *right*.

He had one arrow left in the quiver. There was a sequence of recordings that Lain had played for him, before that meeting with Karst and Vitas: the last transmissions of the moon colony they had set up back in Kern's system. It had been Lain's secret weapon, to persuade him that Something Must Be Done. It had worked, at the time. She had been merciless, and Holsten had been left as depressed and miserable as he ever had been. He had heard the desperate, panicking voices of the people Guyen had left behind: their pleas, their reports. Everything had been failing, the infrastructure of the colony had simply not been self-sustaining. Long decades after the base was established, it began to die.

Guyen had left a community there, some awake, some in suspension. He had abandoned them to live there, and to raise their children to replace them at the helm of that doomed venture. Then the *Gil*'s commander had listened to their dying cries, their frantic begging, enduring the cold, the foul air . . . The lucky ones would have just rotted in their cold coffins once the power failed.

The last message had been a distress beacon, automated, repeated over and over: the successor – humanity's version of Kern's thousand-year call. Finally even that had ceased. Even that had not stood the test of that little span of time.

'I heard the recordings from the moon base,' he told Guyen.

The commander's leathery visage swung towards him. 'Did you?'

'Lain played them to me.'

'I'm sure she did.'

Holsten waited, but there was nothing more forthcoming. 'You're . . . what? You're denying it? You're saying Lain faked it?'

Guyen shook his head, or something else shook it for him. 'What was I supposed to do?' he demanded. 'Go back for them?'

Holsten was about to say that, yes, that was exactly what Guyen should have done. Instead, a little scientific awareness coloured his passion, and he began, 'The time . . .'

'We were decades away,' Guyen agreed. 'It would have taken decades to return to them. By the time they found there was a problem, they didn't have anywhere near that long. You wanted me to go through the colossal exercise and waste of turning this ship around, just to bury them?'

Guyen almost managed it then. Holsten's perceptions of right and wrong flipped and flopped, and he found he *could* look into that grey, dying face and see the saviour of mankind – a man who had been trained to make tough decisions, and had made them with regret but without hesitation.

Then a real expression finally clawed its way on to Guyen's face. 'And, besides,' he added, 'they were traitors.'

Holsten sat quite, quite still, staring at the horrible rearrangement of the commander's features. A kind of childish, idiot satisfaction had gripped the old man, perhaps entirely without his knowledge.

There had been mutineers, of course, as Holsten had more cause than most to remember. He recalled Scoles, Nessel and all that rhetoric about being sacrificed to an icy grave.

And they were right.

And, of course, most of the actual mutineers had been killed. The cargo decanted out to form the moon base crew had not been traitors; in fact they would have had very little idea of what was going on before learning of their fate.

'Traitors,' Guyen repeated, as if savouring the word. 'In the end, they got what they deserved.' The transition from earnest, martyred leader to raving psychopath had simply happened without any discernible boundary being crossed.

Then people started entering the chamber, Guyen's people. They shuffled about in their robes, and swirled and milled into a ragged congregation before the great mechanical majesty of Guyen's dais. Holsten saw them arrive in their hundreds: men, women, children.

'What's happening?' he demanded.

'We're ready,' Guyen breathed. 'The time has come.'

'Your upload?'

'My ascension, my eternal duty that will enable me to guide my people forever, in this world and the next.' He began to take the steps stiffly, one at a time.

From somewhere, Vitas and a handful of her team had appeared, hovering about the machines like a priesthood. The science chief glanced once at Holsten, but incuriously. Around the edges of the wider chamber, there stood a score or so of men and women in armoured shipsuits – Karst's security team. One of them must be the man himself, but they had their visors lowered.

So the old gang's together again, all but one. Holsten was acutely aware that Lain would expect him to buy her some time, although he had no idea if she was even on her way.

'Guyen,' he called after the commander. 'What about them?' His gesture took in the massing congregation. 'What happens to them when you're . . . translated? Do they just keep multiplying until they overrun the ship? Until there's nothing left to eat? What happens?'

'I will provide for them,' Guyen promised. 'I will show them the way.'

'It'll be the moon colony all over again,' Holsten snapped. 'They'll die. They'll eat all the food. They'll just . . . *live* everywhere until things break down. This isn't a cruise ship. The *Gil* isn't supposed to be *lived* in. They're cargo. We're all cargo.' He took a deep breath. 'But you'll have your electronic avatar by then. So long as the power holds, you'll be fine. Probably most of the ship'll be fine, the cargo in suspension . . . but these people, and their children, and – then what? – maybe one generation after that, they'll die. Your followers will die a drawn-out death of starvation and failing machinery, and cold, and suffocation, and all the other things that can happen because we're out in fucking *space!*' He had shocked himself with the vehemence of his tirade, thinking, *Do I actually care about all these lunatics that much?* But apparently he did.

'I will provide!' Guyen's voice rose to a boom without effort, channelled through speakers about the room. 'I am the last shepherd of the human race.'

Holsten had expected his own words to start a riot of fear and uncertainty among the congregation, but they seemed weirdly placid, accepting what Guyen said and barely seeming to register a word said against him. In fact the only reaction he got was that suddenly a couple of the larger sheep in Guyen's flock were standing at his shoulders, laying hands on him as if about to bundle him away. He needed more ammunition. He would have to fight dirty now.

'One more thing!' he shouted, just as Guyen reached the top step. 'You do know that Karst and Vitas have been working with Lain behind your back?'

The dead silence that followed this pronouncement was spoiled by Karst's helmet-muffled voice spitting out, 'Oh, you fucker!'

Guyen had become quite still – and so everyone had become quite still. Holsten stole a look at Vitas, who was observing the situation around her with a calmly inquisitive air, as if she could not feel the sudden change of mood in the crowd. Karst's people had begun to bunch up. They all had guns, and now these were mostly pointing at the faithful.

Have I just done the most sensible thing that I could, under the circumstances?

'I don't believe you,' Guyen's voice croaked, although if his disembodied voice was indeed devoid of belief, it was full to the brim with electronic doubt. Guyen's paranoia clearly had a 360-degree field of vision.

'When your clowns grabbed me, I was just coming back from a meeting – of me, Lain, *her*, *him*,' pointing out the guilty for the court.

'Mason, shut up or I will shoot your fucking head off!' Karst bellowed, neatly erasing any lingering suggestion of innocence.

The congregation was mostly armed, even if it was with knives and makeshift spears and maces. They outnumbered Karst's squad heavily, and the quarters were close.

'You will go back into suspension!' Guyen snapped. 'You, Vitas, all of your people!'

'Piss off! And what then?' Karst snapped. 'You think I trust you?'

'I will be the *ship*!' Guyen fairly howled. 'I will be *everything*. I will have the power of life and death over every member of the human race. Do you think that simply staying out of suspension will save you from my wrath, if you defy me? Obey me now and I will be merciful.'

'Commander—' Vitas started. Above the rising mutter of the congregation Holsten did his best to read her lips.

'You too, traitor!' Guyen levelled a twig-thin finger at her.

Then either Karst or one of his people – Holsten didn't see which – tried to level a gun at Guyen, and the fighting started. A few shots went off, striking sparks from the ceiling, some ripping hungrily into the crowd, but matters degenerated into a brawl almost immediately, the untrained but fervent masses ranged against Karst's few.

That was when Lain chose to make her move.

A knot of robed acolytes burst from the throng, bounding up the steps towards Guyen, and even Holsten thought they were fanatics heading to protect their leader, to form some sort of human shield. Only when their leader dragged some sort of makeshift weapon out, and her cowl slipped back, did he realize his mistake.

Moments later Lain had her weapon – some sort of industrial nail-gun – against the side of Guyen's head and was yelling for everyone's attention.

They were about twenty people down to injury or death by that point – a couple of Karst's band, and the rest luckless followers of the Church of Guyen. Lain never got her requested silence – there was sobbing, cries for help, at least one keening wail that spoke of desolated loss and grief. The bulk of the faithful, however, were frozen in place, seeing their prophet about to be struck down at the very point of his transcendence.

'Now,' Lain shouted, as best she could. Her voice wasn't made for public declamation or for confrontational heresy, but she did her utmost. 'Nobody's going anywhere, and that includes into that fucking computer.'

'Karst . . .' It was Guyen's voice, although his lips hadn't moved. Holsten looked over to the security team, backed into a tight knot with their leader in its midst. If there was any reply, it was too quiet to be heard, but it was plain that there would be no help for Guyen from that quarter, not any more.

'Vitas, disconnect this shit,' Lain instructed. 'Then we can start to sort out the mess.'

'Hmm.' The science chief cocked her head on one side. 'You have some sort of plan then, chief engineer?' It seemed an odd thing to say, for someone with no small-talk. Holsten saw the frown on Lain's face.

And, of course, Vitas had *wanted* the upload to go ahead. She had wanted to see what would happen.

'Lain!' Holsten shouted. 'It's happening! He's uploading now!' It was a lengthy process, but of course Guyen had been plugged in all this time. He had probably been feeding his brain into the *Gil*'s memory for ages, a bite-sized piece at a time.

The realization hit Lain at the same time and she pulled the trigger.

Vitas's face was a picture in that split second: real shock gripping her at last, but at the same time a kind of prurient interest, as if even this twist would yield valuable data for her studies. Guyen's face, of course, joined the rest of his head in painting the upload facility red.

There was a colossal groaning noise that echoed through the room, twisting and garbling and collapsing into static, but rebuilding itself jaggedly until at last it became a voice.

'I!' shouted Guyen even as his body collapsed back into its cradle of tubes and wires. 'I! I! I!'

The lights died, sprang back, flickered. Screens about the chamber suddenly sprang alive with random vomitings of colour and light, fragments of a human face, and that voice stuttering on, 'I! I! Mine! Obey! I!' as though Guyen had been distilled down to the basic drives that had always motivated him.

'Damage report!' Lain's team were all up on the dais now, accessing the *Gil* through the machinery there. 'Karst, get control, you useless fuckwit!'

Karst pointed his rifle at the ceiling and loosed a handful of shots, the roar of the gun scouring the room free of any other human noise, but unable to blot out the tortured glossolalia of the speakers. On the screens, something was trying to form itself into Guyen's face, a proof of ascension for the true believers; it failed and failed again, incomplete and distorted. Sometimes, Holsten thought, it was Kern's face instead.

He lurched his way up the steps to join Lain. 'What's going on?'

'He's in the system, but . . . it's another incomplete copy like his test runs. Only it's more . . . there's more of him. I'm trying to isolate him, but he's fighting me – they're all fighting me. It's like he's seeded the fucking computer with his people, sent them ahead to clear the way. I—'

'You shall not prevent me!' boomed the virtual Guyen, his first complete sentence. 'I! Me! I am! Eternal! I! I am!'

'What's—?' Holsten started but Lain gestured him away.

'Just shut up, will you? He's trying to get control over life-support.'

Karst's people were clearing out Guyen's followers, who seemed a lot less exultant about the partial ascension of their leader than they had probably anticipated.

'Vitas, *help*, will you?'

The science chief had simply been staring at the screens, but now she appeared to come to a decision. 'I agree, this has gone far enough.' As though it was simply a matter of an experiment that had outlived its time.

'What can I—?'

Lain hushed Holsten then, trusting her team enough to take a moment away from the consoles. 'Seriously, you've done what you could. You did what had to be done. You did well. But now? This is out of your area, old man. If you want, go help Karst, and hope we can contain Guyen-the-fucking-virus before he does too much—'

There was a shudder through the substance of the ship, and the colour drained from Lain's face.

'Shit. Just go, Holsten. Be safe.'

Words from one eggshell-dweller to another.

5.8 CONQUERING HERO

Fabian has come to the gates of Great Nest with an army.

It is not his army, technically. Seven Trees is not so desperate that it would give over this force to the official command of a male. Viola, one of that city's most powerful females, is the speaker for her home and therefore nominally in control. Fabian himself is there to put into effect her commands. He had expected this arrangement to rankle more than it has.

It helps that Viola is calm, long-sighted and intelligent. She does not try to tell him how to do his job. She gives him the broad sweep of strategy, bringing to the table an understanding of conflict and of spider nature that is far in excess of his own. He attends to the tactics, playing an army of thousands of ants like a maestro with his fluid, adaptable chemical architecture. The two of them work surprisingly well together.

Another reason that he is glad not to have the final authority is that he is similarly denied the final responsibility. To get this far, Seven Trees and its allies have tallied up a butcher's bill of the enemy that leaves Fabian shaken every time he considers it. Aside from numberless dead ants, several hundred spiders have perished in the fighting, some by design, others by happenstance. Great Nest has done its best to reverse the tide by killing the Seven Trees leaders, hampered in its belief that those leaders must necessarily be female. Fabian has thus been bypassed by assassins on several occasions, whereas Viola has lost two legs and has personally ended the lives of three attempting to kill her. It is a terrible truth they have discovered about themselves – all the participants in this conflict – that they are of a race that does not kill lightly, and yet give them a cause and they will.

And now they are at Great Nest itself, their army facing a host of ants dredged from that larger city's colonies, most of which are not even conditioned for military service but will fight against enemy ants if they must.

Ahead of them, the vast conurbation that is the spiders' greatest city seems fragile, like mere tatters of silk that the wind might blow away. For most of his life this was Fabian's home. There are hundreds of thousands of spiders currently crouching in their peer houses, beneath their canopies, against the tree trunks and branches, waiting to see what will happen next. There has been almost no evacuation, and Fabian has heard that the Temple has done its best to prevent anyone leaving.

Viola has sent a messenger to the peer houses of Great Nest, with a list of demands. The messenger was a male, therefore Fabian does not envy his chances. When he himself complained, Viola stated darkly that if Fabian truly wished all the freedoms of a female for his gender, then his fellow males must take the same risks.

Fabian can only try to imagine the debate going on in Great Nest even now. Portia and her temple priestesses must be urging resistance. Perhaps they believe that the Messenger will save them, even as She once interceded for Her people in the great war with the ants in ancient times. Certainly the Temple radio frequencies must be crammed with prayers for deliverance. If the Messenger has the power to aid Her faithful, then what is She waiting for?

Radio . . . ? And then Fabian is lost briefly in a dream of science, where every ant soldier could be fitted with a radio receiver, and somehow could write its own chemical architecture according to the urgings of signals sent out over that invisible web. A colony of ants that could be orchestrated swift as thought . . . ? He trembles at the thought. *What could we not do?*

And it nags at him, and nags at him, that he has come across such a thought before. And with a sudden jolt, he realizes that the great project of the Messenger, which Portia and her fellow zealots have given their all to realize – the indirect cause of this war – could itself be just such a thing. No ants, no chemicals, but that net of copper would carry impulses just as the radio would, just as the individual ants in a colony would. And were there not switches, forks, gates of logic . . . ? It seems to him that such a design would have the virtue of speed, yet surely it could not be as versatile and complex as an ant colony working at full efficiency?

You know Portia. Will she yield? Viola prompts him. They have been waiting for a response for so long that the sun is now going down. Full dark was their deadline, for the ants can fight perfectly well at night.

If she is still in control, she will not. The Seven Trees forces will tear Great Nest open, if they have to, and Fabian is very afraid that within the close, confused confines of a city he may lose control. Scraps of his army may end up cut off from him, unable to be directed, still following their last conditioning. The death toll, amongst those whose only crime is to have made Great Nest their home, will be horrifying. Fabian would almost rather turn back.

Viola has explained things patiently, though. Great Nest's influence has been cut back to the city's very boundaries, but it must still concede defeat. There are tens of other temple-dominated cities across the world. They must be taught this lesson.

Fabian has already heard the outcome of other conflicts. Entire cities have been burned – by design or by simple acci-dent, given how voracious fire is and how flammable much of spider construction can be. There have been massacres on both sides. There have been ant armies gone wild, reverting to their old ways, breeding unchecked. The radio brings in daily stories of worsening warfare.

Great Nest stands as the symbol of defiance for the cru-saders, though. If Great Nest submits, then perhaps sanity might be salvaged from the chaos.

They will have to kill her themselves, Viola considers.

It is a moment before he understands to whom she is referring: *Portia*. He himself cannot think of Portia without a stab of guilt. She is the cause of this war, as much as any individual spider is, but Fabian knows bitterly that she has done all she has for what she considers the best of reasons. She has hazarded her entire city because she *believes*. And he still feels respect for her, and also that curious coiling sense affecting males, that here is a female to dance for and offer his life for. It is a shameful, backwards feeling, but it has been driving the males of his species to engage in the dangerous pursuit of continuing the species for millions of years.

Fabian wishes things could be different, but he can plot no

path from where he stands now, to any outcome that would see him reconciled with Portia.

Prepare our vanguard, then. Viola knows that he will already have considered the terrain, the opposing forces and the capabilities of their own troops, and formulated some custom conditioning for the initial assault – to be refined and amended as the war goes on. His revolutionary techniques have won battles against massively superior forces before. Now he will employ them against a defending force that is itself outnumbered and outclassed.

He releases his scents. He has refined the technique. As well as airborne pheromones a host of Paussid beetles are lined up, pressed into service to carry his instructions across the breadth of the army. They are buying their continued survival with their usefulness, their services offered with a spark of awareness of the deal, disturbingly clever insects that they are.

Then there is a bright flash from one of Viola's spotters, palps signalling a clear message.

A party is on its way out of Great Nest, twenty or more strong. At their head is the male emissary Viola sent in.

Fabian feels a gripping tension leach out of his limbs. Great Nest wants to talk.

He does not recognize the bulk of the enemy delegation. Certainly none of the females now apparently in control are familiar. There are a handful he does recall, Portia's cronies from her peer house or from the temple. They are hobbled with silk and herded out by their erstwhile political opponents. They are being given over to the enemy.

The story spills out swiftly. There has been a changing of

the guard in Great Nest. There has been fighting within the city, spider against spider, at the highest level. The priesthood has been broken and cast down. Some remain in hiding, sheltered by those who still believe in the sanctity of the message. Some are believed to have fled. The balance are here, as a token of goodwill.

Of Portia, there is no word. Fabian imagines her alone and on the run. She is resourceful enough to survive and now, without the infrastructure of the Great Nest Temple, she is not the threat to the world's peace she once was. No doubt Viola and the others will hunt her down, or her former fellows in Great Nest will, but he hopes that she survives. He hopes that she escapes to find some quiet living somewhere, and does something good.

Terms are then negotiated, punitive but not impossible. The new clique ruling Great Nest treads a delicate line between defiance and acquiescence; Viola knows the game and plays along. It is only in watching the Seven Trees female throw herself into negotiations that Fabian realizes how much she, too, had wanted to avoid taking that final, unthinkable step.

This is not the end of the war of doctrine, but it is the beginning of the end. The fall and conversion of Great Nest is both the catalyst and a model for the future. Fighting continues in various parts of the world but those who still believe that the Messenger's message is all-important only lose ground.

This does not mean that nobody is talking to God, of course, but they no longer listen with the same single-minded purpose that Portia and her fellows did. Progress on the Messenger's machine loses its original frantic fervour, although it does not grind to a halt. There will always be scientific minds willing to take up the challenge, who continue to speak in guarded, monitored terms to the Messenger and try and reduce the complex, technical language into something fitting spider technology. The irony is that in now taking a layman's view of the instructions, some progress is being made that the faithful might never have achieved with their more doctrinal approach.

And, quite soon after Great Nest capitulates, Fabian finds himself crouched before the leading females of Seven Trees: a very similar gathering to the one he faced during the war. Viola is dominant, her war-heroine status confirmed, and they all remember the deal they signed in adversity. He has been expecting this moment, when the great and good try to go back on their word.

Has he allies? Perhaps. Bianca is there, one of the lowliest of the great, but great nonetheless, and as much through her connections with him as due to her own scientific achievements.

The female magnates shuffle and settle, murmurs passing around the web. Viola brings them to order neatly.

Of course, Seven Trees and our allies owe a great debt to your discoveries, she allows. *Our own chemical architects are already considering all the other aspects of daily life that could be improved by such fine control as you can offer.*

I never intended my work to be used as a tool of violence, Fabian confirms calmly. *And, yes, the possibilities are near endless.*

Perhaps you will share your plans with us?

They all become very still, waiting for his first wrong move.

I have my own peer house, he tells them, reminding them right at the start of one of their major concessions. He feels the dislike and the unease ripple out and then vanish back into their accomplished composure. *I have my peers, who have shared in my Understandings. As you say, there is so much that can be revolutionized. I have already begun.*

He remembers Bianca in Great Nest, calling him a dangerous little monster. They all see him that way now. More, they fear him, and perhaps this is the first time females have ever feared a male, in his world. They must wonder whether, if he called, an army would come against them, slaved to his will and his new architecture.

This is not his intention, however, and Fabian suspects that if he makes them too fearful of him, they will kill him and all his followers outright, whatever the loss to posterity. He must make up ground quickly. *My peer house will help make our city the greatest the world has ever seen. Whilst it is true that my discovery must eventually spread to the wider world, whoever has first use of it will always remain its mother, and thus need never fear the armies of those who lack it.*

Much muted messaging vibrates around the edge of the web. Hard, calculating female gazes study Fabian, a mere morsel before them. He can see that most of them want to put him in his place, to take back what was previously given under duress. Probably they would do it with the best intentions, under the long-ingrained assumption that a male simply could not be allowed responsibility for such weighty matters. Probably there are a dozen separate equivocations ongoing in the minds around him, to justify their now withholding what was promised to him. They will offer him

Portia's deal: *Let us feed and value and protect you; what else can you want?*

I would prefer that city to be Seven Trees, Fabian taps out, and hunches against the possible response.

A twitch of Viola's palps prompts him to continue.

I cannot hold you to our bargain, he says simply. *I have asked more of you than the Messenger Herself. I have asked you to extend to me and my whole gender the freedoms that you yourselves live and breathe by. It is no small request. It will not be easily made real. Generations from now, there will still be those for whom these reforms rankle, and places where a matter of gender still determines whether one may be killed out of hand.* The concepts themselves are hard to phrase, since gender is integral to so much of their language, so Fabian must tread the long way round to explain his meaning. *All I can say is this: that city which extends to me and mine these basic rights will have my service and that of my peers, and will gain all the profit that ensues. If Seven Trees will not, then some other city, more desperate, shall. If you should kill me here, you will find some of my peers already outside the city, carrying my Understanding with them. We will go where we are made welcome. I would like you to make us welcome here.*

He leaves them arguing fiercely over his fate. The decision, he hears later, is close, almost as many against as for. Seven Trees nearly has its own schism there and then. Respected matriarchs resort to measuring legs against one another like juvenile brawlers. In the end, solid mercenary interest outweighs outraged traditional propriety – but only just.

Fabian himself does not live to see the world he has helped create. Two years after Great Nest's surrender, he is found dead in his laboratory, drained to a husk by parties unknown. Many believe that resentful traditionalists from Seven Trees are responsible. Others claim that Temple fanatics from some defeated city had tracked him down. By that time the war is won, though, and the spiders are not normally given to exacting vengeance for its own sake. Their nature tends towards the pragmatic and constructive, even in defeat.

There are some who say that the perpetrator was Portia herself, whose name has since acquired a curious mystique – often spoken of but never seen, her final whereabouts and fate a mystery.

By then, however, Fabian's new architecture cannot be put back in its box. His extensive peer house, mostly but not uniformly male, has spread well beyond Seven Trees, the Understanding carefully guarded, but its advantages aggressively exported as stock in trade. A technological revolution is sweeping the globe.

Already it has reached those who speak to the Messenger. The application of Fabian's genius to matters of the divine is still in its infancy, but his wartime revelation – that his new architecture could in some way approximate to what God wishes them to build – is the dream of a number of other enquiring minds.

And out in cold orbit is the fused thing that is Avrana Kern and the Sentry Pod, its computer system and the Eliza mask that it sporadically dons. She is desperate to communicate with her creation. She has taught her monkeys, as she thinks of them, a common language. Originally a stripped-down Imperial C, it has mushroomed into a dense field of unfamiliar concepts, as the monkeys have run away with it. She is aware that, in opening communications with the inhabitants of the green planet, she has broken new ground in the long history of the human race. Having no other humans (in her view) to share it with, she finds the triumph lacking. She is also increasingly aware that the frame of reference of her new people seems very different. Although they share a language, she and they do not seem to have the commonality of concept that she would have expected.

She is increasingly concerned about them. They seem further away from her than she would have anticipated from fellow primates.

She is aware that direct interference from her, in the sense of shoehorning her desires directly into their nascent culture, is entirely against the dictates of the Brin's mission, which was to gently encourage them, and always let them come to her. There is no time. She has been away for far too long, aware that the Sentry Pod's power reserves have dwindled during her long sleep, and have subsequently been drained almost to nothing by her showdowns with the *Gilgamesh*, its drones and its shuttles. The solar cells recharge slowly, but the energy deficit has already taken its toll, starving the auto-repair systems which have slowly accumulated a colossal and continual workload just to keep the pod's vital systems going.

She is increasingly, miserably aware that she herself is now better classified as a vital system than anything truly living. There is no line where the machine leaves off and she begins, not any more. Nothing of Avrana Kern is so viable as to be able to stand on its own. Eliza and the upload and the withered walnut that is her biological brain are inseparable.

She has been trying to transmit to the monkeys her plans

for an automated workshop, which she could then instruct to start building things down on the planet. She could then transfer herself, datum by datum, down into the gravity well. She could finally meet her arboreal people. Most importantly, she could communicate with them properly. She could look into their eyes and explain herself.

The monkeys have made draggingly slow progress, and time is one of many things that Avrana Kern simply does not have enough of. She cannot understand it, but the technology that seems to have arisen on her planet has gone in a wildly different direction to that of Earth. They do not even seem to have invented the wheel, yet they have radios. They are slow to understand much of the task she has set them. She, in turn, cannot follow much of what they say to her. Their technical language is a closed book.

And that is a shame, because she needs to prepare them. She needs to warn them.

Her people are in danger.

The *Gilgamesh* is coming back.

6
ZENITH / NADIR

6.1 THE BALLOON GOES UP

Portia is watching art being made.

She is fidgety, nervous – not the fault of the art itself, but she has a great task in front of her, which occupies most of her mind. She never had much patience with sculpture-telling at the best of times. A shame that all this is being done in her honour.

Not just hers, of course. All twelve of her crew are here, being seen and being lauded. Portia is not even nominally in command of the voyage. However, hers is the task of great-est risk. Hers is the name being drummed about the Great Nest district of Seven Trees.

She tries to shrug off her nerves and concentrate solely on the performance. Three nimble male artists are telling the story of the martyr Fabian, the great scientist and enfran-chiser. Starting with just a few support lines they have spun themselves a three-dimensional narrative, their threads cross-ing and knotting and intersecting in a constantly evolving kinetic sculpture of silk that suggests scenes from the famous pioneer's life, and finally death. Each scene is built on the bones of the last, so that the ephemeral and delicate sculp-ture they create grows and branches, a constantly evolving visual narrative.

Portia is ashamed to find she is bored. She does not have

that poetic turn of mind to properly appreciate this art form – the allusions and memes required to follow the story are not found in her Understandings. She is a pragmatic creature of simple, visceral pleasures. She hunts, she wrestles, she climbs, she mates; traditional pursuits and perhaps a little old-fashioned. She prefers to think of them as timeless.

She could, of course, go to the city library and obtain an Understanding that would immediately allow her to appreciate this art in all its glory, but what would she lose? Some less-regarded ability or knowledge would be shouldered out, for her mind has finite limits on what it can retain. Like many of her kind, she has grown comfortable with what she is, and loathe to change if there is no grand need for it.

She stays still for as long as she can bear, politely eyeing the ever-more-complex structure, while feeling the appreciative stir and tremble of the audience, knowing only that it is something denied to her. At last, she simply cannot stay any longer in that crowd under that grand, tented ceiling, and creeps out as covertly as possible. This is her night, after all. Nobody is going to deny her.

Outside, she finds herself in the centre of the great conurbation that is Seven Trees' scientific district. Struck by a need for greater height and clear air, she ascends limb over limb, by line and by branch, until she can see the darkness of the sky above, seeking out the pinpoint bright dots that are stars. She knows, by learning and by Understanding, that they are so far away as to make any concept of the real distance meaningless. She recalls nights spent in the wilderness, though – for there is still wilderness despite the growth of the spider communities and their attendant support structures. Once away from the constant glare of the bioluminescent city lights, the stars can seem clear and close enough to touch.

Here, though, she can barely see them at all, with everything around her lit up in a hundred shades of green and blue and ultraviolet. A strange thing that she, whose work places her at the very fang-point of scientific advance, feels that life is outstripping her, actually leaving her behind.

Within her she has Understandings that were first held by some distant hunting ancestress whose life was constant toil: working to feed herself and her kin, fighting off ancient enemies who are now safely domesticated or extinct or driven to the wildest corners of the map. Portia – this Portia – can look back at the simplified, even romanticized, recollections of that time that she has inherited, and yearn for a less complex life.

She feels tremors from below, and sees someone climbing up towards her. It is Fabian – *her* Fabian, just one of countless males named after the great liberator. He is one of two males in her twelve-strong crew, and her personal assistant – chosen for his quick mind and agile body.

It is overwhelming, is it not?

He has a knack for saying the right things, and it doesn't matter whether he means the performance below or the great lit-up tangle that is the city around them. Tomorrow, history will be made.

Fabian dances for her, then, because he senses that she is unhappy, and a little flattery and attention tonight will help her on the morrow. Away from the crowd, he now performs for her the ancient courtship of their kind, and is received in turn. Monogamy – mon*andry*, rather – is not a concept the spiders have much familiarity with, but some pairs grow used to each other. Fabian dances only for her, and she rebuffs the advances of any other.

As always, at the height of his performance, when he has set down his offering before her, she feels that deep-buried jab to push the matter on to a fatal consummation. But this is all part of the experience, adding zest and immediacy before swiftly being overridden by her more civilized nature. These days such things hardly ever happen.

Below them, the performance also reaches its climax. Later, the artists will take it all down, consume their swathes of webbing and dismantle their masterpiece. Art, like so much else, is transient.

Elsewhere in the city, in the hub of learning and research that is also the Great Nest temple for the dwindling number of parishioners who still need to embrace the unknown in their lives, Bianca is at work making her last minute preparations. She is not one of Portia's select crew, but she has had a hand in the mission as a whole. Her interest in tomorrow's departure is almost maternal, for she has been the motivating force behind so much that is about to happen. Her true intentions are not quite what others suspect – nothing nefarious – but she has an unusual mind equipped for thinking broader thoughts and seeing further.

Bianca is a born polymath, in this context meaning she is able to absorb far more Understandings than the average spider. Unlike Portia, she changes her mind regularly. The core of what she considers herself to be is simply her capacity and desire to learn, not any individual facility she might briefly take within her. Currently she is an expert radio operator, chemist, astronomer, artificer, theologian and mathematician, her mind crammed to bursting with a complex interlacing of knowledge.

Now, long past the time when her kin are all resting, she checks and rechecks her calculations, and designs trouble-shooting architecture for the ant colony she has instructed to model and double check her figures.

Her newfound theology combines with the basic thought-fulness of her nature to give her a sense of awe and reverence about the venture in hand. Hubris is not quite a concept she grasps, but she comes very close here, alone in her control centre, as she walks through the complex stages of the plan within her mind.

She has a rare perspective that enables her to look back on so many generations of struggle and growth and be able to give a shape and a texture to history, to appreciate the incremental contributions of all those Portias and Biancas and, yes, Fabians down through the generations. Each has contributed Understandings to the sum total of arachnid knowledge. Each has been a node in the expanding web of progress. Each has planned out the path one step beyond their ancestors. In a very real way, Bianca is their child, the product of their learning, daring, discovery and sacrifice. Her mind throngs with the living learning of dead ancestors.

She understands, in a real and immediate way, how she stands on the backs of giants, and that her own back, too, will be strong enough to bear the weight of many genera-tions to come.

Next morning Portia and her crew assemble at a point beyond where the last buildings of the city taper into noth-ing, in the midst of a great swathe of farmland, among stands of stubby, warty trees stretching to the horizon, separated by firebreaks and the well-trodden pathways of the farming ants. The weather is fine: cloudy but with only a little breeze, as predicted. This moment has already been put off twice previously owing to inclement conditions.

Portia remains tense and still. The others deal with their nervousness each in their own way. Some crouch, some run about, some tussle or talk nonsense, feet stamping out a fretting staccato. Viola, the leader, goes from each to each, with a touch, a stroke, a twitch of palps, reassuring them.

Fabian is the first to see the Sky Nest.

Even at this distance, it is absurdly huge as it floats majestically over Seven Trees, coasting smoothly over the Great Nest district like an optical illusion. The vast, silvery bulk of its gasbag is currently three hundred metres long, dwarfing the long, slender cabin suspended beneath. Later, they will extend the envelope to twice its current size until the lift-to-weight ratio reaches the extreme proportions that their project will require.

The spiders have been using silk for gliding since before the earliest Understanding, and their increasing intelligence has led to multiple refinements of this art. Their chemical synthesis meanwhile gives them access to as much hydrogen as they need. With a technology of silk and lightweight wood, even their experiments with powered heavier-than-air flight result in something feather-light and buoyant. Constructing dirigibles is something they have taken to readily.

Lines are dropped by the skeleton flight crew, unravelling a hundred metres to reach the ground. Glad to be in motion at last, Portia and the others scramble up, a climb barely worth mentioning. There is a brief, ceremonial handover from the flight leader to Viola, and then the flight crew abseil down their own lines and leave the Sky Nest to its new occupants.

The airship is a triumph of engineering, rugged enough to withstand the turbulent weather of the lower air, and yet – with the gasbag fully extended and filled – capable of ascending to previously inaccessible heights. The aerodynamic profile of the entire vessel is fluid, and determined, moment to moment, by the tensioned cords of its internal structure. Now it is lifting into a stiffening breeze, its structure shifting in automatic response as the new crew settles in.

Their target height is so far above their world that it barely qualifies as *height* at all. And even then there will be a greater journey for the most adventurous of them: for Portia.

Viola checks that her crew members are in place, and then joins Portia at the forward edge of the cylindrical crew compartment, gazing out through the faintest shimmer at the receding ground below. Already the gasbag is expanding further, bloating out with more hydrogen, its leading edge reshaping itself for streamlining, as the Sky Nest lifts away faster and faster. Here, in the bows, is the radio and also the main terminal for the airship's brain.

Viola places her palps into paired pits in the lectern before her, and the Sky Nest tells her how it feels, how all its component pieces are holding up. It is almost like speaking on the radio, almost like talking to a living thing. She spoke to the Messenger once, did Viola, and communicating with the Sky Nest feels much like that.

Tiny antennae brush and twitch the sensitive hairs of her palps, feeding her information by touch and by scent. Two of her crew stand ready to give chemical commands to the terminal here, which will swiftly spread across the ship.

The ongoing calculations required to take an object of gossamer and hydrogen to the upper reaches of the atmosphere would challenge even the polymath Bianca, who therefore designed the ship to think for itself: a patient, dedicated intelligence subordinate to the commands of its spider crew. The airship is crawling with ants. This particular species is small – two centimetres at most for the workers – but bred to be receptive to complex conditioning. In fact the colony writes much of its own conditioning, its standing chemical architecture allowing it to receive direct information about the ship's situation and constantly respond to it without the intervention of the crew.

Although the ants can go everywhere, their physical pace would be too slow to coordinate the vast ship's constant metamorphoses. Spider bioengineering sidesteps this problem with cultured tissue. Just as, for generations, artificial muscle has been used as a motive source for their monorail capsules and other brute-force devices, so Bianca has pioneered artificial neural networks that link to chemical factories. Hence the ants in the crew capsule do not need to walk to the other widely spaced elements of their colony. Instead they send impulses through the ship's nerves, and these are translated to chemical instructions at the other termini. The neural network – unliving and living all at once – is a part of the colony, as if it was some bizarrely over-specialized caste. The ants are even capable of altering its complex structure, severing links and encouraging the growth of others.

Bianca is probably the only spider to wonder if the thing

she has created – or bred perhaps – may one day cross some nebulous line that separates the calculating but unaware from what she herself would understand as true intellect. The prospect, which will probably alarm her peers when they consider it, has been working on her mind for some time now. In fact, her current private project has a great deal to do with some of her more speculative thoughts in that direction.

Aboard the Sky Nest, the crew are preparing for the conditions of the upper atmosphere. The capsule is double-hulled, a layer of air between the sheets of silk providing the insulation they will need in the thinner reaches of the atmosphere. The outer skin of capsule and balloon is woven with silvery, glittering thread, an organic material that disperses and reflects the sunlight.

The Sky Nest carries them on up towards the light dusting of clouds. Two of the crew don suits of light silk to pass through the airlock and check on the operation of the god-engines, so called because they are a development of an idea apparently received direct from the Messenger. Before it was dictated as part of the old divine mandate, nobody had considered the idea of rotary motion. Now, bioelectric fields spin light metal propellers that steadily separate the Sky Nest from the ground.

Some of the crew gather at the shimmering windows, crowding for a view of the city as it shrinks from a vast swathe of layered civilization to an untidy scrawl like a child's knotted picture. The mood is high and excitable. Portia is the only one there who does not share it. She remains serious, inward-looking, trying to prepare herself for her own task. She seeks solace away from the others, and carefully knots and picks her way through a mantra that has travelled alongside her people for centuries, the ancient, reassuring mathematics of the first Message. It is not that she is some atavistic true believer, but that tradition comforts and calms her, as it did her distant ancestors.

In the fore-cabin space, Viola gestures to her radio operator, and they signal that all's well. Down in Great Nest district, Bianca will receive their message and then send a communication of her own, not to the Sky Nest but further still.

Bianca is hailing God with a simple announcement: *We are coming.*

6.2 AN OLD MAN IN A HARSH SEASON

He woke to the smell of burning. For a moment, lying there with the faint reek of overstressed-electrics infiltrating his nostrils, he began thinking, quite calmly: *cold suspension, hot smell, cold suspension, hot smell, funny* . . .

Then he realized it wasn't funny at all. It was the opposite of funny, and *once again* here he was in his coffin, only the burial had now become a cremation and he'd come back to life at just the wrong moment.

He opened his mouth to cry out, and instead choked helplessly on the acrid fumes that were filling his tiny allotment of world.

Then the lid came off, with a shriek of tortured metal and snapping plastic, even as he pressed against it. It was as though he had briefly been given superhuman strength.

Holsten yelled: no words, not even a sound that had any particular emotion behind it – neither fear, triumph nor surprise. It was just a noise, loud and pointless, as though his mouth had been left tuned to a dead channel. Kicking and clawing, he slid over the edge of the suspension chamber, and nobody caught him this time.

The hard impact brought him back to himself properly, to find he was lying on the floor of Key Crew feeling not only like a fool, but a fool in pain and with an audience. There were three other people there, who had stepped back prudently as he flailed his way to freedom. For a moment he didn't even want to look at them. They might be mutineers. They might be weird Guyenites here to offer him up to their dead but ever-living cybernetic god. They might be spiders in disguise. It seemed to him that there was precious little good that could come of there being other people around him, just then.

'Classicist Doctor Holsten Mason,' said a voice, a woman's voice. 'Do you answer to your name?'

'I . . . Yes, what?' The question was on the pivot point between normal and strange.

'Note that as a positive,' a man said. 'Doctor Holsten Mason, please stand up. You are being relocated. There is no cause for alarm, but your suspension chamber has become unstable and is in need of repair.' Nothing in this speech made any acknowledgement of the fact that these clowns had just had to rip the lid off his coffin to get at the meat within. 'You will be taken to another chamber and returned to suspension or, if no functioning chamber is available, you will be taken to temporary accommodation until one is. We understand that this must be distressing for you, but we assure you that everything is being done to restore normal ship operation.'

At last, Holsten looked up at them.

They were wearing shipsuits, and that had to be a good thing. He had half expected them to be dressed in hides and skins, a doubly unpleasant thought given that the *Gilgamesh* had only one animal in abundance.

They were two women and one man, and they looked surprisingly neat and clean. For a moment he could not work out why that alarmed him so. Then he clicked that, had this been some random emergency, and if these were crew, he would have expected them to be dishevelled and tired about the eyes, and for the man to be unshaven. Instead, they had taken the time to smarten themselves up. The shipsuits, on the other hand, were plainly not new: worn and scuffed and patched – and patched again.

'What's going on?'

The man who had reeled off his reassuring little speech opened his mouth again, but Holsten put up a hand to stop him, hauling himself to his feet.

'Yes, yes, I got it. What's going on?'

'If you would come with us, Doctor Mason,' one of the women told him.

He found his hands had formed pathetic little fists and he was backing away. 'No . . . No, I've had enough of being hauled out every century by another band of halfwit clowns who've got some stupid idea of what they want to do, without telling me anything. You tell me what's going on or I'll . . . I swear I'll . . .' And that was really the problem, because he'd what? What would the great Holsten Mason then do? Would he throw a tiny tantrum, out here in the vastness of space? Would he go back to his lidless coffin and fold his arms across his chest and pretend to be sleeping the sleep of the dead?

'So help me, I'll . . .' he tried again, but his heart wasn't in it.

The three of them exchanged glances, trying to communicate by grimace and eyebrow. At least they were not trying to haul him anywhere by force, just yet. He cast a desperate glance around Key Crew to see what there was to see.

At least half the suspension chambers were lying open, he saw. Some others remained closed, the panels on their exteriors displaying the cool blue glow of good functioning. Others were shading into green, and even towards the yellow that his own had perhaps been displaying. He went over to one, looking down at the face of a man he thought he recalled as being on Karst's team. The panels had a host of little alerts indicating what Holsten assumed was probably bad news at some level.

'Yes,' one of the women explained, noting his gaze. 'We have a lot of work to do. We have to prioritize. That's why we need you to come with us.'

'Look . . .' Holsten leant forwards to peer at the name on her shipsuit, 'Ailen, I want to know what the situation is with the *Gil* and . . . you're not Ailen.' Because abruptly he remembered the real Ailen, one of the science team: a sharp-faced woman who hadn't got on much with Vitas, or with anyone else.

He was backing away again. 'How long is it?' he demanded of them.

'Since when?' They were advancing on him slowly, as if trying not to spook an excitable animal, fanning out around the broken coffin to pin him.

'Since I . . . Since Guyen . . .' But they wouldn't know. Probably they didn't even remember who Guyen was, or perhaps he was some demon figure in their myth cycles. These people were ship-born, *Gilgamesh*'s children. All that smooth patter, the shipsuits, the appearance of neat competence, it was all an act. They were nothing but monkeys aping their long-vanished betters. The 'new suspension chamber' they would take him to, after destroying the real thing, would be nothing but a box with a few wires attached to it: a cargo cult coffin built by credulous savages.

He looked around for something to use as a weapon. There was nothing to hand. He had a mad idea of waking up others of the Key Crew, of popping out the security man like some sort of guardian monster to scare them away. He had a feeling that his persecutors were unlikely to wait patiently while he worked out how to do it.

'Please, Doctor Mason,' one of the women asked patiently, as though he was just some confused old man who wouldn't go back to his bed.

'You don't know who I am!' Holsten yelled at them, and then he ducked and somehow came up holding the whole jagged-hinged lid of the suspension chamber, the unbalancing weight of it a weird reassurance that there was something solid in the world that he had control over.

He threw it. Later, he would look back with amazement, watching this raging stranger he had briefly become, heaving the ungainly missile over the open coffin towards them. He got it bang on target, striking their upraised arms, knocking them out of the way, and then he rushed past them, sleep-suit flapping open at the back as he dashed out of Key Crew.

There was absolutely nowhere he could think of heading, so he just went, stumbling and staggering and pelting down the corridors that he remembered, but that had been transformed in his absence into something strange and broken. Everywhere there were wall panels removed, wiring exposed, some of it ripped out or cut through. Someone had been flaying the *Gilgamesh* from the inside, exposing its organs and inner workings at countless junctures. Holsten was irresistibly put in mind of a body giving way to the last virulent stages of some disease.

There were two people ahead of him, yet more manicured savages in orange shipsuits. They had been tinkering with a mess of tangled wiring, but stood up abruptly at the shouts issuing from behind Holsten.

He would have to go through them, he knew. At this stage his only hope was to keep running, because that might at least get him somewhere other than this. *This* was not a place he could be. *This* was all too clearly a great and delicate space vehicle that was being torn apart from the inside, and how could any of them last after that?

What happened? he was asking himself frantically. *Lain was working to contain the Guyen infection. There was nothing I could do. I had to go back to sleep, in the end. So how did it come to this?* He felt that he was developing some hitherto unknown ailment, some equivalent of motion sickness caught from too many dissociated moments of history crammed into too little personal time.

Is this the end, then? Is this the human race in the end?

He got ready to put his shoulder up against the two primitives ahead of him, but they refrained from getting in his way, and he just stumbled on past them as they stared at him blankly. For a moment he saw himself through their eyes: a wild-eyed old man bouncing off the walls, with his arse hanging out.

'Doctor Mason, wait!' they were calling from behind him, but there was no waiting permitted to him. He ran and he ran, and eventually they cornered him in the observation cupola, with the starfield drifting behind him, as though he was about to hold them off by threatening to jump.

There were more than three of them, by then: the commotion had brought along maybe a dozen – more women than men, and all of them unfamiliar people in old shipsuits with dead names on them. They watched him cautiously, even though there was nowhere else he could go. The three who had woken him were notably neater than the rest, whose garments and faces looked decidedly more lived-in. *Welcoming committee*, he thought drily. *Awards for the best-dressed cannibals of whatever stupid year this is*.

'What do you want?' he demanded breathlessly, feeling himself at bay against the universe.

'We need to reallocate you a chamber—' started the man from the welcoming committee, in those same bright, calm, false tones.

'No,' said one of the others. 'I told you, not this one. Special instructions for this one.'

Oh, of course.

'So, tell me?' Holsten broached to them. 'Tell me who you really are. You!' He pointed at not-Ailen. 'Who are you? What happened to the real Ailen that you're wearing her skin – *clothes*, her clothes?' He could feel a deep craziness trying to shake itself loose inside him. This crowd of serious, well-mannered people in stolen shipsuits was beginning to frighten him more than the mutineers, more than the ragged robes of the cultists. And why was it always like this? 'What's *wrong* with us?' And only from their expressions did he realize that he had just spoken aloud, but the words wouldn't stop. 'What is it about us that we cannot live together in this fucking eggshell ship without tearing at each other? That we have to try and control one another and lie to one another and hurt one another? Who are you that you're telling me where I have to be and what to do? What are you doing to the poor *Gilgamesh*? Where did all you freaks come from?' The last came out as a shriek that appalled Holsten, because something in him seemed to have snapped beyond any control or repair. For a moment he stared at his audience of the young and alien, with his mouth open, everyone including himself waiting to see if more words would be forthcoming. Instead he could feel the shape of his mouth deforming and twisting, and sobs starting to claw and suck at his chest. It was too much. It had been too much. He, who had translated the madness of a millennia-old guardian angel. He who had been abducted. He who had seen an alien world crawling with earthly horrors. He had feared. He had loved. He had met a man who wanted to be God. He had seen death.

It had been a rough few weeks. The universe had been given centuries to absorb the shock, but not him. He had been woken and pounded, woken and pounded, and the rigid stasis of suspension offered him no capacity to recover his balance.

'Doctor Mason,' said one of them, with that relentless, brutal courtesy. 'We are Engineering. We are crew.' And the woman he had singled out added, 'Ailen was my grandmother.'

'*Engineering?*' Holsten got out.

'We are fixing the ship,' explained another of the youngsters, so very earnestly.

This new information spun about inside Holsten's skull like a flock of bats trying to find a way out. *Engineering. Grandmother. Fixing.* 'And how long will it take,' he said shakily, 'to fix the ship?'

'As long as it takes,' said Ailen's granddaughter.

Holsten sat down. All that strength, the rage and the right-eousness and the fear, it all drained from him so viscerally that he felt he should be surrounded by a visible pool of spent emotions.

'Why me?' he whispered.

'Your suspension chamber required urgent attention. You had to be retrieved,' said the welcoming-committee man. 'We were going to find you somewhere to wait while a new chamber was prepared, but now . . .' He glanced at one of his fellows.

'Special instructions,' one of the newcomers confirmed.

'Let me guess,' Holsten broke in. 'Your chief wants to see me.'

He could see he was right, although they stared at him with something approaching superstition.

'It's Lain, isn't it,' he said confidently, and the words unleashed a sudden jagged onset of doubt. *My grandmother*, not-Ailen had said. And where was Ailen now? 'Isa Lain?' he added, hearing a renewed tremble in his voice. 'Tell me.'

In their eyes he could see himself: a terrified man out of his time.

'Come with us,' they urged him. And this time he went.

6.3 COMMUNION

Bianca has spoken to the Messenger before, and she has taken on a set of Understandings donated by researchers who have distilled the wide history of contact with the artificial god into an easily analysed format. To Bianca, the results are fascinating, and she is not sure any other before her has come to quite the same conclusions.

The Messenger is plainly a sentient entity orbiting her world at a distance of around three hundred kilometres. The earliest extant Understandings record that, for an unknown period of time, the Messenger was sending a radio signal to the world consisting of a series of mathematical sequences. A relatively short time ago, historically speaking, an answering transmission was sent out by one of Bianca's forebears, and a strange and unsatisfactory dialogue commenced.

It is the character of this dialogue that Bianca has been obsessing over. She has mulled over the second-hand experiences of those who came before, felt their distant conviction that the curious voice they heard belonged to some manner of intelligence, one that was deeply interested in her kind, intent on communicating, and that had a wider purpose. These conclusions seem unarguable from the facts. Bianca is also aware, from the Understandings she has known, that her ancestors constructed a number of beliefs that are, in

442

retrospect, less verifiable. Many came to believe that the Messenger was responsible for their existence, a belief that their God actively fostered. Furthermore, they believed that the Messenger had their best interests at heart, and that the plan they were following so diligently – and, later, at such cost – was one that, could they only understand it, was for their express benefit.

Bianca has considered all of that, and finds none of it supported by fact. She is aware that a great many of her species are still invested in Temple, and the belief that the Messenger is in some way looking out for them, even though that belief is only a wishful shadow of the fervour that once existed. She has been relatively tactful about her conclusions, therefore, but she has made it plain that the traditional, antiquated view of the Messenger as something like their own kind writ large – some great spider in the sky – is absurd.

That the Messenger is an entity of great breadth of intellect, she cannot contest. Potentially it is a superior intellect, but that is a harder judgement to make because she can only conclude that it is a very different type of intelligence from her own. There is plainly a vast amount that the Messenger takes for granted which even Bianca, stretch her mind as she might, cannot grasp. Conversely, there is much that has been said *to* the Messenger that has evidently been misunderstood, or met with blank incomprehension on the part of God. The capabilities of the divine are apparently limited in curious ways. There are concepts that the most ignorant spiderling would intuitively understand that clearly pass the Messenger by.

And this, of course, is with a common language painstakingly hammered out between the two ends of the twitching radio waves. Ergo, as Bianca is not the first to consider, the Messenger is far from all-seeing or all-knowing. It must feel its way; it must work to understand, and all too often it fails.

Where comprehension is most lacking is in basic everyday matters. The Messenger is plainly unaware of most events occurring on the world it orbits. Moreover, descriptive language is usually lost on it. It is able to deal with visual descriptions in relatively basic ways, but any language coloured by the rich sensorium of a spider – the touch, the taste – tends to lose itself in translation. What is received most readily is numbers, calculations, equations: the stuff of arithmetic and physics.

Bianca is familiar with that sort of communication from other sources. Out in the sea is a thriving civilization of crustaceans that her species has been in sporadic contact with for centuries. A basic gestural language has been negotiated over the years, and the submerged stomatopod state has experienced its own dramas and crises, its upheavals, coups and revolutions. Now they have radio, and scientists of their own, albeit their technology is constrained by their environment and their limited ability to manipulate that environment. They are a world apart, though, not just in being aquatic but in their priorities and concepts. The one thing that Bianca can discuss with them readily is mathematics, something for which the stomatopods have a passion.

She has spent many years refining and elevating the complex architecture of the ant colonies in order to create the tools she needs for her cutting-edge experimentation. The most complex systems, such as the self-regulating flight control-colony aboard the Sky Nest, work on highly mathematical principles, and their chemical architecture is able to receive numerical information and act upon it, even to performing intricate calculations played out in ant bodies and the neurons of individual ant brains.

Bianca is living with a recurring thought concerning the theoretical similarity between the Messenger and an ant colony grown sufficiently advanced and complex. Would it feel the same, to communicate with both?

These days, active communication with the Messenger is strictly limited. There are always odd sects: recidivist peer houses who have somehow nurtured and become consumed by a deviant Understanding. As any reply from the Messenger is received wholesale across most of the planet, such closet zealots are quickly uncovered and hunted down the moment it becomes apparent that someone has opened an unauthorized channel to God. Instead, the major cities each have a say in who has access to the Messenger. Some temples, notwithstanding, attempt to find the divine truth behind the bewildering plan that is still broadcast entreatingly from time to time. Mostly, though, the privilege falls to enquiring scientists, and Bianca has schemed, plotted, flattered and performed favours to buy herself the chance for a free and frank exchange of views.

The Sky Nest is making good progress on its historic mission, rising steadily into the atmosphere. The onboard colony reports on its own radio frequency to Bianca, confirming that all is well, and data from three other distant transmitters triangulate the airship's position. This is the easy stage of the journey. Barring unforeseen weather, the Sky Nest should reach its effective operational ceiling on schedule.

The Messenger will be clearing the horizon, and Bianca

sends a signal to Her, inviting dialogue. She includes a certain amount of the formalities that Temple once used, not because she believes there is any need for them, but because God is better disposed towards those who feign the right humility.

The Messenger is patient enough to outlast generations of Bianca's kind, and Her thoughts have a momentum that does not take note of developments on the world below – or so runs the theory. Bianca is not so sure. It is certainly a matter of fact that, despite the fall in Temple's fortunes, the Messenger continues to exhort its congregation to work further on its machine. The demands have become all the more insistent since Bianca's peers of a generation or so ago essentially ceased to make progress on any literal translation of the Messenger's desires: neither faith nor ingenuity being able to bridge the gap between divine will and mortal comprehension. Bianca is well aware of the threats and imprecations that have come from on high. The Messenger has preached the coming of a terrible catastrophe. These days, Bianca's peers believe that this is little more than a crude attempt to motivate them into throwing further resources at an impossible errand.

Again, Bianca is not so sure. She has a gift for seeing problems from unusual angles, and imagining radical possibilities.

The difficulty now, she believes, is not understanding the Messenger, but getting the Messenger to understand her. She needs to break through what appears to be a deeply ingrained train of thought. Historical example – remembered blurrily through the medium of Understanding – shows that the Messenger was not always so single-minded. Obsession or frustration have made Her so. *Or perhaps desperation*, Bianca reflects.

She intends to show the Messenger something new.

One of the giants whose shoulders she stands on is a still-living colleague who has bred a colony of seeing ants. Their sight is feeble compared to the spiders' own, but the individual pinpoints of what the colony perceives can be assembled, by fearful mathematical effort, into a complete picture. Moreover, this picture can be encoded into a signal. The code is simple: a sequence of dark and light dots, spiralling outwards from a central point, that together build up into a wider picture. It is as universal a system as Bianca can conceive of.

She has just such an encoded image that has been received into her working colony. Appropriately, it is a view of the Sky Nest itself, viewed just as it was lifting away from the city.

She tells the Messenger that she intends to transmit a picture. There is no obvious sign that she has been understood – since God's needy tirade continues unabated – but Bianca can only hope that some part of the celestial presence understands. She then instructs her colony to transmit, knowing that several hundred of her species' top scientists will be listening in on any reply.

The Messenger falls silent.

Bianca cannot contain her excitement, and she races frantically around the silken walls of the room. Whilst it's not the reaction she was hoping for, it is at least a reaction.

Then the Messenger speaks, requesting clarification. The scientific world holds its breath. God has understood, at least, that something new is in the air, and has replied in that odd unemotional style that Bianca recalls from antique conversations, when She was teaching this common language to Her chosen. This is God at Her most procedural, seeking to understand what has just been received.

Bianca tries, and tries again. The Messenger can grasp that the information transmitted is intended to be a visual image, but decoding it seems insurmountable. In the end Bianca breaks down the task into its simplest elements, bringing the whole operation as close to that universal mathematics as she can, by sending out formulae to describe the spiral that is the blindingly obvious way the image should be read.

Bianca can almost *feel* the moment when the fulcrum of God's awareness tilts. A moment later, the response arrives and she learns that God's language already contains a word for airship.

By this time the Messenger has passed beyond the horizon, but God is insatiable. *Show me more* is the unmistakable meaning, but Bianca transmits to her peers, cautioning them from further feeding the fire just yet. Privately, she is jealous of her newfound privilege in finally cracking the composure of God. She could continue speaking to God across the far side of the planet, by passing her signal hand-to-hand across other transmitters until it could be sent out towards space once again, but she is willing to wait until God returns to communicate directly with herself, and her peers grudgingly defer to her suddenly elevated eminence.

The Messenger bombards the planet insistently for more information, during which time Bianca comes to a startling conclusion: that the Messenger *cannot* see what goes on upon the planet right beneath Her. Far from being all-seeing, and despite being readily familiar with the concept of sight, the Messenger is blind. Radio is Her only means of sight.

Bianca has another picture sent to her ant colony, and she transmits it as soon as God returns to the skies above her. It is a simple enough sight, a view of Seven Trees from within, showing the intricate splendour of its scaffolding and the bustling industry of its inhabitants. The developer of the encoded picture originally used it as a test image in her experiments.

God is silent.

Far distant, the Sky Nest finally reaches the heights it was designed for, and finds equilibrium in the upper reaches of the air, its gasbag now expanded to half a kilometre in length. Bianca absently monitors its progress, knowing that the ship's crew will be testing their mechanisms and colony conditioning in the thin air, ensuring everything is ready for the most dangerous part of the mission, to be undertaken by Portia. Despite the double-hulled insulation of the cabin, the cold is causing some discomfort. Their species has some ability to regulate its body heat and keep its metabolic rate up, but they still grow sluggish whenever the temperature drops. Viola, in charge of the mission, reports that the work is going more slowly than anticipated, but is proceeding within tolerance.

Bianca is still waiting. The progress of the Sky Nest is now of secondary concern. She has silenced the Messenger. Nobody in all the history of her kind has done the like. The eyes of the world are on her with a judgemental gaze.

So she waits.

6.4 EPIPHANY

High above the green world, high above the Sky Nest and all the other industrious endeavours of its inhabitants, Doctor Avrana Kern tries to come to terms with what she has just been shown.

She has seen these things before, these scuttling, spinning monsters. The drone sent from the *Gilgamesh* saw one briefly, before its demise. Cameras from the shuttle that she downed caught sight of some before it burned. She has known that there were *things*, unintended things, down on Kern's World, the serpents in her garden. They were not part of the plan: the ecosystem so carefully designed to provide a home for her chosen.

She has known for lifetimes that they were there, but she has found within herself an almost infinite capacity to overlook. She can reel back in horror one moment, demanding, *What have you done with my monkeys?* and a mere decade later she has almost forgotten, hidden subroutines coating this offending memory until it no longer irritates the oyster of her mind. The electronic interior of the Sentry Pod is cluttered with such cast-off memories, the understandings that she cannot bear to have as part of herself. They are lost thoughts of the home that she will never see, they are pictures of arachnid monsters, they are images of a barrel

450

burning as it strikes atmosphere. All gone, excised from her functioning mind, and yet not lost. Eliza never throws anything away.

Avrana has always returned to the certainty that her plan for this world has succeeded. What else is there for her, after all? For untold ages she has orbited in silence, broadcasting her never-ending examination questions at a heedless planet. For untold ages she slept, the robust systems of the Sentry Pod doing their diligent best to stave off the inching encroachment of decay and malfunction. Whenever Avrana woke, at longer and longer intervals, screaming and clawing at the inside of her tiny domain, it was to cringe before an indifferent cosmos.

The pod systems themselves, running on minimal power, did their best to keep everything going, but still there were sacrifices: she is blind, she is fragmented, she is not sure where she ends and where the machines begin. The pod is playing host to a multitude, each sub-system devolving into some crude autonomy: a community of the half-witted holding everything grimly together. And she is one of those shards. She occupies a virtual space, crowded and cramped as a rookery. She and Eliza and the many, many systems.

The passing of the *Gilgamesh* – with all that undignified shouting and begging, even down to the colossal energy expenditure it took to bring their intruding shuttle down – it seems like a dream now, as though the would-be humans had wandered in from some parallel reality that had so very little to do with her. All they had taught her was that she had not known despair until they arrived. A silent planet was preferable to a planet bustling with human life, for human life would preclude the success of her mission entirely. Let her circle the globe until the Sentry Pod fell apart, so that still she could hope her monkey subjects would eventually call out to their creator. An absence of success did not mean her experiment was a failure.

At no time has she examined her motives or priorities or asked herself why she is so rigidly dedicated to carrying out this mission to the exclusion of all else. While she was speaking with those alleged humans from the ark ship, it was almost as if she was two people: one that remembered what it was like to live and breathe and laugh, and one that remembered the importance of scientific success and achievement. She wasn't sure where that first Avrana had come from. It didn't seem like her, somehow.

Then the monkeys had answered, and everything changed.

True, they were late. The projected few centuries had been and gone, and the Sentry Pod was long past the lifespan its creators had envisaged for it. Still, they built things to last, in those days. If the monkeys had needed their hundreds or even their thousands of years, Avrana and Eliza and their myriad support systems were ready for them.

But they had been so dense, and their thinking had been so strange. She had tried and tried, and so often seemed to be getting somewhere, but the monkeys had their own ideas – and such strange ideas. Sometimes they could not understand her superior intellect. Sometimes she could not understand them. Monkeys were supposed to be the easy first step to a universe of uplift. Everyone had assured her they would be close enough to humans to understand, yet far enough to remain a valid and worthwhile subject. Why could she not see eye to eye with them?

Now she sees their eyes. She sees all eight of them.

The image sent to her is insane, fantastical, a vast, layered, tangled structure of lines and links and enclosed spaces that exist only because they have been pulled into temporary arrangements of tension. The spiders are all about it, caught in mid-creep. The words that heralded this image were simple, clear beyond mistaking: *This is us.*

Avrana Kern flees into the limited depths of her remaining mind and weeps for her lost monkeys, and knows despair, and she does not know what to do.

She consults with her council of advisors, the others who share her deteriorating habitat. Individual systems tell her that they are still doing their jobs. The main control is keeping a log of transmissions sent from the surface. Others record the progress of celestial bodies flagged as of interest, including a distant – a very distant – speck that calls itself the last hope of the human race.

She presses further, seeking that other large focus of calculation she shares this pod with, and must occasionally negotiate with. They are legion, in there, but there are two poles to the Brin 2's Sentry Pod, and she reaches for the other carefully.

Eliza, I need your assistance. Eliza, this is Avrana.

She touches the stream of that other mind, and is momentarily immersed in the tumbling river of thought constantly flowing there: *my monkeys where are my monkeys cannot help me now I'm cold so cold and Eliza never comes to see I can't see can't feel can't act I want to die I want to die I want to die . . .* The thoughts flowing, helpless and unconstrained, out of that broken mind as though it is trying to pour itself empty, and yet there is always more. Avrana recoils and, for a terrible, frozen moment knows that if what she has touched is an organic mind, then *I must be* . . . but she has, after all, an almost infinite capacity to overlook, and that moment of self-reflection is gone, and along with it any threat of revelation.

She is left merely with that intolerable image, reconstructed pixel by pixel inside her mind.

This is what she has been communicating with. The monkey mask has been lifted, and *that* appalling visage is revealed instead. Every hope she had for her grand project – quite literally the one thing in the universe left to her – is now dashed. For a moment she tries to imagine that her simian protégés are out there somewhere else, hiding from the festering civilization of the spiders, but her memory has had enough of playing games. They burned. She remembers now. The monkeys burned, but the virus . . . the virus itself got through. That is the only explanation. Oh, perhaps what she has seen could arise spontaneously, given millions of years of the right conditions. The virus is the catalyst to condense all that span of time into mere millennia, though. The agent of her triumph has become instead the agent of something weird and strange.

She tilts on the fulcrum of decision. She sees clearly the path of rejection: those squabbling ape-things of the *Gilgamesh* will return eventually and make an end of it all in that mindless way that humans always have done. Monkeys or spiders, it will not matter to them. And she, Avrana Kern, forgotten genius of an elder age, will slowly decay into senescence and obsolescence, orbiting a world given over to the thriving hives of what she must nominally allow to be her own species.

Her long history will be done. This last corner of her time

and her people will be overwritten with the fecund hosts of her distant and undeserving descendants. All of it will be lost, and there will be no record of her long and lonely aeons of waiting and listening, of her breakthroughs and her triumphs and her eventual horrifying discovery.

There are few immutable boundaries inside the Sentry Pod. The various entities, electronic and organic, have no firm divisions any more, each leaning on and borrowing from the others for simple everyday functionality. Similarly the past bleeds into the present at the slightest invitation. Avrana Kern – or the thing that considers itself to be her – relives her history with the green planet and its denizens: their mathematical reply; teaching the monsters to speak; her painful, difficult conversations; their worship, their entreaties, the baffling, half-incomprehensible tales they told her of their exploits. She has spoken with uncounted numbers of their great minds: votaries and astronomers, alchemists and physicists, leaders and thinkers. She has been a cornerstone of a civilization. No human being has ever experienced what she has, nor touched anything so alien. Save that they are not alien, of course. In the end, undeniably, their stock arose alongside hers. She and they share ancestors five hundred million years old, before the stuff of life separated into those who would forever carry their nerves upon their back and those that would carry them within their belly.

There are no aliens that her people ever met or heard from. Or, if there were, their signals were overlooked, passed by: alien in a way that meant no human could see them and recognize them as evidence of life from elsewhere. Kern's faction and her ideology already knew this, which was why they intended to spread Earth life across the galaxy in as many varied forms as possible. Because it was the only life they had, they had a responsibility to help it survive.

She has lived lifetimes along with the people of the green planet. She and her host of companion systems have soared on their triumphs, shaken under their defeats, sought always to bridge what has ever been a troubled and incomplete understanding. She sees them now, yes. She sees them for what they are.

They are Earth. Their form does not matter.

They are her children.

She backtracks, calling up logs of centuries of conversations from where they are crammed into her electronic memories, having overwritten all the last desperate radio songs of old Earth. She reviews all the baffling mystery of the monkey dialogues now seen under a harsh and uncompromising new light. She stops trying to tell them things, and starts listening.

Much as the spiders can use their Understandings to write new knowledge into their minds – though Kern has no idea of this – so Kern's current state means that she can rewire her own mind far more readily than a human brain could be reconditioned. She models generations of conversations, changes her perception of the senders, ceases trying to cast her protégés as something one step down from human.

She understands, not perfectly – for great swathes of their talk remain a mystery – but her comprehension of what they are saying, their preoccupations, their perceptions, all of it suddenly falls that much more into place.

And at last she answers them.

I am here. I am here for you.

6.5 THINGS FALL APART

They gave him a shipsuit. He could hardly present himself in his flimsy sleeping garb, open at the back where the tubes had gone in, for all he had already paraded his pockmarked old backside through half of the crew quarters before they caught him.

The name on his new outfit was 'Mallori'. Searching his fragmented memory Holsten had no idea who Mallori might have been, and did not want to think about whether there *was* even a Mallori any more. Would he prefer to be wearing the clothes of a corpse, or those of someone who might any moment wake up and need them back?

He asked after his own suit, but apparently it had been taken away and worn out long ago.

When they were getting him clothes, he saw other people. This generation's engineers left him in one of the science rooms that had been converted into a dormitory. At least forty people were crammed in there, the walls studded with hooks for hammocks that a few were still sleeping in. They looked frightened and desperate, like refugees.

He spoke with a few. When they found out he was actually crew, they bombarded him with questions. They were insistent. They wanted to know what was going on. So did he, of course, but that answer did not satisfy them. For most of them, their last memory was of a poisoned, dying old Earth. Some even refused to believe how much time had gone by since they had closed their eyes in the suspension chambers that first time. Holsten was appalled at how little some of these escapees had actually known about the endeavour they were embarking on.

They were young: most of the cargo would need to be young, after all, to be able to start anew in whatever circumstances they were thawed out for.

'I'm just a classicist,' Holsten told them. In truth there were a thousand things he knew that would be relevant to their predicament, none of which he felt like talking about or thought would much reassure them. The most important question – that of their immediate future – he could not help with, at all.

Then the ersatz engineers came with the shipsuit and led him off, against the complaints of the human cargo.

He had his own questions then; he was feeling calm enough to deal with the answers.

'What will happen to them?'

The young woman who was leading him glanced grimly back the way they had come. 'Returned to suspension as soon as chambers are available.'

'And how long will that be?'

'I don't know.'

'How long has it been?' He was picking up ample cues from her expression alone.

'The longest anyone has been out of suspension was two years.'

Holsten took a deep breath. 'Let me guess: there are more

458

and more you're having to thaw out, right? Cargo storage is deteriorating.'

'We're doing all we can,' she snapped defensively.

Holsten nodded to himself. *They can't manage it. It's getting worse.* 'So where . . . ?'

'Look,' the woman rounded on him. Her badge said, 'Terata,' another lost, dead name. 'I'm not here to answer your questions. I have other work to get to, after this.'

Holsten spread his hands appeasingly. 'Put yourself in my position.'

'Friend, I have enough trouble just being in my *own* position. And what's so great about you, anyway? Why the special treatment?'

He nearly responded with, 'Don't you know who I am?' as though he was some grand celebrity. In the end he just shrugged. 'I'm nobody. I'm just an old man.'

They passed a room of perhaps a score of children, a sight so unexpected that Holsten stopped and stared, and would not be moved on. They were aged around eight or nine, sitting on the floor with pads in their hands, watching a screen.

On the screen was Lain. Holsten choked at seeing her there.

There were other things, too: three-dimensional models, images of what might be the *Gil's* schematics. They were being taught. These were engineers in training.

Not-Terata tugged at his arm, but Holsten took a step into the room. The students were nudging each other, whispering, staring at him, but he had eyes only for the screen. Lain was explaining some piece of work, demonstrating by example and expanded diagram how to enact some particular sort of repair. She was older, on the screen: not the chief engineer, not the warrior queen, just . . . Isa Lain forever doing her best with the shoddy tools the universe gave her.

'Where do they . . . ?' Holsten gestured at the now fatally distracted children. 'Where do they come from?'

'Friend, if you don't know *that*, then I'm not explaining it to you,' not-Terata told him acidly, and some of the kids smirked.

'No, but seriously—'

'They're our children, of course,' she told him sharply. 'What did you think? How else were we going to keep the work going?'

'And the . . . cargo?' he asked her, because he was thinking about those people stuck outside suspension for months, for years.

By then she had managed to drag him away from the schoolroom, directing the students' attention back to the teaching display with a stern gesture. 'We have strict population controls,' she told him, adding 'We're on a ship, after all,' as if this was some sort of mantra. 'If we need fresh material from cargo, then we take it, but otherwise any excess production . . .' and here her clipped, professional voice faltered just a little, touching on some personal pain so unexpectedly that Holsten stumbled slightly in sympathy.

'Embryos are put on ice, to await future need,' she finished, with a scowl at him to cover up her own awkwardness. 'It's easier to store an embryo before a certain point in its development than it is a full human being.' Again, this sounded like some rote-learned dogma that she had grown up with.

'I'm sorry, I—'

'We're here.'

They had reached Communications. Until he actually stood there, he had not realized where they were going.

'But what—?'

'Just go in.' Not-Terata gave him quite a hard shove, and then she walked away.

For a long time Holsten stood outside the door to Comms, obscurely fearful of crossing the threshold, until at last the hatch slid aside of its own accord and he met the gaze of the woman inside.

He had not known what to expect. He had thought there might be no living being at all, just a face on a screen that was perhaps something like Lain's death mask, perhaps with taints inherited from Guyen and Avrana Kern and who-knew-what-else that was rattling about in the system. If not that, then he had been terrified that what would meet his gaze might be something like Guyen had become: a withered lich that had once been human, sustained by and inseparable from the mechanisms of the ship itself, harbouring dreams of immortality in its curdling skull. To see the woman he had known curtailed to that would have been bad. Worse would be for the door to open and show him someone else entirely.

But this was Lain – Isa Lain. She was older, of course. She must have been fifteen years his senior by now, a veteran of the long battle against entropy and hostile computer intrusion that she had been fighting, on and off, since they last parted. Fifteen more years would have been almost nothing to the people of the Old Empire. All the myths of that elder age confirmed that the ancients had lived far longer than a natural human span. In these reduced days, however, fifteen more years had made Lain old.

Not ancient, not decrepit – not yet. She was a working woman in the last days of her strength, staring down time's inevitable slope which would rob her of her abilities piecemeal with every step. She was heavier than she had been, and her face was written over in that universal human language of hardship and care. Her hair was grey, long, tied back in a severe bun. He had never seen her with long hair before. She was Lain, though: a woman he had seen evolve in snapshot over the course of so short a time for him, but a lifetime for her. He felt an upsurge of feeling in just looking at her face, the lines and weathering doing their best to hide her familiarity from him, and failing.

'Look at you, old man,' she said faintly. She seemed as affected by his years as he was by hers.

She was wearing a shipsuit with the name ripped off, a garment fraying at the elbows, patched at the knees. The ragged remains of another suit hung about her shoulders, reduced to something like a shawl that she fingered thoughtfully, while looking at him.

Holsten stepped inside, looking at comms, noting two dark panels and one that had been gutted, but the rest of the stations seemed to be operational. 'You've been busy.'

A nameless expression flickered across her face. 'That's it, is it? All this time, and it's still the old flip remarks?'

He gave her a level look. 'Firstly, it's not been "all this time". Secondly, it was always you ready with the lip, not me.'

He was smiling as he said it, because that kind of banter he was used to from her was something he dearly wanted to hear just now, but she just stared at him as though he was a ghost.

'You haven't changed.' And, as she said it, it was plain she knew how fatuous a remark it was, but still something she needed to get out. Holsten Mason, historian, had now outlived the histories. Here he was, bumbling through time and space, making mistakes and being ineffectual, the one stable point in a moving universe. 'Oh, fuck, come here, Holsten. Just come here.'

He didn't expect the tears, not from her. He didn't expect the fierce strength of her arms as she held him to her, the shaking of her shoulders as she fought against herself.

She held him out at arm's length, and he was struck with how alien this situation must be for her. How normal for him to meet an old friend and find her changed and aged, and search the lines of her face for the woman she had been. How wrenching it must be for her to try and find the older man he might one day become in his untouched features.

'Yes,' she said at last, 'I've been busy. Everyone's been busy. You've no idea how lucky you are that you get to travel freight.'

'Tell me,' he encouraged her.

'What?'

'Tell me what's going on. Please *somebody* tell me something, at least.'

She lowered herself carefully into what had once been Guyen's seat, gesturing to another for him. 'What? Situation report? You're the new commander? The scholar doesn't like being kept in the dark?' And that sounded so like the old – the young – Lain that he smiled.

'The scholar does not,' he confirmed. 'Seriously, of all the people left in the . . . on the ship, it's you I trust. But you're . . . I don't know what you're doing with the ship, Lain. I don't know what you're doing with these . . . your people here.'

'You think I've gone like *him*.' No need to name any names there.

'Well, I wondered.'

'Guyen fucked over the computer,' she spat out. 'All his upload nonsense, it went just about like I said it would. Every time he tried to grow, in there, it shut off more of the *Gil*'s systems. I mean, a human mind, that's a fuckload of data – and there were four or five separate incomplete copies fighting for space in there. So I set to work, trying to contain them. Trying to keep the essentials running: keeping the cargo cold; stopping the reactor getting too hot. You remember, that was the plan when you went under.'

'Seemed like a good plan. I remember you said you'd be going into suspension yourself, soon enough,' Holsten noted.

'That *was* the plan,' she confirmed. 'Only there were complications. I mean, we had to find cargo space for Guyen's crazies. Karst had great fun rounding them up and putting them on ice. And by then some of them were working with my people in keeping a lid on the hardware situation. And Guyen – the fucking Guyen archipelago strung out through the system – kept getting out, trying to copy itself, eating up even more space. We purged and we isolated and we set packs of viruses on the bastard, but he was seriously entrenched by then. And when my team was up and running and I had faith in them, I went under like I said I would. And I set myself a wake-up call. And when I woke again, things were worse.'

'Guyen still?'

'Yeah, still him, still clinging on by his electronic fucking fingernails, but my people were finding all sorts of other shit going wrong too.' Holsten had always found Lain's swearing faintly shocking, but weirdly attractive in a taboo sort of way. Now, from her old lips, it was as though she had been practising all those years for just this level of bitter world-weariness. 'Problems from losing more cargo, and other systems going down that Guyen and his halfwit reflections weren't responsible for. There was a bigger enemy out there all along, Holsten. We were just kidding ourselves that we'd got it beaten.'

'The spiders?' Holsten demanded immediately, all of a sudden imagining the ship infested with some stowaways from the green planet, no matter how impossible that seemed.

Lain gave him an exasperated look. 'Time, old man. This ship's close to two and a half thousand years old. Things fall apart. Time is what we're running out of.' She rubbed at her face. The mannerism made her look younger, not older, as though all those extra years might just be scrubbed away. 'I kept thinking I'd got a lid on it. I kept going back to sleep, but there was always something else. My original crew . . . we tried taking it in shifts, parcelling out the time. There was just too much work. I lose track of how many generations of engineers there have been now, under my guidance. And a lot of people didn't want to go back under. Once you've seen a few failed suspension chambers . . .'

Holsten shuddered. 'You didn't think about . . . about upload?'

She eyed him sidelong. 'Seriously?'

'You could watch over everything forever, then, and still stay . . .' *Young*. But he couldn't quite say that, and he had no other way of ending the sentence.

'Well, apart from adding to the computer problem about a hundredfold, fine,' she said, but it was plain that wasn't it. 'And, it's just . . . that copy, the upload, over all those years . . . I'd have set it on a task that would include killing itself off, at the end, leave no survivors in the mainframe. And would it? Because if it wanted to live, it could sure as hell make sure *I* died in my sleep. And would it even remember, in the end, who was the real me?' There was a haunted look on her face that told Holsten she had thought long and hard about this. 'You don't know what it's like . . . When those bits of Guyen got loose, when they hijacked the comms, listening to them . . . even now I don't think the system's right. And the radio ghosts, mad transmissions from that fucking satellite or something, I don't know . . . and . . .' Her shoulders slumped: the iron woman taking her mail off, when it was just him and her. 'You don't know what it's been like, Holsten. Be thankful.'

'You could have woken me,' he pointed out. It was not the most constructive thing to say, but he resented being cast as the lucky survivor with no choice in the matter. 'When you woke, you could have woken me.'

Her gaze was level, terrible, uncompromising. 'I could. And I thought of it. I came so close, you wouldn't believe, when it was just me and these know-nothing kids I was trying to teach my job to. Oh, I could have had you at my beck and call, couldn't I? My personal sex-toy.' She laughed harshly at his expression. 'In and out of sleep, and in and out of me, is that it?'

'Well I . . . ah, well . . .'

'Oh, grow up, old man.' Abruptly she ceased finding herself so funny. 'I wanted to,' she said softly. 'I could have used you, leant on you, shared the burden with you. I'd have burned you up like a candle, old man – and for what? For this moment when I'd still be old, and you'd be dead? I wanted to spare you. I wanted to . . .' she bit her lip, 'keep you. I don't know. Something like that. Perhaps knowing I wasn't putting you through this shit helped keep me going.'

'And now?'

'Now we had to wake you, anyway. Your chamber was fucked. Irreparable, they tell me. We'll find you another.'

'Another? Seriously, now that I'm out—'

'You go back. I'll have you drugged and stuffed into a pod by force, if I have to. Long way to go yet, old man.' When she smiled like that, a hard woman about to get brutal with whatever part of the universe stood in her way, he saw where a lot of the new lines on her face had come from.

'Go where?' he demanded. 'Do what?' he demanded.

'Come on, old man, you know the plan. Guyen surely explained it to you.'

Holsten boggled. '*Guyen?* But he . . . you killed him.'

'Best crew appraisal ever,' she agreed mirthlessly. 'But his *plan*, yes. And he was thinking that up without realizing how the ship was starting to fail. What else is there, Holsten? We're it. This is us, the human race, and we've done really fucking well to make it this far against all the odds. But this piece of machinery simply cannot keep going forever. Everything wears out, old man, even the *Gilgamesh*, even . . .'

Even me, was the unspoken thought.

'The green planet,' Holsten finished. 'Avrana Kern. The insects and things?'

'So we burn them out a bit, get ourselves established. Hell, maybe we can domesticate the fuckers. Maybe you can milk a spider. If the bastards are big enough, maybe we'll be riding around on them. Or we could just poison the fucks, scrub the planet clean of them. We're humans, Holsten. It's what we're good at. As for Kern, Guyen had put in most of the groundwork before. He spent generations fucking with the *Gil*, shielding the system from her. That old terraforming station she sent us to, it had all the toys. She can try taking over and she can try frying us, and we'll be ready for both. And it's not like we have anywhere else to go. And, as luck would have it, we're already on the way there, so it all lines up nicely.'

'You've got it all worked out.'

'I reckon I'll let Karst sort out the frontier-spirit end of things, once we're there,' she told him. 'I reckon I'll be ready for a rest by then.'

Holsten said nothing, and the pause lengthened uncomfortably. She did not meet his eyes.

At last the words fought themselves free, 'Promise me—'

'Nothing,' she snapped instantly. 'No promises. The universe promises us nothing; I extend the same to you. This is the human race, Holsten. It needs me. If Guyen hadn't fucked us up so badly with his immortality scheme, then maybe things could have gone differently. But he did and they haven't, and here we are. I'm going back to bed soon, just like you, but I'm setting my alarm early, because the next generation's going to need someone to check their maths.'

'Then let me stay with you!' Holsten told her fiercely. 'It doesn't sound like anyone's going to need a classicist any time soon. Or at all, ever. Even Guyen only wanted me as his biographer. Let's—'

'If you say grow old together I am going to thump you, Holsten,' Lain returned. 'Besides, there's still one thing you'll be needed for. One thing I need you to do.'

'You want your life story set down for posterity?' he needled, as nastily as he felt able.

'Yeah, you're right, I always was the funny one. So shut the fuck up.' She stood up, leaning against the consoles, and he heard her joints pop and creak. 'Come with me, old man. Come and see the future.'

She led him through the cluttered, half-unmade chambers and passageways of the crew area, heading towards what he recalled were the science labs.

'We're going to see Vitas?' he asked.

'Vitas,' she spat. 'Vitas I made use of right at the start, but she's been sleeping the sleep of the not particularly trusted ever since. After all, she'd not soil her hands with maintenance, and I've not forgotten how she was egging Guyen on all the while before. No, I'm taking you to see our cargo extension.'

'You've put in new chambers? How?'

'Just shut up and wait, will you?' Lain paused, and he could see she was catching her breath, but trying not to show it. 'You'll see soon enough.'

In fact, he did not *see*, when she eventually showed him. Here was one of the labs, and here, taking up much of one wall, was a specimen chamber: a great rack of little containers, hundreds of little organic samples kept on ice. Holsten stared and stared, and shook his head. And then, just as Lain was about to lay into his lack of perception, he suddenly connected the dots and said, 'Embryos.'

'Yes, old man. The future. All the new life that our species couldn't stop itself putting out but that we had no space to raise and bring up. As soon as some over-eager girl decides she wants a family that I, in my wisdom, don't think we can afford, it's out with the surgery and it comes here. Harsh world, ain't it?'

'Alive?'

'Of course, alive,' Lain snapped at him. 'Because right now I'm still hoping the human race has a future, and we are frankly still kind of short on people from a historical perspective. So we put them on ice, and hope that one day we can fire up the artificial wombs and bequeath a load of orphans to the universe.'

'The parents must have . . .'

'Argued? Fought? Kicked and screamed?' Her stare was barren. 'Yeah, you could say that. But also they knew what would happen ahead of time, and they still did it. Biological imperative's a funny thing. The genes just want to squeeze themselves into another generation, no matter what. And, of course, we've had generations growing up here. You know how kids are. Even when you offer 'em countermeasures, they won't use them half the time. Ignorant little fucks, so to speak.'

'I don't understand why you thought I so desperately needed to see all this,' Holsten pointed out.

'Oh, yeah, right.' Lain bent over the console and skimmed

through various menus until she highlighted one of the embryo containers. 'That one, see it?'

Holsten frowned, wondering if there was some mutation or defect that he was supposed to be noticing.

'What can I say?' Lain prompted. 'I was young and foolish. There was this lusty young classicist, he swept me off my feet. We had dinner by the light of dying stars in a ten-thousand-year-old space station. Oh, the romance.' Her deadpan delivery never wavered.

Holsten stared at her. 'I don't believe you.'

'Why?'

'But you . . . you never said. When we were up against Guyen, you could have . . .'

'Right then I wasn't sure we *had* a future, and if Guyen had found out, and got control of the system . . . It's a girl, by the way. She's a girl. *Will* be a girl.' And it was that repetition that told Holsten how close to the edge Lain was now skating. 'I made the choice, Holsten. When I was with you, I chose. I made this happen. I was going to . . . I thought there would be time later . . . I thought there would be a tomorrow when I could go back to her and . . . but there was always some other damned thing. The tomorrow I was waiting for never came. And now I'm not sure I . . .'

'Isa—'

'Listen, Holsten, you're going back under as soon as they find you a chamber, right? You're priority, fuck all the rest. There are some perks to being me right now, and first off is that I call the shots. You go under. You wake up when we hit the green planet system. You make planetfall, and you make sure everything is done to make that place *ours*, come crazy

471

computers or monster spiders or whatever. And you make it somewhere *she* can live. You hear me, old man?'

'But you—'

'No, Holsten, this thing you get to take responsibility for. I'll have done all I can. I'll have done everything humanly possible to bring about this tomorrow. It'll be down to you after that.'

Only later, after she saw him to his newly restored suspension chamber, did he glimpse the name still tagged on the ragged shawl of shipsuit she wore about her shoulders. The sight of it froze him just as he was about to get a leg up into the refurbished coffin. *Really? For all this time?* Facing that long, cold oblivion, with no certainty that he would wake up again, it was curiously warming to know that someone, even if it was this cynical bitter woman, had been holding a torch for him all those unfelt years.

6.6 AND TOUCHED THE FACE OF GOD

Portia wants to go out along with the rest of the crew, but Viola has forbidden it. She is being saved for her own private ideal. Until then, Portia is to be as cosseted and pampered as a sacrificial king.

This high up, the Sky Nest's colony needs physical help to keep the airship envelope in shape, and to keep the ship maintained. Even working from within, the cold is getting to the ants. Tiny and unable to regulate their own temperature, they cannot accomplish much outside the core of the ship itself, and so the spiders have donned their special suits and gone out to crawl about the exterior of their floating home, entering and leaving through pressure doors of their own weaving and re-weaving, temporary airlocks appearing and disappearing as needed. They stumble and stutter back in twos and threes, their work done for the moment. Some return bound to their comrades' backs, overcome by the cold, despite the layers of silk swathing their bodies and the chemical heaters slung beneath their bellies. Portia feels uncomfortable at not being able to assist, for all she understands that she is being saved for another ordeal.

There were a few who had clung to the idea that being closer to the sun would be to feel its unmitigated heat. They have been roundly disabused of this notion. Up here the thin air leaches at their bodies like a sightless vampire. And, despite this, Portia would have joined them, worked knee to knee alongside them and pulled her weight, even as the airship is pulling all of their weights.

The other reason that she wants to work is to take her mind off what is going on down below – or up above, depending on perspective. The sudden silence of the Messenger has affected them all. Reason dictates that their mission is no more than peripherally connected – in that both events involve the erratic brilliance of Bianca – but, like humans, the spiders are quick to see patterns and make connections, to extract untoward significance from coincidence. There has been a curious anxiety about the crew, for all that those glory days of Temple are long gone. Being this much closer to the essential mystery of the Messenger, and so cut off from all they know, arouses strange thoughts.

At last Viola is confident that the Sky Nest will coast stably in the thin air, and she liaises with radio beacons on the ground. The air currents – that have been mapped out crudely over the last few years – are carrying them closer to the crisis point.

Portia, Fabian, go to your station, she orders.

Portia questions her respectfully, signalling with terse passes of her palps that she feels the mission could be achieved single-handed as easily as it could with two. It is not a lack of faith in Fabian's abilities that moves her, but a fear for him. Males are so frail, and she feels protective.

Viola indicates that everything will proceed according to the plan, and that plan calls for two of them to enter the smaller craft mounted atop the Sky Nest. The Star Nest, they call it, and it will carry them where no spider has ever been

– into regions that have been the province of myth and imagination since their records began. Some small unpiloted vessels have coasted close to that boundary. Now, the scientists believe they have come to an understanding of the conditions at the very edge of the world's reach, and have planned accordingly. Portia and Fabian will have to wrestle with the truth of their beliefs, and they go as a pair in case one of them should fail.

The Sky Nest is robust, able to survive the hectic and turbulent weather conditions extending all the way down to the surface of their world. It is still a great, almost weightless object: a cloud of silk and wood and hydrogen; a small crew of spiders and a handful of engines are the heaviest things aboard. Still it is not light enough. When fully inflated, the Star Nest will be a reasonable fraction of the Sky Nest's size, and carry a much smaller fraction of its weight: a truncated onboard colony to handle life-support, a radio, two crew, the payload.

This is one of the things that Bianca and her peers have discovered, that there is a tapering edge to the sky, that the air diminishes as a traveller grows more distant from their world, thinner and colder and more unreliable until . . . Well, there remains some disagreement as to whether it actually *ends*, or whether it simply grows so rarefied that no instrument exists able to detect it. How many molecules of air in a square kilometre of space constitute a continuation of the atmosphere, after all?

Portia makes her way to the robing chamber, to be fitted into her suit. This is not simply an insulating covering, such as the sailors have worn, but a cumbersome and curious outfit that is bulky about the joints, and bloated about the abdomen where the air tanks are housed. At the moment it is depressurized, and hangs flaccid about her, feeling surprisingly heavy, interfering with her movements and making a mumble out of her attempts to speak. On this mission she will be reduced to palp signals and radio.

Fabian joins her, similarly caparisoned. He flicks her an encouraging gesture to keep her spirits up. He has been chosen as her second because they work well together, but also because, small even for a male, he is half her size and less than half her weight. The Star Nest has a long way to haul them; after all, the stars are very far away.

Even the Messenger is far away, passing across the sky far higher than the Star Nest could ever reach. Philosophical quibbles aside, there is no atmosphere there at all. The Messenger is a form of life dwelling in the harshest, most life-negating environment a spider can imagine.

And Portia cannot help wondering: *Have we silenced Her by reaching as high as we are? Are we measuring legs with Her by simply doing so?*

The crew cabin of the Star Nest is terribly cramped. The ceiling is swollen with the airship's systems: its heater, chemical factory, transmitter/receiver and a population of ants of limited capacity, dedicated only to keeping it all running. Portia and Fabian settle themselves as best they can, nestling into the limited give that the walls allow them.

The radio pulses the instructions from Viola, back in the long crew compartment of the Sky Nest, putting Portia through a long series of checks, cross-referenced with the reports of both vessels' onboard colonies that are, in any event, mother and daughter, which kinship aids in linking communications between the colonies.

Viola signals that the crisis moment is reached: given best estimations of air-current movement, this is when the craft must separate for the Star Nest to obtain the optimum chance of success. Viola's words, transmitted as electronic pulses that strip the information of all the sender's character and personality, sound dreadfully efficient.

Portia responds that she and Fabian are ready for separation. Viola starts to say something, then stills the words. Portia knows that she has just reined in some platitude concerning the Messenger's goodwill. Such sentiments seem inappropriate just at this moment.

Down on the surface, dozens of observatories and radio receivers are awaiting developments, agog.

Star Nest has been clinging to the upper surface of Sky Nest's gasbag like a benign parasite. Now its crew have effected the climb to it and set themselves in place, it is detached gently by the Sky Nest ants, a host of tiny lines severed, so that all at once the Star Nest's superior buoyancy tells, and it floats free of the mothership with jellyfish-like grace. Immediately it ascends higher than the more robust vehicle could follow, caught in the upper air currents, holding – for now – to the models of its movements set out by scientists who are not having to trust their own lives to the thing.

Portia and Fabian make regular radio reports back to Viola, and the wider world. In between, they mostly amuse themselves. Their ability to communicate is limited to palp-signalling, any greater subtlety being stifled by their close quarters and the cumbersome suits. The cold is infiltrating despite the layers of silk cosseting the crew compartment. They are already breathing stored air, which is a limited resource. Portia is aware that there is a strict timetable by which their mission must be fulfilled.

The chemical light of her instruments tells her of their swift ascent. The radio confirms the Star Nest's position. Portia feels that curious sensation that is so much of what she is: she is walking where no other has walked. This sense of opportunistic curiosity that has been with her ancestors since they were tiny, thoughtless huntresses, is strong in her. For Portia there is always another horizon, always a new path.

It is around this time that the Messenger breaks radio silence. Portia is not tuned to God's frequency, but the tumultuous response from the ground tells her what has happened. She herself is not fluent in God's difficult, counter-intuitive language, but translations come through swiftly, passing across the face of the planet as swift as thought.

God has apologized.

God has explained that She has previously misunderstood some key elements of the situation, but has now gained a clearer understanding of how things are.

God invites questions.

Portia and Fabian, locked in their tiny, ascending bubble, wait anxiously to hear what will be said. They know that Bianca and her fellows on the ground must be feverishly debating what comes next. What question can possibly mark the start of this new phase of communication with the Messenger?

But of course, there is only one vital question. Portia wonders if Bianca will actually canvass anyone else's opinion in the end, or whether she will simply send off her own demand to God to prevent anyone else doing likewise. It must be a grand temptation to every other spider with access to a transmitter.

What Bianca asks is this:

What does it mean that you are there and we are here? Is there meaning or is it random chance? Because what else does one ask even a broken cybernetic deity but, *Why are we here?*

From her high vantage point Doctor Avrana Kern readies herself to make full disclosure: here is a question she can answer in more detail than all the spiders in the world could ever want. She, Avrana Kern, is history itself.

She takes the equivalent of a deep breath, but no answers come to mind. She is replete with the assurance that she *knows*, but such confidence is not backed by the knowledge itself. The archive of data that she thinks of as *my memories* is unavailable. Error messages leap out when she seeks the answers. It is gone. That trove of what-once-was has *gone*. She is the only witness to a whole age of mankind, yet she has forgotten. The unused records have been overwritten in her thousands of years of sleep, in her centuries of waking.

She knows she knows, and yet in truth she does *not* know. All she has is a patchwork of conjecture, and memories of times when she once remembered the things she can no longer recall first-hand. If she is to answer the planet, it will be with those pieces stitched together into a whole cloth. She will be giving them belated creation myths, high on dogma but low on detail.

But they are so desperate to know, and it *is* the right question. Would she have them ask for technical specifications or serial numbers? *No*. They must know the truth, as best as she can tell it.

So she tells them.

She asks them what they think those lights in the sky are: those below are astronomers enough to know that they are unthinkably distant fires.

They are like your sun, she says. *And around one such was a world much like your own, on which other eyes looked up at those distant lights, and wondered if anything looked back down.* She has slipped into the past tense naturally, although her concept of a linear past is a little at odds with the spiders' own concepts. Earth itself is dead to her.

The creatures that lived on that world were quarrelsome and violent, and most of them strove only to kill and control and oppress each other, and resist anyone who tried to improve the lot of their fellows. But there were a few who saw further. They travelled to other stars and worlds and, when they found a world that was a little like their own, they used their technology to change it until they could live upon it. On some of these worlds they lived, but on others they conducted an experiment. They seeded those worlds with life, and made a catalyst to quicken that life's growth; they wanted to see what would emerge. They wanted to see if that life would look back at them, and understand.

Something moves within what is left of Avrana Kern, some broken mechanism she has not used for such a long, long time.

But while they were waiting, the destructive and wasteful majority fought with the others, the right-thinkers, and started a great war. She knows now that her audience will understand 'war' and 'catalyst', and the bulk of the concepts she is using. *And they died. They all died. All the people of Earth save just a few. And so they never did come to see what grew on their new-made worlds.*

And she does not say it, but she thinks: *And that is you. My children, it is you. You are not what we wanted, not what we planned for, but you are my experiment, and you are a success.* And that jagged-edged part moves once again and she knows that some part of her, some locked-away fleshy part, is trying to weep. But not from sorrow; rather from pride, only from pride.

In her tiny, insulated world, Portia listens to what God has to say, and tries to assimilate it – as other spider minds across the world must also be trying to grasp what is being said. Some of it is incomprehensible – just as so much of the Messenger's message is – but this is clearer than most: God is really *trying* to be understood, this time.

She asks the next question almost simultaneously with Bianca:

So you are our creator? With all the baggage that comes with it: *made why? For what purpose?*

And the Messenger responds: *You are made of My will, and you are made of the technology of that other world, but all of this has been to speed you on a path you might have taken without me, given time and opportunity. You are Mine, but you also belong to the universe, and your purpose is whatever you choose. Your purpose is to survive and grow and prosper and to seek to understand, just as my people should have taken these things as their purpose, had they not fallen into foolishness, and perished.*

And Portia, for all that she was never a temple-goer, feels that she – as she ascends into the sparse reaches of the upper air – is fulfilling that very mandate in pushing the frontiers of understanding.

Their ascent has been rapid; God has been long-winded.

They are slowing now, and the colour of the altimeter suggests that even the tenacious Star Nest, which is merely a thin skin around a great mass of hydrogen from which dangles a very little weight, is reaching its ceiling, out where the atmosphere is almost nothing, and therefore there is nothing for the light gas to be lighter than. They are still far, far short of the orbiting Messenger – barely a third of the distance to that distant spark – but this is as far as they themselves can go.

Their payload, however, is intended to go further. Deploying it is the riskiest part of a risky journey, out here where no spider was ever intended to travel. Portia will be sending into orbit the first ever artificial object originating on her world. The spiders have built a satellite.

It is a double-hulled glass ball containing a radio transmitter/receiver and two colonies: one of ants, one of algae. The algae is a special breed cultivated by the sea-going stomatopods, designed to adjust its metabolism to regulate the proportions of the surrounding environment. It will flourish in the sunlight, expanding into the hollow silk vanes that the satellite will spread, and regulated by the ant colony who will feed on it as well as breathe its oxygen. The satellite is a tiny biosphere, intended to last perhaps a year before falling out of balance in some way. It will act as a radio relay, and the ants can be conditioned from the ground to perform a number of analytical tasks. In respect of its capabilities, it is not revolutionary, but in what it represents it is the dawn of a new era.

It is intended to detach itself from beneath the gondola, where it has been hanging, as the single densest part of the Star Nest expedition. It has chemical rockets to push it that little step further into a stable orbit, the ants already pre-armed with the calculations they will need to adjust its trajectory as it flies. Despite their chemical expertise, the spiders have a limited ability to produce combustion-based rockets, hence the entire Sky Nest/Star Nest project. Kern and her people never considered this, but life on the green planet is young by geological standards – too young to have produced anything in the way of fossil fuels. Biotechnology and mechanical ingenuity have had to take up the slack.

The payload is not detaching.

Portia registers the fact dully. She and Fabian are weathering the conditions only with difficulty. The long cold ascent has taken a great deal out of them both. As a species, they are inefficient endotherms. By now both of them are ravenously hungry, consuming their internal food stores yet still growing sluggish with the cold. Now something has gone wrong, and Portia must leave the crew cabin and go out into the vanishingly thin air to see if it can be rectified. The danger is increasing every moment: if it is the satellite that has malfunctioned, it may try to fire its rockets without detaching from the Star Nest, which would shrivel away the cabin and then ignite the hydrogen cells. Fabian informs the ground of their situation, breaking into the general babble that the Messenger's revelations have sparked off. Bianca and her peers, those directly involved in the Star Nest project, quieten down rapidly.

Communication is difficult. Fabian repeats himself over and over as Portia prepares her suit for exit into the hostile near-space around them. The Star Nest's transmitter is having difficulties reaching as far as the planet's surface, another piece of technology creaking under the strain.

Portia positions herself where she intends to exit, near the bottom of the crew cabin. She spools out a safety line attached to the cabin interior, then spins a second wall over herself, before sealing her spinnerets inside her suit. Then she cuts her way out of the cabin and into the space between the hulls, next repairs the rip left behind her, and then performs the same procedure again to let herself out into the killing cold of beyond.

Her suit inflates instantly, her internal air supply reacting to the thin atmosphere and expanding, mostly about her abdomen, mouth, eyes and joints: those parts which might suffer from a sudden loss of pressure. Portia has several advantages over a vertebrate right now: her open circulation is less vulnerable to frostbite and to gas bubbles caused by changes of pressure, and her exoskeleton retains fluids more readily than skin. Even so, the inflated suit reduces her movement to a crippled shuffle. Worse, she starts to heat up almost immediately. She has – just – been able to keep her body temperature *up*, but she has no ready way to bring it down. The heat that she is generating has nowhere to go, being surrounded by so little air. She begins the slow process of boiling within her own skin.

She crawls painfully down to find the satellite, seeing through her filmy viewport that it is glued to the hull with ice. She has no way of communicating this to anyone, and can only hope that the payload itself is still functioning. Grimly she begins chipping and cutting at the ice with her forelimbs. Still the glass sphere remains anchored to the silk of the Star Nest. Portia is distantly aware that its rockets may trigger at any moment, and will likely burn up the entire Star Nest before melting the ice. Even as this thought fights its way into her broiling mind, she sees the first dull glow, a mixing of chemicals giving rise to sudden heat.

This is her job. This is why they chose her. She is a pioneer, a risk-taker, a spider never satisfied with simply sitting and waiting for the world to come to her. She is a hero, but one more envied than emulated.

She clumsily enfolds the satellite, and succeeds in finally wrenching it away from its icy holdfast. Bunching her rear legs, she takes aim into clear space and puts everything she has into one grand jump.

She feels her suit rip about one of her rear legs, the sudden leap having been more than the stressed silk can take. The chill that now seizes the exposed limb is almost welcome. Then she is springing out and into the thin, thin air, out and arcing downwards towards the patient pull of the planet beneath them. With a spasmodic motion of six limbs she throws the satellite away from her.

Its rockets flare. The extreme edge of their fiery tail singes her as the satellite corkscrews madly away, under and out from the over-reaching canopy of the Star Nest. She has no idea if it will be able to correct its course enough to make the intended orbit.

In her mind arises the surprisingly rational thought: *There must be an easier way than this.*

Then she is falling, and falling, and although her legs go through the stuttering motions of spinning a parachute, she creates nothing.

Her descent comes to a sudden jolting stop, dangling beneath the Star Nest. Her safety line has caught her, but it doesn't matter. The air in her suit is depleted, and she is too hot now to move or think. She gives herself up for lost.

★

Fabian is already at work by this time. He has followed very little of what has gone on, but the sudden pull on Portia's line alerts him, and he follows it out, self-made airlock by airlock, until – his own suit puffed out and constricting – he can haul her up. With what feels like the last of his strength he is able to roll her inside, and then uses his fangs to tear open both their suits once the cabin is re-sealed.

He lies there on his back, limbs tangled with Portia's. She is not moving save for a shallow pulsing of her abdomen.

Somehow he reaches the radio transmitter, sending a semi-incoherent report of their situation. He catches a faint confirmation that the satellite has been successfully deployed, but no indication that they have heard him.

He tries again, sends gibberish with shaking palps, and eventually manages: *Can you receive me? Can anybody receive me?*

Nothing from the ground. He does not even know if the radio is working now. He is desperately hungry, and Portia's extra-vehicular excursions mean that they have very little air left. He has initiated venting of the hydrogen, as swift as is safe, but there is still a long way to go down. He and Portia do not have either the energy or the oxygen to reach hospitable altitudes.

Then the voice comes: *Yes, I receive you.*

The Messenger is listening. Fabian feels a religious awe. He is the first male ever to speak with God.

I understand your position, the Messenger tells him. *I cannot help you. I am sorry.*

Fabian explains that he has a plan. He spells his scheme out carefully. *Can you explain to them all?*

That I can do, the Messenger promises, and then, with a

sudden access of old memory, *When my ancestors reached for space, there were deaths among those pioneers too. It is worth it.* The next phrase is alien to Fabian. He will never know what was meant by, *I salute you.*

He turns to Portia, who has nothing more left to give. She lies on her back, senseless, stripped of everything but her most basic reflexes.

With slow, difficult movements, Fabian begins to court her. He moves his palps before her eyes and touches her, as if he were seeking to mate, triggering slow instinct that has been built over by centuries of civilization but has never quite gone away. There is no food to restore her, save one source. There is not enough air for two, but perhaps sufficient for one.

He sees her fangs unclench and lift, shuddering. For a moment he contemplates them, and considers his regard for this crewmate and companion. She will never forgive him or herself, but perhaps she will live nonetheless.

He gives himself up to her automatic embrace.

Later, Portia returns to consciousness aboard the Sky Nest, feeling gorged, damaged, strangely sensual. She has lost one rear leg entirely, and two sections of another limb, and one of her secondary eyes is out. She lives, though.

When they tell her what Fabian did to secure her survival, she refuses to believe it for a long time. In the end, it is the Messenger Herself who brings her to an acceptance of what happened.

Portia will never fly again, but she will be instrumental in planning further flights: safer and more sophisticated methods of reaching orbit.

For now that the Messenger has found the patience and perspective to properly understand Her children, She can finally communicate Her warning in a way they can understand. At last the spiders appreciate that, even aside from their orbiting God, they are not alone in the universe, and that this is not a good thing.

7
COLLISION

7.1 WAR FOOTING

They were packed into the briefing room. It was like déjà vu, but these days that seemed a good thing. Holsten was a citizen of a tiny world of cycles and repetitions, and where events failed to repeat themselves, it meant deterioration.

Some of the lights were out and that really brought it home to him. All the miracles of technology that had made the *Gilgamesh* possible, all the tricks they had stolen from the gods of the Old Empire . . . and right now they either couldn't get all the lights working, or there were simply too many higher-priority things to be doing.

He recognized a surprising number of faces. This was clearly a Command meeting. These were Key Crew – or who was left of them. He saw the science team, a handful of Engineering, Command, Security, all people who had got on board when Earth was still a place where humans lived. These were people who had been granted custodianship over the rest of the human race.

With some notable omissions. The only department chief present – assuming you discounted Holsten himself and his department of one – was Vitas, orchestrating the bleary, recently awoken muster, ordering people according to some idiolectic system of her own. There were a handful of young faces in old shipsuits helping her – Lain's legacy, Holsten guessed. They could have passed for the mob that he remembered from so recently, but he guessed they must be at least a generation further on from that. They had persevered, though. They had not turned into cannibals or anarchists or monkeys. Even that fragile appearance of stability gave him some hope.

'Classicist Mason, there you are.' It was hard to say what Vitas felt about seeing him present. Indeed it was hard to say what she felt about anything. She had aged, but gracefully and only a little it seemed. Holsten found himself indulging in the bizarre speculation that she was not human at all. Perhaps she was her own self-aware machine. Controlling the medical facilities, she would be able to hide her secret forever, after all . . .

He had seen a lot of mad things since setting foot on the *Gilgamesh*, but that would have been a step too far. Even the Old Empire . . . unless she *was* Old Empire, some anachronistic ten-thousand-year survival, fusion-driven and eternal.

Finding himself momentarily adrift from reason, he grasped for Vitas's hand and snagged it, feeling the human warmth, willing himself to trust to his own perceptions. The scientist raised her eyebrows sardonically.

'Yes, it's really me,' she remarked. 'Amazing, I know. Can you use a gun?'

'I very much doubt it,' Holsten blurted out. 'I . . . What?'

'The commander wanted me to ask that of everyone. I had already guessed the answer in your case.'

Holsten became cold and still, all at once. *The commander . . .*

Vitas watched him with dry amusement, letting him hang

in suspense for a few long seconds before explaining. 'Lem Karst is the acting commander, for your information.'

'Karst?' Holsten felt that was hardly better. 'How bad has it got that Karst gets to call the shots?'

There were a lot of looks from the rest of Key Crew at that remark, some frowning, others plainly sharing his opinion – including even one of the security team. It was a rare moment when Holsten would far rather be in the minority.

'We're travelling into the Kern system,' Vitas explained. She turned to the console behind her, gesturing for Holsten's attention. 'Not to put too fine a point on it, but once we're in orbit around the green planet, the Gilgamesh's wandering days are likely to be done.' The oddly poetic turn of phrase gave her clipped tones an unexpected gravitas. 'Lain's tribe have done a remarkable job in keeping him together, but it really has been damage control, quite literally. And the damage has begun to win. There's quite a population of ship-born now, because the suspension chambers are failing beyond the point of repair. Nobody's going to be heading off on another interstellar jaunt.'

'Which means . . . ?'

'Which means there's only one place left for us all, yes, Mason.' Vitas's smile was precise and brief. 'And we're going to have to fight the Old Empire for it.'

'You seem to be looking forward to it,' Holsten observed.

'It's been the goal of a long, long plan, Mason, and centuries in the making. The longest of long games in the history of our species, except for whatever that Kern thing has been doing. And you were right, in a way, about the commander. He's not here to see it but it's Guyen's plan. It was so from the moment he set eyes on that planet.'

'Guyen?' Holsten echoed.

'He was a man with vision,' Vitas asserted. 'He cracked under the strain at the end, but given what he'd gone through that's hardly surprising. The human race owes him a great deal.'

Holsten stared at her, remembering how she had treated the disastrous upload of Guyen's mind as some sort of hobby experiment. In the end he just grunted, and something of his feelings were plainly visible on his face, judging by the scientist's reaction.

'Karst and some of the tribe have jury-rigged a control centre in the comms room,' Vitas said, somewhat coldly. 'You're Key Crew, so he'll want you there. Alpash!'

One of the young engineers appeared at her elbow.

'This is Alpash. He's ship-born,' Vitas explained, as though excusing some congenital defect. 'Get Mason here, and the rest of Key Crew, up to the commander, Alpash.' She spoke to the young man as though he was something less than human, something more like a pet or a machine.

Alpash nodded warily at Mason. If Vitas was his exemplar for Key Crew, he probably didn't expect much in the way of manners. There was a distinct skittishness about him as he gathered up the recently woken engineers, security men and the like. It reminded Holsten of the way that Guyen's cultists had treated him. He wondered what legends of Key Crew had Alpash been brought up on.

Over in comms, Karst looked refreshingly the same. The big security chief had been given the time to get some stubble going on his ravaged face, and he had obviously not been wheeled out much since Holsten last saw him, because he had barely aged.

As the surviving Key Crew filed in, he grinned at them, an expression equally of anticipation and strain.

'Come in and find a seat, or stand, whatever you like. Vitas, can you hear me?'

'I hear,' the science chief's voice crackled and spat from an unseen speaker. 'I'll continue to supervise the unpacking, but I'm listening.'

Karst grimaced, shrugged. 'Right,' he turned to address them all, looking from face to face. When he met Holsten's eyes there was none of the expected dislike. Gone was any hint that the security man had never much cared for Holsten Mason. Absent, too, was the expected air of dismissal, that of a man of action who had no use for the man of letters. Instead, Karst's grin dwindled to a smaller but much more sincere smile. It was a look of things shared, a commonality between two people who had been there right at the start, and were still here now.

'We're going to fight,' the security chief told them all. 'We've basically got just one good chance at it. You all know the score, or you should do. There's a satellite out there that can probably rip open the *Gil* in a blink if we give it the chance. Now, we bolted on some sort of diffusion shielding, back when we were pirating that terraforming station – some of you maybe weren't awake for that, but there's a summary in the system of the changes we made. We also hardened our computer systems, so that bitch – so the satellite – can't just shut us down or open the airlocks, that sort of trick. We've taken every precaution, and I still reckon toe-to-toe we might be screwed.' He was grinning again, though.

'But I've had some drones fitted out in the workshops. They've got shielded systems as well, and lasers that I think can burn the satellite. That's the plan, basically. Best defence is a good offence, and so on. As we come in towards our orbit, we burn the fucker up and hope it's enough. Otherwise it's down to using the *Gil*'s forward array, and that puts us within range of retaliation.' He paused, then finished: 'So you're probably wondering what the fuck I need with all of you guys, yeah?'

Holsten cleared his throat. 'Well, Vitas asked me if I could use a gun. I appreciate I'm no great tactician, but if it comes to needing that against the satellite, we've probably already lost.'

Karst actually laughed. 'Yeah, well, I'm planning ahead – planning to win. Cos if we don't win against the satellite, there's no point in planning anyway. So let's assume we burn it out. What next?'

'The planet,' someone said. There was a curious ripple through the room, of hope and dread together.

Karst nodded moodily. 'Yeah, most of you never saw it but, believe me, it's not going to be an easy place to settle down on, at least at the start. Am I right, Mason?'

Holsten started at unexpectedly having his opinion solicited. *But, of course, there's just him and me who were down there on the surface.* 'You're right,' he confirmed.

'That's where guns come in, for those that feel they can lower themselves to use them.' Karst, already pre-lowered, winched his grin up a notch. 'Basically the planet's full of all sorts of beasties – spiders and bugs and all manner of shit. So, while we get ourselves set up, we're going to be burning *them* out, too: clearing forest, driving off the wildlife, exterminating anything that looks at us funny. It'll be fun. Frankly it's the sort of thing I've been looking forward to since I first got aboard. Hard work, though. And everyone works. Remember, we're Key Crew. Us and the chiefs of the new engineers, like Al here, it's our responsibility. We make this work. Everyone's depending on us. Think about that: when I say *everyone* I really mean it. The *Gilgamesh* is all there is.'

He clapped his hands, as though that entire speech had reinvigorated him and boosted his personal morale. 'Security team, whoever's got the pad with our new recruits, sort them out and get them armed. Teach them which end not to look down. You lot all get to join us on the bug hunt, afterwards.'

Holsten assumed that meant everyone fool enough to say 'yes' when Vitas had asked them if they could use a gun.

'Tribe,' Karst added, then seemed to lose momentum. 'I won't bother telling you, as you know what you're doing. Been doing it long enough, anyway. Alpash, stick close, though. I want you as liaison.'

'Tribe' seemed to be the engineers, or those descendants of theirs currently keeping the ship together. The few of them still there now bolted off, with the air of people who had found the entire proceedings boring and unnecessary, but had been aware that they should be on their best behaviour nonetheless, like children during a religious service.

'Right, Mason . . . Harlen?'

'Holsten.'

'Right.' Karst nodded, unapologetic. 'Something special for you, right? You actually get to do your job. The satellite's transmitting all sorts of shit, and you're the only person who might know what it's saying.'

'Transmitting . . . to us?'

'Yes. Maybe. Alpash?'

'Probably no,' the young engineer confirmed.

'Anyway, whatever, take Mason here and plug him in. Mason, if you can make anything out of it, let me know. Personally I reckon it's just gone mad.'

'Madder,' Holsten corrected and, although this hadn't been a joke, Karst laughed.

'We're all in the boat, aren't we?' he said almost fondly, glancing around at the battered confines of the *Gilgamesh*. 'All of us on the same old boat.' The mask slipped, and for a second Holsten was looking into the stress-fractures and botch-job repairs that made up Karst's over-strained soul. The man had always been a follower, and now he was in charge, the last general of the human race facing unknown odds with the highest possible stakes. His somewhat disjointed briefing now looked in retrospect like a man fighting for his composure – and holding on to it, just. Against all expectations, Karst was coping. Come the hour, come the man.

Also, he might be drunk. Holsten realized he couldn't tell.

Alpash led him to a console, still acting as though Holsten and Karst and the rest were heroes of legend brought to life, but turning out to be somewhat disappointing in the flesh. Holsten wondered, with a professional curiosity, whether some crazy myth cycle had grown up amongst the Tribe, with himself and the rest of Key Crew as a pantheon of fractious gods, trickster heroes and monsters. He had no idea how many generations had gone by since their last actual contact with anyone not born on the *Gilgamesh*, since . . .

He had been about to ask, but a piece clicked into place and he knew that he wouldn't ask, not now. Not when he had thought of Lain at last. For Lain must have died long,

long ago. Had she thought of him, at the end? Had she come to look into the cold stillness of his coffin, her sleeping prince who she had never permitted to come back for her?

Alpash gave a nervous cough, picking up on Holsten's suddenly changed mood.

The classicist scowled, waved off the man's concern. 'Tell me about these transmissions.'

With a worried look, Alpash turned to the console. The machinery looked battered, something that had been taken apart and put back together more than once. There was some sort of symbol and some graffiti stencilled on the side, which looked new. Holsten stared at it for a moment before disentangling the words.

Do not open. No user-serviceable parts inside.

He laughed, thinking that he saw the joke, the sort of bleak humour that he recalled engineers resorting to in extremis. There was nothing on Alpash's face to suggest that he saw any humour in it, though, or that the slogan was anything other than a sacred symbol of the Tribe. Abruptly Holsten felt bitter and sick again. He felt like Karst must feel. He was just a thing of the lost past trying to recapture an almost-lost future.

'There's a lot of it,' Alpash explained. 'It's constant, on multiple frequencies. We can't understand any of it. I don't know what this Avrana Kern is, but I think the commander may be right. It sounds like madness. It's like the planet is whispering to itself.'

'The planet?' Holsten queried.

'We're not getting these signals direct from the satellite, as far as we can understand.' Now that Alpash began speaking more, Holsten heard unfamiliar rhythms and inflections in his words – a little of Lain, a little of the *Gilgamesh*'s automatic systems, a little of something new. There was obviously a ship-born accent now.

Alpash brought up a numerical display that was apparently intended to be educational. 'You can see here what we can tell from the transmissions.' Holsten was used to the *Gilgamesh* sugar-coating that sort of data in a form that a layman could understand, but that concession was apparently not something the Tribe felt it needed.

Seeing his blank look, the engineer went on, 'Our best bet is that these are transmissions being directed at the planet, just like the original numerical sequence, and we're now catching bounce-back. They're definitely coming to us by way of the planet, though.'

'You've had any other classicists working on this, out of cargo? There must be a few students or . . .'

Alpash looked solemn. 'I'm afraid not. We have searched the manifest. There were only a very few at the start. You are the last.'

Holsten stared at him for a long while, thinking through the implications of that: thinking about Earth's long history before the fall, before the ice came. His society had possessed such a fragmented, imperfect understanding of the predecessors that they were constantly trying to ape, and did even that poor record now boil down to just himself, the contents of one old man's head? *All that history, and if . . . when I die . . . ?* He did not see anyone having time to attend history classes in Karst's survivalist Eden.

He shivered – not from the usual human sense of mortality, but from a feeling of vast, invisible things falling away into oblivion, irretrievable and irreplaceable. Grimly he turned to the messages that Alpash was now showing him.

After some work, Holsten finally deciphered the display enough to register just how many of the recordings there were, and these presumably just a fraction of the total. *What's Kern playing at? Maybe she has gone off the deep end, after all.* He accessed one, but it wasn't anything like the other transmissions from the satellite which he remembered. Still . . . Holsten felt long-unused academic parts of his brain try to sit up and take notice, seeing complexity, repeated patterns. He performed whatever analysis and modelling the console allowed him. This wasn't random static, but nor was it the Old Empire messages that Kern/Eliza had used previously. 'Perhaps it's encrypted,' he mused to himself.

'There's a second type as well,' Alpash explained. 'This is how the majority go, but there are some that seem different. Here.'

Holsten listened to the chosen recording, another sequence of pulses, but this time seeming closer to what he would actually recognize as a message. 'Just this, though? No distress signal? No number sequences?'

'This – and as much of this as you could want,' Alpash confirmed.

'How much time do we have before . . . before things start?'

'At least thirty hours.'

Holsten nodded. 'Can I get something to eat?'

'Of course.'

'Then leave me with this and I'll see if I can find anything in it for Karst.' Alpash moved to go, and for a moment Holsten was going to stop him, to ask him that impossible question that historians can never ask, regarding the things they study: *What is it like to be you?* A question nobody can step far enough out of their own frame of reference to answer.

With some help from the Tribe, he was able to hunt through the *Gilgamesh*'s systems for at least some of his electronic toolkit to try and unpick the messages. He was given what he wanted, then left alone to work. He had a sense that, across the ship, a great many ship-born and woken were bracing themselves for the moment their lives had been leading up to for generations, and during sleeping centuries, respectively. He was happy to be out of it. Here, at this failing end of time, the classicist Holsten Mason was glad to be poring over some incomprehensible transmissions in a futile search for meaning. He was not Karst. Nor was he Alpash, or his kin. *Old, I'm old, in so many ways.* Old, and yet still lively enough that he was even going to outlive the ark ship itself, by the look of things.

He realized he could make nothing out of the majority of the messages. They were generally faint, and he guessed that they were being sent from the planet in all directions, just radiating out into space.

Rather, bounced off the planet. Not sent, of course not sent. He blinked, obscurely uncomfortable. Whatever their source, though, they were sufficiently far from anything he knew that he could not even be sure that they *were* messages, couched in any kind of code or language. Only a stubborn streak of structure to them convinced him that they were not some natural interference or just white noise.

The others, though, they were stronger, and recent analysis conducted by the Tribe suggested that they might actually be targeted towards the *Gilgamesh*'s line of approach, as though Kern was using the planet as a sounding board to rant incomprehensibly at them. Or the planet itself was shouting at them.

Or the planet was shouting?

Holsten rubbed at his eyes. He had been working for too long. He was beginning to come adrift from rational speculation.

These transmissions, though – at first he had thought they were as much babble as the rest, but he had cross-referenced them with some old stored records of messages from the satellite, and tried to treat them in the same way, varying the encoding by trial and error until something like a message had abruptly sprung out from the white noise. There had been words, or at least he had fooled himself that he had decoded words there. Imperial C words, words out of history, the dead language given new and mutated life.

He thought again about Alpash's accent. These transmissions seemed almost as if someone out there was speaking some barbarous version of that ancient language, encoded just as Kern encoded her transmissions; some degraded or evolved or simply corrupted attempt at the ancient tongue.

It was proper historian work, just poring over it. He could almost forget the trouble they were all in, and pretend he was on the brink of some great discovery that anyone would care about. *What if this isn't just the crazed gibberish of a dying computer? What if this means something?* If it was Kern trying to talk to them, though, then she had obviously lost most of what she was – the woman/machine that Holsten remembered had no difficulty in making herself understood.

So what was she trying to say now?

The more he listened to the clearest of those decoded transmissions – those sent directly along the line of the *Gilgamesh's* approach – the more he felt that someone was trying to speak to him, across millions of kilometres and across a gap of comprehension that was far greater. He could even fool himself that little snippets of phrasing were coming together into something resembling a coherent message.

Stay away. We do not wish to fight. Go back.

Holsten stared at what he had. *Am I just imagining this?* None of it had been clear – the transmission was in poor shape, and nothing about it fitted in with Kern's earlier behaviour. The more he looked, though, the more he became sure that this *was* a message, and that it was intended specifically for them. They were being warned off again, as though by dozens of different voices. Even in those sections he could not disentangle, he could pick out individual words. *Leave. Peace. Alone. Death.*

He wondered what he could possibly tell Karst.

He slept on it for a while, in the end, and then shambled off to find the acting commander in the comms room.

'You're cutting it fine,' Karst told him. 'I launched the drones hours back. I calculate about two hours before they do what they do, if it can be done at all.'

'Burning Kern?'

'Fucking right.' Karst stared at the working screens surrounding him with haunted, desperate eyes that belied the easy grin he kept trying to keep pinned on his face. 'Come on then, Holsten, out with it.'

'Well, it's a message and it's intended for us – that much I'm reasonably certain about.'

'"Reasonably certain"? Fucking academics,' but it was almost good-natured, even so. 'So Kern's down to basically bombarding us with baby talk, wanting us to go away.'

'I can't translate most of it, but those pieces that make any sense at all seem to be consistently along that theme,' Holsten confirmed. In fact he was feeling unhappy about his own efforts, as though in this, the last professional challenge of his career, he had made some student-level error and failed. The transmissions had been in front of him, a large body of material to cross-reference, and he had constantly felt on the edge of a breakthrough that would make it all crystal clear to him. It had never come, though, and now there was no time to go back to it. He felt that he had shackled himself too much to the way the Old Empire did things, just as everyone always had. If he had come to those transmissions with more of an open mind, rather than trying to recast them in the shape of Kern's earlier work, what might he have found?

'Well, fuck her,' was Karst's informed opinion. 'We're not going anywhere. We don't have that option any more. It all comes down to this, just like it was always going to. Am I right?'

'You are,' Holsten replied hollowly. 'Are we getting anything from the drones?'

'I don't want them transmitting anything until they're close enough to actually get to work,' Karst said. 'Believe me, I remember what fucking Kern can do. You weren't in that shuttle where she just took the whole thing over, remember? Just drifting in space with nothing but life-support, while she worked out what she wanted to do with us. That was no fun at all, believe me.'

'And yet she let you come down and pick us up,' Holsten recalled. He thought Karst might come back at him angrily for that, accuse him of going soft, but the security chief's face took on a thoughtful air.

'I know,' he admitted. 'And if I thought that there was any chance . . . but she's not going to let us on to that planet, Holsten. We tried that one, over and over. She's going to sit there and hoard the last chance for the human race, and let us all die out in space.'

Holsten nodded. His mind was full of that planet balefully whispering for them to go away. 'Can I send from the ship? It might even take her attention from the drones . . . I don't know.'

'No. Complete silence from us. If she's so crazy that she hasn't seen us, I don't want you clueing her in.'

Karst could not keep still. He checked with his seconds in Security; he checked with the senior members – chiefs? – of the Tribe. He paced and fretted, and tried to get some passive data on the drones' progress, without running the risk of alerting Kern.

'You really think she won't see them coming?' Holsten objected.

'Who can know? She's old, Holsten, really old – older than us by a long way. She was crazy before. Maybe she's gone completely mad, now. I'm not giving her anything more than I have to. We get one shot at this before it's down to the *Gil* itself. Literally one shot. Seriously, you know how much power a decent laser takes up? And believe me, those are our two best functioning drones – fucking patchwork jobs from all the working bits we could find.' He clenched his fists, fighting against the weight of his responsibilities. 'Everything's falling *apart*, Holsten. We've got to get on to that planet. The ship's dying. That stupid moon base thing of Guyen's – that died. Earth . . .'

'I know.' Holsten hunted about for some sort of reassurance, but he honestly couldn't think of anything to say.

'Chief,' interrupted one of the Tribe, 'transmissions from the drones, coming in. They're coming up on the planet, ready to deploy.'

'At *last*!' Karst practically shouted, and stared about him. 'Which screen's best? Which is working?'

Four screens flared with the new images, one flickering and dying but the other three holding steady. They saw that familiar green orb: a thing of dreams, the promised land. The drones were following their path towards the satellite's orbital track, darting in to intercept it and bring an end to it. They didn't care about what they were seeing, unlike the human eyes now watching vicariously through their lenses.

Karst's mouth hung open. At this moment, even the ability to curse seemed to have deserted him. He fumbled backwards for a seat, and then sat down heavily. Everyone in comms had stopped work, instead staring at the screen, at what had been done to their paradise.

Kern's satellite was not alone in its vigil.

Around the circumference of the planet, girdling its equator in a broad ring, was a vast band of tangled lines and strands and nodes: not satellites, but a whole orbiting network, interconnected and continuous around the entire world. It flared bright in the sunlight, opening green petals towards the system's star. There were a thousand irregular nodes pulled into taut, angular shapes by their connecting conduits. There was a bustle to it, of constant activity.

It was a web. It was as though some unthinkable horror had begun the job of cocooning the planet before it fed on it. It was a single vast web in geostationary orbit about the planet, and Kern's metal home was just one pinpoint within its myriad complexity.

Holsten thought about those thousand, thousand transmissions from Kern's World, but not from Kern herself. He thought about those hateful whispers telling the *Gilgamesh*, impossibly, to turn around and go away. *Abandon hope, all ye who enter . . .*

The drones were arrowing in now, still seeking out Kern's satellite, because their programming had somehow not prepared them for this.

'Spiders . . .' said Karst slowly. His eyes were roving around, seeking desperately for inspiration. 'It's not possible.' There was a pleading edge to his voice.

Holsten just stared at that vast snare laid around the planet, seeing more detail every second as the drones closed with it. He saw things moving across it, shuttling back and forth. He saw long strands reaching out into space from it, as though hungry for more prey. He thought he saw other lines reaching down towards the planet itself. His skin was crawling, and he remembered his brief stay on the planet, the deaths of the mutineers.

'No,' said Karst flatly, and, 'No,' again. 'It's ours. It's *ours*. We *need* it. I don't care what the fuck the bastards have done with it. We've nowhere else to go.'

'What are you going to do?' Holsten asked faintly.

'*We* are going to fight,' Karst stated, and his sense of

purpose returned with those words. 'We are going to fight Kern, and we are going to fight . . . *that*. We are coming home, you hear me? That's home now. It's all the home we'll ever have. And we will mass-driver the fucking place from orbit if we have to, to make it ours. We'll burn them out. We'll burn them *all* out. What else have we got?'

He rubbed at his face. When he took his hands away, he seemed composed. 'Right, I need more minds on this. Alpash, it's time.'

The engineer nodded.

'Time for what?' Holsten demanded.

'Time to wake up Lain,' Karst replied.

7.2 WHAT ROUGH BEAST

Far beyond the physical tendrils with which they have ringed their planet, the spiders have extended a wider web. Biotechnological receptors in the cold of space hear radio messages, await the return of soundless calls into the void, and reach out for disturbances in gravity and the electromagnetic spectrum – the tremors on the strands that will let them know when a guest has arrived in their parlour.

They have been preparing for this day for many generations. The entire planet has, ever since they finally bridged that gap with God, fingertip to leg-tip. Their entire civilization has come together with a purpose, and that purpose is *survival*.

The Messenger had forever been trying to prepare them, to mould them into Her image and give them the weapons She thought they needed, in order to fight back. Only when She stopped treating them like children – like monkeys – was She able to do what perhaps She should have done from the start: communicate the problem to them; let them find a solution that was within the reach of their minds and their technology.

One advantage of God ceasing to move in mysterious ways is that the entire planet has found a hitherto unknown unity. Little focuses the collective mind more decisively than the threat of utter extinction. The Messenger was unstinting in Her assurances that the spiders would have nothing else to look forward to if the *Gilgamesh* was allowed to return unopposed. She had racked her piecemeal recollection of her species' history and found only a hierarchy of destruction: of her species devastating the fauna of planet Earth, and then turning on its own sibling offshoots, and then at last, when no other suitable adversaries remained, tearing at itself. Mankind brooks no competitors, She has explained to them – not even its own reflection.

For generations, then, a political unity of the spider cities has worked towards creating this vast orbital presence, using all the tools available. The spiders have entered the space age with desperate vigour.

And Bianca looks up at the darkening sky, at the unseen filigree of Great Star Nest, the orbital city, and knows that she would rather this had not come about in her lifetime.

The enemy is coming.

She has never seen this enemy, but she knows what it looks like. She has sought out ancient Understandings, preserved across the centuries, that reach back to a time when her kind faced extinction at the jaws of a much more comprehensible foe. For, during their conquest of the ant supercolony, Bianca's species encountered what she now knows as humanity. There were giants in the world, back in those days.

She now sees, through the long-gone eyes of a distant ancestor, the captive monster that had fallen from the sky – not from the Messenger, as had been believed, but from this approaching menace. Little did they know it was a herald of the end.

It seems so hard to believe that such a huge, ponderous thing could have been sentient, but apparently it was. More than sentient. Things like *that* – just as the Messenger had once been a thing like that – are the *ur*-race, the ancient astronauts responsible for all life that has evolved on Bianca's world. And now they are returning to undo that mistake.

Bianca's musings have taken her out of the vast reach of the Seven Trees conurbation and on to the closest anchor point, travelling swiftly by wire in a capsule powered by artificial, photosynthetic, self-sufficient muscle. Now she disembarks, feeling the great open space around her. Most of her world's tropical and temperate land area is still forested, either for agricultural purposes, as wild reserves, or serving as the scaffolding that her species use to build their cities. The areas around the elevator anchor points are all kept clear, though, and she sees a great tent of silken walls a hundred feet high, culminating in a single point that stretches ever away into the high distance, beyond the ability of her eyes to follow it. She knows where it goes, though: heading up, up out of the planet's atmosphere, then up further and further, as a slender thread that reaches halfway to the arc of the moon. The equator is studded with them.

That long-ago balloonist was right: there was an easier way to claw one's way up and out of the planet's gravity well and into orbit, and all it took was spinning a strong enough thread.

Bianca meets with her assistants, a subdued band of five females and two males, and they hurry inside to another capsule, this one moving by little more than simple mechanical principles utilized on a grand scale. Unimaginably far away is a comparable weight even now descending inwards towards the planet's surface. By exercise of the sort of mathematics that Bianca's species has been fluent in for centuries, Bianca's own car begins its long, long ascent.

She is the general, the tactician. She is going to take her place amidst the bustling community known as Great Star Nest to mastermind the defence of her planet against the alien invaders: the Star Gods. She has ultimate responsibility for the survival of her species. A great many better minds than hers have formulated the plan that she will attempt to carry out, but it will be her own decisions that will make the difference between success and failure.

The journey up is a long one and Bianca has plenty of time to reflect. The enemy they face is the child of a technology she cannot conceive of, advanced beyond the dreams of her own kind's greatest scientists, using a technology of metal and fire and lighting, all fit tools for vengeful deities. At her disposal is fragile silk, biochemistry and symbiosis, and the valour of all those who will put their lives at her disposal.

Fretting, she spins and destroys, spins and destroys, as she and her fellows are hauled towards the open darkness of space, and the gleaming grid of her people's greatest architectural triumph.

Already in orbit on the globe-spanning three-dimensional sculpture they think of as Great Star Nest, Portia is steeling herself for a fight.

The great equatorial web is studded with habitats that trail out from one another, interconnect, are spun up or taken down. It has become a way of life for the spiders, and one they have taken to remarkably quickly. They are a species that is well made for a life of constant free-fall around a planet. They are born to climb and to orient themselves in three dimensions. Their rear legs give them a powerful capacity to jump to places that their keen eyes and minds can target precisely, and if they get it wrong, they always have a safety line. In a curious way, as Portia and many others have considered, they were born to live out in space.

The old cumbersome spacesuits, which once took those pioneering balloonists to the outer reaches of the atmosphere, are things of the past now. Portia and her squad traverse the lattice-strung vacuum quickly and efficiently, setting out on manoeuvres to ready themselves for the coming conflict. They carry most of their suit about their abdomens: book-lungs fed by an air supply that is chemically generated as needed, rather than stored in tanks. With their training and their technology and their relatively undemanding metabolisms, they can stay out in raw space for days. A chemical heating pack is secured beneath their bodies, along with a compact radio. A lensed mask protects their eyes and mouths. At the tip of each abdomen their spinnerets connect to a little silk factory spinning chemical silk that forms strands – formidably strong strands – in the airless void. Lastly, they have packs of propellant with adjustable nozzles, to guide their silent flight in the void.

Their exoskeletons have been coated in a transparent film, a single molecule thick, which prevents any decompression or moisture loss without diminishing much in the way of feeling. The tips of their legs are sheathed in insulating articulated sleeves to guard them from heat loss. They are the complete astronaut-soldiers.

As they cross from line to line, judging each leap effortlessly, they are swift and agile and utterly focused.

The enemy is coming at last, just as the Messenger foretold. The concept of holy war is alien to them, but this looming conflict has all the hallmarks. There is an ancient enemy that they know will negate their very existence if they cannot defend themselves. There are weapons that, try as they might, they cannot even conceive of. The Messenger did Her best to set out for them the technical and martial capabilities of the human race. The overwhelming impression received was of a terrifying and godlike arsenal, and Portia is under no illusions. The best defence her people have is that the invaders want their planet to live on – the worst excesses of Earth technology cannot be deployed without rendering the prize that both sides fight for worthless.

But there are still a great many unpredictable weapons the *Gilgamesh* could conceivably possess.

The spiders have done what they could in the generations allowed to them, having considered the threat and prepared what is to them the best technological and philosophical response.

There is an army: Portia is one of hundreds who will serve on the front line, one of tens of thousands whose turn will likely come to fight. They will die, many of them, or at least that is what they expect. The stakes are so high, though: individual lives are ever the chaff of war, but if there was ever a just cause, it is this. The survival of an entire species, of a whole planet's evolutionary history, is now at stake.

She has heard that Bianca is on her way up. Everyone is glad, of course, that the commander of their global defence will be up here alongside them, but the simple fact that their leader is *on her way* brings it home to all of them. The time is finally here. The battle for tomorrow is beginning. If they lose, then there will be no future for them and, with that severed tomorrow, all their yesterdays will be undone as well. The universe will turn, but it will be as though they had never existed.

Portia knows that the great minds of her species have considered many diverse weapons and plans. She must take it on faith that the strategy she has now been given is the best: the most achievable and the most acceptable.

She and her squad gather, watching other bands of soldiers surge and spring across distant sections of the webbing. Her eyes stray to the high heavens. There is a new star up above, now, and it foretells a time of terrible cataclysm and destruction simply by its appearance. There is no superstitious astrology in such predictions. The end times are truly here, the moment when one great cycle of history grinds inexorably into the next.

The humans are coming.

7.3 MAIDEN, MOTHER, CRONE

'What do you mean, "Wake Lain"?'

Karst and Alpash turned to Holsten, trying to read his suddenly agonized expression.

'What it sounds like,' the security chief replied, baffled.

'She's *alive*?' Holsten's fingers crooked, fighting the urge to grab one or other of them and shake. 'Why didn't anyone . . . why didn't you . . . why only wake her *now*? Why isn't she in charge?'

Karst obviously took issue with that, but Alpash stepped in quickly. 'To wake Grandmother is not something to be done lightly, by her own orders. Only in matters of emergency, she said. She told us: when I next wake, I want to walk upon a green planet.'

'She told you that, did she?' Holsten demanded.

'She told my mother, when she was very young,' the engineer replied, meeting the classicist's challenging stare easily. 'But it is recorded. We have records of many of Grandmother's later pronouncements.' He bent over a console, calling up a display that shuddered patchily. 'But we should go now. Commander . . . ?'

'Yeah, well, I'll hold the fort here, shall I?' Karst said, plainly still smarting somewhat. 'You get the woman up and on her feet, and then link to me. Give her the situation and tell her that Vitas and I need to touch heads with her.'

Alpash headed off into the ship, away from Key Crew and most of the living areas that Holsten was familiar with. The classicist hurried after him, not much wanting to be left with Karst, still less wanting to get lost within the flickering, ravaged spaces of the *Gilgamesh*. Everywhere told the same story of slow autolysis, a cannibalism of the self as less important parts and systems were ripped out to fix higher-priority problems. Walls were laid open, the ship's bones exposed. Screens flared static or else were dark as wells. Here and there huddled small pockets of the Tribe, still about the essential business of keeping the ship running, despite the immediate crisis, their heads close together like priests murmuring doctrine.

'How do you even know how to fix the ship?' Holsten asked of Alpash's back. 'It's been . . . I don't know how long it's been. Since Guyen died, even, I don't know. And you think you can still keep the ship running? Just by . . . ? What do you . . . ? You're learning how to make a spaceship run by rote or . . . ?'

Alpash looked back at him, frowning. 'Don't think I don't know what the commander means, when he says "Tribe". The chief scientist, too. It pleases them to think of us as primitives, inferiors. We, in turn, are bound to respect their – your – authority, as our precursors. That is what our grandmother laid down. That is one of our laws. But we do nothing "by rote". We learn, all of us, from our youngest age. We have preserved manuals and lectures and tutorial modules. Our grandmother has provided for us. Do you think we could do all we have done if we did not *understand*?'

He stopped, clearly angry. Holsten had obviously touched a nerve already rubbed raw by the other Key Crew. 'We are of the line of those who gave their lives – *all* of their lives – to preserve this vessel. That was and is our task, one to be · undertaken without reward or hope of relief: an endless round of custodianship, until we reach the planet we were promised. My parents, their parents and theirs, all of them have done nothing but ensure that *you* and all the other cargo of this ship shall live, or as much of them as we could save. And it pleases you to call us "Tribe" and consider us children and savages, because we never saw Earth.'

Holsten held his hands up appeasingly. 'I'm sorry. You've taken this up with Karst? I mean, he's kind of depending on you. You could . . . make demands.'

Alpash's look was incredulous. 'At this time? With the future of our home – our old home and our new – hanging in the balance? Would you say that was a good time for us to start arguing amongst ourselves?'

For a moment Holsten studied the young man as though he was some completely new species of hominid, separated by a yawning cognitive gulf. The feeling passed, and he shook himself. 'She did well when she set down your laws,' he murmured.

'Thank you.' Alpash apparently took this as a validation of his entire culture – or whatever it was that had developed amongst his weird, claustrophobic society. 'And now at last I get to meet her, here at the end of everything.'

They passed on through a wide-open space that Holsten suddenly recognized, the remembrance coming to him half-way across it, looking at the raised stage at one end where stubs of broken machinery still jutted. Here Guyen had stood and made his bid for eternity. Here the earliest pro-genitors of Alpash's line had fought alongside their warrior queen and Karst's security team – some of whom were surely recently reawakened, possessing living memories of events that for Alpash must be song and story and weirdly twisted legend.

A lone screen hung at an angle above the torn-up roots of the upload facility, flickering malevolently with scattered patterns. *As though Guyen's ghost is still trapped inside there,* Holsten thought. Almost immediately, he thought he did see, for a broken moment, the rage-torn face of the old com-mander in the flurrying striations of the screen. Or perhaps it had been Avrana Kern's Old Empire features. Shuddering, he hurried on after Alpash.

The place he ended up in had been a storeroom, he guessed. Now they stored only one thing there: a single sus-pension chamber. At the foot of the pedestal was a huddle of little objects – icons heat-moulded in plastic into an approxi-mation of the female form: offerings from her surrogate children, and their children, to the guardian-mother of the human race. Above that desperate little display of hope and faith were tacked little scraps of cloth torn from shipsuits, each bearing some close-written message. This was a shrine to a living goddess.

Not only living but awake. Alpash and a couple of other young engineers were standing back respectfully while Isa Lain found her balance, leaning on a metal spar.

She was very frail, her earlier heaviness eaten away from her frame, leaving skin that was bagged and wrinkled and hung from her bones. Her near-bald scalp was mottled with liver spots, and her hands were like bird's claws, almost fleshless. She stood with a pronounced hunch, enough that Holsten wondered if they'd altered the suspension chamber to let her sleep out the ages lying on her side. When she looked up at him, though, her eyes were Lain's eyes, clear and sharp and sardonic.

If she had said, then, 'Hello, old man,' like she used to, he was not sure that he could have borne it. She just nodded, however, as though nothing was to be more expected than to find Holsten Mason standing there, looking young enough to be her son.

'Stop your bloody staring,' she snapped a moment later. 'You don't look such a picture yourself, and what's your excuse?'

'Lain . . .' He approached her carefully, as though even a strong movement of air might blow her away.

'No time for romance now, lover boy,' she said drily. 'I hear Karst's fucked up and we've got the human race to save.' And then she was in his arms, and he felt that fragile, thin-boned frame, felt her shaking suddenly as she fought the memories and the emotions.

'Get off me, you oaf,' she said, but quietly, and she made no move to push him away.

'I'm just glad you're still with us,' he whispered.

'For one more roll of the dice, anyway,' she agreed. 'I really did think that I might get some honest natural gravity and decent sunlight when they cracked me open. Was that too much to ask for? But apparently it was. I can't believe that I even have to do Karst's job these days.'

'Don't be too hard on Karst,' Holsten cautioned her. 'The situation is . . . unprecedented.'

'I'll be the judge of that.' At last she shook him off. 'I

swear, sometimes I think I'm the only competent person left in the whole human race. I think that's the only thing keeping me going.' She made to stride past him, but stumbled almost immediately, and her next step was decidedly less ambitious, a careful hobble while leaning on her stick. 'Never grow old,' she muttered. 'Never grow old and then go into suspension, that's for sure. You dream young dreams. You forget what you're coming back to. Fucking disappointment, believe me.'

'You don't dream in suspension,' Holsten corrected her.

'Look at you, the fucking expert.' She glowered at him. 'Or am I not allowed to swear now? I suppose you expect some sort of fucking *decorum*?' Behind her defiance there was a terrible desperation: a woman who had always been able to simply physically impose her will on the world, who now had to ask its permission and the permission of her own body.

Holsten brought her up to date with developments on the way back to join Karst. He could see her determinedly fitting each piece into place, and she wasn't slow to stop him and ask for clarification.

'These transmissions,' she prompted. 'Do we reckon they're actually from the planet, then?'

'I have no idea. It's . . . it explains why most of it's completely incomprehensible, I suppose. It doesn't explain the stuff that sounds a bit like Imperial C – so maybe *that* is Kern.'

'Have we tried talking to Kern?'

'I think Karst was pinning everything on mounting a sneak attack.'

'How subtle of him,' she spat. 'I reckon now's about the

time to talk to Kern, don't you?' She paused, breathing heavily. 'In fact, go do it now. Just get on with it. When we hit comms, I'll talk guns with Karst. You can talk whatever-the-fuck with Kern, find out what she's saying. Maybe she doesn't actually like spiders crawling all over her. Maybe she's an ally now. You never know until you ask.'

She had so much of her old sense of purpose still clinging to her, like the tatters of a once-magnificent garment, that Holsten was considerably heartened up until the moment that she reached comms and saw what the drones were transmitting. Then Lain stopped in the hatchway and stared, exactly as aghast and lost as all the rest of them. For a moment all eyes were fixed on her, and if she had declared it all a lost cause then and there, there might have been nobody else willing to take up the baton.

But she was Lain. She endured and she fought, whether satellites or spiders or time itself.

'Fuck,' she said expressively, and then repeated it a few more times, as if taking strength from the word. 'Holsten, get on the comms to Kern. Karst, get Vitas over here, and then you can start telling me just what the fuck we can do about that mess.'

With the comms at his disposal – or at least after Alpash had explained half a dozen workarounds the engineers had come up with to deal with system instability – Holsten wondered what he could possibly send. He had the satellite's frequency, but the space around the planet was alive with whispering ghosts: those faint transmissions that were, he had to admit now, not just signals from the satellite bouncing off the planet below it.

He tried to feel some sort of awe about that, and about

the unprecedented position that he was in. The only emotion he could muster was a worn-out dread.

He began to assemble a message in his impeccable Imperial C, the dead language that looked to be about to survive the human race. *This is the ark ship* Gilgamesh *calling for Doctor Avrana Kern . . .* He stumbled over '*Do you require assistance,*' his mind thronging with inappropriate possibilities. *Doctor Kern, you're covered in spiders.* He took a deep breath.

This is the ark ship Gilgamesh *calling Doctor Avrana Kern.* And, face it, she knew them and they knew her; they were old adversaries, after all. *We are now without any option but to land on your planet. The survival of the human race is at stake. Please confirm that you will not impede us.* It was a wretched plea. He knew that, even as he let the message fly off at the speed of light towards the planet. What could Kern say that would satisfy them? What could he say that would dissuade her from her monomaniacal purpose?

Vitas had arrived by then, and she, Karst and Lain had their heads close together, discussing the important stuff, whilst Holsten was left babbling into the void.

Then a reply arrived, or something like it.

It was sent from the point in the web that Karst had figured to be the satellite, and it was far stronger than the feeble transmissions he had been analysing before. There seemed little doubt that it was directed at and intended for the *Gilgamesh*. If it was Kern, it seemed she was long gone: it was not her crisp, antique speech, but more of the weird, almost-Imperial that he had caught before, a jumble of nonsense and letter-strings that looked like words but weren't, and in the midst of them all a few words and what might even be sentence fragments, like an illiterate aping writing from memory. An illiterate with access to a radio and the ability to encode a signal.

He re-sent his signal, asking for Eliza this time. What was there to lose?

The return was more of the same. He contrasted it with its predecessor: some repeated sections, some new ones, and by now his professional eye was seeing certain recurring patterns in those sections he could not interpret. Kern was trying to tell them something. Or at least *something* was trying to tell them something. He wondered if it was still simply 'Go away' and, if that was the case, would it now be a warning for their benefit? Turn back before it's too late?

But there was no *back* for them. They were now on a one-way journey towards the only potentially viable destination they could possibly reach.

He pondered what he might be able to send, so as to jolt Kern into some semblance of comprehensible sentience. Or was Kern, too, now a failing machine. Was the end coming for all of the works of human hands, even as it was for their masters?

It seemed intolerable that the universe could be left to the creators of that planet-spanning web, to a legion of insensate crawling things that could never know the trials and hardships that poor humanity had suffered.

A new message was being broadcast at them on the same frequency. Holsten listened to it dully: not even a mimicry of language now, just numerical codes.

To his shame, it was the *Gilgamesh* that recognized it, rather than he himself. It was the signal that Kern had, once upon a time, been sending down towards the planet. It was her intelligence test for monkeys.

Without much examination of his motives, Holsten composed the answers – with help from the *Gilgamesh* towards the end – and sent it back.

Another battery of questions followed – new ones this time.

'What is it?' Lain was at his shoulder, just like old times. If he didn't look back, he could even fool himself that rather less water had flowed under the bridge since they were first playing this game.

'Kern's testing us,' he told her. 'Maybe she wants to see if we're worthy?'

'By setting us a maths exam?'

'She never made much sense at the best of times. So why not?'

'Get her the answers, then. Come on.'

Holsten did so – finding it so much quicker to assemble a response once the complexities of actual language were removed from the equation. 'Of course, we have no idea of the purpose of this,' he pointed out.

'But we can still hope it has a purpose,' she replied crisply. Holsten was vaguely aware of Vitas and Karst hovering in the background, impatient to get on with talking about the offensive.

There was no third round of the test. Instead they got another blast of the maddeningly near-to-Imperial C that Holsten had seen before. He analysed it swiftly, passing it through his decoders and pattern-recognition functions. It seemed simpler than before, and with more repeated patterns. The phrase came to him, *like talking to a child*, and he experienced another of those vertiginous moments, wondering who or what it was that was speaking, far out there. *Kern, surely? But Kern made strange – stranger – by the curdling effects of time and distance.* But, even though Kern's little Sentry Habitat was the origination point of the signal, a part of him understood already that this was not so.

'I can identify some words used frequently,' he announced hoarsely, after he and his suite of programs had finished their work. He could not keep the quaver out of his tones. 'I've found what's definitely a form of the verb "approach" and the word "near", and some other indicators I'd associate with "permission" or "agreement".'

That pronouncement got the thoughtful silence it deserved.

'They've changed their tune, then,' Karst remarked at last. 'You said it was all "fuck off" before.'

'It was.' Holsten nodded. 'It's changed.'

'Because Kern's in desperate need of our superior maths skills?' the security chief demanded.

Holsten opened his mouth, then shut it, unwilling to make his suspicions real by voicing them aloud.

Lain did it for him. 'If it's actually Kern.'

'Who else?' but there was a raw edge to Karst's voice that showed he was not such a blunt tool, after all.

'There's no evidence that anything but Kern exists to transmit from there,' Vitas said sharply.

'What about that?' Holsten jabbed a finger at the screen still showing the drone's images.

'We have no way of knowing what has transpired down on that planet. It was an experiment, after all. It may be that what we are seeing is an aberration of that experiment, just as was the grey planet and its fungal growth. The point remains that the Kern satellite is still present there, and it's where the signal comes from,' Vitas set out doggedly.

'Or it may be—' Lain started.

'It's possible,' Vitas cut her off. The very suggestion seemed abhorrent to her. 'It changes nothing.'

'Right,' Karst backed her up. 'I mean, even if they're – if *Kern's* – saying, yeah, come on down, what do we do? Because, if she's got all her stuff, she can cut us up as we touch orbit. And that's not even thinking about *that* bastard mess and what that could do. I mean, if it's something that's grown up from the planet, well, it's Kern's experiment, isn't it? Maybe it does what she says.'

There was an awkward pause, everyone waiting to see if someone, anyone, would argue the other side, just for the form of it. Holsten turned the words over, trying to put together a sentence that didn't sound flat-out crazy.

'There was a tradition the Old Empire once had,' Vitas stated slowly. 'It was a choice they gave to their criminals, their prisoners. They would take two of them and ask them to spare or to accuse each other, each making the decision quite alone without a chance to confer. All went very well indeed if they both chose to spare one another, but they suffered some degree of punishment if they both accused each other. But, oh, if you were the prisoner who decided to spare his friend, only to find you'd been accused in turn . . .' She smiled, and in that smile Holsten saw suddenly that she *had* grown old, but that it showed so little on her face – kept at bay by all the expressions she did not give rein to.

'So what was the right choice?' Karst asked her. 'How did the prisoners get out of it?'

'The logical choice depended on the stakes: the weighting of punishments for the different outcomes,' Vitas explained. 'I'm afraid the facts and the stakes here are very stark and very plain. We could approach the planet in the hope that we were, against all past experience, now being welcomed. As Karst says, that will leave us vulnerable. We will put the ship at risk if it turns out that this is really a trick, or even that Mason has simply made some error in his translation.' Her eyes passed over Holsten, daring him to object, but in truth he was by no ways that confident of his own abilities. 'Or we attack – use the drones now, and prepare to back up that first strike when the *Gilgamesh* reaches the planet. If we do that, and we are wrong, we are throwing away a priceless chance to reach an accommodation with an Old Empire intelligence of some sort.' There was genuine regret in her voice. 'If we go in peace, and we are wrong, we are most likely all dead, all of us, all the human race. I don't think we can argue with the weighting that we have been given. For me there is only one rational choice at this point.'

Karst nodded grimly. 'That bitch never liked us,' he pointed out. 'No way she'd suddenly change her mind.'

Several centuries later and a lot of spiders is a long way from 'suddenly', Holsten thought, but the words stayed unspoken in his head. Lain was looking at him, though, obviously expecting a contribution. *So now people actually want to listen to the classicist?* He just shrugged. He suspected that the loss, if they went to war on false pretences, might be far greater than Vitas claimed, but he could not argue with her assessment of the complete total loss of everything there was if they erred too far on the path of peace.

'More importantly, the logic is universal,' Vitas added,

looking from face to face. 'It truly doesn't matter what is waiting for us at the planet. It's mathematics, that's all. Our adversary faces the same choice, the same weighting. Even if to welcome us with open arms and have us then play the responsible guest may give the best results all round, the cost of being betrayed is too high. So we can look into the minds of our opponents. We know that they must make the same decision that we must make: because the cost of fighting needlessly is so much less than the cost of opting for peace and getting it wrong. And that same logic will inform the decision of *whatever* is there, whether it's a human mind or a machine, or . . .'

Spiders? But it was plain that Vitas wouldn't even utter the word, and when Lain spoke it for her, the science chief twitched ever so slightly.

So Vitas doesn't like spiders, Holsten considered morosely. *Well, she wasn't down on the bloody planet, was she? She didn't see those bloated monsters.* His eyes strayed to the image of the webbed world. *Can it be sentience? Or is Vitas right and it's just some mad experiment gone wrong – gone right, even? Would the Old Empire have wanted giant space-spiders for some purpose? Why not? As a historian I must concur that they did a lot of stupid things.*

'Come on, then,' Karst prompted. 'I'm pressing the button, or what?'

In the end everyone was looking at Lain.

The old engineer took a few careful steps forward, stick clacking on the floor, staring at the drone's camera image of the shrouded planet. Her eyes, that had witnessed centuries pass in a kind of punctuated stop-motion, tried to take it all in. She had the look of a woman staring bleak destiny in the eye.

'Take out the satellite,' she decided at last, quietly. 'We go in fighting. You're right, there's too much at stake. There's everything at stake. Bring it down.'

Karst sent the order briskly, as though afraid that someone would get cold feet or change their mind. Millions of kilometres away, in the direction of the *Gilgamesh*'s inexorable progress, the drones received their instructions. They already had the metal fist of the satellite targeted, trapped as it was in that vast equatorial web.

They carried the best lasers that the Tribe had been able to restore, linked to the remote vessels' little fusion reactors. They had already drifted as close as they dared, jockeying for geostationary orbit above the trapped satellite with as little expenditure of energy as they could get away with.

They loosed, the two of them together, striking at the same spot on the satellite's hull. Somewhere far distant, Karst would be tensing, but the image he would be reacting to would already be old by the time he saw it.

For a moment nothing happened, as energy was poured into the ancient, ravaged shell of the Brin 2 Sentry Pod. Karst would have his fists clenched, staring at the screens with veins standing out on his forehead, as though his will could cross space and time in order to make things happen.

Then, with a silent flowering of fire almost instantly extinguished, the drilling beams reached something vital within, and the millennia-old home of Doctor Avrana Kern was ripped open, the webs on either side shrivelling and springing away under the sudden excess of heat. Still gouting out its contents into the hungry emptiness of space, the shattered satellite slipped free from its tangle of moorings, burning a hole in the great web, and was propelled away from the drones by the outrush of material from its jagged wounds.

The drones themselves had given their all, the discharge of their weapons leaving their reactors cold and draining them dry. They tumbled off across the face of the web, to fall or to drift away.

The satellite, though, had a more definite fate. It fell. Like Kern's experimental subjects so very very long before, it was jolted out of its orbit, to be gathered up by the arms of the planet's gravity, spiralling helplessly into the atmosphere, where it streaked across the sky, just an old barrel with a single ancient monkey in withered residence, delivering a final message to the anxious eyes below.

7.4 END TIMES

They watched it burn its way across the sky.

Although active Messenger-worship was almost non-existent in these more enlightened times – what need of faith when there was ample proof of the precise nature of God? – the spiders watched that fiery trail, either with their own eyes or through the surrogate eyes of their biological systems, and knew that something had gone out of their world. The Messenger had always been there. They retained the memories of distant, primitive times when that moving light in the heavens had been both compass and inspiration to them. They recalled the heady days of Temple, and the earliest communications shared between God and Her congregation. Something that has been a part of their cultural consciousness from their earliest times; something that they know, rationally, to be older than their very species; and now it is gone.

In the quiet dark of his work-chamber, Fabian feels a shock of emotion go through him that he had not expected. He, of all spiders, is not religious. He has no time for the unknowable, save to pin it down by experiment and reason, and thus make it knowable. Still . . .

He has been watching on a filmy screen, the image formed from thousands of tiny chromatopores of various colours expanding and contracting to form pinpoint parts of the overall picture. Deep underground, as his chambers are, there is no chance of him witnessing this first-hand. He is a pallid, angular, unkempt specimen of his species, and seldom cares much about seeing the sun; instead he works to his own rhythms that have little to do with day or night.

Well, he remarks to his only constant companion, *I suppose that backs up everything you have told us.*

Of course. The response comes from the very walls, an invisible presence all around him like a familiar demon. *And you must retaliate at the first opportunity. They will give you no chances.*

The connection peer group seemed to be having some success, just before, Fabian notes. The curved walls of the chamber around him seethe and crawl; a thousand thousand ants engaged in the inscrutable bustle of activity that allows this colony – a super-colony really, risen again after all this time – to function in the unique way that it does.

There was never any chance of their success. I am only glad that they have been shown this unequivocal demonstration of the enemy's intent. I am concerned about the strategy to be employed, however. It is a strange thing, this bodiless speech. Muscular pistons in the walls create the vibrations that simulate a spider's elegant footfalls. Elsewhere, the thing communicates by radio still, but here Fabian can speak to it as though it was a spider: a particularly aloof, temperamental female, he considers, but still a spider.

It speaks in that curious negotiated language that was long ago devised for communication between the spiders and their God, but recently it has taken to bringing up a pair of phantom palps on the screens to add emphasis to its language, adopting a bizarre pidgin of the spiders' own visual language. Fabian, who has never been comfortable much with his own kind, finds it congenial company. That, and his unarguable skill with chemical architecture and conditioning, has earned him this vital role. He is the hands and the confidant of the Messenger, as she is now.

I wonder if there was anything left, at the end, of me. The words were slow, hesitant. At first Fabian wonders if another glitch has developed in the machinery, or possibly in the colony's conditioning. Then he decides that this is one of those times when his companion is dredging up some remnant intonation or rhythm of speech that it might have used in another age, in another form.

Doctor Avrana Kern, he addresses it. It does not like him to call it God or Messenger. After long haggling, they have found a form of arbitrary movements that seem to recall to it the name it once went by. It is one of many idiosyncrasies that Fabian is happy to indulge. He has a special relationship with God, after all. He is Her closest friend. He is responsible for maintaining Her proper functioning and untangling any errors in Her conditioning.

Around him, in a network of tunnels and chambers the geography of which is constantly being altered, dwells a colony of hundred million insects. Their interactions are not as fast as an electronic system built by human hands, but each insect's tiny brain is itself a capable engine for data storage and decision making, and the overall calculating power of the colony as a whole is something that even it cannot assess. Cloud computing: not speed but an infinitely reconfigurable breadth and complexity. There is more than enough room for the downloaded mind of Avrana Kern.

It took a long time to work out how to do it, but in the end she was only information, after all. Everything is only information, if you have sufficient capacity to encompass it. A long time, too, to copy that information from satellite to a holding colony on the surface. A long – a much longer – time for what they had downloaded to organize itself to the extent that it could say *I am*. But it *is*, now, and they have had a long time. The colony that Fabian lives within and tends is God made flesh, the incarnation of the Messenger.

Fabian opens radio contact with one of the orbital observatories and checks on the approach of the enemy, which is in a trajectory that confirms it will be seeking orbit around their world. This is a time for waiting, now. Across the planet, they are all waiting: not just the spiders, but all those species they have connected with. They will all be under the hammer soon, facing with their numbers and their ingenuity a species that created them without ever meaning to, and now seeks to erase them just as thoughtlessly. There are spiders, ant colonies, stomatopods in the ocean, semi-sentient beetles and a dozen others of varying proportions of intellect and instinct, all in some faint way aware that the end times are here.

Up on the orbital web, Bianca can plan no more. Portia waits with her peers, ready to fight the returning space-gods. For now they can only cling to their webs, as the extended senses their technology gives them track the approach of the end.

And then the great bulk of the *Gilgamesh* is drawing close, at the end of its long deceleration, its ailing thrusters fighting to slow it to the point where the momentum of a dive past the planet will mesh with the reaching gravity and bring the ark ship into orbit.

Although they have been aware of the dimensions of the enemy, from their own measurements and Kern's records, the sheer scale of the *Gilgamesh* is awe-inspiring. More than one spider must be thinking, *How can we fight such a thing?*

And then the ark ship's weapons unleash their fire. Its approach has been calculated to put the equatorial web in the sights of its forward-facing asteroid lasers and, in that fleeting pass, the *Gilgamesh* makes full use of its window of opportunity. The web has no centre, no vital point where a surgical strike might cause widespread damage, and so the lasers just sear out indiscriminately, frying strands, cutting open nodes, tearing great gashes in the overall structure of the web. Spiders die: exposed suddenly to vacuum, thrown out into space or inwards towards the planet, some few even vaporized by the incendiary wrath of the lasers themselves.

Portia receives damage reports even as she and her warrior peer group prepare for their counterattack. She is aware that they have just lost, in one searing instant, a certain number of soldiers, a certain proportion of their weapons – all just blindly snuffed out. Bianca confers with her, her radio vibrating with electric current to simulate the dancing rhythms of speech.

The battle plan is unchanged, Bianca confirms. She will already have a complete picture of what they have lost and what they still have. Portia does not envy her the task of coordinating all their orbital defences. *Are you ready for deployment?*

We are. Portia feels a swelling of angry determination at the destruction. The deaths, the destruction of the Messenger, the heedless brutality of it all, fire her up with righteous zeal. *We will show them.*

We will show them, Bianca echoes, sounding equally determined. *You are the swiftest, the strongest, the cleverest. You are the defenders of your world. If you fail, then it will be as though we never lived at all. All our Understandings will be nothing but dust. I ask you to keep the plan in mind at all times. I know that some of you have qualms. This is not the time for them. The great minds of our people have determined that what you are to do is what must be done, if we are to preserve who and what we are.*

We understand. Portia is aware that the great star-blotting form of the ark ship is nearing. Already other detachments are launching.

Good hunting, Bianca exhorts them all.

All around, the orbital weapons of the web are in action. Each consists of a single piece of debris, a rock hauled up by the space elevator or captured from the void, held under enormous tension within the net – and now suddenly released, hurled at great speed into the vacuum towards the ark ship.

But tiny, Portia considers. Those vast boulders she remembers seeing are nothing to the ark ship. Surely its shell must be proof against any such missiles.

But the spiders are not simply throwing rocks. The hurled missiles have multiple purposes, but mostly they are a distraction.

Portia feels the webbing tense around her. *Ensure your lines are properly coiled,* she sends to her peers. *This will be rough.*

Seconds later, she and her peers are flung into the void on an oblique line that will intercept the *Gilgamesh*'s pass as it enters a stable orbit.

She clutches her legs tightly into her body by instinct at first, a shock of terror erupting in her mind and threatening to overwhelm her. Then her training takes over and she begins checking on her soldiers. They are spreading out as they fall towards their rendezvous with the *Gilgamesh*, but they are still linked by lines to a central hub, forming a rotating wheel, just one of many now spinning towards the *Gilgamesh*.

The ark ship's lasers burn the first few rocks, heating them explosively at carefully calculated points to send them tumbling out of its path. Others slam into the vast vessel's sides, rebounding or embedding. Portia sees at least one thin plume of lost air from a lucky or unlucky strike.

Then she and her peers are bracing for impact. Her radio feeds them second-by-second instructions from the computing colonies on the orbital web, to help them slow down their approach with their little jets and their meagre supply of propellant. Portia is very aware that this is quite likely to be a one-way trip. If they fail, there will be nothing to journey back to.

She has slowed as much as she is able, spinning out more line from the centre of the wheel to put her further away from her sisters. She spreads her legs and hopes that she has managed to do away with just enough momentum.

She lands badly, fails to catch hold with the hooks of her insulated gloves, bounds back from the *Gilgamesh*'s hull. Others of her team have been luckier and now they latch on with six legs and reel in their errant peers, Portia included. One is unluckier, landing at an angle and smashing her mask. She dies in an agonized flurry of twitching legs, her helpless cries coming to her companions through the metal of the hull.

There is no time for sentiment. Her corpse is secured to the hull with a little webbing, and then they are on the move. They have a war to fight, after all.

We will show them, Portia thinks. *We will show them the error of their ways.*

7.5 MANOEUVRES

'Rocks! They're throwing *rocks* at us!' Karst declared incredulously. 'They're space-age stone-age!'

One of the console displays flickered and went out and others began to dot with baleful amber displays.

'Karst, this isn't a warship,' Lain's brittle voice snapped. 'The *Gilgamesh* wasn't designed for any sort of stresses except acceleration and deceleration, certainly not impact—'

'We have a hull breach in cargo,' Alpash reported, sounding as though someone had trampled over his holy places. 'Internal doors are . . .' For a moment, apparently, it wasn't clear whether they were or weren't, but then he got out, 'Sealed off, the section's sealed off. We have . . . cargo loss—'

'Cargo is already in vacuum, or close to. Exposure shouldn't cause any harm,' Vitas broke in.

'We have damage to forty-nine chambers,' Alpash told her. 'From the impact, and from electrical surges resulting from the damage. Forty-nine.'

For a moment nobody felt up to following that. Half a hundred deaths from a single hit. Trivial, compared to the overall cargo manifest. Horrifying, though, to go behind that word 'cargo' and think about the implications.

'We're in orbit, one hundred and eighty kilometres out

from the web,' Karst said. 'We need to fight back. They'll be throwing more stones at us.'

'Will they?' Holsten's meagre contribution.

'Maybe they're reloading.'

'What other damage?' Vitas asked.

'I . . . don't know,' Alpash admitted. 'Hull sensors are . . . unreliable, and some have been lost. I don't believe any essential systems have been damaged, but there may be weakening of the hull in other areas . . . our damage-control systems have been refined so as to concentrate on emergencies and critical areas.' Meaning that they simply hadn't been able to properly maintain the entire network.

'We can reposition the lasers,' Karst stated, as though it was a natural sequitur to what had last been said. Perhaps in Karst's head it was.

'We can probably reposition the ship rather more easily,' Lain told him. 'Just turn him round so that the asteroid arrays are aiming towards the web. In orbit, our orientation doesn't matter.'

Karst blinked at that, obviously still somewhat married to the idea that the front end should go first, but then he nodded. 'Well, let's start on that, then. How long?'

'Depends how responsive the systems are. We may need to do some spot repairs.'

'We may not have—'

'Fuck off, Karst. I am literally in the same boat as you. I will do it as fast as it can be done.'

'Well, right.' Karst grimaced, apparently remembering that his status as acting commander had been sidelined once they woke up Lain.

The ancient engineer lowered herself in front of one of

the working consoles, a handful of her Tribe gathered around her to do her bidding. She looked terribly tired, Holsten thought, and yet there was still an energy to her he recognized. Time had fought with Lain for possession of this bent, fragile body, and so far time had lost.

'We are simply not going to be able to burn our way to control of the planet,' Vitas stated.

'Sure we are,' Karst said stubbornly. 'Seriously, we can probably cut across that entire web, just send it fucking off into space like an old . . . sock or something.' And then, 'Shut up, Holsten,' when the classicist seemed about to take issue with his simile.

'Karst, please check the available power to the asteroid array,' Vitas said patiently.

Karst scowled. 'So we recharge them.'

'Using all the energy that is currently ensuring that systems like life-support or reactor-containment keep working,' Vitas agreed. 'And, even if you get it right, what then? What about the planet, Karst?'

'The planet?' He blinked at her.

'You were planning to just trip down there in a shuttle and plant a flag? If *that's* what near-orbit looks like, what do you think you'd find on the surface? You're going to laser all of that, too, are you? Or will you take a disruptor, or a gun? How many bullets do you have, precisely?'

'I've already got the security team and some auxiliaries woken up and armed,' Karst said stubbornly. 'We'll go down and make a beachhead, establish a base, start pushing out. We'll burn the fuckers. What else can we do? Nobody said it was going to be easy. Nobody said it would happen overnight.'

'Well, it might come to that,' Vitas conceded. 'And if it does, I shall stay up here and coordinate the assault, and good luck to you. However, I hope there will be a more efficient way to dispose of our pest problem. Lain, I'll need at least one of the workshops up and running at my direction, and access to all the old files – anything we've still got regarding Earth.'

'What's the plan?' Lain asked without looking back at her.

'Brew up a present for the s-s- . . . for them, below.' This time Vitas's stutter was clear enough that everyone noticed it. 'I don't think it should be impossible to put together some sort of toxin that will target arthropods, something to eat away at their exoskeletons or their respiratory system, but that won't have any ill effect on us. After all, assuming they're derived from actual Earth spiders, they're essentially a completely different form of life to us. They're not like us at all, in any way.'

Holsten, listening, heard too much emphasis on those words. He thought of broken messages in Imperial C. Had it been Kern herself, or something just parroting Kern's words?

In the end, he supposed, it didn't matter. Genocide was genocide. He thought of the Old Empire, which had been so civilized that it had in the end poisoned its own homeworld. *And here we are, about to start ripping pieces of the ecosystem out of this new one.*

Nobody was paying attention to him, especially as he wasn't voicing any of these thoughts that entered his head, so he found a console that looked halfway operational and got into the comms system.

As he had expected, there was a great deal of broad-frequency radio activity issuing from the planet. The destruction of the Sentry Habitat meant that nothing was coming to them now as clearly – possibly it had been merely a powerful transmitter for the planet, at the end. But the green world itself was alive with urgent, incomprehensible messages.

He wanted to think of something wonderful, then: some perfect message that would somehow bring comprehension in its wake, open a dialogue, give everyone options. The cruel arithmetic of Vitas's prisoners locked him down, though. *We couldn't trust them. They couldn't trust us. Mutual attempts at destruction are the only logical result.* He thought of human dreams – both Old Empire and new – of contacting some extra-terrestrial intelligence such as nobody had ever truly encountered. *Why? Why would we ever want to? We'd never be able to communicate, and even if we could, we'd still be those same two prisoners forced to trust – and risk – or to damn the other in trying to save slightly more of our own hides.*

Then there came a new transmission, from the planet direct to the ship, fainter than before, but then it was not using the satellite as a relay any more. One word in Imperial C, but absolutely clear in its meaning.

Missed.

Holsten stared, opened his mouth two or three times, about to draw someone's attention, then sent a simple message back on the same frequency.

Doctor Avrana Kern?

I told you to stay away, came the immediate, baleful response.

Holsten worked swiftly, aware that he was negotiating now not for the *Gilgamesh* but as Earth's last classicist in the face of raw history. *We have no option. We need to get off the ship. We need a world.*

I sent you to a world, ungrateful apes. The transmission came from the planet, pulsing strongly out of the general riot of signals.

Uninhabitable, he sent. *Doctor Kern, you are human. We are human. We are all the humans there are left. Please let us land. We have no other choice. We cannot turn back.*

Humanity is overrated, came Kern's dark reply. *And, besides, do you think that I am making the decisions? I'm only an advisor, and they didn't like my preferred solution to the problem that is you. They have their own ways of dealing with trouble. Go away.*

Doctor Kern, we are not bluffing, we really have no option. But it was just like before: he was not getting through. *Can I talk to Eliza please?*

If there was anything left that was Eliza and not me you've just destroyed it, Kern responded. *Goodbye, monkeys.*

Holsten sent further transmissions, several times over, but Kern was apparently done with talking. He could hear the woman's contemptuous voice as he read through the impeccable Imperial C, but he was far more shaken with the ancient entity's suggestion that the creatures on the planet would not be held back even by her. *Where has her experiment taken her?*

He glanced about him. Vitas had gone now, heading off for her workshop and her chemicals, ready to sterilize as much of the planet as was necessary so that her species could find a home there. Holsten wasn't sure how much would be left of what made the place attractive for habitation, after she was finished. *But what other choice have we? Die in space and leave the place to the bugs and to Kern?*

'We're still losing hull sensors,' Alpash noticed. 'The impacts may have caused more damage than we thought.' He sounded genuinely worried, and that was a disease that others caught off him almost immediately.

'How can we still be losing them?' Lain demanded, still concentrating on her own work.

'I don't know.'

'I'm sending out a drone, then. Let's take a look,' Karst stated. 'Here.' After some fumbling, he got the drone's-eye-view up on one of the screens as it manoeuvred somewhat shakily out of its bay and coasted off down the great curving landscape of the ship's hull. 'Fuck me, this is patched to buggery,' he commented.

'Mostly from what we installed after the terraform station,' Lain confirmed. 'Lots of opening her up and closing her back down to get new stuff in, or to effect repairs . . .' Her voice trailed off. 'What was that?'

'What now? I didn't see—' Karst started.

'Something moved,' Alpash confirmed.

'Don't be stupid . . .'

Holsten stared, seeing the lumpy, antennae-spiked landscape pass. Then, at the corner of the screen, there was a flurry of furtive, scuttling movement.

'They're here,' he tried to say, but his throat was dry, his voice just a whisper.

'There's nothing out there,' Karst was saying. But Holsten was thinking, *Was that some kind of thread drifting from that antenna? Why are the hull sensors going down, one by one? What is that I see moving . . . ?*

'Oh, fuck.' Karst suddenly sounded older than Lain. 'Fuck fuck fuck.'

In the drone's sight, a half-dozen grey, scrabbling forms passed swiftly over the hull, running with slightly exaggerated sureness out in the freezing, airless void, even leaping forwards, catching themselves with lines, leaving a tracery of discarded threads latticing the *Gilgamesh*'s exterior.

'What are they doing?' Alpash asked hollowly.

Lain's voice, at least, was steady. 'Trying to get in.'

7.6 BREAKING THE SHELL

One of Portia's peers operates a bulky device of silk-bound glass that acts as an eye, containing a colony of tiny ants whose sole function is to create a compound view of the sights before them and relay it back to the orbital web and to the planet. Bianca can then give moment-to-moment orders to best exploit their new position up on the exterior of this vast alien intruder. This is just as well, for Portia would not have the first idea what to make of anything she sees. Every detail is bizarre and disturbing, an aesthetic arising from the dreams of another phylum, a technology of hard metal and elemental forces.

Bianca herself has little better idea what to do with it, but the images are being routed down to the vast colony-complex that is Doctor Avrana Kern, or what is left of her. Kern can make an educated guess at what Portia is seeing, and offers her recommendations, some of which are taken, some of which are discarded. Kern has fallen far from her status as God. She and the leaders of her erstwhile flock have undergone some bitter disagreements about the fate of the human race currently aboard the *Gilgamesh*. She argued and threatened, and in the end she begged and pleaded, but by then the spiders had their assault planned, and were not to be swayed. In the end Kern was forced to accept the hard decisions of those that had once been her faithful, and were now her hosts.

Now she has identified the hull sensors for Portia and the other bands of orbital defenders. They have been busy crossing the hull to put out the *Gilgamesh*'s eyes.

Portia has little concept of the living contents of the ark ship at this point. Intellectually, she knows they are there, but her mind is focused on this stage of her duty, and the concept of a vast ship of giants goes further than her imagination will stretch. Nonetheless, her mental picture of the processes going on within is surprisingly accurate. *They will detect us, and they will know that we will try and break in.* In her mind, the *Gilgamesh* is like an ant colony, one of the bad old kind, and any moment the defenders must boil out, or else some weapons will be deployed.

There will be a small number of hatches that lead to the interior, Bianca instructs. *Continue to destroy sensors as you travel, to hamper their ability to respond. You are looking for either a large square . . .* With meticulous patience Bianca gives concise descriptions of the various possible means of access to the *Gilgamesh*'s interior, as dredged from Avrana Kern's memory of her own encounter with the ark ship: where they launch their shuttles, where there are maintenance hatches, airlocks, drone chutes . . . Much is conjecture, but at least Kern was once of the same species as the ark ship's builders. She has a common frame of reference, while Portia cannot even guess at the purpose or function of the profusion of details on the *Gilgamesh*'s hull.

If the spiders possessed a certain form of determination, then they would be able to enter the ark ship without needing to find a weak point. After all, they have access to chemical explosives that carry their own oxygen and would trigger in a vacuum. Their space-age technology has its limits, though. Tearing the ship open is not a preferred option. If nothing else, Portia and her peers are intending to rely on the ark ship's air, even though it is short of oxygen compared to their usual needs. The respirators about the spiders' abdomens have a limited lifespan, and Portia is keenly aware that they would prefer to return home across the void as well. Better to establish a controlled breach, and then seal it off once her spiders are inside.

A curious sensation washes over her, like nothing she has experienced before, setting her tactile sense organs quivering. The nearest equivalent she could name would be that a wind had blown past her, but out here there is no air to move. Her fellows, and other peer groups currently engaged on the assault, have felt it too. In its wake, radio communications become patchy for a brief while. Portia cannot know that her adversaries inside the ship have improvised an electromagnetic pulse to attack the spiders' electronics. The two technologies have passed each other in the night, barely touching. Even Portia's radio is biological. What little the pulse can touch of it is instantly replaced; the technology is mortal, born to die, and so every component has replacements growing behind it like shark's teeth.

Portia has located a hatch now, a vast square entryway sealed behind heavy metal doors. Immediately she broadcasts her position to nearby teams who begin to converge on her position, ready to follow her in.

She calls forwards her specialist, who begins drawing the outlines of the hole they will make with her acids. The metal will withstand them for a while yet, and Portia steps from foot to foot, anxious and impatient. She does not know what will greet them once they get inside – giant defenders, hostile environments, incomprehensible machines. She has never been one to just sit and wait: she needs to plan or she needs to act. Denied either, she frets.

As the acid begins to work, reacting violently with the hull and producing a frill of vapour that disperses almost immediately, others of the team begin weaving an airtight net of synthetic silk between them, which will close up the breach once the team is inside.

Then radio contact is gone abruptly, swallowed by a vast ocean-wash of white noise. The denizens of the ark ship have struck again. Immediately Portia begins searching for clear frequencies. She knows the giants also use radio to speak, hence it seems likely that they may have held some channels open. In the interim, though, her squad is cut off – as are all of the hull squads. But they know the plan. They already have their instructions on precisely how to deal with the human menace – both the waking crew and the vastly greater number of sleepers that Kern has described. The precise details will now be down to Portia's discretion.

Uppermost in her mind at this point is that the inhabitants of the *Gilgamesh* are taking an active hand in their own defence, at last. She has no idea how this might manifest, but she knows what she would do if an attacker were gnawing at the walls of her very home. The Portiid spiders have never been a passive or defensive species. No patient web-lurkers they – they attack or counterattack. They are made to go on the offensive.

Without the radio, close-range communication remains possible, just. *Be ready, they will be coming*, she taps out on the hull, flashing her palps for emphasis. Those not directly involved in breaching the hull fan out, watching to all sides with many eyes.

7.7 THE WAR OUTSIDE

'Hah!' Karst shouted at the screens. 'That screws over their fucking radio.'

'It's not exactly a killer blow.' Lain rubbed at her eyes with the heel of one hand.

'It doesn't deal with the implications of them having radio in the first place,' Holsten remarked. 'What are we dealing with here? Why aren't we even asking that question?'

'It's obvious,' came the terse voice of Vitas from over the comms.

'Then please explain, because precious little is looking obvious to me right now,' Lain suggested. She was concentrating on the screens, and Holsten had the impression that her words had more to do with being irritated at Vitas's superior manner.

'Kern's World was some sort of bioengineering planet,' Vitas's disembodied voice explained. 'She was creating these things. Then, knowing we were returning, she's broken them out of stasis at last, and has deployed them against us. They're fulfilling their programming even after the destruction of her satellite.'

Holsten tried to catch the eyes of Lain or Karst or, indeed, anyone, but he seemed to have faded into the background again.

'What does that mean the surface is going to be like?' Karst asked uneasily.

'We may have to conduct some widespread cleansing,' Vitas confirmed with apparent enthusiasm.

'Wait,' Holsten muttered.

Lain cocked an eyebrow at him.

'Please let's . . . not repeat their mistakes. The Empire's mistakes.' *Because sometimes I feel that's all we've been doing.* 'It sounds like you're talking about poisoning the planet to death, so we can live on it.'

'It may be necessary, depending on surface conditions. Allowing uncontrolled biotechnology to remain on the surface would be considerably worse,' Vitas stated.

'What if they're sentient?' Holsten asked.

Lain just watched, eyes hooded, and it looked as though Karst hadn't really understood the question. It was now Holsten versus the voice of Vitas.

'If that is the case,' Vitas considered, 'it will only be in the sense that a computer might be considered sentient. They will be following instructions, possibly in a way that gives them considerable leeway in order to react to local conditions, but that will be all.'

'No,' said Holsten patiently, 'what if they are actually sentient. Alive and independent, evolved?' *Exalted*, came the word inside his head. *The exaltation of beasts.* But Kern had spoken only of her beloved monkeys.

'Don't be ridiculous,' Vitas snapped, and surely they all heard the tremble in her voice. 'In any event, it doesn't matter. The logic of the prisoners' choice holds. Whatever we are ranged against, it is doing its best to destroy us. We must respond accordingly.'

'Another drone gone,' Karst announced.

'What?' Lain demanded.

'With the hull sensors being picked off I'm trying to keep tabs on the fuckers with drones, but they're taking them out. I've only got a handful left.'

'Any armed like the ones that took down Kern?' the old engineer asked.

'No, and we couldn't use them, anyway. They're on the hull. We'd damage the ship.'

'It may be too late for that,' Alpash commented levelly. He showed them one of the last drone images. A group of spiders was clustered at one of the shuttle-bay doors. A new line in the metal was visible, flagged by a ghost of dispersing vapour down its length.

'Fuckers,' said Karst solemnly. 'You're sure we can't electrify the hull?' That had been a hot topic of conversation before they tried the EMP burst. Alpash had been trying to work up a solution for a localized electrical grid around wherever the spiders were located, but the infrastructure for it simply was not there, let alone the enormous energy that would be needed to accomplish it. Talk had then devolved towards lower-tech solutions.

'You've got your people armed and ready?'

'I've got a fucking army. We've woken up a few hundred of the best candidates from cargo and put disruptors into their hands. Assuming the little bastards *can* be disrupted. If not, well, we've broken out the armoury. I mean,' and his voice trembled a little, small cracks evident from a deep, deep stress, 'the ship's so fucked a few more holes won't make any difference, will they? And anyway, we can still stop them getting in. But if they do get in . . . we may not be able to contain them.' He fought over that 'may', his need for optimism crashing brutally into the wall of circumstances. 'It's not like this ship was laid out with this kind of situation in mind. Fucking oversight, that was.' And a rictus grin.

'Karst . . .' Lain began, and Holsten – always a little behind – thought she just wanted to shut him up and spare him embarrassment.

'I'll get suited up,' the security chief said.

Lain just watched him, saying nothing.

'What?' Holsten stared. 'Wait, no . . .'

Karst essentially ignored him, eyes fixed on the ancient engineer.

'You're sure?' Lain herself seemed anything but.

Karst shrugged brutally. 'I'm doing fuck all good up here. We need to go clear those vermin off the hull.' There was precious little enthusiasm in his voice. Perhaps he was waiting for Lain to give some convincing reason that he should stay. Her creased face was twisted in indecision, though, an engineer seeking a solution to a technical problem she could not overcome.

At that point Holsten's console flickered into activity again, and he realized the attackers on the outside had located the clear channels that Karst had been using to control his drones; and that Karst would soon be using to communicate with the ship. It was Holsten's job to notify everyone the moment the spiders made this discovery, but he said nothing, part of him staring at the sudden patchy scatter of signals being picked up by the *Gilgamesh*'s surviving receivers, the rest of him listening to the conversation going on behind him.

'Your team?' Lain prompted at last.

'My core team are suited and ready,' Karst confirmed. 'It looks like we might have a fight the moment we open the airlock. Little bastards could be out there already, cutting *in*.' Nobody was arguing with him, but he went on, 'I can't ask them to go and me stay behind,' and then, 'This is what I'm for, isn't it? I'm not a strategist. I'm not a commander. I lead people: my team.' He stood before Lain like a general who had disappointed his queen and now felt that he had only one way to redeem himself. 'Let's face it. Security was only ever here to keep Key Crew and cargo in place for the duration of the trip. But if we have to be soldiers, then we'll be soldiers, and I'll lead.'

'Karst . . .' Lain started, and then dried up. Holsten wondered whether she had been about to say something bizarrely trite, some piece of social ornament like, *If you don't want to go, then don't.* But they were long past what people did or didn't want to do. Nobody had wanted the situation they found themselves in now, and their language, like their technology, had been pared down to only those things essential to life. Nothing else, none of the fripperies and flourishes, had been cost-effective to maintain.

'I'll get suited up,' the security chief repeated tiredly, with a nod. He paused as though he wanted to throw out some more military form of acknowledgement, a salute from those about to die, and then he turned and left.

Lain watched him go, leaning on her metal stick, and there was a similar ramrod stiffness to her bearing despite her crooked spine. Her bony knuckles were white, and everyone in that room was watching her.

She took two deliberate steps until she was at Holsten's

shoulder, then glowered about her at the handful of Tribe engineers still left in comms.

'Get to work!' she snapped at them. 'There's always something that needs fixing.' Having dispersed their attention, she took a deep breath, then let it out, close enough to Holsten's ear that he heard the faint wheezing of her lungs. 'He was right, wasn't he?' she said very softly, for his ears only. 'We need to clear them from the hull, and the security detail will fight better if Karst's out there with them.' It was not that she had told the man to go, but a word from her might have stopped him.

Holsten glanced up at her and tried to make himself nod, but something went wrong with the motion, and the result was meaningless and noncommittal.

'What's this?' Lain demanded abruptly, noticing the stream of signals on his screen.

'They found our gap. They're transmitting.'

'Then why the fuck didn't you say?' She called out, 'Karst?' then waited until Alpash confirmed that she was connected to the man. 'We're changing frequencies, so get your people ready,' next giving him the new clear channel. 'Holsten—'

'Vitas is wrong,' he told her. 'They're not biological machines. They're not just Kern's puppets.'

'And how are you supposed to have worked that one out?'

'Because of how they communicate.'

She frowned. 'You've cracked that now? And didn't think to tell anyone?'

'No . . . not what they're saying, but the structure. Isa, I'm a classicist, and a lot of that is a study of language – old languages, dead languages, languages from an age of humanity that doesn't exist any more. I'd stake my life that these signals are actually language rather than just some sort of instructions. It's too complex, too intricately structured. It's inefficient, Isa. Language is inefficient. It evolves organically. This is language – real language.'

Lain squinted down at the screen for a few seconds until the transmissions abruptly cut off, as the jamming switched frequencies. 'What difference does it make?' she asked quietly. 'Does it get Vitas's fucking prisoners out of their cells? It doesn't, Holsten.'

'But—'

'Tell me how it helps us,' she invited. 'Tell me how any of this . . . speculation does us any good. Or is it just like all the rest of your bag of tricks? Academic in every sense of the word.'

'We're ready,' came Karst's voice at that moment, as though he had been politely waiting for her to finish. 'We're in the airlock. We're about to open the hatch.'

Lain's face was like a death mask. She had never been intended as a commander, either. Holsten could see every one of those centuries of hard decisions in the lines on her face.

'Go,' she confirmed, 'and good luck.'

Karst had a squad of twenty-two ready to go, and that used up all the heavy EVA suits that were still functioning. Another twelve were currently being worked on, and he was only grateful that the Tribe had needed to go out and make patch repairs on the hull, or he might not even be able to field that many soldiers. *Soldiers*: he thought of them as soldiers. Some of them actually were soldiers, military woken up from cargo either this time or the last time, added piecemeal to the security detail whenever he had needed a bit more muscle. Others were veterans of his team: Key Crew who had been with him from the start. He was taking only the best, which in this case meant almost everyone who had the appropriate EVA training.

He remembered very clearly when he himself had gone through that training. It had seemed a complete waste of time, but he had wanted to win a place in Key Crew on the *Gilgamesh* and it had been something they had been looking for. He had spent months bumbling about in orbit, learning how to move in zero gravity, how to step with magnetic boots, acclimatizing to the nausea and the disorientation of such a hostile and inimical environment.

Nobody had mentioned fighting an army of spiders for the survival of the human race, but Karst half-fancied he might have imagined it, day-dreamed it back when he was young and the *Gilgamesh* project was still just an idea. Surely he had seen himself standing on the hull of a mighty, embattled colony ship, weapon to hand, beating away the alien horde.

Now, in the airlock, his breath loud in his ears and the suit's confines pressing and leaden, it didn't seem at all as much fun as he had imagined.

The hatch they were about to exit through was set in the floor, from where he was standing. There would be a vertiginous shift of perspective as they got out, carabinered to one another and trying not to be flung off the ship's side by the rotating section's centripetal force. Then they would have to trust to their boots to hold them, progressing along a surface that would constantly try to dislodge them. Things would have been easier, perversely, had they been accelerating or decelerating in deep space, with the inner sense of 'down' falling towards the front or the rear of the ship, and the rotating sections stilled, but they were in orbit now, free falling around the planet, and therefore forced to fake their own gravity.

'Chief!' one of his team warned. 'We're losing air.'

'Of course we're—' Then he stopped, because he hadn't given the order to open the external doors. They had been standing here on the brink for some time and the words had been reluctant to emerge. Now someone – some*thing* – was forcing his hand.

Somewhere on the hatch there must be a pinhole letting out their air. The spiders were out there, right now, trying to claw their way in.

'Everyone latch down and lock your boots,' he ordered and, now he was faced with action, the thoughts were coming smoothly and without undue emotional embroidery. 'You'd better crouch low. I want the outer door opened quick as you like, without the air venting first.'

One of the Tribe confirmed his instructions in his ear, and Karst followed his own advice.

Instead of the steady grinding of the hatch that he expected, someone had obviously taken that 'quick as you like' to heart and activated some sort of emergency override, snapping the hatch open within seconds so that the pressurized air around them thundered through the resulting breach like a hammer. Karst felt it raking at him, trying to drag him out with it, to enjoy the vast open vistas of the universe. But his lines and boots held, and he weathered the storm. One of his team was immediately torn loose beside him, yanked halfway through the opening and only saved by her anchoring line. Karst reached out and grabbed her glove, clumsily pulling her back until she was against the subjective floor beside the gaping hole.

He saw some fragments, then: jointed legs and a torn-open something that must have been most of a body caught by the mechanism of the hatch. Beyond . . .

Beyond were the enemy.

They were in disarray, crawling over one another. Several had been battered away by the decompression, and he hoped that a few had been lost to space, but there were at least three or four dangling out at the end of threads and beginning to climb back up towards the hatch. Karst aimed his gun. It was built into his glove, and was a refreshingly simple piece of kit, overall. Nothing in the airless wastes of vacuum would stop a chemical propellant working if it contained its own oxygen, and the airless void should be a perfect marksman's paradise, his range limited only by the curve of the *Gilgamesh*'s hull.

He wanted to say something inspiring or dramatic but, in the end, the sight of the creeping, leg-waving, spasmodically scuttling monsters so horrified him that, 'Kill the fuckers,' was all he could manage.

He shot but missed three times, trying to adjust for the surreal perspective and mistaking the distance and size of his quarry, his suit's targeting system mulish about locking on to the little vermin. Then he caught it, sending one of the beasts that still remained on the hull spinning away. His team were shooting as well, careful and controlled, and the spiders were plainly utterly unprepared for what was happening. Karst saw their angular, leggy bodies being hurled away on all sides, the dead ones dangling straight out from the hull like macabre balloons.

Some of them were returning fire, which gave him a nasty turn. They had some sort of weapons, though the projectiles were slow and bulky compared to the sleek zip of bullets from the human-made guns. For a moment Karst thought that they were throwing stones again, but the missiles were something like ice or glass. They shattered against the armoured suits, causing no damage.

The spiders were unexpectedly resilient, clad in some sort of close-woven armour that had them dancing about under the impact of the bullets without necessarily letting any penetrate, and Karst and his fellows had to hose several of them with shot before something got through.

They exploded quite satisfactorily, though, once they died.

Soon, if there were any enemy survivors, they had fled; Karst paused a moment, reporting back to Lain before taking the big step of putting himself outside on the hull, out before the curtailed horizon of the *Gilgamesh*.

Then there was nothing for it – so he went.

The heavy EVA suits were proper military technology, although most of the actual military systems Karst would have liked to have accessed were not online or had been removed entirely. After all, the engineers had not needed sophisticated targeting programs when going out to make repairs. Like everything else that survived of the human race, a tyranny of priorities had come into force. Still, the suits were reinforced at the joints, and armoured everywhere else, with servos to help the determined space warrior actually move about in them. They had an extended air supply, recycled waste, controlled temperature and, if the hull sensors had actually been left intact, then Karst would have had a lovely little map of everything around him. As it was, he climbed laboriously through the hatch in a second skin that bulked out his torso and each limb to twice its actual circumference, feeling hot and cramped, sensing the slight shudder as ancient and lovingly maintained servomotors considered each second whether or not they would relinquish the ghost and seize up. Some of the suits still had functioning jet packs to allow for limited manoeuvring while away from the hull, but fuel was at a premium, and Karst had given the order to save it for emergencies. He was unconvinced that using the antiquated, oft-repaired flight packs was not just one step too far towards a death-trap.

His image of his surroundings was the cluttered and narrow view from his faceplate, and a handful of feeds from cameras on his squad-mates' suits, which he was having difficulty matching up to the actual individuals concerned.

'Lain, can you send everyone instructions on a formation, and their place in it?' It felt like admitting defeat, but he did not have the tools that the suit's inventor had anticipated to hand. 'I need eyes looking out every way. We're heading for Shuttle Bay Seven doors. Close this airlock behind us. And the outer door's compromised somewhere—'

'It's not closing,' came Alpash's voice. 'It . . . something's gone wrong.'

'Well . . .' and then Karst realized he had nothing much to say to that. He could hardly demand they came out and fixed it right now. 'Well, seal the inner door until we return. We're going now.'

Then Lain's instructions came through: showing them her

best guess at a route to take, and a formation for the security team to fall into, eyes focused all around.

'We've got another drone launching,' she added. 'I'll send it far out to look down on you, and patch it into your . . . fuck.'

'What?' Karst demanded immediately.

'No drone. Just get to the shuttle bay, double-time.'

'You try fucking double-time in these things.' But Karst was moving, the point of the arrow, and his team shambled into place, step after hulking metal step along the hull. 'And let me guess: drone bay after the shuttle, right?'

'Well done.'

The drone had simply not got out of the bay, hanging tangled in webbing that its sensors could not even detect, its launch hatch still open. Holsten had no idea what sort of access the drone bays gave to the rest of the ship, but Lain was already sending people that way, so presumably that meant the creatures were aboard.

They had camera feeds from Karst and a handful of his people, though by no means all, recording their slogging progress outside on the hull, constantly surveying the ground before them over that truncated horizon.

'Blind!' hissed Lain furiously. The network of hull sensors was in pieces, hundreds of maintenance-hours of damage inflicted in just minutes. 'Where are they, then? Where else?'

Holsten opened his mouth – another chance for a trite and meaningless remark, and then alarms began to go off.

'Hull breach in cargo,' Alpash said flatly, and then, with a curious deadness to his tone, 'That's a second breach, of course. After the impact earlier.'

'There's already a hole in cargo,' Lain echoed the sentiment, eyes seeking out Holsten's. 'They're probably already inside.'

'Then why make another hole?'

'Cargo's big,' Alpash said. 'They must be boring in all over the ship. They don't need hatches. We . . .' His eyes were wide as he looked at Lain beseechingly. 'What are we going to do?'

'Cargo . . .' Holsten thought of those thousands of sleepers, oblivious in their little plastic coffins. He thought of spiders descending upon them, coasting in the gravity-free vacuum towards their prey. He thought of eggs.

Perhaps Lain harboured similar thoughts. 'Karst!' she snapped. 'Karst, we need your people inside.'

'We're coming up on the shuttle-bay hatch now,' Karst reported, as though he hadn't heard.

'Karst, they're inside,' Lain insisted.

There was a pause, though the clomping progress of the cameras didn't slow. 'Get people there from the inside. I'll deal with this, then we'll head back in. Or do you want them actually right outside your door?'

'Karst, cargo is without gravity and atmosphere, I can't just send—' Lain started.

'Let me kill this nest and then we'll be back,' Karst spoke over her. 'We'll keep a lid on it, don't worry.' He sounded maddeningly calm.

Then another transmission came in from aboard the ship, a moment of garbled shouting and screaming . . . then nothing.

Silence followed. Lain and Alpash and Holsten stared at one another, appalled.

'Who was that?' the ancient engineer asked at last. 'Alpash, what did we . . . ?'

'I don't know. I'm trying . . . Call in, please, call in, all . . .'

There was a flurry of brief acknowledgements from different groups of the Tribe and reawakened military across the ship, and Holsten could see Alpash checking them off. Even before they had finished someone was shouting, 'They're here! Get out, get out. They're inside!'

'Confirm your position.' Alpash's voice was strained. 'Lori, confirm your position!'

'Alpash—' Lain started.

'That's my family,' the younger engineer said. He was away from his station, suddenly. 'That's our living quarters. They're all in there: my kin, our children.'

'Alpash, stay at your post!' Lain ordered him, hand trembling on her stick, but her authority – the leverage of her age and pedigree – was right now just smoke. Alpash had the hatch open and was gone.

'There they are,' came Karst's triumphant shout over the comms, and then: 'Where are the rest of them?'

Lain's mouth opened, her eyes dragged irresistibly towards the screens. There was a handful of spiders about the shuttle-bay hatch, caught in the glare of the sun, long, angular shadows cast down the length of the hull. Less, though, than there had been, and perhaps that just meant that the others had gone for easier access points. The chaos over the comms showed that the creatures were establishing beachheads all over the ship.

'Karst . . .' from Lain, surely too quietly for him to respond.

Holsten saw one of the spiders abruptly shatter, torn open

by a shot from Karst or one of his team. Then someone shouted, 'Behind us,' and the camera views were swinging around, giving wheeling views of the hull and the stars.

'I'm caught!' came from someone, and others of the security team were no longer moving. Holsten saw one man, pinned in the camera view of a comrade, fighting something unseen, slapping and pulling at his suit, the drifting net of threads that had ensnared him invisible yet too strong to break.

The spiders were emerging then, racing along the curve of the hull with a speed that laughed at Karst's plodding progress. Others were steering down from above, where they had been drifting at the end of more thread, climbing up against the outwards force of the rotating section; climbing to where they could leap on Karst and his men.

Karst's upraised gun/glove, at the corner of his camera, flashed and flared, trying to track the new targets,' killing at least one. They saw one of Karst's people being hit by friendly fire, boots torn off the hull by the impact, falling away from the ship to end up jerking on the end of an unseen line, as an eight-legged monster came inching up towards his helpless, flailing form. Men and women were shouting, shooting, screaming, trying to run away at their leaden, crippled pace.

Karst stumbled back two heavy paces, still shooting, seeing his helmet display record the remaining rounds in his helical magazine. More by luck than judgement, he picked one of the creatures off as it alighted on the woman next to him, spraying freezing pieces of carapace and viscera that rattled as they bounced off him. She was caught in the webbing the little bastards had seeded the hull with, just great loose clouds of the fine stuff that had half his people now completely ensnared.

His ears were full of people shouting: his team, others from inside the ship, even Lain. He tried to remember how to shut down the channels: it was all too loud; he couldn't think. The thunder of his own hoarse breathing roared over it, like a hyperventilating giant bellowing at each ear.

He saw another of his people fly loose from the hull, cancelling the grip of his boots without anything else to secure him. He just flew away, ascending into the infinite. If his suit had thrusters, they weren't working now. The luckless man just kept going, receding into the infinite, as though he just could not abide to share the ship with the busy monsters intent on getting inside it.

Another spider landed on the trapped woman beside Karst, just sailing in at the end of a colossal leap, its legs outstretched. He could hear her screaming, and he stumbled forwards, trying to aim at the thing as the woman flailed and bludgeoned at it with her gloved hands.

It was clinging to her, and Karst saw it carefully line up its mouthparts, or some mechanism attached to them, and then hunch forwards, lancing her between the plates of her suit with sudden, irresistible force.

The suit would seal around a puncture, of course, but that would not help against whatever she had been injected with. Karst tried to call up medical information from her suit, but he could not remember how. She had gone still, just swaying limply against the anchor point of her magnetic boots. Whatever it was, it was quick-acting.

He finally managed to turn off all the voices in his head,

leaving only his own. There was a moment of blessed calm in which it seemed possible, somehow, that he could regain control of the situation. There would be some magic word, some infinitely efficacious command that a truly gifted leader could give, one that would restore the rightful arrow of evolution and allow humanity to triumph over these aberrations.

Something landed on his back.

7.8 THE WAR INSIDE

Like an ant colony, is Portia's thought. It is not true, though, just something she tells herself to counter the vastly alien surroundings that weigh upon her.

She comes from a city that is a forest, filled with complex many-sided spaces, and yet the architects of her people have cut even that three-dimensional geography down to their own size, compartmentalizing the vast until it is manageable, controllable. Here, the giants have done the same, making chambers that for them are perhaps a little cramped and constricting, but to Portia the exaggerated scale of it all is frightening, a constant reminder of the sheer size and physical power of the godlike beings that created this place, and whose descendants dwell here still.

Worse is the relentless geometry of it. Portia is used to a city of a thousand angles, a chain of walls and floors and ceilings strung at every possible slant, a world of taut silk that can be taken down and put back up, divided and subdivided and endlessly tailored to suit. The giants must live their lives amongst these rigid, unvarying right angles, entombed between these massive, solid walls. Nothing makes any attempt to mimic nature. Instead, everything is held in the iron hand of that dominating alien aesthetic.

Her peer group is through the savaged shuttle-bay doors,

the breach sealed up behind them to minimize pressure loss. She has just had a brief window of radio contact with other groups, a hurried catch-up before the giants change their own frequency and obliterate all the others with their invisible storm. There are six separate peer groups within the great ship now, several of them in a section that had no air of its own. Attempts to coordinate are hopeless. Every troop is on its own.

They encounter the first defenders shortly afterwards: perhaps twenty giants arriving with violent intent before the spiders can set up their large-scale weapons. The vibrations of the enemy's approach serves as forewarning of an almost absurd degree, and Portia's band – a dozen of them now – are able to set an ambush. A hastily woven spring trap catches the front-running giants in a mess of poorly constructed webbing – not enough to hold them for long, but enough to drag them to a stop where their fellows will crash into them. They have weapons – not just the lethally swift projectiles of their compatriots outside, but also a kind of focused vibration that runs like mad screaming through every fibre of Portia's body, shocking all the spiders into motionlessness, and killing one outright.

Then the spiders begin shooting back. The weapons slung beneath their bodies are far slower than bullets, closer to the ancient slingshots Portia's ancestors used. Their ammunition is three-pronged glass darts, formed to spin in flight. Here, in gravity, their range is relatively short, but the interior of the *Gilgamesh* does not allow for much long-distance marksmanship anyway. Portia and her peers are, at the very least, extremely good shots, excellent judges of distance and relative motion. Some of the giants wear armour like those outside; most do not.

When the darts draw blood, they snap, tips shearing off and their contents being forced into the curiously elaborate circulatory systems the giants boast, to be hurried about their bodies by their own racing metabolisms. Only a tiny amount is needed for full effect, and the carefully measured concoction works very swiftly, going straight for the brain. Portia watches the giants drop, spasming and going rigid, one by one. The few armoured enemy are dealt with by the more risky approach of direct injection. Portia loses four of her squad and knows that, if the ambush had failed, they might all have died.

Still, their numbers within the ship are growing steadily. Whilst she would rather survive, she has always accepted the reasonable chance that this mission would mean her death.

Her field-chemist is still alive and ready for orders. Portia does not stint. *The Messenger said there will be vents to allow circulation of air about the vessel.* The precise logistics of keeping the living quarters of an ark ship supplied with breathable air are somewhat beyond Portia's understanding, but Avrana Kern's information has been understood to the degree required.

Their hairy bodies sensitive to movement even through their vacuum coating, the spiders quickly track down the faint motion of air from the vents. Out there, Portia knows, there will be armies of giants mustering, no doubt expecting the spiders to come against them. But that is not the plan.

The field-chemist sets up her weapon swiftly, preparing the elegantly crafted mixture to discharge into the air ducts, where it will find its way around the ship.

Move on, Portia orders when she is done. They have plenty more such chemical weapons to put in place. There are a large number of giants on the ship, after all.

When they understood at last what Avrana Kern had been trying to communicate with them; when it became obvious that the path their species travelled would bring them inevitably into collision with a civilization of giant creator-gods, the spiders turned to the past for inspiration, seeking out learning buried since the early days of their history. But, for them, history could be remembered like yesterday. They had never suffered the problem with human records: that so much is lost forever as the grinding wheel of the years groans on. Their distant ancestors, in conjunction with the nanovirus, evolved the ability to pass on learning and experience genetically, direct to their offspring, a vital stepping stone in a species with next to no parental care. So it is that knowledge of far distant times is preserved in great detail, initially passed from parents to their brood, and later distilled and available for any spider to incorporate into mind and genes.

Globally, the spiders have assembled a vast library of experience to draw upon, a facility that has contributed to their swift rise from obscurity to orbit.

Hidden in this arachnid Alexandria are remarkable secrets. For example: generations ago, during the great war with the ants, there were giants that walked briefly upon the green world, crew from the self-same ark ship that Portia has now invaded.

One of those giants was captured and held for many long years. The Understandings of the time did not include the belief that it was sentient, and scientists now twitch and skitter in frustration at what might have been learned had their forebears only tried a little harder to communicate.

However, that is not to say that nothing was learned at all from the captive giant. During its lifetime, and especially after its eventual death, the scholars of the time did their best to examine the creature's biochemistry and metabolism, comparing it to the small mammals they shared their world with. In their library of first-hand knowledge, the spiders uncovered a great deal of how human biochemistry works.

Armed with that knowledge, and a supply of mice and similar animals as test subjects – not ideal but the best they had – the spiders developed their great last-ditch weapon against the invaders. There was much argument between the chosen representatives of cities and great peer groups, and between them all and Avrana Kern as well. Other solutions and possibilities were pared away until the spiders' nature and the extremity of the situation left only this one. Even now, Portia and the other assault squads are the first to find out that their solution works, at least for now.

The *Gilgamesh*'s sensors barely register the concoction as it passes into the ship's circulation, creeping about the rotating crew section one chamber at a time. There are no overt toxins, no immediately harmful chemicals. Some readouts across the ship begin to record a slight change in the composition of the air, but by then the insidious weapon is already wreaking havoc.

The giant warriors Portia has just defeated have been injected with a concentrated form of the drug. Portia now examines them curiously. She sees their strange, weirdly mobile eyes twitch and jerk, dragged up and about and around by the sight of invisible terrors, as the substance attacks their brains. Everything is going according to plan.

She wants to stay and bind them, but they do not have the time, and she does not know if mere silk could restrain such gigantic monsters. She must hope that the initial incapacity – seen in the mammal test subjects as well – has the intended permanent consequences. It would be inconvenient if the giants somehow recovered.

Portia's people move on, swift and determined. The substance is harmless to their own physiology, passing over their book-lungs without effect.

Shortly after, they come to a room filled with giants. These are not armed, and they are in several sizes which Portia surmises to be adult and juveniles of various moultings. They are already succumbing to the invisible gas, staggering drunkenly about, collapsing on suddenly fluid legs, or just lying there, staring at sights that exist only in their own minds. There is a strong organic scent in the air, though Portia does realize that many of her victims have soiled themselves.

They check that there is nobody left to fight them, then they move on. There are plenty more giants to conquer.

7.9 LAST STAND

They could hear Karst shouting and screaming for an appallingly long time, his microphone fixed on an open channel. His suit camera gave them blurred glimpses of hull, stars, other struggling figures. Lain was shouting at him in a cracked voice, urging him to get inside the ship, but Karst was past hearing her, instead fighting furiously with something they could not see. From the fumbling of his gloves, glimpsed briefly in the periphery of the image, it looked as though he was trying to pry his own helmet off.

Then abruptly he cut off, and for a moment they thought he had simply ceased transmitting, but his channel remained open, and now they heard a gurgling sound, a wet choking. The wild movement of the camera had ceased, and the starfield drifted past Karst's view almost peacefully.

'Oh, no, no, no . . .' Lain got out, before a segmented leg arched up from beyond the camera's view to plant itself on Karst's faceplate. They only saw a piece of the thing as it crouched on his shoulder, bunching itself for better purchase. A hairy arachnid with a shimmering exoskeleton, and a suggestion of curved fangs within some kind of mask: man's oldest fear waiting for him here at the outer reach of human expansion, already equipped for space.

There were reports coming in from all across the ship, by

then. Teams of engineers were suiting up – lightweight work suits without any of the armour or systems that had done Karst so little good – and heading into the hostile, contested territory of the cargo holds. Others were trying to repel boarders wherever the scuttling creatures had entered. The problem was that, with the hull sensors torn up in so many places, the *Gilgamesh* could only make a poor guess at precisely where they *had* broken in.

For bitter minutes Lain tried to coordinate the various groups, some of them out there on Command orders, others just vigilantes from the Tribe, or woken cargo who had been awaiting a replacement suspension chamber.

Then something changed around them. Holsten and Lain exchanged glances, both knowing instantly that something was wrong, but neither able to quite say what. Something ubiquitous, never consciously noted and always taken for granted, had gone away.

And at the last Lain said, 'Life-support.'

Holsten felt his chest freeze at the very thought. 'What?'

'I think . . .' She looked at her screens. 'Air circulation has ceased. The vents have shut off.'

'Which means—?'

'Which means don't do any more breathing than you have to, because we're suddenly short on oxygen. What the fuck is . . . ?'

'Lain?'

The old engineer screwed her face up. 'Vitas? What's going on?'

'I've shut the air off, Lain.' There was a curious tone to the scientist's voice, somewhere between determined and frightened.

Lain's eyes were fixed on Holsten, trying to take strength from him. 'Would you care to explain why?'

'The spiders have released some sort of chemical or biological weapon. I'm segmenting the ship, cutting off areas that haven't been infected yet.'

'Cutting off areas that *haven't* been infected?'

'I'm afraid it's quite widespread,' Vitas's voice confirmed almost briskly, like a doctor trying to cover bad news with a smile. 'I think I can work around those areas and restore a limited air circulation that's uncontaminated, but for now . . .'

'How do you know all this?' Lain demanded.

'My assistants in the lab here have all collapsed. They're suffering some sort of fit. They're completely oblivious.' A tiny, swiftly quashed tremor lay behind the words. 'I myself am in a sealed test chamber. I was working on a biological weapon of my own to win the war, annihilate the species without having to fire a shot. How could we know they'd beat us to it?'

'I don't suppose that's near completion?' Lain asked, without much hope.

'I'm close, I think. The *Gilgamesh*'s records on old Earth zoology are rather incomplete. Lain, we're going to have to—'

'Route uncontaminated air,' the engineer finished. She was hunched over a console, trembling hands stabbing at it in desperate, jagged flurries. She looked older, as though the last hour had loaded another decade on to her shoulders. 'I'm on it. Holsten, you need to warn our people, get them to put on masks, or fall back to . . . to . . . to wherever I'll tell you in . . .'

Holsten was already doing his best, fighting the *Gilgamesh*'s intermittently unreliable interface, calling up each group he could locate on the system. Some did not answer. The spiders' weapon was spreading invisibly from compartment to compartment even as Vitas and Lain fought to seal it off.

He raised Alpash with a surge of relief. 'They're using gas or something—'

'I know,' the Tribe engineer confirmed. 'We're masked. Won't work for long, though. This is emergency kit.' His voice sounded weirdly exhilarated, despite it all.

'Lain's preparing a . . .' the proper words fell into place just in time '. . . fall-back position. Have you seen any—?'

'We just shot the fuck out of one bunch of them,' Alpash confirmed fiercely. It occurred to Holsten that the fight was different for the Tribe. Yes, intellectually he knew that the *Gil* was the only haven for all mankind, and that his species' survival depended on it right now, but it was still just a ship to him, a means of crossing from one place to another. To Alpash and his people it was *home*. 'Right, well you should fall back to . . .' and by that time Lain had prepared a route, working with furious concentration while her breath wheezed in and out between her lips.

'Vitas?' the old engineer barked.

'Still here.' The bodiless voice sounding no more distant than the scientist's usual tones.

'All this compartmentalization is going to hamper your own weapon's dispersal, I take it?'

Vitas made a curious noise: perhaps it was meant as a laugh, but there was a knife edge of hysteria to sabotage it. 'I'm . . . behind enemy lines. I'm cut off, Lain. If I can brew something up, I can get it to the . . . to *them*. And I'm close. I'll poison the lot of them.'

Holsten made contact with another band of fighters, heard a brief cacophonic slice of shouting and screaming, and then lost them. 'I think you'd better hurry,' he said hoarsely.

'Fuck,' Lain spat. 'I've lost . . . we're losing safe areas.' She bunched her crabbed hands. 'What's—?'

'They're moving through the ship,' came Vitas's ghostly voice. 'They're cutting through the doors, the walls, the ducts.' The shakiness was growing in her tone. 'Machines, they're just machines. Machines of a dead technology. That's all they can be. Biological weapons.'

'Who the fuck would make giant spiders as biological weapons?' Lain growled, still recalibrating her sealed areas, sending fresh instructions for Holsten to relay to the rest of the crew.

'Lain . . .'

There was something in the scientist's voice that made the two of them stop.

'What is it?' Lain demanded.

There was a long gap into which Lain spoke Vitas's name several times without response, and then: 'They're here. In the lab. They're here.'

'You're safe? Sealed off?'

'Lain, they're here,' and it was as though all the human emotion that Vitas so seldom gave rein to had been saved up for this moment, just to cram into her quivering voice and scream out of every word. 'They're here, they're here, they're *looking at me*. Lain, please, send someone. Send help, someone, please. They're coming towards me, they're—'

And then a shriek so loud that it cut the transmission into static for a second. 'They're on the glass! They're on the glass! They're coming through! They're eating through the glass! Lain! Lain, help me! Please, Lain! I'm sorry! I'm sorry!'

Holsten never got to know what Vitas was sorry for, and there were no more words. Even over the woman's screaming, they actually heard the almighty crack as the spiders broke into her test chamber.

Then Vitas's voice abruptly died away, just a shuddering exhalation left out of all that terrified noise. Lain and Holsten exchanged glances, neither of them finding much to be hopeful about.

'Alpash,' the classicist tried. 'Alpash, report?'

No more words from Alpash. Either the ambusher had become the ambushed, or perhaps the radio wasn't functioning any more. Like everything else, like their defence of the ship itself, it was falling apart.

The lights were going out all over the *Gilgamesh*, one by one. The safe zones that Lain set up were compromised just as quickly, or were not as safe as the computers told her. Each band of defenders encountered its final battle, the spiders within the ship becoming only more numerous, more confident.

And in the hold, the tens of thousands who were the balance of the human race slept on, never knowing that the battle for their future was being lost. There were no nightmares in suspension. Holsten wondered if he should envy them. He didn't, though. *Rather face the final moment with open eyes.*

'It's not looking good.' It was a rather laboured piece of understatement, an attempt to lighten Lain's mind just for a moment. Her creased, time-worn face turned to him, and she reached out and clasped his hand with her own.

'We've come so far.' No indication as to whether she meant the ship or just the two of them.

They each spent a few moments in assessment of the spreading damage, and when they next spoke, it was almost together.

'I can't raise anyone,' from Holsten.

'I've lost integrity in the next chamber,' from Lain.

Just us left. Or the computers are on the blink again. We lasted too long, in the end. Holsten the classicist felt that he was a man uniquely qualified to look down the road that time had set them all on. *What a history!* From monkey to mankind, through tool-use, family, community, mastery of the environment around them, competition, war, the ongoing extinction of so many of the species who had shared the planet with them. There had been that fragile pinnacle of the Old Empire then, when they had been like gods, and walked between the stars, and created abominations on planets far from Earth. And killed each other in ways undreamt of by their monkey ancestors.

And then us; the inheritors of a damaged world, reaching for the stars even as the ground died beneath their feet, the human race's desperate gamble with the ark ships. *Ark ship, singular now, as we've not heard from the rest.* And still they had squabbled and fought, given way to private ambition, to feuding, to civil war. *And all that while our enemy, our unknown enemy has grown stronger.*

Lain had stalked over to the hatch, her stick clacking on the floor. 'It's warm,' she said softly. 'They're outside. They're cutting.'

'Masks.' Holsten had located some, and held one out to her. 'Remember?'

'I don't think we'll need a private channel any more.'

He had to help her with the straps, and eventually she just sat down, hands trembling before her, looking small and frail and old.

'I'm sorry,' she said at last. 'I led us all to this.'

Her hand was in his, cold and almost fleshless; like soft, worn leather over bone.

'You couldn't have known. You did what you could. Nobody could have done any better.' Just comforting platitudes, really. 'Any weapons in here?'

'It's amazing what you don't plan for, isn't it?' something of Lain's dry humour returning. 'Use my stick. Squash a spider for me.'

For a moment Holsten thought she was joking, but she proffered him the metal rod, and at last he accepted it, hefting its surprising weight. Was this the sceptre that had kept the nascent society of the Tribe in line, from generation to generation? How many challengers for leadership had Lain beaten down with it, through the ages? It was practically a holy relic.

It was a club. In that sense, it was a quintessentially human thing: a tool to crush, to break, to lever apart in the prototypical way that humanity met the universe head-on.

And how do they meet the world? What does the spider have as its basic tool?

Briefly he entertained the thought, *They build*. And it was a curiously peaceful image, but then his console sounded, and he almost fell over the stick in lunging for it. A transmission? Someone was alive out there.

For a moment he found himself trying to drag his hand back, thinking that it would be some message from *them*, some garbled mess of almost-Imperial C within which that inhuman intelligence, malign and undeniable, would be hiding.

'Lain . . . ?' came a soft and wavering voice. 'Lain . . . ? Are you . . . ? Lain . . . ?'

Holsten stared. There was something dreadful about the words, something shuddering, damaged, unformed.

'Karst,' Lain identified it. Her eyes were wide.

'Lain, I'm coming back,' Karst continued, sounding calmer than he had ever been. 'I'm coming back in now.'

'Karst . . .'

'It's all right,' came the voice of the security chief. 'It's all right. It's all going to be all right.'

'Karst, what happened to you?' Holsten demanded.

'It's fine. I understand now.'

'But the spiders—'

'They're . . .' and a long pause, as though Karst was fumbling through the contents of his own brain for the right words. 'Like us . . . They're us. They're . . . like us.'

'Karst—!'

'We're coming back in now. All of us.' And Holsten had the terrifying, irrational thought of a sucked-dry, withered husk within an armoured suit, but still impossibly animate.

'Holsten,' Lain clutched at his arm. There was a kind of haze in the air now, a faint chemical fog – not the killer weapon of the spiders, but whatever was eating away the hatch.

Then there was a hole near its lower edge, and something was coming through.

For a moment they regarded one another: two scions of ancient tree-dwelling ancestors with large eyes and inquisitive minds.

Holsten hefted Lain's stick. The spider was huge, but only huge for a spider. He could smash it. He could sunder that hairy shell and scatter pieces of its crooked legs. He could be human in that last moment. He could exalt in his ability to destroy.

But there were more of them crawling through the breach, and he was old, and Lain was older now, and he sought that other human quality, so scarce of late, and put his arms around her, holding the woman as tightly to him as he dared, the stick clattering to the floor.

'Lain . . .' came Karst's ghostly voice. 'Mason . . .' and then, 'Come on, pick up the pace,' to his own people. 'Cut yourself free if you're stuck.' And the spark of impatience there was Karst's, through and through, despite his newfound tranquillity.

The spiders spread out a little, those huge saucer eyes fixed on the two of them from behind the clear masks the creatures were wearing. Meeting that alien gaze was a shock of contact Holsten had only known before in confronting his own kind.

He saw one of the creatures' rear legs bunch and tense.

The spiders leapt, and then it was over.

7.10 THE QUALITY OF MERCY

The shuttle seems to take forever to fall from the clear blue sky.

There is quite a crowd gathered here, on a cleared field beyond the edge of the Great Nest district of Seven Trees City. On the ground and in the surrounding trees and silk structures, thousands of spiders are clustered close and waiting. Some are frightened, some are exhilarated, some are less than well informed regarding what precisely is about to happen.

There are several dozen seeing-eye colonies, too, and these capture and send images to chromatopore screens across the green world – to be viewed by millions of spiders, to be pored over by stomatopods beneath the waves, to be gazed at with varying degrees of incomprehension by a number of other species who stand close to the brink of sentience. Even the Spitters – the neo-Scytodes on their wilderness reservations – may see images of this moment.

History is being made. Moreover, history is beginning: a new era.

Doctor Avrana Kern watches, omnipresent, as her children prepare themselves. She is still not convinced, but so many millennia of cynicism will take time to wash away.

We should have destroyed them, is her persistent thought, but then, and despite the dispersed form she currently inhabits, she is only human.

Her surviving files on human neurochemistry, together with the spiders' own investigations of their long-ago captive, have wrought this. She has not been its prime mover, though. The spiders themselves argued long and hard over how to respond to the long-awaited invaders, discounting her advice more than following it. They were aware of the stakes. They accepted her assessment of the path the humans would follow, if given free rein over the planet. Genocide – of other species and of their own – was ever a tool in the human kit.

The spiders have been responsible for a few extinctions along the way, too, but their early history with the ants has led them down a different road. They have seen the way of destruction, but they have seen the way the ants made use of the world, too. Everything can be a tool. Everything is useful. They never did wipe out the Spitters, just as they never exterminated the ants themselves, a decision that later would become the basis of their burgeoning technology.

Faced with the arrival of humanity, the creator-species, the giants of legend, the spiders' thought was not *How can we destroy them?* but *How can we trap them? How can we use them?*

What is the barrier between us that makes them want to destroy us?

The spiders have equivalents of the Prisoners' Dilemma, but they think in terms of intricate interconnectivity, of a world not just of sight but of constant vibration and scent. The idea of two prisoners incapable of communication would not be an acceptable status quo for them, but a problem to overcome: the Prisoners' Dilemma as a Gordian knot, to be cut through rather than be bound by.

They have long known that, within their own bodies and in other species across their planet, there is a message. In ancient times, when they fought the plague, they recognized this as something distinct from their own genetic code, and took it to be the work of the Messenger. In a manner of speaking they were correct. Long ago, they isolated the nanovirus in their systems.

It had not escaped their notice that creatures formed like the giants – mice and similar vertebrates seeded across their world – did not carry the nanovirus, and so lacked a commonality that seemed to bind the spiders to each other and to other arthropod species. Mice were just animals. There seemed no possibility of them ever becoming anything else. Compared to them, the Paussid beetles – or a dozen other similar creatures – were practically bursting with potential.

The spiders have worked long and hard to craft and breed a variant of the nanovirus that attacks mammalian neurology – not the full virus in all its complexity but a simple, single-purpose tool that is virulent, transmissible, inheritable and irreversible. Those parts of the nanovirus that would bolster evolution have been stripped out – too complex and too little understood – leaving only one of the virus's base functions intact. It is a pandemic of the mind, tweaked and mutated to rewrite certain very specific parts of the mammal brain.

The very first effect of the nanovirus, when it touched the ancient *Portia labiata* spiders so many thousands of generations ago, was to turn a species of solitary hunters into a society. Like calls out to like, and those touched by the virus knew their comrades even when they did not have enough cognitive capacity to know themselves.

Kern – and all the rest – watches the shuttle land. Up on the *Gilgamesh*, orbiting a hundred kilometres beyond the equatorial web and its space elevators, there are many humans, all infected, and thousands still sleeping who will need to have the virus introduced to them. That task will take a long time, but then this landing is the first step towards integration, and that will also take a long time.

Even within the spiders, the nanovirus has fought a long battle against ingrained habits of cannibalism and spouse-slaying. Its notable success has been mostly within-species, though. Portiids have always been hunters, and so pan-specific empathy would have crippled them. This was the true test of their biochemical ingenuity. The spiders have done their best, conducting what tests they can on lesser mammals, but only after Portia and her peers had taken control of the ark ship and its crew could the truth be known.

The task was not just to take a cut-down version of the virus and reconfigure it so as to attack a mammal brain: difficult enough on its own, but essentially useless. The real difficulty for that legion of spider scientists, working over generations and each inheriting the undiluted learning of the last, was to engineer the human infection to know its parents: to recognize the presence of itself in its arachnid creators, and call out to that similarity. *Kinship* at the sub-microbial level, so that one of the *Gilgamesh*'s great giants, the awesome, careless creator-gods of prehistory, might look upon Portia and her kin and know them as their children.

Once the shuttle has landed, the spiders press closer, a seething, hairy greyish tide of legs and fangs and staring, lidless eyes. Kern watches the hatch open, and the first humans appear.

There is a handful of them only. This is, in itself, an experiment simply to see if the nanovirus fragment has produced the desired effect.

They step down among the tide of spiders, whose hard, bristly bodies bump against them. There is no evident revulsion, no sudden panic. The humans, to Kern's reconfigured eyes, seem entirely at ease. One even puts her hand out, letting it brush across the thronging backs. The virus in them is telling them all, *This is us; they are like us*. It tells the spiders the same, that crippled fragment of virus calling out to its more complete cousins: *We are like you*.

And Kern guesses, then, that the spiders' meddling might go further than they had thought. If there had been some tiny bead present in the brain of all humans, that had told each other, *They are like you*; that had drawn some thin silk thread of empathy, person to person, in a planet-wide net – what might then have happened? Would there have been the same wars, massacres, persecutions and crusades?

Probably, thinks Kern sourly. She wants to discuss it with Fabian, but even her faithful acolyte has crept out into the sunlight to watch this first-hand.

At the shuttle's hatch, Portia steps out after the humans, along with some of her peer group. The enormity of what she has played a part in is mostly lost on her. She is glad to be alive: many of her fellows are not so lucky. The cost of bringing the human race around to their point of view has been high.

But worth it, Bianca had assured her, when she aired that thought. *After this day, who knows what we may accomplish together? They are responsible for our being here, after all. We are their children, though until now they did not know us.*

Amongst the humans is one who Portia had thought was injured or ill, but now understands to be simply at the end of her long giant's life. Another, a male, has carried her from the shuttle and laid her on the ground, with the spiders forming a curious, jostling but respectful circle around them. Portia sees the ailing human's hands clench at the ground, gripping the grass. She stares up at the blue sky with those strange, narrow eyes – but eyes in which Portia can find a commonality, now that the bond of the nanovirus runs both ways.

She is dying, the old human – the oldest human there ever was, if Kern has translated that correctly. But she is dying on a world that will become her people's world: that her people will share with its other people. Portia cannot be sure, but she thinks this old human is content with that.

8
DIASPORA

8.1 TO BOLDLY GO

Helena Holsten Lain reclines in her webbing, feeling at ease in the zero gravity, whilst around her the rest of the crew complete their pre-launch checks.

The ship has two names and they both mean the same thing: *Voyager*. Helena does not know that this was once, in a long-ago age, the name for a pioneering human space vehicle, one that might, millennia after its launch, still be speeding through the cosmos somewhere, a silent record of achievement long forgotten by its makers' descendants.

There is nothing of the long-dismantled *Gilgamesh* in the *Voyager*, save the ideas. The old technology of Earth, so painstakingly husbanded by Helena's great-great-grand-mother, has been resurrected, rediscovered, built upon and advanced. The scientists amongst the spiders first learned what the humans could teach, about their technology of metal and electricity, computers and fusion drives. After that, they taught it back to their tutors' children, broadened and enhanced by a non-human perspective. In the same way, human minds have unravelled the threads of the spiders' own complex biotechnology and offered their insights. Both species have limits they cannot easily cross: mental, physical, sensory. That is why they need each other.

The *Voyager* is a living thing with a fusion-reactor heart, a vast piece of bioengineering with a programmable nervous system and a symbiotic ant colony that regulates, repairs and improves it. It carries a crew of seventy, and the stored genetic material of tens of thousands of others, and hundreds of thousands of Understandings. This is a vessel of exploration, not a desperate ark ship, but the journey will last many sleeping years, and the precautions seemed wise.

The two peoples of the green world work together in easy harmony now. There was a generation of wary caution on both sides, but once the nanovirus had taken down those barriers – between species and between individuals – so much potential tragedy was already averted. Life is not perfect, individuals will always be flawed, but empathy – the sheer inability to see those around them as anything other than people too – conquers all, in the end.

Communication was always the great problem at the start, Helena knows. Spiders lack the ability to hear speech as anything more than a tickling of the feet; while humans lack the sensitive touch required to detect the wealth of arachnid language. Technology on both sides came to the rescue, of course, and there was always the sour, recalcitrant presence of Avrana Kern. The common language, everyone's second language, is that curious mangled Imperial C that Kern and the spiders worked out between them when she was still the Messenger, and they her faithful. The dead language lives on. Helena's great-great-grandfather would find that thought hilarious, no doubt.

All of the living ship's systems are within tolerance, the organic readouts confirm. Helena adds her own confirmation to the chorus, waiting for the word. She is not the commander of this mission. That honour goes to Portia, the spiders' first ever interstellar pioneer. Hunched in her own webbing slung from the ceiling – or at least the curved side of their chamber that faces Helena's, the spider considers the moment for a few seconds, exchanges quick radio communication with the dock and with the world below, and then speaks to the ship itself.

When you wish.

The ship's response, though positive, has a fragment of the dry wit of Doctor Avrana Kern. Its biomechanical intelligence is extrapolated from what she once was: a child of Kern budded off her, with her blessing.

With awesome, colossal grace, the *Voyager* reconfigures its shape for optimum efficiency and detaches itself from the orbital web, a structure vastly grander than when the *Gilgamesh* first saw it, and now blooming with green solar collectors, dotted with other amorphous spacecraft that have already plotted the extent of the green planet's solar system.

The *Voyager* is more fuel-efficient than the *Gilgamesh* – or even than the Old Empire's vessels, according to Kern. Sometimes all it takes, to crack a problem, is a new perspective. The vessel's reactor can accelerate smoothly and constantly for far longer, decelerate likewise, and the ship's fluid internal structure will protect the crew from extremes of acceleration far more effectively. The journey out will be a sleep of mere decades, not millennia or even centuries.

Still, it is a grand step, and not to be taken lightly. Although returning to the stars was always a certainty that both species had worked hard towards, nobody would ever have suggested reaching out there quite yet, if it had not been for the signal, the message.

Out of all the points of light in the sky, one of them is

talking. It is not saying anything comprehensible, but the message is plainly something more than mere static, something more structured than the orderly calls of pulsars or any other known phenomenon of the universe. The work, in short, of intelligence, where there should be none. How could the people of the green planet ignore such a beacon?

The *Voyager* begins its long acceleration, gently stressing the bodies of its crew, realigning its internal geometry. Soon they will sleep, and when they wake there will be a new world awaiting them. An unknown world of perils and wonders and mystery. A world that calls out for them. Not an alien world, though, not entirely. The ancient progenitors of the people of the green planet walked there once. It exists on the *Gilgamesh*'s star maps, another island in the strung-out terraformers' archipelago that was left to its own devices by the collapse of the Old Empire.

After all the years, the wars, the tragedies and the loss, the spiders and the monkeys are returning to the stars to seek their inheritance.